Dear Anton

# TELONAUT

## (Teloverse Series)

Thanks for the
support!

## MATT TYSON

*For Ellis and Ripley*

# Contents

# PROLOGUE

"They did it for their kids. Like their kids were more important than them. Can you believe that they used to live like that, every dad working his whole life just to give his kid a chance to grow slightly taller than he was? Every mum hoping that her little girl would marry better than she had—correct the mistakes that they'd made in their own lives."

"That's what she told us."

"I don't believe it," said the boy. "How could it be? Look around. All those towers back in town. My old man's energy plant. How would the Race have built the things it has?"

"I don't think she'd lie. What would be in it for her? To lie, I mean? Unless she just enjoys tricking students." The other boy was skipping flat stones out across the Atlantic, south towards Antarctica. "Can you think of anything else that any of them have lied to us about? I can't."

"It might not be a *lie*; she might believe it, even if it isn't true." He threw a flat pebble underarm, tracing the same path as his friend's effort, ripples still dissipating on the surface.

"Hah. Nine! Maybe she had her own mistress who told it to her once, and she never thought about it?"

"And the video she showed us? The trip next week to Amasia and the tower grid? That's so old it was around before the Race even started. So they must have been able to build stuff somehow. Maybe we were less organised then than your dad or WorldGov," the other boy offered, "but we still built tall buildings and airplanes."

"It doesn't seem right though. Think it through. If there were so many people that were only thinking about themselves and their own families, why would anyone team up to do anything together? She made it sound like a big game, everyone trying to take as much as they can from everyone else. There'd have to be so many losers— too many to make it work at least. It would explode before anyone built anything. Why would they have settled for it? Why would they have settled for a life where the best they could hope for at the end of it all was to make the lives of their kids slightly easier than their own?" The boy had ceased looking for flat stones now. He was looking at his friend, caught up in making his gist clear.

"I think that was her point, wasn't it? It *did* explode. If there hadn't been a problem, the Saints wouldn't have had anything to fix, and we've never have ended up with the

Race. That was the lesson of the whole module, I think? It was called 'Race History.'"

The boy was quiet at that. Stilled, sat on the beach, his legs outstretched in a wide V. He began piling the stones between his feet, larger ones first, and then filling the gaps with smaller pebbles to make a raised square shape. He was creating the base of a pyramid.

The other boy saw what his friend was doing and sat opposite him, touching his feet to the soles of his class-mate's boots to form a diamond shape with their four legs. He cleared away a space with his hands, smoothed it flat, and took off his jacket, laying it flat on the ground. He began building his own pyramid in the centre of the ma-terial. The two worked quietly for several minutes before the other boy spoke out. "What would you've done? If you were alive back then, I mean. Born somewhere where the best you could hope for was kicking your kids one rung up a ladder from you?"

The first boy moved a large stone from hand to hand, left to right and back. The stone would complete the next layer of his construction. He didn't place it down in the spot left for it. Instead, he toyed with it as he thought, weighing the question as he moved the heft of the stone from palm to palm. Silence overtook them. The other boy patiently waited, beginning the second layer of his own pyramid. When the boy did answer, it was with con-viction. "I wouldn't have kids. Six or seven billion people, right? How many would be part of something special?

Really contribute? You'd have to accept that it's not possible to do both things. To have kids *and* be significant."

"Significant?"

"You know. To a large number of people. Important. You'd have to choose, right? The fantastic or the family." The boy placed the final stone of the second layer down onto his pyramid. "I'd choose fantastic. Anyone can have kids, but not everyone can write history." The boy looked pleased with himself, nodding sagely in agreement with his own statement. "What about you?"

"I was thinking about it during the lecture," said the other boy. "The Race is basically a big team-up, right? There are rules and reasons that the team doesn't break down, systems that keep us together—"

"*Citizenry*," the boy interrupted, an imitation of his mistress.

"Yeah, that. But the point of it is that the Race started out as a team. Everything that's happened in the last few centuries has only been about making the *team* stronger. So, I think I'd've started a team. You're right, you'd only have a tiny chance of being…*significant*. I'd've wanted to leave a bigger legacy than just some kids, just like you said. So I'd've increased my chances by starting a team, getting together with some people that wanted the same thing as me, and creating something all together. Even if the whole thing was a big near-unwinnable game, surely having more people on your side would've brought you closer to winning? I reckon that's ultimately what the Saints were all about. A team."

The boy looked impressed. "I guess that still works now, right? I mean, my dad still needs a team to help him convince the Race to spend their Red on the project he's working on."

The tide was coming in, the frigid water of the Atlantic Ocean reaching towards them.

"Maybe *we* should start a team. Now. Right here," said the boy.

The other boy carefully picked up the edges of his jacket, holding the material taut underneath his newly built beach-pebble monument. He rose to his knees, retreating from the encroaching water, and then leant forward and placed his pile of stones on top of his friend's, doubling its height. "All we need to do now is to decide what to build."

*Sequens Mirabitur Aetas.*

—Latin Motto

# ONE

*B*lue...*blue*...*blue*...*blue*...*blue*. The light circled, appearing on the left of his vision, too bright for him to keep his eyes open but still recognisable as a colour. Aware of his breathing and heartbeat, Sero focused on their rhythms, using the inferred echo to imagine the shape and extent of the body they powered. Two more blues passed. Confident of his sense of self, Sero followed his training, relevant synapses in his brain firing as he remembered the ten times he had been exposed to this situation before. As blue became cyan and then black, his eyelids rose, lifting the curtain of darkness to reveal the semidark of the bubble's interior. Sero's vision was made up of two sections. In the upper half, the shimmering falling-water effect of the bubble's wall obscured the reception facility outside. The centre of the remainder was made up of a solid-pink parabola with translucent edges. He assumed it was his nose. Routine was comforting. Closing his eyes once more, Sero prompted further potassium gates to open within the front section of his brain. Electrical impulses were generated and propagated to further cells for the first time in this particular incarnation. The memories that formed in Sero's mind's eye were far from new, however. Blue again.

The blue had slowed to less than one flash a minute as the energy vibrating the strings dissipated, returning the bubble to a sapien timeframe. The shimmer of the bubble wall had reduced to a slightly opaque tint. No longer looking down his face, Sero was free to look around and notice the translucent gaps appearing in the bubble wall. At knee level a dark-grey metallic floor became visible through a nonshimmering half-metre-square window in the bubble. The opening elongated, offering further views of hard, rough flooring and a basic, square cable conduit tracing towards Sero's feet. The window increased in height, first meeting the floor and then joining another smaller gap appearing at face level. As the remaining shimmer effects faded, he felt confident in raising his left hand to his chin and manipulating his jaw and neck, testing their range of movement. *Perfect; not a flicker of pain or stiffness.* Every time he had done this, he had feared, even expected, some terrible side effect. Every time he was pleased to be proved wrong. Reassured of his health, he appraised his new surroundings. A Postbox. Perhaps on Wolf 359D, perhaps not. It was the same as every reception room he'd ever landed in: blank walls, cabling, and the pedestal—the kill switch.

On ten occasions Sero had stood in Postboxes, contemplating activating the kill switch. Each time he'd operated the control panel to send a brief pulse of light through the switch, Sero had imagined the familiar view he knew was behind steel doors somewhere—wondering if the doors he could see at that moment were doors to that same somewhere or doors to another colony, another episode, another world. *What's behind these doors, eh? Pale-white seas of the Arctic cap or something new?* Images of the moments before postage flashed through his mind: the isolation bridge retracting, an oval of red lights winking away into the distant gathering lights of Telosec, his last line of defence during postage. *Only a few minutes ago to me. Cell samples turned in, best long-hop strides for the cameras, and close the doors without glancing back. A quick rest in the spidering chair, and we're golden. Easy. Take a nap.*

Now he looked out into an identical room, possibly the same room, looking at a spidering chair which might be the one he'd sat in five years ago. *No point dallying now, though, Novak; wherever you are, your legs and head seem to be working, so there's only one option. Push the button.*

# Two

Seven point eight light-years away in Telospace's vision and broadcasting centre, Minnus watched the postage facility's quantum-linked indicator with one eye and a broadcast of a popular current-affairs feed with the other. The audio from the newsCast was playing in his ear, and he could hear the host's commentary.

"Anywhere between ten and twenty seconds later, a world audience of ten billion souls will see the same images on NeuroVision sets in homes and offices."

Minnus tried to turn down the audio to only base awareness in his mind and instead focus on the indicator dial, but the commentary kept mentioning his name and dragging his attention towards it.

"Minnus Mbeki is an NV broadcaster and producer of experience. Today he is direct streaming memories and thoughts almost 'as occurred' via an active spidering process that constantly assesses changes in the brain from second to second."

*Argh! Head in the game, man; everything is being recorded here.* Minnus focussed on the dial. Still "1." As required by his contract, he also glanced at the station's timekeeper every thirty seconds. The newsCast's nasal tones continued to intrude.

"Earlier this century, Mbeki generated several million Red in a venture that image rendered the experiences of five-hundred-metre sprinter Joules Chavez from promising teenager to nine-hundred-and-thirty-fourth Olympic champion. By spidering young Joules each day with a home-use kit, Mbeki created a complete record of the sights and sounds experienced by an extraordinary man. From puberty to all powerful, Joules had shared like no man before him. By the time of the Northwest Demisphere trials for his first Olympics, Joules Chavez had the support in both goodwill and Red of the majority of people on the planet, regardless of affiliations otherwise. Minnus Mbeki had created a man more popular than any world leader had ever been—except the Saints, of course. Debate sessions occurred in schools, system wide, about whether Joules Chavez would ever have been a champion without a planet behind him. Mbeki was immune to this controversy, though, repeatedly stating that he was simply a proud citizen happy to support the Race's knowledge chase."

*Good times. Fun times. Ultimately meaningless. This matters. SapienCam on the longest-running project the Race has ever known and Sero's quickest link back to the masses. We just had to decide what to build, eh?* The indicator dial still read "1." Just above the dial, Minnus could see in the screen of his commSheet that the news host had brought another "expert" into his commentary, and the focus of the piece had shifted. A woman was answering leading questions for the benefit of the audience.

"That's right, Michele. Before Mbeki's intervention, TeloSpace Direction and Processing had been asking Mr. Universe to standardCam his experiences on colony using two-hundred-year-old nanoBot-built technology."

"Well, I work in the business, Sheila, and I can tell you that would mean a whole heap of editing. An entire year's worth of standardCam footage?"

"Not anymore, Michele—that's the genius of this work. We all know how much the Race enjoyed the serialisation of the last audit Mr. Universe undertook—"

"The Rigil Kentaurus audit."

"Right. Well, that serialisation was done the hard way. As you say, an entire audit's worth of footage reviewed and edited together into something coherent that you and I would be able to follow. Worth it, of course, given all we learned about the Race's exploration programme—but hard work. Mbeki's background in active spidering allows him to use the technology within the telonaut transmission process itself to let Race members experience another world through the eyes of Mr. Universe. The best part is that we'll live the journey along with him, experiencing a day's worth of his audit each day here on Earth, autoedited and packaged up for us without the delay of previous audits."

"Just to be clear though, we won't see anything from Mr. Universe today. Only Mbeki, right?

"You got it, Michele. Kind of a publicity thing. The data that represents Mr. Universe's experiences still needs to travel to us through space, and remember, the colony is light-years away. What we're seeing here is Mbeki's experience of watching the lighthouse. The lighthouse is quantum linked to the colony, you see? Instant information transfer. As soon as Mr. Universe presses the kill switch, and we know he's been transported safely, Mbeki will see the indicator dial move, and the Race will experience the same thing in their NV sets just a few seconds later."

"Although right now it looks like Minnus is actually watching us watching him, Sheila."

Minnus managed to wrest his attention wholly to the indicator as the programme host chuckled. *Yeah. Either the dial will move, or Mr. Universe will open the door of the postage facility here on Earth, and the Race will get to experience me face palming.* The dial still read "1." Getting close to the upper limit now. He should have been out of the bubble for three minutes. *Come on, Sero. Don't let us all down here.* Sheila left the set of the feed, replaced by large, thick-set man with an awful moustache and a brick-top haircut. He and the host were silently watching a montage of catch-up material along with the audience. The words WHITE DAISY ACTIVITY were looping across the bottom of the images. Minnus recognised the recording location of one segment as the base of the postage facility, hundreds of metres below him. A woman with a southern Amasian accent was sound bitten: "And into that Postbox to destroy that travesty of nature and spiteful creation of the hellnaut programme."

*What the frak is wrong with those people? We're exploring the galaxy, and they want to commit murder over it?* He kept his eyes on the dial but could still passively hear the newcomer's exposition interview with Michele.

"Well, Michele, this group are motivated by an idealistic interpretation of the past. They're not really signed up to the Race."

"How so, Buzz?"

"Their ultimate aim is to go back to centuries-old ways of living; back to market economies and excesses; back to base, mistrusting and separate societies; even back to religion. But for the present, they like to take issue with and oppose individual projects and certain select aspects of good Citizenry."

"Such as the telonaut survey effort?"

"Amongst other things, yes. They don't like the income cap. They don't like the idea of central control or even the idea of the Race collectively deciding where to invest our efforts. Telospace is just one outcome of the Race's leaps in social equality, so it's an example that the White Daisies find easy to dislike. Ultimately, they're just not with us on the mission of discovery for discovery's sake, challenge, or the search for the Race's limits."

"Devolutionists?"

"Yeah, Michele, if you like."

*Petty and small minded, seeking some personal concept of private gain by claiming the vision of the Saints had failed. Disgraceful. I hope you feel satisfaction at challenging facts with dangerous arguments based on disproved, faith-based rhetoric, because it just fires me up to push on with building the Saints' flat universe.* Glancing at the clock again, Minnus waited. *Come on, Sero.*

# THREE

One hundred and seventeen years had passed since Sero's birth. His eleventh copy body was aged forty-six years, two months, and fourteen days, exactly the same as his tenth copy body, blank bubbled in the Postbox on Earth. The mind that occupied the brain of his eleventh copy body had spent 69 years of those 117 occupying nothing more than a permaDrive, a spider map, waiting to be re-introduced to a human body. The latest permaDrive had been here in this room.

He shivered. The grey floor was cold and hard. The control panel was simple: a smooth magSteel plate with a single depression button. Behind the plate was a light isolator, shielding a single quantum-linked carbon atom. As he lifted his right arm so that the back of his hand was at eye level, between his face and the depression button, a memory, stored for years in a permaDrive on 359D, was triggered in copy body eleven's brain. He saw a clean, smooth hand extend its index finger and remembered a very similar bloodied and scarlet hand slip from its mark and drop her. He stopped moving and stared vacantly, remembering. *No. She's gone. Move forward. There's a mission here. Stick to the schedule.* Blinking and removing the image, Sero pressed the kill switch.

"Welcome to NineDee. I am 359 Central, administration and facilities manager on colony." The voice was male and well defined, with the structured pronunciation of an individual that has learnt a language later in life. "Please orientate yourself towards the door to this reception facility, currently on your right. Thank you. All reception protocols are complete; please state your name and specialism for entry into colony facility databases. This will allow access to NineDee habitation."

"Sero Novak. Telonaut lead auditor," he retorted to the ethereal voice.

The doors, now in front of him, thudded mechanically. The locking mechanism disengaged at four levels. Once free of the lock bolts that tethered the doors to the interior of the reception facility, the metre-thick panels began to fall away under their own weight. Clear of the adjoining walls, the door continued to fall away, more quickly at the top than at the bottom and hinged at the base, becoming a drawbridge onto which Sero could walk. He did. The view that greeted him was definitely not the Arctic Cap on Earth.

A familiar oval force shield was present, but rather than protecting the walkway in front of him from the harsh weather of the Arctic Cap, this shield was keeping the surrounding sea away from the walkway. He was underwater.

"That's a first."

With the second sentence from his current incarnation, Sero's voice broke. No muscle in this body, including those of his voice box, had ever been moved by impulses generated in the body's brain. The impulses applied to the body during its final growth period were technically exactly the same as the impulse that originated in Sero's brain now as he moved across the drawbridge and onto the walkway. However, in every body he'd previously grown, he had experienced random failure of muscles to respond to his commands, at least in the first few hours. *First test drive. Here goes.* Coughing and clearing his throat, Sero continued along the walkway.

He could see no sign of movement, but scanning directly above him, he saw a web of fine filaments, silhouetted by a pale-green light. *The surface of a sea? A lake, perhaps?* How far away? He was sure that the filaments that he could see weren't *immediately* beyond the force field above him, as none extended to the sides of the walkway or level with his eyes. However, with no idea of the size of the filaments, he couldn't even guess how far away the surface was. They could be as thick as tree trunks and metres apart or as thin as noodle mesh and ten to the hand.

Coughing again and checking the walkway horizon, Sero began walking more quickly and training his voice by counting. At 112, the walkway began to incline. At 332, its grade became very steep. *OK, voice works. Let's test the danger-evasion systems.* He broke into a brisk jog.

At 843, a glint appeared at the end of the walkway, reflecting the dim-green light filtering through the filaments from above. *Steel is polished here. Regular human presence, then? Wouldn't be the first time, I suppose.* This wasn't strictly supposed to be the case; the reception facility on all colonies was designated as generally off limits to all at all times after they'd first entered habitation. However, on Sero's five previous colony audits, several changes had been made to standard operating procedure as was necessary. He followed the glossy steel to the door. Its exterior seemed to move as the pale reflection of the water's surface ran across it. Standing fully erect, at 910, Sero stopped counting.

"Sero Novak. Telonaut lead auditor."

"Welcome to NineDee Habitation," 359 Central replied.

The polished doors retreated to reveal the wide sweep of an open, clearly public space. He remained as upright and dignified as possible, striding forward to present himself to the twelve hundred colonists gathered in the park. At the head of two cohorts, all facing Sero, stood an elderly man. He was dressed in a purple robe of a type that had been fashionable in Sero's youth. His hands were clasped together, intimating thanks, as he stepped slowly towards Sero.

"Nine hundred and ten," the old man enunciated. "I counted to three thousand before opening those doors."

The voice was recognisably the same one as 359 Central, although a little breathier, slower to complete words and with a more pronounced Northern Eurasian lilt.

"I am Patriarch Zwolf, and these are my children."

Zwolf made a sweeping motion with his arm, lifting the long, gaping sleeve of his robe as a toreador would in Western Eurasia back on Earth. At the end of the sweep, he stepped back to allow Sero to fully view the assembled ranks of faces that focused on him.

Sero assessed the many faces. All were calm and respectful; not one face looked away. All eyes and minds were concentrated towards the front of the park. *Attentive bunch. OK, royal wave.* Sero held his arm at full length above his head, waving once in greeting. As he lowered his arm slowly, exaggerating his initial salutation to the colony, three standard hoverCams swooped silently and gracefully from the rear of the park. Two faced Sero, one in close up, he knew; a second encompassing the scene; a third faced the ranks of on-looking families in the park's panorama. He smiled at the standardCam he assumed was cut tight to him, as he'd agreed with Minnus before postage eight relativistic years previously. *Righto, Novak, your best commSheet voice, please."*

"Patriarch Zwolf. My thanks for your welcome. However, despite my hurry to reach your facility and the hospitality with which you receive me, I am cold. May I trouble you for some clothes?"

# Four

Minnus stopped broadcasting barely a minute after the indicator read "0." No longer Man One and therefore free from all the constraints of his contract, he jumped and jerked around the vision centre, swearing and making as much noise as possible. Most of the swearing and noise were directed at the White Daisies that were amplified into his view by the standardCam at the base of the postage facility. They were as aware of the transmission success as the rest of the planet and had lit afire a two-headed effigy underneath the mushroomed canopy of the Postbox hundreds of metres above their heads. Smoke from the dual-faced sack cloth body billowed green as the bulk of it burned. *Simple images for simple people.*

"Frak! Let the Saints watch, idiots," Minnus bellowed at his screen. He clicked it off with a wave of his rolled up commSheet. Rotating in his chair, a sleek Plastische recliner that he'd had transported from his own home, Minnus looked again at the indicator. Still zero. He allowed himself a further single exclamation of his delight, relief overcoming him.

"Yes! Let's see what the masses think of that!"

Unrolling his commSheet and informing the processor of what he wished to see, Minnus expanded the number of the news feeds. Each one was now enthusiastically describing what their particular expert believed the scene that Sero was now viewing would be like.

Switching to the environment channels, he pulled locations from around the globe. Amasia square in Nouveau Delhi; the Thames Tunnel Holo; the Near Earth Cable Tether in Houston; every location was teeming with people who knew of the success of Sero's latest transmission. Large screens in public places generated conversation; people who'd networked their commSheets to share Minnus's broadcast were now using those networks to congratulate each other, simply for having been present. *Winner.*

Elated, Minnus rerolled his commSheet and leaned fully into the bespoke form of his chair. The Plastische gripped his shoulders as his weight displaced some of the chair's bulk from its spine to its neck. Sparked by the debate ensuing around the globe, he allowed his own mind to drift into its perception of Sero's new environment. Basing his concept on the Kentaurus audit, he saw swirling red mists bounded by a deep crevasse that had once been an ocean floor, viewing it all from his friend's perspective.

His imaginings were interrupted as the end of the pencilled commSheet, laid on the table to Minnus's left, expanded to form a red holographic ball, indicating a queued communication. Lifting the silver-coloured tube to his face, Minnus greeted the caller, whom he knew would be his wife.

"Hello, dear, job done…yes…thank you…well, I always said he would, didn't I? You know I will…two…well, keep it clipped. I'll see you then…me too."

The holographic ball, now green, retracted into Minnus's commSheet as he slid it into his cover pocket. His wing was already prepped and cleared to leave from the more convenient platform on the roof of the facility. He wouldn't need to travel down through Telosec proper to the more heavily used lower levels. He stood and strode briskly to the exterior gantry, which spiralled around the Telosec's mushroom's upper levels and became a wide plateau of steel on the roof of the building. Reaching the wing, Minnus paused and looked at the smoke dwindling from the bottom of the Postbox facility's stalk. Calmer now, he laughed rather than cursed, directing his favourite gutter salute of fingers made orifices at the miniscule dots moving around the smoke source, before turning and walking along the length of the lowered wing. Dropping into pilot, Minnus closed the winglid and spoke a single word.

"Home."

# FIVE

aving walked from his arrival assembly wearing a robe similar to Zwolf's, Sero now stood in what he understood would be his personal quarters, browsing a rail of clothing for something less ceremonial. Selecting plain, dark clothes and heavy-soled boots, he appraised himself in the polished steel mirror on the interior side of the door of his quarters. *Same old, same old. Old man.*

Sero was a man of small physique. One hundred and eighty-three centimetres tall, eighty-three kilograms. While bubbled, his body was allowed to develop to the full limit of its genetic code, maximising each physical variable. In Sero's case that was a low maximum. He'd chosen his muscle mass himself, coded the electrical impulses that would create the body shape that stood before him now. It was suitable to his role, but knowing the capabilities of the technology, Sero always felt a pang of regret that each copy body wasn't a Mr. Universe to complement the title he was given in the press on Earth.

Cupping his hands to his ears, Sero manipulated this head about the neck, appraising both sides of his face. Just as when he'd last arrived back on Earth, the scars on his face had gone. Sero knew that they were never actually there, the scars had been destroyed along with the version of himself that had been laser-incinerated on Rigil Kentaurus, ruined the moment that he'd activated the kill switch on Earth reception. *Just a memory now. Nothing physical to show for it all. Stop it. Move forward. Audit.*

Sero arranged his hair using a steel comb from the cabinet beside the mirror. As he did so, he ran through the protocols for first contact. He'd broken one already by not requesting a formal update upon arriving on colony, but he wasn't concerned. The current popularity of both the telonaut programme and, indeed, himself allowed him more freedom with Telospace leadership than he'd been able to acquire before. Maintaining public interest in a programme that began over two hundred years ago was top priority for Johnson and the rest of the telonaut bureau so that they could keep the Red coming in every five years as part of the global Mission Selection process. For this latest mission, Sero received an official request to continue the *exciting* speed at which his last audit had progressed. *Exciting. Dicks.*

Spinning away from the mirror, he surveyed the room that would be his home for the next twelve months. Similarly to the rest of the facility, the walls were plain, unpolished steel. The room had three sections and was the largest room he'd ever been allocated while on a colony.

It was also the sparsest. Lighting was of a similar fashion to the rest of the facility: beam illumination running from wall to wall in pairs. Sero had already noticed that around half of the beams were switched off. *Too much reflection from the steel, perhaps? Maybe not. It's pretty dull in here.* Energy shouldn't be a problem. Millions of miniSuns populated the sea that Sero had arrived in, generating energy from hydrogen-splitting reactions. He knew that this was the case without asking for the formal report he'd omitted from the arrival proceedings. Without the suns, the nanoBots that had built the facility would never have been able to make it ready for the first transmission, and there would have been no colony at all.

As he finished arranging himself, the frame of the door to his quarters vibrated. As he turned his head towards the door, it became instantly transparent. It was Patriarch Zwolf, composed and smiling, flanked by two large gentlemen in similarly coloured drill suits to the patriarch's robes.

"Auditor Sero, we are delayed in completing our protocols. Are you suitably attuned to your new environment?"

Sero made a lifting motion through the air with his left hand, and a blue line of light appeared at ground level, rising slowly to the top of the doorframe.

"Welcome to my home. After a few wash, rinse, and repeats of waking up on a new planet every couple of years, I find myself pretty much instantly at home wherever I lay my hat."

"One of us, eh? A hardy pioneer seed?"

"Oh no, not as hardy as all that. I've measured myself against many colonists on many worlds. I've never met a single colonist who didn't dwarf me for personal resilience. I'm sure you guys here on 359D are no different."

"We hope so, Auditor. We do pride ourselves on our mental strength. Holding course and eating the terraforming elephant in small bites, as you might say."

*True to type. A world builder.* Only the most ambitious applicants were chosen for delivery to a colony, but the ambition was filtered. Of a type. *Mutually supportive social animals. All bricks in the same wall here, just like on the other colonies? We'll see. Hopefully there'll be at least some room for experimentation around the edges.* "I can't wait to discover more. Where are we off to?"

"We would like for your first impression of NineDee to be centred on our proudest achievement, the thing that our family is most involved in, the item that you will see separates us from any other settlement in the history of our Race. We will now take our leave to the plait-city of NineDee, Gesponnen."

*Separate from any other city in history? Pride. Sounds good. They should put that on the brochure.*

# Minus Six

The boy was bored. He already understood everything the teacher was explaining. He'd learned it at home from his father. He didn't see why he even had to complete this part of the curricula. He tried to communicate his boredom by sliding right back in his chair and huffing exaggeratedly, but the lady at the front of the class droned on.

"…shielding a single quantum-linked carbon atom. After so many years and several million generations of nanoBot replication and expiration, the carbon atom is one of only two original Earthborn items on each of our colonies…"

He wondered when they'd get on to the practical stuff, the stuff that would allow him to show off, show what he knew. Nobody was paying attention to him here.

"…carbon B, sent as a backup via a completely different solar sail…"

The boy looked around at his classmates, busily tapping out notes on their cSheets—like all this wasn't already available elsewhere. He wanted to build something new, not read about what others had built before.

"…nanoBots begin replicating and becoming either miniSun or construction units to create a reception facility around carbon A…"

Maybe he'd ask his father to help him move forward a year. But that would mean moving away from his friend. That wouldn't do. They'd promised to work together.

"…Sapien Filtering has allowed for the elimination of inherited disease, but we stop there…"

Maybe they could both move forward a year together?

"…for two reasons: The Race prizes diversity and also wants to protect against one individual making an ownership claim over another individual's genetic material…"

The boy closed his eyes and waited for the lesson to finish.

# Six

**Minnus was woken** by the heat of the reflected sunlight warming his face. Sleeping on the balcony of his thirtieth-floor apartment had become a habit in recent months. The glass-walled buildings that surrounded his home reflected and dispersed light throughout it, especially the small covered area that Minnus now lay upon in his portable bunk pod. Nombre Mbeki was up and cooking in the kitchen. Minnus waved weakly as he rose, watching her watch him stand. His wife gestured back with a smile. She wore only a thermaRobe, silk thin but regulating her temperature by absorbing light and passing a slight electrical current, created by the sun's energy, through the fibres of the mesh. The robe bunched on her hips where she'd tied it with an equally light transparent belt.

Clearing his vision by blinking away the sun and focussing on the darker environment inside the apartment,

Minnus beamed his best smile to his wife. "You are as beautiful now as the day I met you."

"When I met you, I was wearing more clothes. You don't have the judgment to tell the difference between beauty and one of your morning moods." Nombre smiled again as she teased him.

"Maybe not, but you give me the same morning moods as you did the day *after* I first met you."

A rouge was added to the right and left of Nombre's persisting smile. "What's in the day today, then, superstar? Any more worldwide broadcasts?"

"Old news, honey. Today I'm inventing." Minnus slipped his right hand into his wife's gown. Resting his index finger on her stomach button, he slipped behind her and reached his left hand around to rest on the granite surface of the preparation area.

Kissing his wife playfully on her cheek as he passed her, Minnus used the distraction to make sure he picked the plate with the biggest duck egg and a little more rocket. He scooped up the plate in one motion and headed back out onto the balcony.

"It *is* for you, ya know?" she called after him.

Reaching his bunk pod again, he fished into the base of it to retrieve the commSheet that he assumed he'd left there the previous night. Finding and unrolling it, he gave a flick of his wrist to make the polymers inside it click rigid and form a full screen. Setting its position on the arm of his chair, he sat down to his day's work. With Sero confirmed on-colony, Minnus was free to rewrite the decipher algorithms used to decode the spider map in Sero's return signal. He had several hundred ideas for process improvement spilling around his head. *Get them in some kind of order though, eh? How is this gonna work? Much of the audit is rote protocol stuff, and after all, nobody wants to watch Sero piss either. You've sold them the bold idea; need to make it happen now.*

Nombre joined him on the deck. "So what are you 'inventing' exactly?"

"Well, I've got to follow through on my promises. I can do it, I'm sure. Just needs a bit of…coarse tuning?"

"Lay it out for me, genius. It always helps thought to say stuff out loud."

"It's the automation I need to sort out. I need a way of interpreting each new digital memory spider map we get from Sero without someone having to actually sit through the memory experience to work out which parts are important. The NV cast has to go out regularly so that by the time Sero steps out of the Postbox here on Earth, everyone is caught up with what happened out there."

"And it's going to be a single narrative, serialised like last time?

"Yeah, only we'll edit a week's worth of experiences every single week and broadcast immediately rather than taking years reviewing and manually editing standardCam footage like we did for Rigil."

"OK. So where's the gap?"

"Erm, I don't have an algorithm to do that?"

"So what *do* you have?"

"I know what I want it to look like? I want it to turn out a little like the hard-work version we did for Rigil." *Hopefully without all the loss and pain.*

"Good. Start with the end in mind. What else do you have?"

"I guess I've also still got all the base material for that version. Before hard work, I mean—the raw footage...*and* I've got Sero's spider maps from the Rigil audit too."

"So?"

"So..." *Here it comes.* "It's a training exercise. Train an algorithm to take base material similar to the Rigil audit, and turn it into NV casts similar to those we made manually." *How does she do that? A handful of questions and all of a sudden everything is so simple. Lots of work still, but you've got eight years until deadline, old man. Just needs a little perseverance.*

Nombre knew him well enough to recognise a breakthrough and leave him to his own thoughts. She finished her breakfast with silent smiles.

Lying comfortably in the bunk pod, sun on his face and his mind sequencing the work ahead of him, Minnus found himself regressing to a sunny day in his childhood. He took the last few leaves of rocket between his thumb and forefinger and used them to mop up the remains of the yolk of his duck egg. He blinked through an image of him and Sero hunched over his pod, teasing out the development of Claudiera the racing duck, his favourite companion for over a year. He'd gestated her himself and loved her like a womb-born child in a manner that a twelve-year-old boy didn't understand, but perhaps his wife now did, having born children of that twelve-year-old boy sixty years later.

"Terrible swimmer, though," he muttered as he returned his gaze to his plate. "You never even made it to a full duck, and I think you could float faster than old Claddy," Minnus said to his egg.

As he dropped the duck-coated rocket into his mouth and licked his fingers, he noticed his wife coming towards him.

"What high and lofty things is my husband now thinking of as he feeds himself like an animal?" Nombre questioned while settling onto Minnus's right knee, opposite his screen.

"A time when I was much shorter, the universe was much smaller, and eggs seemed much bigger." Minnus blanked his screen and turned to face her. "A time when I'd yet to develop my moods and was glad of my innocence."

"Rather be there or here?" Nombre let the clear belt, which she'd loosened on her route to his chair, fall away completely.

"Here."

"Sure?"

"As sure as eggs are eggs." Minnus opened the thermaRobe.

# SEVEN

Zwolf's companions had taken positions to the front and rear of Sero and the patriarch as they walked.

The standardCams, which had down-timed outside Sero's quarters, now hovered back at face height. They floated, dispersed along the departure route that the four walkers had taken. One eyeballed Sero as he looked back at what it appeared would be his home for the next twelve relativistic months. A second traced the path in front of the group. The final cam had remained at the quarter's exit, framing the quartet in retreat.

The track they walked upon was the same dull steel as the walls and floor of every other room Sero had seen on colony so far. The only polished surfaces here were two stripes shined into the floor from the shuffling feet of other passersby in the same way he'd seen on crossing the arrivals bridge. On either side of the track were the squares of each family and couple on

NineDee. Each square had a door and wall made from the same material as Sero's quarters. Some were transparent, often with a young face staring out enquiringly at the newly arrived alien.

The artificially regular pattern of the sleeping quarters' layout was in contrast to the haphazard, vertical dwellings of the inhabitants of Rigil Kentaurus, Sero's previous destination colony. *Well, at least it won't be another yearlong audit spent clambering from sky-tree to ledge and ledge to sky-tree again. Thin air, thick air, thin air, sick.* A blue line in the periphery of his vision warned Sero that someone was about to exit from a room adjacent to the corridor. Flitting his eyes, Sero saw glimpse of a glistening, scarlet hand reflected in foot-polished floor. *Get a grip. You've got the tools to handle this.* Stopping walking for the anticipated oncoming individual and taking the opportunity to close his eyes, he willed the image away, consciously replacing it in his mind with the strangely old face of his friend Minnus as they'd agreed. *It's over, Sero; she's gone.*

"We have twelve hundred and fifty three living here on NineDee. Of those, some two hundred and eighty are original transmissions, with the remainder the product of the unions established here on our colony. Our family."

Patriarch Zwolf smiled and nodded at a couple, who both looked middle aged, around one hundred body years old. They were standing in the doorway Sero had stopped short of a moment before. The female reached out to touch the patriarch's arm, to which he conceded with an air of royal assent. *OK, back in the game, Novak. This is colony first contact here. Shake it off.*

"Hello, Auditor. Welcome to our home. I'm Divis, and this is Sana."

Divis tilted her head backwards and to the left in a corkscrew nod towards her partner, still standing in the doorway. Sero smiled. *This'll get you back in the groove. Meeting new people. Frontier people. Volunteer frontier people.* He was envious. The pride that Sero felt as Telospace lead auditor was difficult to eclipse, but an element of insecurity cast a shadow over the corner of his ego. *If I were to be out here permanently, an envoy of the Race, a galactic seed, would I flourish? Would my principles be retained?* The self-doubt amplified his respect for colonists.

Divis was a tall lady, taller than Sero. She didn't carry herself in an effeminate manner but strode to meet Sero with a forceful gait, as though rather than her legs carrying her forward, her shoulders were restrained from getting to where they wanted to go by hips and feet that were the last to know where that was. She wore a robe similar to Zwolf's but of a lighter colour. The lower-cut sections of the robe had been buttoned up over Divis's shoulders across her back, forming what looked like an empty pack hanging to her waist.

Sero decided he would forget auditing for the present and measure his insecurities against this lady's accomplishments. *Relax. Enjoy it! You can do this.* He touched Divis's hand, laying his knuckles flat on her outstretched palm

"Thank you, Divis, Sana. I'd say we were probably born about the same time, you and I, relativistic aging excepted, of course. Good to meet a fellow Telopreneur." *Smiles all around. Good, going well.* "So, 'home' being the colony or 'home' being your square?"

"The Race's home is the *galaxy*, Auditor, but our family's home is here on NineDee. The square behind me is simply a room in our community's grand house, a drawer in which a section of us are kept. Although perhaps the larger that section becomes, the more the collective focus of our wider family will be placed there.

"Ah, I see." But he didn't see. *More like a poem than a conversation.*

It wasn't unusual for colonists of all ages to be philosophically heavily socially focused. They were, after all, selected for their ability to live in self-governing teams at the boundary of the Race's reach. When left in isolation for long periods, this did sometimes produce kibbutz-proselytisers with a limited memory of alternative social groupings. Perhaps in that there was respite from his insecurities. His was a role in the progression of the collective of the entire Race, rather than a small community. *This work is grand; significant. You* are *important.*

"You say your section is becoming larger? Are you to play a more important role here on NineDee? Scratch that. Putting first things first, what *is* your role here? Divis, do you have a specialism?"

Sero didn't really need to hear her answer. As she was an Earthborn colonist, he'd been proscriptively briefed on everything from her hydromics research profile to culinary likes and dislikes. He knew the stock description of the work that a hydrologist living on a wetworld might perform. *I do want to know how she feels about it, though.*

"...and so I offer the raw premise to Sana. I define the boundaries of what can be created from our planet, and Sana designs our vision of the future state of our family's infrastructure, aided by NineCents, of course." Divis finished her description with a flourish, tapping her feet alternately, pivoting at the heel, the three-note "rat-a-tat" echoing slightly along the solid steel of the corridor.

"I see." this time Sero did see. *A family cell. Interesting approach. Probably allows for increased adaptive focus on ad hoc terraforming? Reacting as and when needed, always available to work, even in the home. Maybe would better speed the development of a planet's habitability—beyond the basics provided by the initial nanoBot burst.*

"I'm told our initial interview will be at 'Gesponnen,' although I don't yet know the features or purpose of the place. Are you involved?"

Both Divis and Sana looked to Zwolf, seemingly unsure of what response to make. Removing his right hand from the left sleeve of his robe, the patriarch took a step towards Sero and reached out to clasp the auditor's hand.

"Auditor, please. Let me maintain the suspense for a few moments longer. Our interview will be a good impression of our plait-city. We've practiced the event using the cameras above. We'd like to record the reaction you have to both our plans and our progress. Live, so to speak."

*Pride.* Sero acquiesced immediately, squeezing Zwolf's hand and smiling at the old man. *Big show planned!*

"Gesponnen, then."

Experience taught him that the endeavours of colonists were akin in their minds to early peacemakers in Amasia, preparing a hostile and unruly place for the peaceable achievements of the Race. He'd read a story in his youth in the Comsease facility about frontiersmen of the old Americas during the precooperative Earth-bound colonial age: the adventures of a travelling man moving from place to place, assisting however he could in each community and leaving behind him a legacy of new laws that would mean that he'd never be needed again to deal with a grasping businessman, or perhaps the strong lawman would legacy a new rail track for transport that would mean his ability to carry heavy loads up mountain tracks to build a dam would be unnecessary. In those tales, the travelling man had been a metaphor for the God that the earlier versions of the Race had believed in, helping them to construct a new and better land of which he would approve. Sero had seen the spirit of the people of the Americas in those tales; however, in every modern colony he'd visited, belief that what they were creating was better than before was important. Such pride often led to a desire to have Sero— representative of the "God" of their time, representative of the Race itself—confirm the colony's importance and success. *Only natural that the leader of such a place is precious over how their achievements are presented. There's twelve months to investigate. Let him grandstand a little.*

He turned to Divis and nodded his head respectfully and then raised his hand to Sana in the doorway of the quarters to bid farewell. As he did so, a previously unseen person darted from behind Sana and through the gap in the doorway created by his raised arm, causing Sana's robe to flap first forward with the impact of the person's head and then to retract and swing backward, revealing the new arrival section by section. Legs were visible first, heavy-looking hydroBoots, taut to the shin. Rather than a robe like the other colonists Sero had met, this individual was wearing a multipocketed pair of tool trousers. The figure's waist became visible from under the retreating robe more quickly than Sero had expected. *A shorty.* Around the waist was a bandolier of canisters hung like the bullets of an antique rotary cannon. There was a muffled noise emanating from the shorter person as he or she entered the corridor, but Sero couldn't make out any distinct words as he got his first glimpse of the face. The girl was maybe fifteen or sixteen years old, her full height reaching only to Sana's underarm. She had short, dark hair, swept to one side of her head and fastened above her right ear in the functional style of a sports competitor.

"Gesponnen?" The muffled word was now clearer. "Fantastic! I'll accompany you, Patriarch Zwolf. I've been promised that I might see the plate a final time before the dissolution."

The young girl walked towards Sero, tracing the path Divis had taken but with infinitely more grace. "Hello, Auditor Novak. My name is Prid. These are my parents."

Zwolf stepped behind Prid, laying a hand on each of her shoulders as though to fix her to the spot in which she stood. As Zwolf's face appeared above that of the teenager's so Sero could see both heads, he noticed the girl's shoulder's reverse from him slightly. *Has the old guy got his thumbs in her shoulder blades there? Ensuring she'll move nowhere else without his permission?*

"Pridescent is, rightly, proud of her section's work and, perhaps due to her youth, sometimes allows her pride to forget proper procedure. Prid, you have been briefed in the gatherings in Park 359. The protocol dictates that the auditor must first interview me for an official record of our progress. Talk of the plate and dissolution must wait, otherwise the narrative of our audit would not be clear to the auditor. Or the rest of the Race."

Zwolf turned and smiled to the close-up standardCam, still hovering to Sero's left and looking over his shoulder directly at Zwolf and Prid.

*He's preening for the camera there. Shall I explain about the sapienCam thing?* This would allow him to speak with whomever he pleased about any subject as Zwolf would know that any staging would be ineffective. *Might make him more guarded, though? Don't want him hiding difficult situations with interesting solutions—that's the Race enrichment that you're supposed to be here for. No. Discretion for now.* He nodded at the patriarch and also turned to recognise the standardCam. As he did so, his gaze passed across the face of Prid. Sero saw a glint of recognition in her eyes as she understood why he was looking towards the camera. She smiled mischievously and bent her legs at the knees, lowering her body away from Zwolf's grip and twisting towards the StandardCam, freeing herself so she could be seen by both the colonists and the levitating recording device.

"I apologise, Patriarch Zwolf. I intended only that my pride not further our problems. I will not allude further to these problems. I'm sure your recognition of them will form part of the interview. However, the promise made that I might visit the scene of our greatest achievement will require the use of a transport to Gesponnen."

*Precocious kid.*

"As you will already be taking two for the purposes of Auditor Novak's interview, I see an opportunity for my own relocation at no further energy cost. I would not like to increase energy costs to our colony, as I am sure that you would not, Patriarch."

Prid smiled at the old man and hooked both thumbs onto her can-bandolier before turning her head to look directly into the camera. Although Sero could only see the back of the articulate young girl's head, he thought he detected a look of faux innocence in the way Prid's ears sat. Beyond the smug-looking rear of Prid's head, Zwolf was displaying obvious fury, attempting to scratch his chest with his upper teeth by clenching his jaw harder and harder.

Seeing a chance to build a relationship with a colony-born, Sero decided to appease both the youth and the elder. "Patriarch, the Race is always keen to know the advancements of a colony but also the personalities born at the edges of our civilisation—to meet minds that have never experienced our ancestral home. Perhaps I could spend some time with young Prid as we journey to our interview? We agree to not discuss Gesponnen. You talked of a *plate* and a process—the *dissolution*, was it? These topics and any other you care to mention would be strictly off limits."

Apparently sensing her chance, Prid ventured a further suggestion. "NineCents could help with that, Auditor Novak. He could monitor our discussions and let you know if we we're straying into territory that the patriarch would rather educate you on."

With Prid apparently on board his vessel of compromise, Sero made an offering to Zwolf. "Of course, whilst I don't know the specifics, I'm also duty bound to ensure that my audit has as little effect on a colony as possible. A blank bubbling reception is quite an energy vampire. If sharing a transport with this young lady would minimise my thermal footprint, it'd make me happy."

He emphasised the "I" ownership in each sentence and made sure that Zwolf saw him look at the nearest standard-Cam on each occasion. *No blame on you for your audience; all my own work, my friend.*

Zwolf's reaction was slow in coming and was preceded by a triumvirate of glancing nonverbal exchanges between the colony adults.

"Auditor, *Negotiator*, let's continue to our transports."

As they left, Sero heard the rat-a-tat of Divis's tapping feet once more.

# Eight

"Did you see the tendrils of the tentaculos as you travelled through the arrival runway?" enquired the faceless voice of 359 Central.

"I did," replied Sero, trying to decide where to look when speaking with the computer. The transport was similar to the racing halos Sero had loved as a boy. The skill required to pilot those unguided halos was immense, powered as they were with antigravity repulsors and little in the way of guidance systems. Sero recalled sitting on Table Mountain in his native Surfaca, watching the Race unfold on the plain beneath him. At the speeds at which the repulsors drove the halos along the expanse, like huge runaway drive wheels, the strength and timing required from the pilot had amazed his younger self. His father had once taken him to a sports halo vendor and allowed him to stand inside one of the stationary halos. When he'd asked if Sero thought he could make the halo turn, Sero had thrown himself against the inner field of the halo with all his might, to predictably comic effect. Although he was bright, the laws of inertia were not yet fully understood in Sero's mind. *Pipsqueak pinball. I should have gotten a tattoo of that nickname. More appropriate than "Mr. Universe."*

"What drives this transport, 359 Central? Repulsors?"

The reply came from behind him, and he twisted his neck as if to face a person seated there. Prid had not spoken since seating herself beside Sero.

"No. The transport is moved forward by applying alternating charge to the foremost and then rearmost sectors of the platform upon which it rests. The platform is constructed of a metallic ore, easily harvested from the ocean bed of the colony."

"It's a large wheel-shaped electromagnet, then?"

"Indeed. As soon as the nanoBots had constructed enough of my processing power to make me 'aware,' I selected this configuration of transport system as the most efficient construction—providing satisfactory mobility for the exploration effort whilst minimising the work required to harvest materials and assemble infrastructure."

"And the tentaculos?"

"The tentaculos are an indigenous species to the colony wetworld. Their existence is endemic to the ninety-five percent surface area of the planet that is liquid based."

"We seem to be displacing quite a few of them in our wake here."

Sero could see a hillock of the tangled, dark-green, rope-like organisms forming six or seven metres behind the halo as he sat in the hoop section, speeding along the steel platform. There was something incongruous about what he was observing. "How long and wide are those tentaculos, 359 Central?"

"Auditor Novak, might I suggest you refer to me in the same manner as the other colonists? I'm informed that they find it expedient whilst also offering me a character that is otherwise difficult to ascribe. Given my generally faceless nature."

"They don't call you 359 Central, 359 Central?"

"No, Auditor Novak. I am, I believe not *without* affection, addressed as 'NineCents.' It is part of our colony's culture. We have developed a branding based on our nearest star. Everything here is NineSomething."

"NineCents, eh? Cheap at twice the price. OK, NineCents, what do you know about those tentaculos? You asked me if I'd seen them on my way in, and they're behaving noncharacteristically for any twine-forming lifeform I've observed, either on Earth or any other colony."

"Would you like a summary or a summation?"

"Just a summary for now, please, NineCents."

"Well, Mr. Novak, 'tentaculos' is a pluralisation. We've catalogued eighteen theoretically singular, extremely large organisms, each made up of millions and millions of similar tendrils. It is the belief of our researchers that each individual animal can only exist by combining to form what is in effect a surface-area-maximising continental land mass. There is a basic form of photosynthesis that occurs only at a very specific wavelength of light on the planet. A refraction occurs in the upper atmosphere of the wetworld, separating the light. In order for photosynthesis to occur, an organism must be very specifically between four and eight metres above the average sea level, taking advantage of light at the appropriate wavelength."

"The animal's source of growth? What does it use for replacement of its tendrils? Photosynthesis only provides energy. How did these tentaculos acquire such vast size?" Sero performed the mathematics quickly in his head. "Eighteen such lifeforms would mean, assuming similar size, an average surface area of...thirty-six thousand square kilometres. Are they carnivorous? Do they compete with each other for protein?"

"An average surface area of thirty-six thousand kilometres square is approximately correct. The simplest form of substrate for growth known to the Race—a simple amino acid soup. Each tentaculo feeds on itself and its neighbours as it and they deteriorate though age and abrasive damage. The seas are layered in the same manner as the light strata on this world. As the tendrils die at upper levels, sections break off and fall though the weave to the lower levels of the tentaculos' network. Just as the surface of the tentaculo must be between four and eight metres above the average sea level, the base of the tentaculo must be no more than eighty metres below sea level. As the broken-off sections fall below this level, they pass through a single-metre layer of amino-acid-rich water to a further layer of digestion enzyme containing seaborne bacteria. The tendril sections are devolved back to their base amino acids, which then filter through to the middle layer of water. The amino acids are then available to make proteins, which can replenish the broken tendrils lost at the surface, maintaining the height of the uppermost tendrils in the tentaculo."

*Fascinating. The Race has never encountered anything like it before.* Sero was beginning to see how this would cause the rolling hill behind him.

"But to spontaneously create a permanently raised level like that hill chasing us, the growth at the lower levels would need to occur really quickly."

"Indeed, instantaneously. The amino broth immediately extends the chains at the bottom of the tendril as soon as it is lifted into the acid level."

Prid decided that now was the time to offer her opinion. "The best part is what you can make from them, though. Watch this." Reaching into a pocket on her tool trousers just above the knee, she retrieved a small piece of bark-like substance. It was basically flat but curved slightly at the edges like a rudimentary canoe. "This is a tendril cutting I took the last time I was out here."

She tossed the cutting across to Sero. Prid's speech was different than it had been in the corridors of the habitation area, less formal, more focused. *The real Prid?*

"So, this is how you really speak, then?"

"Yeah, I suppose."

"You sounded more like a politician of a very old republic back there with your parents and your colony patriarch. You switch back and forth much?"

"It's necessary, you know? When I'm with people my own age, colony-born, we can talk however we like—be ourselves. But the older guys, my parents included, they all talk the same way. It's very...accurate. I don't think I know I'm *switching*, really, as you put it—just blending in with whoever is around me. Making it easier to get along. Sometimes I even walk like them. You know how it works. You do it too. I saw you work out how I was going to get on board here, and you spoke to everyone as they expected: me, them, all of us. It's subtle, but I see it."

*Clever girl.* Sero smiled as Prid unclipped herself from her seat and stepped into the flat space behind the chairs they had been seated in. Rummaging in two pockets on her other leg, she produced something that looked like a small stencil and a sharp-looking scapula. The stencil looked like a large arrowhead, about the size of Sero's palm. Laying these out on the floor, she unclipped one of the canisters from the can-bandolier around her waist and set it next to them.

"Very perceptive, Prid. Do you think you get that from your mother or your father? I've read their backgrounds, at least the background they had before they were transmitted here from Earth; they're both very intelligent people."

Now it was Prid's turn to smile, through comic exasperation. "I'm not sure that my parents could be described as subtle! They don't have a *feel* for things—they have a *map* for things!. I had a friend Dini, and we worked out that it was probably part of the selection process. If you're coming to a place with no rules yet, or at least none that you know about fully, then you'd better be pretty good at making up rules and structure. We figured that's why all the Earthborn are tied up so tight. It was always in their nature to map things out and interpret things they come across using only their own map, sticking to its direction and dismissing the rest as unnecessary. My parents are just the same, but that's probably why they're here and therefore probably why *I'm* here, right? Confluence of circumstance."

"And Dini's parents?"

"They're the same, although we don't really talk anymore. She's a little older than me and is fully involved in the dissolution now."

"Prid, remember that topic is not something that can be discussed at this time." The voice of NineCents echoed into the transport, this time seemingly from the ceiling.

"Sorry, 'Cents. Didn't mean to."

Sero was distracted by NineCents's interruption. "NineCents, where is your voice coming from? It seems to jump around me, originating from all directions, but I can't see any kind of terminal."

"It's in the steel, Mr. Novak," Prid said.

"Call me Sero, please, Prid. NineCents, please explain."

"Well, Mr. Novak, our transport grid is now rather extensive, covering a large part of the megafauna that we are currently above. Following the decision that the transport systems should be constructed from a single metallic material, it was further decided, by me, that rather than overlay a complicated communications infrastructure upon it—with the associated complexity and maintenance—I might more simply use the metal itself. As you are by now aware, much of the colony is constructed from a conterminous solid piece of metal, extended and modified to whatever purpose the colony requires. The rail upon which the transport you are currently located in sits is in fact the same piece of metal that you walked upon in your new quarters and also the same piece of metal that surrounds my central processors in Park 359. So I cause the metal to vibrate so that to your hearing, the vibration sounds like a voice. I pulse sound towards the most convenient metal surface using a focused soundwave from one of one hundred orbitals we have constructed."

"Elaborate, no? Sure, it's elegant, but I can't think that this is the design that would have been arrived upon from the first planning session you had, NineCents. Why so fancy?"

"Quite correct, Auditor. However, I am unable to elaborate on this further until you have completed your conversation with Patriarch Zwolf. I may state that the existence of orbitals with the capability to produce audio waves is not simply because of our need to communicate with the fringes of our transport system. There is a more primary purpose to them. Their use for communication is simply an efficient by-product."

"And how do you—"

"Under your collar," Prid said, hopping up to just in front of Sero's seat as he sat, twisting from the trunk to observe the tools she had laid out on the transport's floor behind him. She lifted his dark jacket collar away from his shoulder and tugged it to show the underside to Sero. A red ring of material the size of Prid's fingernail was visible. "It's a simple audio relay—radio waves. Hops from person to person usually, finding the nearest one that's nearer to 'Cents each time until it reaches him, but out here where there are no people, we have to build the railmen." Prid pointed behind Sero to a man-height outgrowth of the rail, standing directly upward. As they sped along the flat magnetic road, he spotted another railman on the horizon. "That's what causes the delay in 'Cents's response as we get further away. Anyway, look at this."

Prid took the tendril cutting from his hand and returned to the workspace she'd created for herself in the rear well of the transport. Sero watched as she held the stencil over the tendril and worked with the cutting tool. The effect was ultimately like taking a bite from a biscuit and then putting the biscuit back in the biscuit cutter that made it. With the broken biscuit tendril inside the stencil, she took a canister from her waist candolier and sprayed a jet of liquid. Instantaneously, the empty space was filled with a new tendril-like material, remaking the tendril biscuit-arrowhead. Prid lifted the stencil, smiled superiorly at Sero's open-mouthed reaction, and headed over to him, pressing the newly shaped tendril cutting out of the stencil and into Sero's open hand.

"I've used it to make loads of stuff. Me and Dini grew a new vest each every day one year."

Sero laughed out loud. *Really clever girl. Glad she tagged along. She's like Minnus. Well, like my energetic young Minnus—not the withered-eyed old man he is now.* Still laughing, Sero got up from his chair and joined Prid in her new mobile work-shop. Sitting on the floor beside her, he tugged at his left boot.

"Well, then, let's see if we can make me some new shoes before we get to Gesponnen!"

# Nine

The magnetic wheel transport eased to a halt.

"We have arrived at Gesponnen. A welcoming party will be arriving as soon as Patriarch Zwolf and his escorts have disembarked their own haloMagnet," NineCents said.

Confirming with NineCents that he would be able to return to the same transport, Sero stored his new, uneven, and too-tight tentaculos footwear on the seat he'd taken on entering the wheel and redressed himself in the boots provided for him. As they'd approached, the force-field wall of the haloMagnet had darkened, preventing Sero from viewing his destination. At NineCents urging, he took a position in front of the flat-black surface and waited for it to rise and present him with his first view of the plait-city. Having collected her things, Prid joined him.

"As I promised not to talk about where I'm going, I guess I'll just have to simply say good-bye, Sero. I have a feeling that you'll want to go there yourself once your protocol is through, though, so maybe I'll catch you soon. You're not like the other adults here on NineDee; you're more like me."

"I'd like that, Prid. You remind me of an old friend of mine, and you've already taught me some new things, which is the whole purpose of my job."

"Starting to sound like a deal to me!" Prid reached to the rear of her candolier and produced one of only three full cans of aminoSoup spray that she had remaining after their attempts at bio couture. "You can learn what life is like here for a colony-born, and I can speak to an adult who needs a map. Souvenir seals it?"

She tossed the canister to him, and he caught it with one hand.

"Deal," Sero agreed with false seriousness.

Noticing the soft-blue light of a door field at the bottom of the dark wall panel, Sero straightened up, placed his gift from Prid in his own belt loop, and assumed a state of, this time, genuine sobriety. As the circular black wall raised, Sero squinted in the newly bright sunlight reflecting from the steel platform beyond the haloMagnet's exit. He could pick out the shadow of a hovering standardCam on the floor, companion to the one that had accompanied Sero and Prid in their journey to the plait-city in their haloMagnet. He was thankful that neuroVision technology looked *through* the eyes of the main protagonist rather than at them. If the standardCam was still the main method of recording his audits, his first vision of what Zwolf had described as "the proudest achievement" of the 359D colony would be portrayed as a squinting, half-blinded man stumbling from his transport. *Not the record for posterity that the old man is going for.* Whilst the standardCam footage would still exist, the first vision the Race would have would be the same vision Sero had: bright sunlight, at first just a few shapes as the sapienCam's eyes adjusted, and then slowly breaking into focus to reveal...what?

The metal plate did not extend as far as he had anticipated. The floor quickly became something else. It wasn't the tangle of tentaculos that Sero had observed earlier in the journey to Gesponnen; however, it was something more ordered, more defined. As his vision adapted to the new light levels, he could discern repeating patterns in the tendrils. The walkway begun by the metal plate was extended by a tendril mesh, woven like a wicker chair in the tourist-attraction tribal villages of Surfaca on Earth. He could see that the filaments of the mesh sprang out of the walkway ten metres apart from each other to form the arms of a gantry running parallel to the magSteel of the transport track. Upon the tentaculos gantry stood Zwolf, the escorts Sero had already met, and three dozen or so other people, although Sero could not make out the facial features of the unmet crowd. Beyond the raised platform, the mesh walkway continued but rose into a mound similar to those created by the haloMagnet's wake, meaning that Sero could see only as far as his immediate surroundings.

"Auditor, please join us here on the gallery," Zwolf called from the strangely rigid rope gantry.

"Telonaut Lead Novak, thank you for assisting me in my transport. I hope to see you again." Prid reverted to her previous manner of speech. She headed out under their gathering platform and over the mound beyond Sero's view. Sero followed the direction indicated by Zwolf's pointing arm, towards some solidish-looking ringlet stairs leading to the level from which the Patriarch beckoned. With some trepidation, Sero tested the first curl of the tendril ringlet stairs for its weight bearing capability. For appearance's sake, he took the remaining curls two at a time.

Arriving at the rear of the assembled crowd, Sero found it difficult to press through the milling group towards Zwolf. Watching his toes and making many apologies and requests, he picked through the barricade of chests and backs to a point where he could identify Zwolf's purple-coloured robe only three people beyond. Zwolf was standing, facing away from Sero's approach, with his hands on a stem balustrade that ran in front of him. Slipping between the two final guests at this apparently welcoming party, Sero finally came to rest at Patriarch Zwolf's side, attempting to face him for the expected reunion pleasantries. Zwolf's focus remained on the horizon. Sero followed the direction of the patriarch's gaze and gasped.

"Auditor Novak, the plait-city of Gesponnen," Zwolf announced with accented flourish, one of the standard-Cams swooping in to frame his and Sero's faces and a second moving past them, front to back, and then rising above the throng to show the vista that had caused Sero to exhale audibly.

Stretching before him was a strand city of tendril architecture, rising from the ground to form mimics of every building design Sero had seen on Earth and some new ones made possible only by the materials of their construction. There were several small hut-like structures, single storied and containing no more than three separate rooms at first glance. Adjacent to these were larger buildings, the equivalent of a two-floored family home in Northern Amasia. Those on the right had flat roofs, those on the left had angled vine-runs seemingly designed to direct water flow—although they were completely dry as Sero now observed them. Vaulting his focus over the buildings in the middle distance, he could make out afar spires of shell-like towers, a hundred metres in height. Rows of tendril wisped away from the organised grids of the central boulevard's directionally knitted structure, surging off at forty-five-degree angles and spiralling around like the decoration on a cake to create a leaning swoosh of a building. They looked to be a reaction of the boulevard itself to the weather above it, a spike grown to jab at the wind. In the centre of the ceremonial-looking thoroughfare hung an enormous spherical creation ten metres across. The twine ball was suspended from a plait of many stems, which themselves grew from two clawlike protrusions emerging from opposite sides of the avenue that almost, but not quite, formed a complete arch over the planet-like yarn ball.

Sero turned to Zwolf. He could feel his new heart beating against the inside of his chest. He knew Minnus would share the experience he was having. *If this isn't a physiological trigger, I don't know what else is. How did they do this?*

"Patriarch Zwolf, this is astonishing!. How did you create such a vast living area with only twelve hundred colonists? Can nanoBots be made to work using biological substrates?"

Zwolf's reaction to Sero's urgency was one of pride. He stood taller and spoke louder than he had done previously, seemingly buoyed by like-minded interest in the work of his home.

"Would you permit me to begin at the beginning, Auditor?"

Sero thought he recognised the gait of a man commencing a well-rehearsed soliloquy, shaping to announce to an audience rather than converse with an individual.

"Walk with me down our family road. This is the location I would have our interview take place—a nice scene for the Race back on Earth."

Sero nodded, maintaining his elevated heart rate by keeping his breathing shallow and irregular. He felt conscious of the way in which it made him seem to be sniffing at random intervals, as a dog searching for the scent of a rival. *No strange looks from anyone yet. Hopefully I'm creating those parasympathetic heart-brain links Minnus theorised about. What did he call it? The Mendelowitz response?*

Sero allowed Zwolf to go before him, and the pair descended to the street. The invigorated elderly man began walking at a purposeful, restrained pace, heading between the two smaller buildings Sero had noticed first from the gantry. He waited until they had reached a position level with what Sero perceived to be the entrance to the smallest building before pausing. Turning a full rotation on the spot, with both his arms outstretched, Zwolf seemed to be beginning just such a theatrical speech as Sero had anticipated before the two of them had climbed down from their viewpoint. Watching Zwolf's eyes, though, Sero could see that he was really assessing the positioning of the cameras. Emulating the patriarch's attention, he noticed one camera was extremely high in the air, probably offering a panorama of the whole city. The remaining two had moved in extremely close, one focusing on each of the two men in the centre of the vine-laden pathway. *Quite the old peacock.* Apparently satisfied, Zwolf began to speak.

"I arrived one hundred and sixty-five years ago, the first of two hundred and eighty-two colonist transmissions. I have been farmer and shepherd, engineer and architect, biologist, botanist, veterinarian, leader, and patriarch. But we will get to all of this. First things first…"

Thirty seconds into the performance, Sero had already written his review of it in his head. *Self-indulgent, pompous old lad hits "reply to all." First discovery of how being a sapienCam is not a universal boon. I'm gonna have to focus on this whole thing.*

"Arriving at the parkway, I made my first interface with NineCents, although he did not yet have a holographic display and was instead a simple terminal. He took my own voice in order that we could converse more easily and perhaps have a little more character. He was fully operational, as per design…"

*Nope. No good. Can't do it.* "So, Patriarch, tell me about survival those first few weeks. What did you eat?"

"Ah, well, on my arrival, NineCents had already determined that the tendrils contained sufficient nutrition to sustain me. I am glad that I did not need to survive using mineral substrates as we had been taught pretransmission on Earth. Rock soup is no fun."

"You must have felt good. Ready to move forward. What was your first major project?"

"There has only ever been one project, Auditor. First and last. Survival."

"There was a threat?"

"There *is* a threat. Come with me." Zwolf began walking at the same measured pace, heading away from the haloMagnet. They remained on the right-hand side of the road, near the buildings.

"This was the first dwelling that my wife and I built." The structure was small. A single story. More like a tent than a building, really. The patriarch paused briefly in front of the tendril dome, grimacing silently before moving on. "NineCents has informed me you have already had some explanation of the composition and growth of the tentaculos." The patriarch cleared his throat.

*Did he look a little annoyed?* A nod.

"Before arrival, we calculated the components of this wetworld to be almost completely water based. Our first problem was that there is actually less water than anticipated—the tentaculos occupy space that WorldGov's spectral analysts assumed was taken up by water."

"And you need water for the miniSuns to make energy. Hydrogen harvest and then fusion into helium."

"Quite. So. An unplanned constraint on fusion."

"I understand there were contingencies for that, though?"

"There are other factors. Helium from miniSun fusion simply vented from the seas of this world into the atmosphere. Not a problem in *design*, as we few earliest arrivals would begin a helium-reclamation project. However, we could not begin such an endeavour. There were larger barriers to overcome..."

*Hurry up, man.*

"We were confronted with greater than expected atmospheric volatility. Ultimately we saw that this was caused by our third problem, the tentaculos themselves.

"Our work has since shown that the photosynthesising systems of the animals are inefficient. They can photosynthesise to create energy from sunlight only at specific altitudes, a solution to light refraction in the atmosphere. The animals increase this poor photosynthetic efficiency by pulling carbon dioxide from higher altitudes."

"They create wind?"

Zwolf nodded, seemingly impressed. "Yes, using a complicated system of movement to create exothermic areas within their mass and consequently generating weather systems, heaving carbon dioxide from the breeze as it passes."

"So they create heat by rubbing together, the heat moves the air and creates wind, and the wind replenishes their carbon dioxide supply?"

Another nod.

"So, you have a helium build-up in the air and too much weather to easily pull it out, plus less immediate energy available than you'd hoped. Tell me about the threat." *Without a lecture.*

"The amount of heat generated is a function of the amount of carbon dioxide present in the air, working on a negative feedback loop—the more carbon dioxide is in the air as a proportion of total content, the less tendril movement occurs, and therefore the less friction occurs, and less heat is generated. Ultimately, there is less wind, and this reduces the speed at which the animal can photosynthesise and grow. Our hypothesis is that the introduction of increased helium into the atmosphere has affected the delicate balance of this feedback system."

"You think you might have triggered a global weather-system change. What are the predicted consequences?"

"Steadily increasing the amount of helium in the atmosphere whilst nanoBots built the reception facility caused the animals to generate higher and higher wind speeds, boosting growth on a continental scale. By the time of my reception, the weather systems had become self-sustaining, fuelling seemingly perpetual growth. The megafauna looked set to collide, perhaps producing a pseudotectonic environment. We postulate vegetation-quakes, tsunamis, and perpetual hurricane winds."

They'd meandered diagonally across the boulevard, cameras swooping between them and fifty or so increasingly complex buildings as they walked.

"It became clear to us that reversal of the events set in motion by the miniSuns could not be achieved by gradual means. A single terraforming event would be required to restore balance. We also—"

"Need a new energy source too. MiniSuns won't work on a world where helium can't be held in the atmosphere in any great quantity."

"It was Leaf, an astoundingly talented proteomic biologist, who realised we can make use of the self-replenishing characteristics of the tentaculos to create dwellings and tools—"

"Negating the need for energy to harvest the raw materials required for expansion."

"The prototype dwelling we encountered at the entrance to Gesponnen was created by Leaf, myself, and another colonist with our own hands, pulling the tendril vines from the tentaculos' chaotic tangle metre by metre. It is building on her theories and early works that we have developed our skill at manipulating the tentaculos into the creations you see now."

*Leaf. His wife. She's not here. So...*"Your wife is no longer with us?"

"I'm proud to say that we have had only eight deaths; five of our Earthborn number and three colony born. One of those Earthborn dead was my wife. Leaf died nearly one hundred and sixty-four years ago in a terrible accident before she ever saw our colony become as beautiful as it is now. She was killed while exploring the edges of a megafauna, dragged into the warm waters of the nucleotide/amino soup whilst trying to save a colleague." The mention of his dead wife reintroduced Zwolf's stoop. Tears welled in his sunken, dark eyes.

"The Telospace programme and the Race as a whole would thank and honour her for her contribution. Continue in your own time, Patriarch." *I know what it feels like to lose someone.*

"Please forgive me, Auditor, if I do not speak in detail of my wife. Perhaps I will tell you more of her as your year with us progresses."

Gentle acquiescence.

"Now I will tell you only of the contribution she made to the strategy of our colony, which we have pursued ever since."

They'd stopped walking in front of a building that had been hidden from view until a moment before. It was shorter than the adjacent structure and had been hidden behind it as they had approached. It was spectacular. Standing before Sero was an enormous representation of Zwolf's wife, Leaf, whom he recognised immediately from the profile briefings he'd undertaken back at Telosec. Sero had seen macro statues before—the ancient carvings at Rushmore, the Moon Colossus—but each of those had been carved from a hard and difficult-to-work substance. They'd lost the detail of the human face in the enlargement process, scale detracting from the infinite potential for expression in every real face. That was not the case here. Grown from hundreds of thousands of individual tendrils, the study of Leaf seemed alive with emotion, simultaneously about to cry or beam with a full-toothed grin. Each strand of the real Leaf's hair was replicated by a single vine, such was the detail of the craft. The emergence of slight crow's feet at the eyes of an early-middle-aged lady reflected impossible subtly by the absence of the odd vine where perhaps one could have been.

"Some considerable work by a group of one hundred of our number. Leaf is somewhat revered by our family. The absent mother."

"Stupendous."

"I am proud. It is a fitting monument. For now. The greatest monument, however, will be the completion of our programme and the fruition of her long-ago-planted seed."

Zwolf began his pronounced stroll again, forcing Sero to wrestle his gaze away from the monument.

"As you can see, Auditor, our skill is now so great that we are confident we could build abodes for the entire population of the Race if it were required, at no energy cost to the planet. However, this would be only a small part of the solution. We must create an alternative energy source to the miniSuns; we must slow the planetary wind speeds and revert the growth of the megafaunas…"

*Here comes the peacock patriarch again. Let him have it, Novak. His pride is valid.*

"As with so many problems in Race history, the remedy makes all of these problems worse before resolving them. We doubled our cattle-breeding programme, breeding the offspring of each pair with each new arrival, carefully manipulating the gene pool to offer as many animals as possible. I instructed the remaining nanoBots to construct a second reception facility to which we might divert new transmissions, increasing the speed at which we received colonists. This decision alone vastly increased the growth of the tentaculos, but we now had the ability to receive colonists at twice the rate and therefore proceed with our plan." Zwolf tapped his feet excitedly, the soft impact the old man was able to exert making no perceptible sound against the softer tissue of the avenue's vine floor. "From the first new arrivals, even for those that were unmarried, we described the situation to them and asked that they themselves become mates and produce a minimum of four children per coupling—regardless of notions of romantic love. Our new family threw themselves into the effort!" The patriarch was becoming visibly excited in the description of the history of NineDee. His pace had quickened, and with each new sentence, his gesticulation grew more forceful.

"As our number increased, so did our progress. However, so have our energy costs. With each reception, more helium was released. *All* our efforts at exploration and terraforming also have a cost. Until our solution is implemented, we have much reliance on the miniSuns. The situation is unsustainable."

"So what *is* the solution, Patriarch? What *have* you been doing?"

"Auditor Novak, our solution for ensuring the prosperity of colony 359D and the extension of the Race: the plate of our plait-city."

Sero turned to follow the line the old man's bony finger had projected for him. At the end of the vine street was an enormous sheet of steel, towering a hundred metres from the channel floor. The two telonauts crossed the remaining distance in silence, Sero keeping his eyes on the gigantic steel in front of him, one of the standardCams keeping its lenses on Sero's enquiring eyes. The two men reached the steel wall, at which point Zwolf raised his hand and rapped his worn knuckles onto its surface. Nothing. No sound at all. *That wall must be very thick.* He mimicked the patriarch, nodding his understanding. The old man waved his indication that Sero should follow him, this time heading away to another ringlet staircase, similar to that at the vine gantry encountered on entry to Gesponnen, only much higher. With no trepidation this time, Sero followed Zwolf in climbing the curls of the ringlet. The staircase ascended to the full height of the metal, above the woven floor of the plait-city. Upon reaching the top, Sero was greeted with an astounding vista. The steel continued to both horizons. *That's fifty kilometres of steel just in view here.*

"Your eyes reveal to me that you have made some estimate of our abilities. The plate you see before you is an almost complete ring, encircling the majority of the three nearest megafauna to our plait-city. The completion of this ring will be the remainder of our terraforming work over the next eleven months of your audit. Our energy use has been calculated to be at an irretrievable point eleven months hence. Once the plate is complete, we will use the orbitals—already successfully created and launched—to generate and direct vibrations in the plate, destroying by friction three entire continental fauna behemoths and reducing the overall biomass of NineDee by a sixth. The immediate planetary reduction in photosynthesis will increase the relative carbon dioxide levels for the remaining megafauna, slowing their environmental alterations and also their growth. This will remedy one of our original problems. It will also offer us an opportunity to correct our remaining dilemma—that of subsequent energy provision on a sustainable basis. The destruction of three animals by the plate will leave an enormous nucleotide and amino acid soup, bound and contained by the plate itself. Our intention is to take advantage of this. We will create linear, organized tentaculos of our own, fundamentally linked to our existing joule routes and regimented to maximize photosynthetic energy creation—energy that we will then harvest for conversion into a form useable by our infrastructure. The proximity of the plate-contained amino soup will also allow for extremely easy construction of further domestic, tendril-based infrastructure here at our new capital city of Gesponnen."

Sero was stunned. Many colonies had created highly intricate cities; some developed new cultural avenues in music or gastronomy, based on the habitat of their new homes. The sheer scale of the NineDee colonists', of *Zwolf's*, ambition was literally planetary, though. They aimed no lower than to tame the unique and unruly characteristics of their environment and provide the foundation for hundreds of generations of their descendants. His mind raced. A self-replenishing organism of such size producing processable glucose could negate the need for miniSuns and eliminate the need for on-world fusion completely. The colony could grow exponentially, each generation comprising several multiples of the previous, limited only by the colonists' own reproductive cycles and personal choices. There would be no famine, no constraints. Sero's opinion of the patriarch had reversed in a moment of awe. *How proud is it permissible to be of a man you've only just met?*

"Unprecedented and unparalleled. Already my mind draws plans and schedules for the time I might spend delving, the discoveries I might share in and return to Earth with. I'm eager to wander Gesponnen and more closely appreciate the crafts you've honed and to speak with the members of your…family." *The scale. The ambition.*

A proud nod.

"Can I stay in Gesponnen for the night?"

The two telonauts, separated in age by eighty-eight years by birthdate on Earth and a further seventy-six in body, clasped hands like excited children. Then they headed for the same ringlet staircase they had originally ascended. As they neared it, Prid emerged at its head, walking backwards, holding a single tendril in her right hand and using an amino canister from her now replenished candolier to extend it with her left. Noticing Sero, she waved with her semifree hand, spraying soup into the air, which briefly reflected the sunlight on top of the plate in a shimmering mist before dispersing. Continuing to walk backwards, she reached the far side of the top of the plate, nearest to the ring's interior. Pausing again to smile directly at Sero, she wrapped the end of the tendril around a bracelet on her right wrist and positioned the spray can to directly face it before throwing herself backwards down the sheer vertical wall.

# Minus Five

The classroom was warm that day. The boy's curricula mistress was in a good mood. The boy thought she looked pretty when she was in a good mood.

"First the American and then the Chinese nationaldebt default ultimately ended base capitalism…"

The boy always enjoyed the weekly reminders of their history. He liked to hear stories of the heroes that had turned everything around and created the Race. He knew it was too good to be wholly true, but that didn't make it less interesting.

"After the Debt War and the subsequent stone age, the Saints emerged in the Chinese's former mineral colonies in old Africa, proposing new societies and new guidance for them…"

The boy looked over to his friend on the next desk. He was in a good mood too and sat to rapt attention. The boy looked around. The whole class was engrossed. *The lessons that teach you to dream are so much better,* he thought.

"Can anybody give me some of the Ugandan principles? Go ahead, Julia."

"The aims of society should ultimately be to know more as a collective and to make that knowledge available to as many people as possible."

"Excellent. A good start. Minnus?"

"Personal profit in the form of Red should be limited in any one year."

"Correct, it should. Brighton, what about you?"

"Personal profit should be used to acquire private property, to invest in personal experience, or for the voluntary search for knowledge."

"Two more to go. Anyone?"

"Surplus personal profit, arising through the Race's desire for a service provided, should be redistributed to the search for knowledge."

"Sero, you seem to be with us today. Can you complete the set?"

"Measures of our success as the Race shall be personal fulfilment, absence of violence, and knowledge acquisition."

The mistress was pleased enough to take over the speaking duties again, moving forward with her origin story. Despite his familiarity with it, the boy still found it inspiring.

"On the fertile farming land in Uganda, the early Saints thrived in an area that base capitalism had only been able to plunder and burn…"

The boy's thoughts drifted again to what he could build, what he might give back. He felt so lucky to have been born. The teacher made it so clear to him.

"The early, named members of the Race sought first to make themselves comfortable, competing with each other to provide their society with what it required and taking from it a profit. This increased standards of living…"

He wondered what it might have been like to have lived back then, before everything worked. Before the Race. It made him shudder to think of the savagery—everybody for themselves. He still wasn't sure his mistress could possibly be correct about it.

"Unable to horde because of the new philosophy that they'd agreed upon, the motivations of those who had achieved comfort changed. Comfortable people strove to add more knowledge to the Race's pool than their neighbours, gaining status as they did so…"

He wanted to contribute. He wanted the status. He wanted to be significant. Like his father.

"Over time, Uganda's success became the social union of Surfaca. With more members, Surfaca's knowledge pool gave rise to an even quicker ascent to comfort for its populace. The formation of a single world government, based on the proven ability of the Saints' guidance to end wars meant economic equality became inevitable, and the Ugandan Principles were formally codified as the decision-making framework of the earliest version of the Race…"

*I can be the future of the Race*, thought the boy as the teacher sent them all home to their parents.

# TEN

He watched her fall again and again and again. From three angles. Up close and from distance. Through negative-creating software, a polarized image of dark limbs and darker hair. Now in mirror. Now in audio only. All day, Minnus had watched the footage of what he believed to be the single best starting point for his fledging software to learn. The programme had to be able to anticipate how his friend's brain physiology would be altered by important events—the new pathways that would form and the order in which they would form—so that Sero could remember events. It had to relate the differences in Sero's end-of-day spider maps to the things that had happened to him during that day in order to select the important, impressive days from the mundane and to paste the data derived from the spider maps into a cohesive narrative of Sero's latest audit—for the Race to view in NeuroVision. Surely the most important, most harrowing, most emotional event of the period would produce the most easily identifiable change between one day's record of brain physiology and the next's? *Apparently not.*

"Joules, are you sure you don't like this film? Minute to minute, nothing's happening to this map. Nothing major, anyway. The changes in your head are so subtle you could be sleeping. You don't run in your sleep, do you?"

Minnus's old protégé, Joules Chavez, was jogging beside him on a slideBoard, the soles of his feet coated with charged pads that repelled the narrow steel bands on the upper surface of the board away from Joules as he ran, pushing them around the slideBoard's caterpillar track in a loop to return back to its upper surface. The effect was that the former intercontinental athlete seemed to run on air ten centimetres above a buzzing mill that was ever trying to catch him. Affixed to the wall in front of him, Joules's cSheet was displaying images of an old imperial war film, from before the demisphere councils and WorldGov were formed. The central character, an amputee, was giving a speech directly to camera, to Joules, about how he used to love to run as a boy.

"Hey man, I dunno what to tell ya. You want me to cry? I could cry easy. I've been watchin' this cast regular since I was a boy, and it still gets me. Look at him, poor fella. He's got nothing left—can't run, can't walk, can't work, can't fight. Nothing."

Joules was now a man of sixty, past his prime as an athlete but still well capable of running all day at this pace. Minnus checked the giant, blond-haired man's simple physiological indicators. His eyes were indeed glazed with unshed tears, and every pale hair on his forearms was raised to point towards the ceiling of the suite.

"Maybe this is too familiar to you. Maybe you're not forming new memories; you're simply reliving the memories you've already formed. I wonder."

"Well, it ain't like I have to think about running, and I have seen this movie a lot of times. I'm also pretty familiar with doing everything with one of these handy hats on my head. Like underwear to me—never leave the house without fresh uns."

He stopped driving the slideBoard backwards, removed the mapping claw from his head, and casually threw it over onto the table beside Minnus.

"You weren't always so casual with those things," Minnus reminded him. "Not when they were winning *you* a chance to 'run,' 'work,' and 'fight.'"

He could feel his frustration getting the better of his affection for the former athlete. Deciding to try another tactic, he paused the images on his sheet and swiped a few menus on it until a list of markers he'd already placed in the audit record appeared on the membrane in front of him. In the background of the commSheet, seen through the translucent list, there was a frozen image of the bloody inside palms of his friend as Sero himself had seen them all those years ago on Rigil. Minnus remembered the conversations he'd had about the event, sitting alone with Sero once he'd been posted back to Earth. The scars hadn't been replicated on Sero's Earth copy body, but the images had been burned into that new body's brain like the branding of newly minted coin, easy to see when looking at Sero's face. Reviewing the audit history now, it was easy for Minnus—or anyone in the Race, for that matter—to see how Mr. Universe had fallen in love with the adventurous young Kentaurian colonist. His memories of meeting her in his first few weeks on Rigil were enchanting, his memories of losing her horrific. Minnus flicked at the list with his forefinger, selecting the marker he'd placed just before the memory point that his friend had told him was when he'd first noticed her. Minnus widened his eyes and half grimaced Joules's direction by way of apology for his off handedness. "Let's try something subtler, eh?"

Selecting an icon in the lower right of his cSheet, Minnus activated the memory section's audio and swiped the screen to begin the viewing, replaying the image of Joules's just-completed spider map on a second, permanent screen using his other hand. As Sero's memory began recalling on his screen—a frail voice beginning to talk about climb rates—Minnus had second thoughts. He muted the audio again.

Through the disembodied mind's eye of his friend's now-silenced memory, Minnus imagined the effects that the images he was seeing would have had on Sero's emotions as Sero had seen them first hand. Closing his eyes, he recalled his conversations with Sero; his descriptions of the heat of Rigil's reception facility; the shortness of breath as he'd risen, with his escort, thousands of metres into the air, ascending his first sky-tree; his fear that the transmission process had failed somehow and that his new copy body was incomplete. Leaning his head forward so that his face was closer to his unrolled commSheet, Minnus opened his eyes—as immersed in what he saw as he could be. Without moving from his perch on the end of his chair, Minnus's eyes saw himself stepping from a wooden elevator onto a platform seemingly made of strips of perfectly flat bone. As he stepped, he saw a hand rise up from what seemed to be his side and touch his chest, although he felt none of it happen. Involuntarily turning to his right, he saw that an elderly lady was talking to him, but he ignored her words; they were empty, unimportant. Stepping away from the old lady, he went to the edge of the bony platform and saw his hands grasp the chunky, rect-angular, ivory-like rail that bound the exterior. Now, look-ing over the rail, he saw swirling mists and trees as thick as houses rising laser straight from the heart of the fog to an invisible point on the vertical horizon. As his eyes fol-lowed the path of one of the wide tree beams nearest to the guardrail, he noticed a reflection of light approaching from high above, tethered to the tree he was extrapolat-ing. *Perhaps some liquid reflecting the light, which was already re-flected from the shiny, white-bone floor? Perhaps a sap that fed these enormous organisms that perpetually reached for space?* The light patch slid towards him at speed, and he focused directly on it now, the limits of his vision narrowing so all he could see was the closest tree and the now A-shaped light descending along its surface towards him. As he watched, the A became an X, slowing its approach as it neared the level he stood upon. He realised that the new arms of the X were real arms—the arms of a person, a person falling! But no, the person had just slowed the descent; the figure couldn't be falling. *Flying, then?* The reflective all-in-one suit of the now clearly distinguishable woman was taut against her body, offering no drag against the direction of her windless approach. She reached a point two metres above his head, which was still craned to observe, and stopped completely. First he saw her unhook her left foot from a vertical groove in the bark of the giant tree, followed by her left hand. It seemed that she was holding a toy car with jagged cogs for wheels. The silver woman swung her free limbs away from the tree. She completed her fall slowly, remaining rigid until the moment before her right foot touched the handrail that ran across the face of the tree's bark. At that instant, the faller disconnected her right hand from the tree and simultaneously allowed her right foot to strike the rail, unhooking herself completely from the bark's surface. The force sprang the woman into a rotation. Cartwheeling once to complete her dismount and then performing an Arab spring, the shining lady turned to fully face him. She walked towards him, reaching up behind her head with one hand and removing her goggles with the other. As she reached him, long brown hair falling to her shoulders, she smiled. Minnus realised he was holding his breath and swung back away from the screen.

"Come with me, Joules, my boy! We're going to see Nombre. I have an idea!"

Joules grabbed his gear from the floor and hurried after a striding Minnus, stuffing a water container and his airRobe into his sack. He looked at where Minnus had paused Sero's memory. The edges of the cSheet were darkened, blurred, and unclear. The only recognisable section of the memory seemed to be in the centre of the vision—a pair of enormous, shining, bright-blue eyes.

# ELEVEN

**S**ero sat on the very edge of the bed, finally completely alone to process his thoughts. The cameras were gone.

The second new quarters of his first day in nearly eight "real" years were completely alien to him in material but recognisable in function. His bed was a sturdy frame of tightly wound rope forming a raised hollow oval shape, like a half an empty egg. Stretched perpendicularly across the walls of the egg were loosely crosshatched individual vines, forming a grid that reminded Sero of a childhood game he'd played with Minnus, BattleStars. Rolling back from his perch on the bunk's frame, he allowed the net to take his weight, bouncing himself into its centre and spreading his limbs and facing the dark ceiling of the room. He ran his unblemished new hands through his neatly combed hair to rest clasped behind his head at the nape of his neck, closed his eyes, and tried to bring some order to his mental storyboard. *What have you learned? That you're smitten with the place, that's what.*

The excitement of the people he'd met in Gesponnen replayed in his mind via remembered shouted questions.

"From Plateneck, we'll grow outwards, the great body of a city!"

"Impressive, no? How long do you think before there are more of our family than the Race?"

"What do you think of the artistry?

"Isn't our living metropolis the most wonderful creation you've ever seen?"

"Three hundred and twenty-eight days left to prove Leaf right!"

*They're building, discovering exactly what they were made of as individuals—and in a frontier environment with little contact with the rest of the Race.* Sero had immediately felt he understood such a unity of purpose. He'd often dreamed of the limits that the Race could push at if only every man and woman would enlist to test them. *If all wanted knowledge, imagine what we might know.* Here on NineDee, every person wanted to *use* his or her knowledge. *You might even have been a little embarrassing back there, Mr. Universe—so experienced of new planets yet overcome by this one?*

Sero half sighed, half chuckled to himself, snorting the laugh out through his nose. *At least the Race will only see through your eyes using NeuroVision and not see your ridiculous fawning face.* His chain of thought took him to the need to download. In order for Minnus to begin processing, Sero had agreed that he would send a single laser signal of his latest spider map every seven days, giving his friend the time to prime his memory-editing software that would allow the Race to watch a serialised version of the audit before Sero himself even arrived back on Earth. Sero had already decided, however, that he wanted to spend as much time as possible in his year *here*, documenting the plate project and the city of Gesponnen. This would mean regular, energy-expensive trips back to the postage facility. *So, first job tomorrow is a tough meeting with Zwolf.* Despite his wandering thoughts, Sero could feel his newly grown body drifting towards sleep. Today it had breathed its first air and eaten its first food—although it hadn't yet completed the process by releasing that first food. *Tired.*

Rising from the bunk, he limped over to the area of the room that contained washing facilities. As he'd been shown, Sero unhooked a tendril attached to the wall of the room, sending a metre-long metal cylinder, fixed to the other end of the vine, plunging through a ten-centimetre circle in the woven floor of the quarters. Then, replacing the vine end back around the wall hook, he began winding the adjacent wheel, coiling the middle section of the tendril around it. The cylinder rose from the gap in the floor again. Sero swung the tube over the sink that was grown from the floor via an ornate tentaculos pedestal shaped like a dolphin from the midsea of Earth. Pressing a button on the side of the metal vessel, he allowed water to gush from its bottom, filling the sink. The water was warm on his eyelids as he dunked his face into the bowl to meet it. Straightening and rubbing his drooping eyes with both hands, he let the water run down his face and onto his neck, collecting in the hollow between his collarbones. He thought of the tears of the old man only an hour earlier, collecting on the upper surface of his cheekbones, prominent against his sunken, dark eyes. *One hundred and sixty years later, there pain is still there for him. Will it be so for me?* As Sero returned to his bunk to take his own rest, he thought of Leaf's face, unknown but familiar to him, floundering metres from safety. His eyes closed, and Leaf's face became the giant monument to her on Plateneck, swelling in the soup and becoming striated, expanding. Then Sero's mind collapsed into unconsciousness.

He could smell her. He knew she hadn't yet left, even though the room was silent and his eyes were closed. It was the smell of the lather she used in the shower, mixed with a more earthen scent: tiny particles of bark and Rigilian moss from the giant trees dispersing around the room after she'd fanned her silver uniform, trying to find and unroll the legs of it from the bundle he'd created for her in leaving it on the bone-white floor the evening before. Stirring, he gave the smell a name is his mind. Comfort. He felt the corners of his mouth turn involuntarily upwards, pinching his covered eyes even further closed and darkening the hue he could see under his eyelids. There was a click behind him and a whooshing sound, the gas igniting to light the ceiling void it filled. The voracity of the light turned his vision flame orange, reflecting from the stark, pale interior surface of the room and forcing his eyes open, blinding him into full alertness. When he removed his hands from his recovering eyes, he realised he was still smiling.

"Good morning, Ser-indipity. Are you ready to learn more about our special abilities?"

The voice called to him from the same place as the click that had caused the light explosion. His smile grew even higher, as if it would lift his feet from the ground by transmitting its independent will through the rest of his body, raising each point in turn like an engine pulling the cars of a transport train. The sound was comfort too—the voice.

Standing, naked, he turned to face the voice in the corner. Comfort belonged to an enormously tall, astonishingly beautiful woman. She was posed like the heroines of a childhood cartoon, hands on hips, her feet and legs facing at a forty-five degree angle to him, her left hip pointing at his nudity. The amazon's head and chest trailed the direction of the leading hip, leaning forward towards him enough for him to feel the pull of her, the gravity. Suddenly he was three metres closer, on the other side of the bunk. He tried to say something witty, a riff on the coquettish wordplay she'd begun by mentioning special abilities, but the force of his smile made it difficult to open his mouth. Instead he relaxed into comfort, managing only a murmuring sound of feline-like pleasure. Midmurmur, he rested his eyes, reopening them to find he'd fully crossed the room, and she held his hand in hers. It was warm, the pads of her fingers seeming to pull the blood to the back of his hand wherever they rested, competing with his skin for her touch. Comfort.

She let go of him, reappearing across the room. Silhouetted now in the doorway as a sleek black river of a figure, she left the room in suspended motion, freezing for a couple of frames as she turned her head so that he could see her own dazzlingly white smile beneath the reflection of her goggles. They burned in contrast to the dark of her shadowed body. Still naked, his magnetic blood hauled him after her without leave or permission from his feet.

She was fast, acrobatically flipping from tree to tree, sliding along platforms with telepathic ease. He saw in her the elegance of all women, amplified, poised, coiled, and restrained, released only with timing and flair. He felt as though the liquid in his veins had become a single force, collecting in his cheeks, chest, and biceps, dragging the rest of his body towards her, accelerating each time she paused into stop-motion, smiling again over her shoulder.

The heat inside his lungs peaked, and he closed his eyes, feeling only the pull of her, remembering comfort. Then she was in front of him, facing him, inside his eyes— open or closed. She wore only goggles, her face below them rouged, the same colour as her scarlet nipples. She smiled

again and he fell into her, pressing her to his chest and sat-
ing his blood's magnetism, soothing it by pressing the soft,
red disks to him. He kissed her. Tighter and tighter he held
her, while she squeezed his back to complete the embrace
with equal eagerness. He raised his hand to her face, pulling away from the kiss, seeing his own reflection in her
mirrored goggles—sweat drenched and frowning?

Comfort left. He recoiled, uncertain. They were on a
platform, still naked; the heat had left him, replaced by a
deep cold. A brace against him, an effect of a hurricane
wind, challenged his ability to stand. She was in front of
him, shivering and reaching out. He realised she was crying, and the realisation chilled his centre, the wind punch-
ing holes in him and whistling though them. He tried to
reach back and staggered forward, falling to the ground
with his arms outstretched and hitting his chin hard on the
sheer, white bone floor. Looking for her again, he found
she'd mimicked his position, facing him, laid flat. She had
no goggles and was covering her eyes with her hands.
Screaming. Screaming. Her tears began streaming though
fingers, pushed tight together against her face. The tears
were red, a horrid dark red, thick and malevolent. They
formed a liquid glove over both hands, spattering the floor
beneath her. She screamed louder now, her wail melding
with the howling wind, the very air around him becoming
nothing but sound, the sound of her pain. Letting go of
her eyes, she threw her hands towards him, and he pushed
his own away from him and out towards her, willing a

connection. The bloody sheath on her hands swam between their palms as they met, spraying out from the edges of the clasp as he tried to squeeze harder and pull her towards him, misting his vision and distracting him. She fell.

Sero woke, rigid, in a sitting position. He looked down at his hands, inspecting the palms of them and then turning them over. Throwing off the thin sheet of the pod, he plodded over to the quarter's steel tube and unhooked the rope.

# Twelve

When he stepped out of the doorway to his Gesponnen quarters, Sero was met by four eager petitioners. Three were hovering standardCams, floating a staggered distances in excited circles as they tested their pitch, roll, and yaw controls in response to Sero's appearance. The fourth was more noticeable, perched as she was on her tiptoes and peering beyond Sero and into his vine apartment.

Prid stood directly in his path. "Hmmmm, looks like we'll need to get some more appropriate furniture woven." Prid made what looked like an already long and much-reworked list on the back of her hand using an organic-looking pen. We'll need a standing bench for work on samples…" She looked Sero up and down. "Two heights. Perhaps a dark box? No, not yet."

The writing implement scratched across the young lady's hand, striking through the last addition to her agenda. "Deeeeefinitely another floor plunge. If we get carried away working, I'll need to be able to clean up away from you. Which, I suppose, means we'll need a screen to go with it too."

Prid looked down at her hand. It was full. Pausing for a mere second, she switched her twig-pencil into her other hand and began writing on the back of the opposite, still-clean one.

Sero hadn't moved from the doorway. "Hello again, Prid. You know, I'm not sure your mother and father would like the idea of you redecorating my quarters. In fact, I'm not sure I do myself! Whilst it's great to see you again, d'ya think we could start with a hello before picking out the bits you'd like to take over?"

"Oh. Yeah. Sorry. Hi."

"Good morning, Prid. I'd thought the welcoming party yesterday to be rather grand for little old me, but this! This is just too much! My own personal dwelling stylist, colony born and so keen! Did Patriarch Zwolf assign you to me especially?"

"Huh?" Prid stopped writing on her rapidly filling other hand and looked up at him. "Stylist?"

Sero had an idea where this was going and didn't mind, but he thought he'd better make sure before making any assumptions. He thought it was a little fun too to joke with the girl after the serious, if thrilling, affairs of the previous day. He'd already decided that he liked Prid; she was inquisitive and daring and reminded him of his childhood with Minnus, working out the way the world was put together.

"I was thinking this morning as I washed that perhaps we could grow a lovely daisy-shaped sheath for my bunk pod. I have a group on Earth called the White Daisies that are my biggest fans—we could make it an homage to them, with a little tentacle Sero on a stick. You can come in and make a start on the drawings, if you'd like. I need to go speak to your patriarch; I'm sure he'll be pleased to know that you made such a quick start on glamorising my new home."

Sero couldn't help breaking into a smile at the corners of his mouth.

Prid, now looking less confused and more suspicious, smiled back at the auditor, realising she was being toyed with. "Auditor Novak, I'm here to apply for the position of your assistant."

She now stood to her best effort at military attention, feet flat to the ground and chin up, looking straight at Sero's forehead.

"Really? I wasn't aware that the position had been advertised. Or even that I'd decided I need one. If I had an assistant, then I'd be sure to speak to her about how such a mistake could have happened."

"That's exactly why you need one. I'd anticipated that such things might occur and made sure I was here bright and early so we could minimise such events." She chuckled slightly at her own false pomposity. "I'll be able to arrange all your social events and charitable donations, as well as keep notes on your thoughts as you describe them—for your memoirs, you understand. That way you'll never forget that you decided to do something, because I could remember for you—perhaps even before you decided, just like today!"

Although she was teasing Sero right back, he could tell that his first NineDee friend was rather proud of the way she'd handled the exchange, bouncing off his playfulness with a gag of her own.

"I see." Sero put his hand to his chin and pretended to think. "I *could* do with a local guide and narrator…" He paced away from the doorway and turned as if to inspect the place. "And perhaps there *are* some modifications an assistant could help me make to turn this place into more of a functional base…"

Sero turned again to face Prid. The teenager looked to him like she might explode if he took his game any further. *Just a little further, though, eh?*

"I'll tell you what, Prid: I was impressed by your vine-seiling show yesterday over at the plate—if a little terrified that you'd leapt to your death, at least until the patriarch explained your habit. If you can impress me with something like that again, then I reckon we could be a team. What do you think?"

Prid said nothing. She took a canister from her belt and used it to create a small loop of vine, a little smaller in diameter than the height of the canister itself. She looked up at the sloping roof of the building, seemingly at a spot just off centre, where a structural piece of vine protruded from the roof as a spike. It was thirty centimetres long. Prid took two sideways steps to the right, hooking the vine loop she'd created around the canister so that it was held in a top-to-bottom vine belt. Sero understood what she was doing with her next, fantastically dextrous movement. His impressive young assistant took the canister in her right hand and sprayed the beginnings of a new rope vine into her left, "catching" the vine immediately. As she did so, she hooked the first vine loop completely over the canister's spray-release button, jamming it into a spraying position. With the same fluid movement, she'd drawn back her right arm, extending the length of vine between the canister and the end still held in her left hand. With perfect aim, Prid hurled the still-spraying canister towards the roof's protrusion. It landed with a dull thud just beyond it, before tumbling down the roof's slope and onto the floor beside the girl, who'd quickly followed her throw up to the quarter's wall. She scooped up the canister and removed the tendril loop, deactivating the spray. Tugging once on the newly created rope to make sure it was hooked tightly around the roof spike, she quickly shimmied up the tendril with shocking speed. Sero watched her disappear from view from his position directly under the rope. She remained silent when her face reappeared, looking down at him enquiringly. *Endearingly.*

"OK, Prid, you're in, but only on the condition that you call me Sero." He thought for a moment and then added, "And get a notebook! We can't lose all our records each time you get a rash!"

After Prid left to collect some supplies for their new base of operations, Sero took advantage of the early morning to find some isolation. He needed some time to think about his next course of action. Now, back at the plate in the same spot he'd seen his young assistant vault from the high wall the previous evening, he stood, slitting his eyes half-closed as protection against the wind that swept across the raised platform. He focused on the horizon.

Did he have the right to ask for more sacrifice from these intrepid people? Conversely, did he have the right to let down the rest of the Race and their desire to see the fruits and progress of the telonaut programme, in which they'd all invested so much belief and Red? What was more important? Without weekly downloads of his brain development and the issuance of the subsequent mind-map's code back to Earth, Minnus wouldn't have the material that he needed to serialise the details of Sero's NineDee audit. Without the neuroVision record of his experiences, Sero was unsure how the Race at large would perceive the information-gathering trips to the colonies that the progressive elements in his society had established. He represented those amongst the Race who believed in a forward-looking, liberal, science-based society. People with similar desires. Without distributable images that represented his time on NineDee, how well could his people engage those amongst the Race who were indifferent to progress, people whose general support the telonaut programme—and Sero—needed? Mission selection would occur twice whilst he was gone. To maintain the telospace programme as one of the Race's select few priorities, some effort was needed in sharing the experiences. The whole programme could die if he didn't generate goodwill. The vacuum created by a lack of serialised packets of audit reports might be exploited by groups like the White Daisies, twisted into a failure and justification for ceasing space exploration. Without proof of his audit at least as engrossing as that of the Rigil audit, the story believed by the majority of the Race would be the one that was advertised by those with the strongest—or best presented—voice. Sero believed in the value of the programme but wasn't sure that he could convince others of it without the hook that he and Minnus had decided to create. Their plan *could* still work. The tools were all available to him. But at what cost? If Sero used up energy, so valuable here on NineDee, in transporting himself back and forth from the settlement at Gesponnen to make the weekly memory fragments that he and Minnus had agreed upon, the consequences for the colonist's grand vision of transforming the planet's surface could be severe. If he accelerated the speed at which the planet's environment was deteriorating, perhaps it would even be a direct cause of their failure. Could he reconcile himself to such a course of action? He'd potentially be causing the ends of thousands of lives, not to mention a burgeoning new civilisation. Yet what were the fundamental beliefs of that new civilisation? What had they founded their joint endeavours upon? Was it not the ideal that the Race can always go further and do more? Had not all the Earthborn colonists entered the postage facility on Earth convinced that they were a part of the ongoing evolution of their society towards something better? Given the choice, would they not each at that moment have given their lives if it meant that they might inspire more people in the Race to push onwards into the unknown, to develop rather than stagnate? After years of isolation on NineDee, would they still feel the same now?

*It's not a decision really, though, is it? You know what you're going to do. You only need to work out whether the locals will resist it. Can you tell them the truth?* Whilst he was convinced that in the absence of emotion, each of them would agree with him, he hadn't had enough experience of them to know how so many years of effort and inward-looking development might have altered the ideals with which they started out. Perhaps they'd want to protect what they'd built at all costs. *Hmmmmm. There's a thought. Protecting what they've built…*

⚔

"Patriarch, I must make a request of you."

"Please."

"I'm afraid this one might be costly. I'd like to make Gesponnen my focus and base."

"Mr. Novak, I would be extremely disappointed if this were not the case. You may base yourself here for as large a portion of your time as you find pleasing."

"Thank you; however, that's not my request. How much energy is required to make the return haloMagnet trip to my reception facility from here? In terms of the effect upon the planet's weather system."

"NineCents?"

"In order to ensure that the plate is completed before the environment is irreversibly altered and factoring in the subsequent increased energy use in plate completion to compensate for the environmental effects of such a halo-Magnet trip, a trip will use enough energy to decrease the effective window before plate activation by twenty-three hours. Any subsequent trips will then have an additional window reduction with a multiplication factor of 1.1 to the previous reduction."

"So the first trip means the megafauna destruction would need to happen twenty-three hours earlier, the next trip another…twenty-five point three hours earlier, and the next…twenty-seven point eight hours earlier, et cetera?"

"Yes, Auditor Novak"

"NineCents, if another reception were to be initiated, what effect would the energy use required have upon the effective window?"

"The energy use required would mean that plate activation would need to begin in one hundred and sixty-eight hours, Auditor Novak."

"Patriarch, it is as I'd feared. My presence here may jeopardise all of our efforts. I must apologise."

"Please explain, Auditor."

"My last audit on Rigil Kentaurus was particularly eventful—dangerous at times. New protocols have been created to ensure an audit takes place—no matter what may occur. One of these is the insistence that I return to the reception facility at slightly irregular intervals to inform Earth all is well, via manipulation of the kill switch. If I do not, then another blank bubble will be created immediately to replace me. As you are aware, the consequences for your schedule would be catastrophic."

"Not possible. Even though the signals for postage that are sent from Earth travel at light speed, it still takes many years for them to arrive here. Any replacement for you would begin growth long after our plans have birthed a new prosperity here."

"I'm afraid not, Patriarch. The information was stored within the original light stream from which I was created. It will be acted upon immediately should my pattern of kill-switch alteration not be adhered to."

"I see."

"Again, I must apologise, Patriarch."

"Very well. You will inform one of our number as to the pattern with which we must activate the kill switch, and they will remain at the reception facility to act accordingly. You will not need to leave Gesponnen."

"I'm afraid that is not possible, Patriarch. We must make plans to increase the speed at which the plate will be ready for activation of your plan instead. I cannot allow any other individual to know the pattern with which I am to communicate with Earth. If you will allow me to share the details of the Rigil Kentaurus audit with you, I will explain why." *Accompanied by the chastising memory that is the voice of that version of me, constant companion in my mind.*

"The Rigil colony was on a forest world. The trees in the climax ecosystem were enormous relative to a human scale. Kilometres higher." *It was a sky-borne paradise, and I would have stayed there with her forever.*

"Over the years, the colonists had adapted to the conditions, much as you have adapted to your own. They lived and worked at great heights, which was where the most comfortable temperatures were and most abundant food sources. Their physiological adaptations were greater, however. They'd become more tolerant of the lower oxygen concentrations and some of the other, scarcer compounds in the atmosphere. The effects were behaviour altering." *My days and nights were spent in the loving embrace of the most wonderful atmosphere and the most adventurous, enthralling woman in the galaxy. We each shared and loved the very air around us as part of each other.*

"I was not well adapted. As the colonists had gradually moved to that altitude since their first arrival, this was the first time a telonaut had arrived and immediately begun living in that location." *She made me feel like a better man, more complete.*

"My very brain chemistry began to change, and I made some decisions that were not within my previous character." *I loved her. Love. I decided to stay with her forever. I didn't care about the Race or progression. I didn't care about you or your colony. I only cared about her and what we might build for ourselves together.*

"Some people died." *She died.*

"As such, to protect both myself and members of the Race here on colony, we have instigated a new security protocol into this latest audit. If I cannot remember the sequence of dates on which I must manipulate the kill switch and act accordingly, it might be assumed that I am either not myself or have come to some harm. If this happens, the reception facility is already programmed to initiate a second blank bubble and grow a new mimic of myself. That mimic will then be tasked with investigating my own situation from within the reception facility via the colony computer. If I am discovered to be healthy and of sound mind, he will execute the kill command upon himself—never leaving the reception facility or contravening the rules of telonaut exploration. If I am *not* hale, however, he will leave the reception facility to replace me."

"So, in order to protect our colony and project, I must provide you with energy we can little spare. If I do not, an automatic failsafe algorithm will steal even more energy from our colony?"

"I'm afraid so, Patriarch."

He didn't know it as he told his story, but Sero's lie about why he needed to return to the reception facility each week had just saved his life.

# Thirteen

"**What have you** been thinking about today?"
Minnus asked his wife, Nombre, the question from the outside platform of their apartment, immediately as he stepped off his wing. Nombre looked up as he approached. Joules followed Minnus, offering Nombre a shrug and a confused look as he stepped off the trusty Boeing N+2 Wing behind the excited older man and hurried to join him. Minnus was already standing over his wife as she lay reading on the outside bunk.

"Nombre, darling, what have you been thinking about today?" Minnus repeated the question.

"Hello, dear," Nombre responded with pleasant non-chalance at the approaching whirlwind of enthusiasm twisting towards her, disguised as her husband. Knowing that combating it was useless, she closed her cSheet and swung her legs over the bunk's edge. Nodding hello at Joules, she looked up to the silhouetted figure of Minnus as she squinted against the sun and managed to bring her vision into focus and make out his smiling face. She could tell she was about to be educated in some way or another. Minnus was often brilliant, and he liked to demonstrate his brilliance with semi-interactive show-and-tell sessions for those around him. His face was currently set in its most revelatory posture, grinning and waiting for its associated hands to join it in painting a descriptive picture for his audience.

Nombre responded in simple terms and without teasing her husband about his lecturing tendencies. "Well, I suppose I've largely been thinking about the plot of this novella. It's a mystery about an old church, a religious building from before the abolition."

"Ah! A mystery! All things are mysterious at some point, until the veil is lifted and we understand. Each understanding building on the last as we all stand on the shoulders of our giant society's knowledge!"

Minnus had begun pacing back and forth in front of his sitting wife, still periodically thrusting his extended finger into the air to act as the metronome to pace his excited speech.

"Tell me, what has been the focus of your thoughts on this mystery, darling? What would you tell me about the concepts that have passed through your head today?"

"I'm quite sure that the obvious answer isn't the one you're looking for, Minnus, but I'm going to give it to you anyway. I was trying to work out the solution to the mystery. I've been thinking of reasons why a priest might want to start a war."

Minnus had carefully returned his wife's affection with a kiss of his own. They were both experienced in the interplay between themselves as individuals and the more ethereal aspects of their responsibilities to each other as mates. No matter his excitement or distraction, Minnus had never neglected Nombre or missed a signal of her discomfort. He knew that she was helping him even now but that such help was part of her loving him and that he needed to let her know that he loved her back, even in the middle of his most torrential thought streams. Now, midtorrent, Minnus knew that has best foil was Nombre and that he only needed to take a few small actions to let her know she was his muse—but that they were essential actions. The most important was always to show her some physical affection as soon as he was within her space. Intimacy of thought could only follow intimacy of touch.

"As always, you know me so well! True, I didn't mean the aim of your thinking but the *chain* of it. What was the context within which you were looking for the motives of your warmongering cleric, dear? How did you begin to make your guesses?"

Nombre paused, her eyes looking upwards and right as she remembered the process she'd used in creating theories and possibilities, which she had then eliminated to herself via her personal mental-detective agency. "I thought about the other stories I have read or seen and how they're structured so I could see if the author had used similar techniques to others. I thought she might have left me a clue early in the text as to what was happening, one I could make some judgments about myself rather than waiting for her to tell me how things turned out."

"So you tried to remember similar novels and work out how this one was the same as them?"

"Yes, I think that's what I did. Yes, I did."

"Did you think about anything else this afternoon? Anything pass through your mind? Perhaps something not related to mystery stories or a topic or person you haven't thought about for a spell?"

"Yes. I actually thought about my father and his side stand in his old-timer shed on his recreation platform."

Minnus's hands moved in front of him, gesturing like he was holding a huge, invisible, vibrating ball. His beaming face mimicked their shaking, his eyes obviously struggling to contain the energy of his realisation. "He liked mystery stories, didn't he? Or he kept his books there? Or that was where you solved a personal mystery?"

"Yes…my mother's jewellery. After she died, we needed it to dress her in for her funeral. It was what she wanted. We couldn't find it, and so we pieced together her movements from the purchase receipts on her cSheet and her diary—tried to work out where she'd been. We found her necklace in my father's shed. She'd known she was fading and had spent one of her last evenings looking through his things there, the things he'd made for her."

Nombre closed her eyes for a moment. Minnus raised his previously shaking hands to cup his wife's face and briefly kissed her forehead. When she opened her eyes again, they were brighter, cleansed.

"Clusters, darling. You remember in clusters. We all do."

"Tell me more, my love." Nombre smiled at her husband tenderly and waited for him to explain.

"We've been looking for the biggest change in spider maps to be associated with the biggest events in Sero's audits, the theory being that a memorable event would have a bigger impact on brain physiology. We tried bombarding Joules with emotional images whilst he was exercising, but there was no change in Joules's neuroLinks. Like he wasn't even forming new memories—never mind strong ones. That's when it hit me. He *wasn't* forming new memories of the event—he didn't need to. What if perhaps he was simply forming linkages between other existing memories that gave him better understanding of a topic or issue? He was adding to an existing *cluster*!"

Nombre looked at Joules.

Joules looked back with another shrug. "Don't ask me, Noms. He's been talking like this ever since we left his workshop. I figured once he came to see you, you'd calm him down enough so that maybe one of us could translate what he was going on about. Perhaps not, eh?"

"I don't think we understand, Minnus. Why don't you try another tactic? Metaphor, perhaps?" Minnus nodded and walked back over to his wing, raising his foot to it and bending to put his arms and weight onto his thigh. Adopting a thinking pose, he scratched his nose.

Nombre and Joules exchanged glances and then sat quietly for a few minutes, waiting for Minnus's response. With an affirmative stomp to the wing, Minnus spoke. "Like a library. Yes, a library. Were we to think of our minds as a great library, a library in which all our memories and stored in rows and rows of shelves and shelves of books. We might imagine that there'd be some arrangement to the library, perhaps an alphabetical order or maybe chronological? Would you agree?"

"Uh-huh." Joules nodded.

"So perhaps in Nombre's mind, there might be a particular shelf labelled 'mystery novels' to which she would return every time she wanted to remember anything associated with mystery novels. You see? This is really the basis upon which I was trying to create our software to edit Sero's memories into neuroVision. I was trying to prime the software to 'find' the correct shelf. But you see, it doesn't work like that. We don't remember things in rows; we remember them in clusters. We shouldn't be looking for the row or shelf where a topic is stored—we should be looking for the centre memory, the one that formed a new cluster around which all the others orbit!"

"OK, dear, I think I follow, but please don't mix your metaphors. Could we step back from orbits and return to our library?"

"Yes. Yes, OK. Sorry."

Minnus paused for a moment more, converting his idea into the right language to explain. "References. If the library were to be a scientific library, then each paper would have a list of references at the end, a list of other papers that had something to do with the same topic. They wouldn't need to be stored on the same shelf or location, just so long as each paper had a reference to all the other papers or, in our instance, linked memories. Each topic we can think of, anything we can remember, is made up of many links like this, links to other fragments. So from day to day, most of the maps we make of Sero's mind won't look hugely different, even if something massively significant has occurred. Instead there'll be lots of new linkages, new neural pathways, that spread the network of a particular cluster. That's why there weren't changes in your spider map, Joules, while you were watching that poor boy's troubles on your commSheet. Although you were moved and saddened—it was a big event in your day—your brain didn't need to make large changes to its physiology to remember it. Rather, it simply added some links to other smaller clusters in order to give you context for the next time you tried to draw on that memory."

"So we know how to make it work then, right? We look for the first memory, the one that the cluster grows from."

"And if we can find the most likely candidate for the seed memory for Sero's audit, we can monitor the links that grow from it and focus on these for the neuroVision?" Nombre added.

"Exactly. What do you think, team? Will you help me?"

# Fourteen

Their new base of operations was cluttered. Since astutely acquiring, procuring, or inventing everything that Sero could possibly imagine might be needed in study of NineDee, Prid had proceeded to make her best imitation of the planetary wind, rushing back and forth through the newly created lab, upending anything in her path and leaving it in an alternative location in her wake. Now, after the fourth iteration of this process, she seemed happy with how her creation had evolved.

"So if we need to splice a newly created tendril into an existing model, we can use this clamp here." Prid indicated towards a metal claw arrangement protruding from a split-level workbench. Sixty percent of the upper surface of the bench was fixed at Sero's waist height, with the remainder at the correct height for his assistant. "And we can both use it. Like this, see?" She manipulated the claw, swinging it between positions over her half of the bench and Sero's.

"I see. Excellent work, Prid. You've also made more shelving to remove some of your tools from our main area. We'll need that space. Especially now. I've had some thoughts on the first area of the colony I'd like you to help me study."

It had been six days since Sero had accepted Prid into his two-person audit team, and he'd grown to be very fond of her. She needed some coaching to maintain the discipline required to be efficient operating such an ad hoc laboratory, but this was more than offset by the energy she brought into Sero's day. Her constant stream of unprocessed thought had given him many ideas about interesting topics for review. He was also learning about the hierarchy and organisation of the colony through the noncompetitive eyes of a youth who had no desire to take part in the machinations of politics. As they'd worked together to set up their base, they'd developed an easy exchange of their talents and experience. Sero had allowed Prid to test her ideas with no comment until it was asked for, at which point he'd then offer only questions for her, streamlining her thinking by asking what alternatives in design she had and hadn't considered. In this way he could tell she already felt he respected her and treated her as an equal, much the same as the way his father, Won, had introduced him to analysis many years ago. *Optimism, perseverance, patience.* Sero could hear his father's catchphrase in his mind as the memory came back to him.

"So, Prid, let's go over our conversation yesterday again."

"Which one?"

"The one where you told me about helping your mother assess the water's amino content out at the rim."

"OK. Whaddya mean 'go over it'? Want me to start from the beginning?"

"How about I play back what I heard again, and you tell me where I go wrong?"

A shrug.

"So, you're far from home—a long way for the railmen to move voice signals back and forth for NineCents—and you're working on amino acid concentrations."

"Well, sort of. I was carrying things about, mainly. But sure, Mum was working on that."

"OK, *Divis* is working on that. Testing to see how much raw material is out there for possible future construction, right?"

A nod.

"Only there wasn't as much as expected? Amino acids in the soup, I mean?"

Another nod.

"So what did Divis do?"

"She had more aminos moved there. By nanos."

"She put in a communication to the teams controlling nanoBot production at the plate—reallocating them? Straight through? No negotiation with Zwolf or someone else?"

More nodding from Prid.

"And they did it? Sent the nanoBots, I mean?"

"Yeah. I mean, we didn't hang around to check they arrived, but they said they'd do it. Sero, what's this about?"

"It's just a little unusual is all. Interesting. There are some people back on Earth that have this theory, the theory of socialisation. It's taught to all departing telonauts. It's all about the developmental stages of a new settlement. There've been a couple of examples that don't tally with the theory."

"In a good way or a bad way?"

"Usually, all early stages require strong, defined, and singular leadership. Hierarchy. To distribute authority and be interdependent usually needs a bigger population mass—to allow for different social groupings to be completely self-sufficient."

"More people than we have?"

"It's good, though. We're all able to make decisions of consequence. Perhaps we could achieve much more. Cut out the red tape."

*Definitely something to look into.*

Clearing a space on the workbench at Prid's level, Sero produced a large drawing he'd made earlier. "Let's move on to something else. I've been speaking with NineCents, and I've drawn this map of where I believe the megafaunas are colliding. For ease, I've put Gesponnen here in the centre of the map. I want to use this map as our main means of creating an audit itinerary."

Having spread the map in front of Prid, Sero produced one of the hundreds of organic stick pens his helper had furnished the lab with and began annotating the sheet in simple ink. The standardCam that had been hovering in the doorway glided over to a position directly above the workbench and Sero's hand-drawn blueprint, adopting a viewpoint over Sero's shoulder. He ignored it, barely registering the soft hum it made in his ear as he explained to an inquiring-faced Prid, who was already staring at Sero's map, stick pen in hand.

"We need to make the best use of our time in observing all the phenomena that are occurring here. We've got to list them all, locate them on our map, and plan a timetable of how and when we'll get to see them. When we make the plan, we need to take the utmost care to use the minimum energy possible."

"OK, well, there's the obvious location of the plate…"

Prid drew a circle around the bulk of the three megafauna nearest to Gesponnen, noting "Dissolution" next to it.

"And there are the two reception facilities—they should be around here. Is that what these red dots indicate?"

"Uh-huh, and the blue rectangle just next to that one shows the boundaries of the habitation centre and Park 359. Which covers what I've already seen, although not yet in enough detail. Now we need to add on the things I haven't seen, starting with one of the collision sites between megafauna and progressing from there with anything that you can think of. Once we've got all the important things down there from you, we can top it off with some others by asking NineCents and people like your mother and father what they think the Race would like to know about."

Prid beamed her pride at having been given first opportunity to define the audit plan. Wide eyed and twirling her stick pen between the fingers of her right hand in excitement, Prid grinned broadly, nodded at her new mentor, and vaulted onto the surface of the workbench itself, landing on her knees at the corner of the map. She assessed it from several angles by rotating her head and shuffling around on her knees, making noises of comprehension periodically. After a couple of minutes, she declared, "OK, Boss, I'm with it. But the first thing we need to do is put the most important feature of the audit on this map!"

"HaloMagnets?"

"HaloMagnets."

Prid reached around her back to a pocket on her utility trousers and produced a second pen. Testing it on the corner of the sheet, she confirmed that this one marked in purple. Satisfied, she began working on adding the steel runways that joined various positions on the map, occasionally noting items adjacent to the straight lines she was drawing, such as "Drop-Dive Ridge" and "Cattle Country." Sero felt teacherly pride as he watched her work. He stepped away from the girl, who was busying herself with plans for the time they would spend together. He noticed the standardCam in the room closing in on his face and allowed himself to be watched by it, watched watching his assistant. Perhaps he would ask Minnus if he could construct a version of the audit for the Race to observe, one that blended the sapienCam sights he was seeing now with those captured by the camera. It would be good for his audience to see him training Prid, operating as a newer and improved version of Mr. Universe. By the time this audit was screened on home neuroVision sets on Earth, Sero's reputation would have had nearly twenty years to fester in the aftermath of the Rigil Kentaurus audit, successful though it was as an information-gathering exercise and entertainment for the Race but devastating to Sero's confidence and sense of mortality. *Perhaps this is personal growth for you, eh? Teaching someone.* A year of discovery. *And the replacement of a part of my soul, scuttled high in a tree on a distant planet.* Nodding to himself, strengthening his resolve with the optimism of a man who has found new belief in his purpose, Sero returned to the table. *You're still you.*

The map had become a spiralling graph of purple lines, with four central thicker lines forming two concentric circles linking the habitation quarters and Gesponnen. There were lines on the outer of these circles that kicked off periodically at tangents, often ending in a destination annotated by Prid, sometimes returning to the thicker line after passing close to another of the handwritten labels. It was one of the later destinations, close to the habitation block, that Prid had her finger on now.

"We're returning to the reception facility tomorrow, right? I think we should set off right now and take a detour.

We need to go here as part of the audit—an absolutely certainty," Prid said. "The sooner we do it, the better, too. I imagine it won't be long before it's impossible to use this rail."

"It's labelled 'Updraft'?"

"You wanted to go to a collision site, right? Well, this is the easiest one to get to. It's nearest to the reception facility, and there was a haloMagnet rail put in there a long time ago by the nanoBots, before any of the other collisions started happening. It's pretty impressive—almost a mountain range by now."

"Is that why you think the rail might become unusable?" Sero asked.

"Maybe, but there's also the wind. It's because of the collision itself. The air around the mountains rises much faster than anywhere else, which helps to destabilise the weather, hence the wind. Sometimes it's so strong that a passing haloMagnet has to lock down, fixing itself to the rail until the winds have reduced enough to allow it to pass. I sat in one with my mother and some other guys from our section for five hours once after we'd been out there to get some samples. Generally, it's getting worse all the time as the megafauna keep growing. The longer we leave it, the less chance it will be passable at all."

"NineCents, calculations, please. What would be the impact of the extra energy usage?" Sero requested of the colony AI.

As the answer to his question was orated to him, Sero began walking for the exit. "Prid, mark up the map with destination one and the date, and then pack a bag for each of us that will allow for twenty-four hours away from the haloMagnet. Include a tent."

"Where are you going?"

"I'm going to find the old man to ask if he'll bring forward his plans just a little more than he already has." Sero disappeared out of the door. "And pack the map and your notebook!" he called from outside.

# FIFTEEN

Prid checked and rechecked the candolier she wore across her chest, sash fashion. Holding her breath and grimacing slightly, she tugged on the lowest strap, tightening the fastening around her body. "No matter what else happens, I won't lose my gear in the wind!"

She was obviously excited. Sero and Prid were speeding towards the area marked as "Updraft" on their now multiple-lined and coloured map. Whilst his companion was busy tying everything she valued to her chest, arms, and legs in some fashion, Sero was selecting individual items from their hastily packed twine satchels. He held up a small handheld spin cutter and a snap light for his own inspection before slotting both into his button-down pocket, observed by a standardCam floating inside the cabin they shared. "How long till we reach the slow point, NineCents?"

Earlier in the journey, the computer had briefed them on the required plan of approach as interpreted from one of NineDee's orbiting satellites. Their haloMagnet would slow five kilometres from the line of impact between the two megafaunas, increasing the magnetic force and holding the vehicle more firmly to its track as the surface wind speed increased. At the point of collision, the huge friction created enough heat to warm the air around the forming twine mountains instantaneously and powering teralitres of air straight up through the wetworld's atmospheric layers. The pressure change caused by the departing volumes of gas caused roaring winds on the surface, racing in from the plains in every direction and ramping up the vine incline to the summit of the growing mountain range to join the superheated air current.

"Fifteen minutes, Auditor Novak. I will begin increasing magnetic force in six."

"Thanks."

Sero saw the silhouette of the range kick up on the horizon at the extreme right of his view. The image reminded him of Surfaca and the cape curve as viewed from the low-approach wing route in from Antarctica. Sero imagined the view he might see here if he approached in a wing rather than his ground transport. With his eyes closed, he visualised the sloping terrain from above. He saw the haloMagnet rail bisecting the otherwise monocoloured, textured vegetation expanse. The rail curved away to the right as the haloMagnet moved onward. He added the winds too, imagining a wave of purple air rushing towards the hills, pushing the huge metal hoop faster along.

Sero guessed that from above, the rail made the shape of a letter "r," banking away to offer the haloMagnet's broadside to the air movement. Sero added a wobble to the path of the illusory disc transport in his mind, a flourish of movement as he saw the transport buffeted by the air. Returning to the use of his eyes, he found that the silhouette had become the central part of his field of view, raising the horizon in front of him. The hump of vine didn't rise evenly from base to summit. Squinting against the sun on the horizon, he could make out lines dividing the incline into ascents and plains. The vines weren't tangled in the manner he'd seen elsewhere on the surface. The winds had combed each strand into a huge track of parallel twine, converging towards a central point like a giant spoked wheel. Running through an accelerated creation of the landscape in his mind, Sero envisaged slight dips in the formation changing the airflow over the surface of the germinating mountain, pushing the air over the vine like a descending aircraft. This would force them to grow into themselves until the mass of sister vines underneath them formed enough of a barrier to alter the growth again, the wind now catching sheets of tendrils like a sail, pushing them vertically onwards as one.

"How old are you, Sero?"

Sero's thought process was interrupted by his companion. He snort-laughed a little in surprise. "Do you often introduce such questions into a conversation by way of a verbal head butt, Prid?"

"Um, yeah, sorry. I didn't mean to be rude; I was just trying to work out the whole relativity thing, you know. I got a little lost with the numbers and thought the best thing to do would just be to ask. Only it came straight out of my mouth as soon as I stopped trying to calculate it myself. Sorry." Prid shifted in her seat, moving away slightly, obviously embarrassed by her sudden query. "What I meant to ask was more like 'Auditor, sir, I'm familiar with the transportation process and understand that whilst in transit and the blank bubble, you have no awareness with which to experience the passage of time. I know you've been transported many times. I'd like to know how many years you remember as an, erm, consciousness and how many years have been spent as a…well, I dunno. A non-consciousness?' I suppose."

"You're not the first colonist to be curious. I got a bit of a shock last year actually. Last time I was on Earth, a chat-show host got me on a broadcast and arranged a personality-based timeline of the years when I'd been on Earth rather than on a colony. Sportsmen and women from each year—reporters who'd experienced significant events, you know? The whole bunch varied in age by over a hundred years. The youngest chap, a techArtist credited with inventing this new thing called the orbital sling, had not even been born when I left for Rigil Kentaurus. Everyone had a good laugh asking about other things that might be new to me." *Like the commSheet. Or the Internet.*

"So you're really old, then?

"Forty-six years," he said. "At least, my mind has been conscious for forty-six years. Nonconsecutive. I don't remember the really early ones, either, when my original body was still developing, as most children don't. So I suppose the answer to your question is about forty years, Prid."

He smiled as he watched the girl performing the mental arithmetic. He cut the process off by giving her the answer.

"One hundred and ten years since birth, seventy-one of those years either blank bubbled or existing only as an information stream, speeding across the galaxy, depending on what you see as the "real" me."

Prid let out a long whistle. "So, for over a third of the time since you were born, you haven't physically existed?"

"It's not that the body doesn't exist really, Prid. If anything, the contents of the blank bubble might be said to *hyper*exist—in seven dimensions rather than the four-dimensional sapien space-time that we're so familiar with."

"This one is going to hurt my brain, isn't it?" said Prid.

"If we were to be truly honest with ourselves as a species, we'd have to admit that we don't fully understand the theory behind the entire process—only that we've had experience of enough reproducible outcomes that we can confidently predict when the process will work and when it won't."

"Have you finished hedging your bets yet, Mr. Universe?"

Sero took the barb on the chin. *She's a good kid, just likes to level things out if she can—make things peer to peer. Charismatic insolence.*

"Just managing your expectations, kiddo. My father invented this process, and even I'm aware that it's too complicated to understand without real study. If there were anyone else at all around to explain it, they'd almost certainly be a better choice."

"So, *no*, hadn't finished hedging your bets."

"All right, here goes. You know about string theory, right?

Prid adopted a mimic of NineCents's voice. "It's the Race's best bet on describing how everything we can observe in our universe fits together. Basically, it supposes that the four fundamental forces of nature—gravity, electromagnetism, and the strong and weak nuclear forces—as well as all matter are simply different manifestations of a single essence: strings. Any given subatomic particle is made of a string that vibrates and rotates at the speed of light. A particular particle gets its unique identity from the manner in which the string rotates and vibrates. The frequency of vibration corresponds to the mass of the particle, so by vibrating and rotating the same basic thing in different ways, we can create all of the mass as we observe it in our three dimensional universe—which we call space-time, if we also add the fourth dimension of time. Yeah. With you on all that—"

"OK, clever clogs." Sero smiled. "Let's try out the more difficult stuff! What about the ten dimensions? Do you understand those?"

Prid shook her head this time, no chirping back at the lecturer.

"Length, width, depth, and duration—or time—are all naturally observable to us. All together, we call them 'three-dimensional space-time.' But there are six other dimensions that we can't observe from our Sapien 3-D space-time."

A blank look.

"Pass me your notebook and tendril pen." Sero tore out a page from the notebook and marked a single straight line on it before holding the page up to Prid.

"You see this page? Imagine that this page is a two-dimensional universe and that the line on this page is an inhabitant of that universe—a 'line worm' living in 2-D space-time. In his 2-D universe, the line worm can move through his length, forwards and backwards…"

Sero moved the tip of the pen to indicate how the "line worm" might move. "He can also turn left and right to curl around, even chasing his own tail to form a circle. But…" Sero rotated the page so that Prid was looking at only the edge of the paper, making it almost invisible to her. "The line worm has no idea that a third dimension exists. He can only move and observe things in the plane of this 2-D piece of paper. For example, imagine my fist here is a perfectly round balloon." Sero held his bunched fingers out above the page that he held in his other hand. "The ballon would be very close to the line worm in 3-D space, but because the line worm can only observe and move in his 2-D space, he doesn't know it's there. See?"

Prid nodded.

"Good. Now let's move the balloon…" Sero lowered his hand so that he could clamp the edge of the paper between the two middle fingers of his still-clenched fist. "Now, we can imagine the 3-D balloon bisected by the 2-D universe. If Mr. Line Worm moved across the paper to reach the edge of the balloon, he still wouldn't be able to understand that it was a balloon. To him, all it would look like is a circle—an infinitely thin slice of a bigger three-dimensional object. He could only perceive a *part* of the balloon—"

"So there are ten dimensions, but the line worm can only experience three of them: length, width, and duration. We humans can only observe four of them: length, width, *depth*, and duration. The other six are not observable by us, but we can use the line worm example to imagine that they might exist."

"Correct," said Sero.

"But what should I call the other dimensions? How should I think of them?"

"Well, the fifth dimension is best thought of as the 'probability' dimension. It's how we describe the multiverse."

"I've heard about that one. That's where there are many universes, and every possible combination of events is played out through one universe each."

"That's right. So there's one universe where I chose for my next word to be…sausages."

"Erm, yeah, this universe," Prid said, back in teenage-mocking mode.

"Yes, but there were multiple other universes where my next word was something else. And the theory plays that kind of thing out infinitely, so that there's a universe somewhere for every possible outcome in every possible situation—but all behaving according to the same laws of physics, *our* laws of physics, just with different probabilities."

"That's sort of helpful, I guess, but it doesn't help me think about it, really. I mean, I can understand the multiverse theory, but it doesn't really feel like a dimension, you know? At least not like length or width does."

Sero smiled. He'd had similar difficulty understanding the workings of the blank bubble when he was a child, even if it was introduced to him at a much younger age than Prid. He used exactly the same demonstration as had been given to him all those years ago.

"Let's see if talking about the sixth dimension helps: the phase dimension. Let's use our 2-D line worm universe as an example again." Sero drew two separate dots on the page at opposite corners and labelled them "A" and "B." "The line worm would say that these two points are completely separate, right? Distinct points in his universe."

Prid nodded.

"Mr. Line Worm is not aware of the third dimension, though," said Sero, folding the paper so that "A" and "B" touched each other. "If we fold through the third dimension, we can make the two distinct points in the 2-D universe become a single point in a 3-D universe. If we call that folding process 'phasing,' then you might be able to imagine what the sixth phase dimension is."

"It's the dimension we would need to fold the multiverse through in order to make two points in the multiverse the same point in a 6-D sea of multiverses?"

"Bang on."

Sero waited for a minute as Prid scrunched up her nose, clearly thinking. When he thought it was safe, he added a complex rider. "The seventh dimension can be thought of as the whole of the 6-D multiverse sea represented as a single point. The seventh and eighth dimensions can then be thought of as lots of those points and the phase space that we'd need to fold through in order to make any two points in 7-D become the same point in 8-D. The differences between the 7-D points would be differences in the fundamental laws of nature for each set of multiverses in the multiverse sea—for example, all the different possibilities for the strength of gravity or even all the different possibilities for the speed of light. Each combination of the variations in the physical laws of nature would give rise to its own infinity of multiverses, all contained within the single point in 7-D space-time that are represented by that version of physical laws. We can get up to ten dimensions thinking in this way before every possible configuration of information can be described."

"Or our heads explode," said Prid. "OK, I think I've got it pictured in my mind. What does this have to do with blank bubbling? Quick, before I lose the image!"

"OK, I'll go as quickly as I can." Sero laughed. "Before your head explodes! So, when my father, Won, invented blank bubbling, he was first trying to make strings vibrate at a certain frequency—increasing the energy of the strings and therefore changing the mass of the resulting particles. It didn't work, but during his research, he discovered that we can use energy to uncurl some of the higher dimensions in a defined space."

"I don't think I follow. What do you mean?"

"I mean that he worked out that we can create a skin around a part of 3-D space, like a bubble enclosing air. We can create a bubble that encloses air, people, nanoBots, whatever inside it. Anything, really. Then, by altering the strings' spin in the particles that make up the skin of the bubble, we can 'uncurl' or 'uncompactify' some of the extra six dimensions for all the mass within that bubble. It's like a chain reaction: each particle with altered strings spin causes the next particle it interacts with to alter its own string spin subsequently—until the reaction reaches the boundary that we've defined for the bubble, and we police it using an energy field."

"OK, so we move the 3-D mass into a higher dimension. Wouldn't that mean that we can no longer observe it? We can only observe 3-D space-time right?"

"You've got it! We can no longer see or sense any energy or mass made up of the strings that were in the bubble before, hence the term 'blank' bubble." *And here human understanding fails, and we begin to rely only on the weight of past experience to predict outcomes.*

"Somehow the information we've encoded into the mass that we move into the unobservable higher dimensions persists. If the mass is a set of cells programmed with information on how to grow—a set of nanoBots programmed with information on how to move to help cells grow or even a bomb programmed to explode—then all the information continues to work whilst the mass is elevated into the higher dimensions. We can't see it play out in the growth of the copy body, but we know that it must happen because when the blank bubble is dropped, an individual steps out of the bubble, back into a Sapien space-time context. Our best guess is that time passes differently in the compacted version of hyperspace that we transport the mass to—so the information we send can self-execute its algorithm, building the body of a telonaut whilst defined in multiple dimensions. Or, conversely, it can simply remain frozen and unaging. Depends what we tell it to do."

"Can I have my notebook back, please? I think I need to write some of this down to make sure it sticks in my mind."

They walked on for ten minutes as Prid scribbled in her pad. Then she asked Sero to stop so she could make tidier notes. When she seemed comfortable to get up and depart, she jerked her head towards Sero accusatorially. "If folding through higher dimensions can bring two points in a lower dimension together, why do we bother with the whole telonaut process? Shouldn't we just fold space-time through a higher dimension and instantly teleport the original body rather than creating copies?"

"Clever girl, Prid. You really have got it. Unfortunately, the Race isn't so clever as to know how to do that. The inability to use the higher dimensions to transfer information or mass from one point to another is one of the frustrations of humanity—we haven't been able to create wormholes that can fold though the higher dimensions to move matter. All we can do is take mass and encode it as a representation of that same mass using more, higher dimensions—rather than only three. We think the blank-bubbling process represents matter and information in a maximum of seven dimensions because the laws of nature and physics probably need to be consistent with our own universe so that we can 'grow' the body and still have it turn out as we'd expected it to. Once we get to the eighth dimension, the laws of physics can be variable, which doesn't tally with what we've observed. The truth is that we don't know, though. Once the blank bubble is up, we've never been able to penetrate it with any kind of probe or even send information through to try to measure what's going on inside."

"The bubble is impenetrable to information, once it's up."

"Uh-huh. If we could penetrate the bubble, we might be able to work out if there was a way to teleport directly as you say, without the information that encodes a human body and mind needing to take a trip the long way around via 3-D space-time to get to somewhere new."

"I don't know that I'll ever be able to truly work that ou—"

Prid was interrupted by a wailing screech of metal on metal. She threw her hands to her ears in instinct, catching one of her fingers in her eye in the rush. Sero had also covered his ears but was on his feet, trying to locate the source of the sound. He thought it was coming from below them and to one side of the vehicle. Keeping hands clamped tightly to the side of his head, he made a single step towards the sound. As soon as he lifted his foot, his whole body was picked up and hurled against the side of the haloMagnet. The impact smashed the broad of his upper back, driving a wave of pain down his spine and forcing the air from his lungs. Sero crumpled to the floor, his arms limp against his stomach, redoubling the disorientation of the piercing scream invading his head. Unable to breathe, he sat for a moment, trying to locate his senses and understand what had happened to him. Across the cabin of the haloMagnet, Prid had pulled her knees to her chest. Her left eye was bloodshot and streaming. She was wailing, but he couldn't hear her over the tin scream raping his brain. Prid wasn't looking at him. She was looking at the floor. He could tell from the look on the top of her head that she was forcing the sound from her lungs as hard as she could, throwing words at the steel bottom of the vehicle.

"Cents. N…eents. Ni…"

Calmer, with oxygenated blood flowing around his body again as he regained the ability to inhale, Sero could pick out some of the sounds Prid was making.

"Nin…ents. Nine…"

The computer. Prid was calling the computer. Sero added his own voice to her call, trying to time his words with those he'd part heard, part inferred from his assistant. No response. At least no response he could hear. Then the screeching stopped.

Relieved that the cacophony had ceased, Sero stood and began to walk towards Prid to check if she was OK. He was confused and uncertain. Something was still wrong. *Uphill?* The whole haloMagnet was tilting. "Prid, look up—look around! We're derailing!"

He knew what had tried to rivet him to the wall. *The wind must be overpowering the magnetic force holding the halo to the rail. That's why we're tilting. That screeching must have been the metal-on-metal contact of the edge of the vehicle, grinding the surfaces closer together than they're built for.*

"NineCents, can you hear me? NineCents, what is the status of the slow point?"

The computer's voice came back through the metal of the transport, weak and intermittent. NineDee was unable to accurately vibrate the metal moving erratically around them in order to communicate.

"Energy    dip…overcome…wind    speed    doubl… inevitable…"

Prid had scuttled down the newly sloping floor of the haloMagnet to join Sero at the low point of the space they were in. Sero imagined the exterior of the circle directly beneath them, friction heating as it rubbed too close to the steel monoroad on which it ran, careening along at an ill-designed angle.

"Cannot slo…cannot stop…haloMag…"

He thought he understood what was happening. They needed to get the haloMagnet off the rail immediately. He grabbed Prid by the shoulders, turning her to face him, and explained rapidly what they were going to do. He barely had time to get his hastily conceived plan through her one-eyed emotional fog before the steel whine began again. Resorting to sign language, he asked Prid if she was ready, forming a circle with his thumb and forefinger. She wiped away the tears streaming involuntarily from her invaded eye, gritted her teeth, and nodded. Sero held up three fingers and let them fall one by one in a visual countdown. When his clenched fist remained, Prid turned away from him and began the climb up the no-longer-vertical side-wall of the haloMagnet. She grasped the sill of the external viewer and clambered on the crouching Sero's shoulders. As he stood, she moved two metres further up the wall to reach a routed depression in the chassis of the halo. Sero leant his body into the wall, stabilising the acrobatic pair enough for Prid to remove one of the spray cans from her sash. Working quickly, she took a tendril cutting from a pocket on her thigh and jammed it into the depression in the wall. Taking a small knife from the same pants pocket, she opened the end of the tendril and filled the depression with aminos from her can-wielding hand, working left to right and using the whole length of the depression as a mould. The resulting "rope" was about two metres long. The young rider spurred Sero in his ribs gently and pulled the best "question" face she could muster with one eye closed, asking silently for approval of the new tool. With some difficulty, Sero looked up and nodded encouragingly.

Prid took a deep breath and closed her good eye, composing herself against the insistent din of the derailing craft. Eyes still closed, she manipulated the can and rope into the same looped arrangement she had used to impress her new boss back in Gesponnen, using her finger to prevent the tendril loop from activating the amino can it was wrapped around. Opening her good eye, Prid fixed her gaze on the rod emerging from the cabin wall near the ceiling, part of the superstructure that suspended the passenger compartment within the rotating outer hull. Holding her breath, she tightened the can-tendril lasso into constant-release mode and hurled the whole complex towards the protrusion. Her aim failed. The can hit the arm of the rod and bounced down to rest between the cabin floor and wall at Sero's feet, now trailing several metres of newly created twine. As she looked down in frustration, the whole halo-Magnet shook violently, reeling from a new blow to its opposite side. Sero could feel the floor becoming hot through the soles of his boots, and the air temperature was raised inside the cabin. If they didn't stop the runaway craft soon, they would be cooked alive inside a huge hooped radiator. The magnets reengaged, and the halo ploughed on, tilting just slightly more than it had before, away from its original centre of gravity. But not enough to defeat the battling magnets of the rail.

Sero squatted again and lifted the trembling Prid from his shoulders. She was crestfallen in failure and obviously frightened. He thought he detected a tear welling in her undamaged eye. Giving her a thumbs up, he smiled, hoping to maintain some hope for her, and then turned to the rope and can at his feet. He took the spin cutter from his pocket and activated it, freeing the tendril from the can. The can had been heated through conduction from the steel floor and was now too hot to touch without gloves. Sero felt his boots stick slightly to the floor as he kicked it away. Holding the freed rope, he turned to Prid and removed an unused amino can from her candolier. Using the can as a weight, he made an anchor of it, tying the tentaculos cord around its centre, much more roughly than Prid's elegant arrangement. Twice Sero threw the can at the rod. Twice it bounced off and back into his hands. The third time he managed to squeeze the can through the gap between the ceiling and the bar, leaving the rope suspended from above. He immediately heaved on the rope, dragging himself upwards towards the corner of the room, increasing the height of the halo's centre of gravity. Reaching the meeting of wall and ceiling, Sero kicked his legs out at the wall, imitating the old-fashioned abseiling technique he'd seen in historyCasts. The halo wobbled, moving away from the rail, but didn't overcome the magnetic field of the rail. The screeching stopped, though. "Well, at least that's something," Sero muttered to himself, as he looked down towards the cabin floor. "Prid! Prid! I need you to come up here too."

The young girl's fearful eyes looked up at him. She was hopping left to right on the hot floor and fully crying now.

"Come on, Prid—we're nearly there now," Sero called down to her. "Just a little climb and we can stop this."

He offered his hand in encouragement, swinging back on his own weight to lower his fingers towards her. Prid had ceased her hot-footed dance was frozen to the spot with fear, despite the heat of the surface searing away the tentaculos-made boots she wore.

Sero took a powerful breath and composed himself. He closed his eyes for a single second, extracting will from the depths of his memory. When he opened his eyes again, all the strength of nearly half a century of experience was pooled in their centres. "Kiddo, I've been in worse spots than this. We *can* do this. Come on!"

He swung his outstretched arm at the young girl again, spreading his fingers, urging her up the rope. Prid nodded, wiped the water from both eyes with the back of her right hand, and started to climb.

She reached him quickly, operating with instinctive efficiency now that her emotional indecision had been overcome. While she climbed, Sero had fashioned and hung a second vine, easier to do now he was nearer the ceiling. As she arrived below him, he passed her the new rope, and she made the transfer from one to the other.

"Prid, I want you to look for a spot in front of you that you could fix yourself to. When this thing comes off the rail, there's going to be some momentum to run down, and we won't be steering. Use your canisters to make a mooring." He'd already created an improvised belt for himself to hook onto a point of the structure. He knew it probably wouldn't hold him fast if things got violent, but a similar job might be enough for the much lighter Prid.

"Looks like there's a sharper bend in the track coming up—might give us more wind on the broadside. This is our chance! Are you ready?"

Prid grimaced before nodding. The look of determination on her face, with one bloodshot eye and tear-streaked cheeks, made Sero snort an appreciative acknowledgment through a smile. Prid noticed and smiled back, a silent essay travelling between them in an instant.

"OK, here it comes. One…two…*three*!" Sero kicked at the halo wall as hard as he could, swinging backwards and flexing his legs again to maximise a second blow. As it hit, the screeching started again. Prid fell in time with the hammering rhythm of his strike at the third push. The heat in the cabin was omnipresent now, and Sero noticed sweat in his eyes and the taste of salt on his lips, pursed through exertion. He looked across to his left and saw that Prid's face was scarlet, and the tracks left by her tears were being overrun by new streams of perspiration. This had to work fast. The combination of heat and effort couldn't be maintained. If they couldn't derail the halo on this bend, they'd cook.

Sero heard his screams in his head as he threw himself at the wall with every neuron of will he possessed. Again and again. Then the pitch of the screeching sound changed.

"It's working!" Sero screamed silently to no ears again, but Prid understood.

Again they swung. Again the noise changed, rising in pitch to a squeal. The wall of the cabin was perceptibly leaning further out over the surface of the tentaculos now. Sero could see the floor outside through the cabin window, a few metres from the rail. He felt for his tethering belt on a backswing and gestured for Prid to do the same. Another impact, another pitch change. A third. He knew the next would do it and held his index finger up to Prid to remind her to be ready. As their boots hit the sidewall at the depth of the final swing, the force of gravity on the halo's mass became stronger than the magnetism holding the steel outer loop to the rail beneath it. The two explorers scrambled for gripping points as the wall descended away from them to become their floor, looping and lashing their belts over two grip handles meant for loading cargo into the vehicle. In the five seconds it took for the magnets to completely lose their hold on the ring and its contents, Sero managed to shimmy across the wall slightly and throw himself over Prid, shielding her from any debris that might come lose should they begin to flip. It wasn't the right strategy. As the outer side of the halo hit the surface of the tentaculo, the impact transferred energy right through the landmass to the water below, and the vehicle bounced, skipping like a flat stone on water. Both Prid and Sero left the wall-floor slightly with each bounce—the full weight of Sero squashing Prid to the floor-wall with every return. Fearing he'd crush her, Sero rolled onto his back as the halo bounced for the fourth time. He thought he heard a four letter Amasian curse coughed at him as he did. Both their tethers held, and the halo didn't begin to flip or rotate as Sero had feared. Instead, it continued to skip along at a slight tangent from the rail it had just left, slowing with each impact. It took twenty seconds to come to a complete halt.

Sero took his spin cutter and freed himself from his belt. "Are you OK, kiddo?"

He stood gingerly and stooped over Prid. She was lying on her back, covering the former window and facing the wall-ceiling with her eyes open, dripping with sweat and holding her chest. "I think it might have been my ribs that slowed us down after you pushed them out of my body and through the window."

A single second and another silent essay passed between them before they both began chuckling in relief. Sero lay back down on the floor-wall next to Prid. They both gazed up at the standardCam hovering above them as they laughed the relief from their bodies.

# Sixteen

"**So you were** a kind of outsider, then?"

Prid was asking questions again. The two companions were walking back towards the monorail, having spent a few hours sat inside the wreckage of the dismounted halo waiting for the wind to abate. It had taken an hour to cut themselves out of the vehicle, tangled up as it was in the twine ball of tendrils that had been pulled from the surface of the tentaculos by the sliding halo. It was slow work in the residual heat, using only Sero's spin cutter to make an exit. Once out, they saw that they'd travelled a greater distance than they thought in the time it had taken the craft to come to a halt. Perhaps three kilometres. It had then taken another hour for them to widen the hole sufficiently to expose enough metal for NineDee to communicate with them. Sero had wanted to get more information about their position before leaving the wreck. In order to try to conserve energy, having promised its patriarch that he would minimise his impact on the grand plans they had, Sero had decided that they would walk back to the rail and then walk halfway to their original destination before meeting a recovery halo. There wouldn't be any extra energy usage than was originally agreed to by Zwolf, but Prid hadn't been happy with the plan initially—it was a fifty-kilometre walk and would mean that neither of them would sleep for a full day. After the near-death experience they'd just had—the first for Prid—he thought that he owed her some patience whist they made the trip, so he was being as thorough and considerate as he could in answering her questions.

"An outsider? Yeah, in some ways, I was. But I felt that I was special because of the responsibilities I'd been given, responsibilities to the Race."

"Even as a kid?"

"I grew up in two places: the facility where my father worked, which was at the very south pole of planet Earth, and a young country called Surfaca. Most of the people around me were either dark skinned, yellow skinned, or a blend of the two. Surfaca has historically been populated by dark-skinned people."

"So you looked different?"

"Back in the old republic days, many yellow-skinned people came to Surfaca because an ancient country called China had bought large areas of it. They wanted to use the minerals found in the ground to make money. It's an old concept, which isn't of much use now, but it motivated a lot of people to move their homes and families a very long way. When the Saints created the Race, it was from these two groups of people. Despite the formation of WorldGov and free movement of all peoples, there are still many more yellow-dark faces in Surfaca than any other types of faces. So I looked very different at least."

"You're not from Surfaca?"

"I was born there, but my mother is from a place called Eurasia, and my father's father was also from Eurasia. Eurasia is very far from Surfaca, and the people there have evolved slightly differently because of the different weather conditions and the historical difficulties in travelling between the two places. So I had the name of my father's father, Novak, and light skin. It meant that I stood out, but it also meant that everyone knew who I was and what my father had contributed to the Race. That generated a lot of affection and meant I learned very quickly about the benefits of generating and sharing knowledge. It probably contributed to me being here, as a telonaut auditor."

"I wonder why we're not taught of all this history here on NineDee. I know we're supposed to collect knowledge, push the Race further and all that, but I'm sure that I could do that better if I knew all about our home planet. I've learned a lot about where I am now and the basics of terraforming from the original colonists, like my mother and father, and of course I know about the Saints and their rules, but they only really taught us about Eurasia."

"Well, Eurasia is where Patriarch Zwolf is from. Even here on the colony, many years after his transmission, you can hear the legacy of his birthplace in the manner of his speech. His accent. You also have a slight Eurasian accent, Prid. I think everyone here seems to. Have you noticed how there aren't any dark- and yellow-skinned people here too?"

"I hadn't until you just told me about Surfaca, but I do now. Everyone here looks like you. You know—light skinned."

"The idea was to create colonies representing the culturally varied areas of Earth, to give those colonies a coherent social framework within which to grow. It was felt that colonists who had shared memories and experiences of life on Earth would be able to more quickly form their new society here. In Earth's history, many wars have been fought between groups of people that look, sound, and think a little differently. The Race has overcome this on Earth, but it was decided that so far from home, humans probably still have the capacity to fight amongst themselves—especially if conditions are difficult. NineDee is a Northern Eurasian colony. Of course, everyone speaks Surfacan in order to more easily relate to the rest of the Race."

"Hmmmm." Prid considered silently as the pair continued to walk on towards the approaching monorail—their route back to the reception facility and Sero's first spider-map download of this audit. She asked a few more questions, largely about what it was like for Sero growing up, when he knew he wanted to be part of the telonaut programme, and how he knew he was ready. Sero could tell that she was perturbed by his answers, though. Eventually she fell back into silence, rubbing at the back of her own neck as they walked. When they reached the rail, she sat on the edge of the metal and indicated she'd like for him to sit too, glancing at the spot beside her.

"I think Zwolf doesn't want us colony-born to know about Earth. I think he's too focused on the dissolution and the rest of the plan to save the colony. Earth and its history are just a distraction." Prid was looking at Sero bluntly.

"Until we're large enough to go out in a team with the Earthborn and contribute to the plan, we're just a problem to be solved. And by limiting the things we know about, he can limit the number of questions we might ask, therefore limiting the problem we represent. I think it's pretty short sighted. When the plan works, and we all have to carry on doing things other than the dissolution, how am I supposed to contribute if I don't have any skills or knowledge of history? I'll need to be out there soon—I'm nearly an adult—but I don't feel like I know anything like nearly enough to be able to do my best." She lowered her head to look at her knees, angry and deflated.

*Way to go, Novak. All this talk of having a special history and place in the Race. Great way to make a teenage girl feel inadequate.* The standardCams flitting around him reminded him that his words and actions might be broadcast to the whole

Race once his spider maps were transmitted. *Hope I don't embarrass her. Think, man.*

"What about your friend Dini? Didn't you say that you used to be close, involved in the same kind of things? She's old enough to be involved in the dissolution now, isn't she? How is she making a contribution?"

Prid raised her head and look upwards and right, towards Sero. He could tell that she was measuring her response against her emotions. Before she spoke, Sero saw an internal conflict resolved on her face. She brightened even as she began. He was relieved but made sure to listen intently to her.

"Actually, she's doing very well, I think. She's officially a hydrobiologist now and spends most of her time out at the plate, but I have spoken to her at Park 359 when she's been back in the habitation section. She was busy and seemed much more serious, but she said that her training had been short but very effective. She seemed…focused. Purposeful, I suppose?" Prid intoned the statement as a question to herself. "Yeah, purposeful. She knew what she was about."

"It *is* important to have goals. I know it can make a big difference to how people feel about themselves." Sero tried to amplify Prid's change in mood.

"Hmmmmmm. I suppose I *could* learn about Earth's history and anything else I wanted from NineCents myself, once I'm old enough to have full record access…and of course I'm a quick learner—much quicker than Dini was, and she became a full hydrobiologist in just a few weeks. Maybe I just need to hurry up and begin training in something—hurry up and…age!"

Sero laughed gently at Prid's conclusion. Still sitting beside her on the rail, he put an arm around her shoulders and shook her lightly. "And in the meantime, I have work for an assistant, and you already have all the training you need for that. You just need to be able to put up with my company for a year."

"Well, I feel much better!" Prid exclaimed, jumping to her feet. "What's next, Boss?" She mimed a comic salute.

"We have a little walking to do, Prid." Sero pointed down the monorail, trailing away over the streaked, green horizon. "And then perhaps you can arrange for me to meet with your friend Dini if she's at the habitation section. I'd like to know how she felt about joining the grand dissolution plan."

"No problem, Boss." Prid saluted again and spun on her heels before marching comically along the steel rail towards the reception facility.

# SEVENTEEN

**Minnus and Johnson** were in the editing suite at Direction and
Processing.

"So, what do you think?" Minnus said.

"There's a lot of change from what they saw before;
I'm worried about the narrative. We *do* need them to feel
like this is a new experience—new *knowledge* as you would
probably say—but it can't look contradictory. Sero's Rigil
audit is folklore now. We have to retain the emotional
thread. This 'director's cut' of the Kentauran audit is supposed to make people more accepting of seeing through
Sero's eyes rather than as a third person, but they've gotta
connect to the guy they already know and love." Johnson
had his feet on the rim of Minnus's favourite plastiche
recliner as he spoke.

Minnus nodded, practising the deferential show of active listening he'd found to be useful with Johnson over the
time the younger man had been running D & P and now,

as head of the entirety of TeloSpace. "I see. I can promise you that the rest of the memories play out that way. It all focuses around *her*, you see—just like the standardCams showed last time. But that's why the first cast is different. Sero meeting her was a new cluster for him. I think *love*. Everything that happened to him on Rigil is therefore centred on her, and the software keys off the detail created in this first cast. Of course, when we began editing the standardCam footage last time, we were focused on the detail of the colony rather than an individual. The NV editor shows us the detail of the colony *through* the context of Sero's memories of an individual. The first meeting with her is therefore key."

"How many more casts can I preview today? I'm not sure we should throw this out relying on just your software. The way you describe it, we might run the risk of broadcasting NV pornography every night as your software only keys on to close-ups of the dive bomber's nipples!"

"Now, Idi, I've been working on this cluster-memory algorithm for seven years, and you know the drill here. We need to test whether the software can run at the right pace. If we're going to run at a rate of one cast a week when the 359D maps begin arriving, I want to be certain that we can turn around the same depth of mapping using the Rigil audit. Seven days of spider map turned into an NV cast in seven days—"

"I know all that. For frak's sake, he physically finished the damn audit six years ago. Whilst you've been busy with your dream weaver, the rest of us have been waiting for the weekly spider maps to begin arriving."

"Light speed not fast enough for you?"

"No. It's not."

Silence.

"Look. This is a big deal for us, OK? We need reraise the visibility of the programme. Whizz things up a little before Sero's copy-body pencil-beam arrival gets back here. I just want to make certain we don't create the wrong kind of visibility. As in 'fraking in space' jokes on global feeds—"

"OK, OK. I knew you'd ask the question, so I've brought the second cast with me. It's ready. Everything else though is in theoretical staging only—it doesn't form a fully coherent narrative yet...*but* it will.

"You've done a fantastic job, Idi. The Race is ready for this now—and excited! You must trust me, though. Nombre, Joules, and I have devoted years of our life to making this work. We've run tests and models on our own memories and maps; we've looked at childhood and adulthood; we've had the code computer checked by intelligence loops; we've each watched Joules's life in serialised form each month as a cast, even rerunning his old sprint development for the Olympics. I *know* this will work."

He knew that Sero's Rigil cluster formed around an emotional nucleus but included more practical and scientific memories in orbital links to the core. He had no doubt that the physical relationship Sero had would form the central part of any serialisation, but he also knew that the sky-trees and star climbers would be in there too.

Johnson had softened a little as Minnus spoke. Minnus knew that his intentions were good, even if his manner was brash and commanding. To achieve his acquiescence took only a little acknowledgment of the new TeloSpace bureau head's ultimate authority, combined with an earnest appeal to his trust. Johnson took his feet from the edge of Minnus's plastiche chair and lifted his personal commSheet from the arm of his own, spinning its rigid form on one finger like an antique circus act.

*Good. He's relaxing. This is going to fly.*

Johnson slowed the cSheet's spin and then collapsed its rigid form into a roll in one smooth motion. "OK, old man, I trust you. We've made a good team so far, you and me. We can do more too. If this goes well, another two years could see us in WorldGov itself, making decisions for the entire Race! It's all about the ends, Minnus!"

"In two years' time, all I'll be interested in will be reminiscing over this with Sero. The bricks we'll have placed in the wall of society will be reward enough for me, Idi."

Johnson was already on his way out of the room. As he disappeared through the doorway, he called over his shoulder. "Like I said, it's all about the ends…"

Minnus leant back and felt the hugging arms of his reclaimed favourite chair close around his shoulders and replayed the conversation in his mind. He felt a twist of discomfort in his stomach at the callous way Johnson spoke of his friend's lover's death. Especially when he remembered the amount of work it had taken to return Sero to a functioning state last time he was on Earth. The memory was so painful for Sero and so visible everywhere in society whilst he was here. *His first love. His only love, perhaps. Such trauma and so many reminders of her everywhere.* The way they'd each experienced women before that was really the only difference between their philosophies. Minnus had been Earthbound his entire life, experiencing relationships that were relativistically constant. He'd had his share of fleeting romances, sure, but when he'd met Nombre, Minnus had known that something was different. That she was special. That he wanted to form a life together and *live* it together, entwined. *You never really had that option, did you, old friend? The very definition of a traveller, the* greatest *hobo, never staying for longer than a year on any colony, never staying for much longer than that on Earth. Just turn around, and he's gone again.* Perhaps more significantly, every time he left a place, Sero stepped out of time. He had been blank bubbled for years as the signal that contained his consciousness and the digital description of his physical form sped through the galaxy on its way to the next destination. All that while, everyone he'd ever met aged disproportionately relative to Sero. *How could you form a life bond with a partner when your job was to regularly disappear for over a decade, returning with only a single year of life experience? How could you learn and grow together when you didn't even age together? You couldn't.* That's why Minnus had understood what others had referred to as Sero's "callous" attitude to relationships with women. His Mr. Universe nickname had been salaciously twisted at the lower end of the media's historical coverage, made to reference his tendency to take lovers both on audits and on Earth and then leave them with a seemingly thoughtless wink. That was a misrepresentation, though. Sero was simply aware that each lover he took was only a stop on his journey and could never be the destination. He'd rationalised it all ahead of time, and Minnus knew that when he met someone, it was one of the first things he explained to them. Sero had once confessed that he thought this early declaration of planning to leave might be one of the reasons he was relatively successful with women. Late one night after Sero's second audit, during one of his spells back on Earth, Sero had made the admission in Minnus's first marital home. Their lives had become very different by then. Minnus was over twenty physical years older than Sero already and had young children in the house. They'd been drinking, reminiscing over old times—when they were both young men completing their curricula and setting life goals for themselves. Those goals including learning more about the opposite sex. Sero had offered his revelation that he wasn't all that different from other men, certainly no more physically attractive, and that even his role as a telonaut auditor wasn't so special. He spent his time with actual telonauts, and therefore his status on colonies wasn't as elevated as it was on Earth. *What did he say? "A natural part of the reproductive dance of the species."* Men tend towards a higher sample rate, trying to find the best chance of a partner that would satisfy them and their life goals. Women tend towards a lower sample rate and trying to convert a man into a partner that would satisfy *them* and *their* life goals. *"The challenge of converting a man who's already stated up front that he's going to leave excites women."* Not intellectually but biologically. Sero's theory, as a younger man, was about a woman's internal drive that wanted to prove the woman's reproductive worth by seducing and entangling the man. Prove that despite being thought of as only a provincial bus stop en route to the big city, it was actually her, *that* woman, who was the metropolis and end destination.

*One day, when you decide to turn this auditing in…*

After so much contribution to the Race's development, it seemed unfair that Sero might not experience the fullest range of personal fulfilment possible—personal fulfilment being one of the three key measures of success that the Race measured itself by each year. At the time, Minnus had tried to convince his friend that Sero's assessment of women's drives was incorrect. He'd used his own self-rating in the last ten annual global personal fulfilment assessments as evidence of the difference to happiness that a woman could make to a man's life, showing him the clear step change upwards in his happiness relative to his unmarried peers since he'd met Nombre. He and Sero had both been a little drunk, of course, and the conversation had quickly turned to other reminiscences. They hadn't revisited the subject the next morning, and Sero had soon been away to his next adventure. *How many times have you replayed that conversation in recent years, Mbeki, watching the Rigil footage in the background? Would it finally make sense to Sero now, even if it would be a conversation about loss rather than happiness? Come home, and stay home, old friend; you've done enough.*

# Eighteen

**Sero was exhausted.** He'd slept a little on the halo transport back to the habitation area, but it was a light, unrefreshing sleep. Prid had collapsed into unconsciousness immediately upon entering the vehicle, and Sero had felt the need to stay as alert as possible given what had befallen them the previous day. After arriving at Habitation, he'd carried Prid to her parent's quarters before moving on to the reception facility. Once inside, he'd taken the precaution of removing all outside communication, shielding the core reception pod from even the inspection of NineCents. He still didn't want the colonists to know that his purpose was to send actual records of his audit back to Earth ahead of him for NeuroVision processing. They were very proud and protective of their dissolution plan, and he still didn't feel confident that he could predict their reaction to what he thought was his logical course of action in furthering the Race as a whole. *Difficult to see the big picture when your work is literally your whole world.*

The process of spider mapping was reasonably quick and even allowed him to relax a little as the electrical-imaging claw developed detail on the changes in neuron makeup since his arrival. As he initiated the pencil-beam transmission back to Telosec, he felt relief at having successfully been able to convey the scale of the colonist's ambition to the Race through his memories. Even if the rest of the audit became a disaster, some knowledge of the Race's efforts at this boundary of their galactic presence would have reached the masses. *Would she be proud of me for carrying on?*

On the walk back to his original quarters, however, Sero's mind turned to the Rigil audit. His near escape at the Updraft and the danger he and Prid had been in only now rested fully upon him, now that his objectives of getting his young charge safely home and sending his first update to Earth had been achieved. Would he repeat his mistakes? Would more people die? *Should you even be out here?* As he stumbled in whilst trying to kick off his boots, Sero's thoughts were already becoming the haphazard chain of memories that leads to dreams. As the standardCam followed him into the room, he fell onto the bunk pod fully clothed and closed his eyes.

$$\lambda$$

Comfort. She was holding him, high in the sky. They were alone.

She held him close to her, tessellating them together like oil on water, fitting in and around each other. He was only dimly aware of the heights reaching down below him, distorting the horizon's deep blackness with the linear, branched trunks of the sky-trees. His focus was here. On Comfort.

Something buzzed past his head. It didn't matter. He ignored it. Comfort.

Comfort was speaking to him now, asking questions. He formed his responses in thought alone. No need to speak to Comfort; she understood. He thought of his home in the ice and the mountains, the wine grown in valleys and on the plains, the roar of the old race starting stadium at Green Point. He just thought about them, and Comfort knew, Comfort understood. Visions and sensations poured into him in return, zipping along tubes of bark and feeling the temperature changes on his skin, falling into the darkness with grace and poise, the glow of admiration on the faces of an audience as he displayed mastery of his tools. He understood Comfort. They were the same. They grew their space and the space of those around them.

Something reflective, distracting him again. What was it? Why was it trying to invade his Comfort? He owned this. It was his. Why didn't it understand? Desperate to prolong the feeling, he fixed his head towards her, blocking out the distraction.

Comfort was beautiful. She reflected his own worth and amplified his sense of self, proving he was valid. She quantified him. He felt the glow of her face on his own. She was warm. She loved him.

The buzzing appeared at his temple. What was it? Then he saw it, a metal eye, round like a sportBall, watching him. Watching them. Trying to steal them, their time, his Comfort. How dare they? This Comfort was his. He owned it. Furious, he flailed at the eye with both hands, releasing his grip on his companion. And then they were two, no longer together as oil and water, but separated over miles as earth and space. His face was cold, air rushing over it. He could see only lines and darkness. He was falling. Until he was bouncing. Branch to trunk to branch and back. His arms, his legs, his face. Pain. Where was Comfort? Then he was still, his face warm again, running with heat from his cheek as he hung limply over something. Rod shaped. Where was Comfort? Who had taken her from him?

Darkness. Then Comfort returned. She was crying. Near to him but not attached. Afraid. Could Comfort be fearful? He didn't know. He was tired. Darkness.

Then Comfort again, closer now. She put gloves and shoes on his hands and feet; they were sticky. She held him to a trunk; he had three points of attachment. But Comfort now had only one. He couldn't move. Comfort was very afraid. Her eyes glistened wet. Her free hand ran red with warmth, his warmth, from his face. Comfort was touching his face.

She dropped. Her shining, wide eyes were now at his hips. Comfort was afraid. He reached out to her. Pain. Atrocious pain. He reached anyway. Her warm, wet hand lunged into his. She loved him. Comfort. They were together.

And then she fell.

# NINETEEN

"Fragment Update One, Wolf359D, Wetworld.
Subject: Telonaut Auditor One. Novak, Sero 400.4
PostSt
Status: Reception complete."

The internal record at Telosec's new NeuroVision processing centre was updated as the pencilled beam of light registered on the photometer of the near-Earth-tethered satellite at the south of the planet. The satellite spun only three times as the photometer, running around its surface like a banded skirt, received the entire short transmission from a sister solar system. Using the tether, the data had been transmitted to Telosec on a secure, physical line.

"Status: Fragment stored and cross-referenced. Telonaut Auditor One. Novak, Sero 395.3 PostSt. Match confirmed. Estimated map growth = eight days."

The internal record ran a new code, which alerted the commSheets of the entire TeloSpace Bureau and the author of its protocols. It immediately received a single return ping from the commSheet of its designer, instructing it to initiate its broadcast construction algorithm.

"Status: Fragment assessed. Cluster Candidate One identified. Memory orbit scenario creation begun."

Meanwhile, Minnus and Bureau Head Johnson hurtled towards the pole in separate wings. Years after Sero had sent his transmission, the first record of his time on 359D had reached Earth. The message was in. Now their work could really begin.

*There is nothing noble in being superior to your fellow man. True nobility is being superior to your former self.*

—Ernest Hemingway

# Minus Four

Why?

What motivated her to be with that old fool? Couldn't she see that she was more compatible, more successful, and more complete when she was with him? He knew she was brilliant. Dazzlingly intelligent, in fact. So why did she persist with such blind loyalty?

Only three people at the end of the populated galaxy. No consequences for the Race because of any mating decisions made out here. No judgement from anyone. No injured pride. So why? *Why!*

He watched them walking along the flat steel floor outside the reception facility. Arm in arm. Measuring the floor plan of the home they planned to build on the other side of continent. Imagining how it would be for them to share the space. Ignoring him. Rapt in each other, oblivious to his pain. How was he supposed to be part of this new world when the very foundations of his understanding of people didn't make sense? What could be built upon anything produced by the efforts of such a sham relationship? He chewed more on the tendril, spitting a ball of amino paste onto the walkway. It became the only dark spot on the consistent magSteel matte finish. Except the spot between them, he thought, immediately after recognising the contrast.

It cannot stand. Leaf should be with me, he determined. All of our personal history shows it. It is obvious. Logical. Right. I will not allow it to be otherwise. Once this obvious wrong is righted, once he is gone, only then can the real building of our new society begin. Leaf was a beautiful, philosophising frontier queen, mother to a whole new arm of the Race. He would not allow that man to purport to sit at her side.

Resolved, he fixed a smile and walked towards them.

# TWENTY

Minnus was exultant.

"We knew they'd be impressed, darling," Nombre said. "It doesn't just work—it works *fantastically*."

"They really love it, though. Maybe even as much as me."

"What's not to love? Slickly produced, stupendous NV broadcasts for three months? Check. Generating pride and renewed commitment to exploration? Check. Swelling the library of achievements that the Race can collectively call ours? Check. It's a masterwork."

"I feel so…so…justified."

"So tell me about it. What exactly did they say?"

"You know, Idi, we started from the outcomes. Looked at what we've seen so far. Idi had personally cut together a highlight reel from the NV footage: Sero travelling the vegetation city, then a cutaway to a panorama of the dissolution plate and some operatic music, a voiceover introduction to Sero's adopted assistant—"

Minnus assumed an actorly stance and mimicked what he'd heard earlier in the Telospace review board with WorldGov. "This has given the Race the benefit of not only experiencing Sero's wonder, amazement, and pride first hand but also having an avatar in young Prid, on whom we can overlay our character and all have a role in the 359D project."

"Stop it, you old fool. Just give me the gist, not a pantomime."

"It's the combination of Sero's narration habit and his conversations with her. One of the WorldGov inspectors said it was 'like a father thinking out loud.'

"Then Idi's trailer skipped through a few different episodes that have had high repeat viewings. The magnet accident and escape, the vine-seiling lesson from Prid, a review of apparel design using ropes of plant material— he cut that with opinion pieces from here on Earth—'The Fashion Culture Connection'—what else? The seismic experiment where the two megafauna were colliding. Oh yeah! He'd even riffed some science-comedy about a herd of cows, vine spaghetti, and how two animals unknowingly eating their ways towards each from opposite ends of the same tendril proved they were 'in love.' They lapped it up."

By now, Nombre had managed to usher the excited Minnus across the balcony and into their home. She gave him a drink as they both sat at the kitchen table. "Sounds a little superficial for your taste, though."

"That's the genius of it. Once he'd teed them up, he gave me the floor to talk about the meat of it."

"Which was?"

"A bit of the 'how'—me and Sero setting up the parasympathetic biological trigger before he left and how even though cluster memories don't quite work how we thought they might, we were still able to use the neurological response to find that first memory to build the NV on.

"Mostly it was a detailed follow-up on the 'what,' though—the project itself. Leveraging how the Leaf Day project is immense and being able to view directly through Sero's eyes gives the Race something truthfully novel. Additive. The colonists' determination to see Leaf Day become a reality—"

"Inspiring."

"Yeah. Exactly. Then Idi came back in with some viewing figures. Forty percent of the population have now NVd the entire series. They're hooked."

Nombre smiled and embraced him. Minnus allowed the delight he felt inside to wash around the pair of them, an outer envelope of shared fulfilment. When Nombre broke the clinch, she headed for the door. "I'm off to lunch with our eldest. Enjoy your afternoon, genius."

Minnus reversed into his chair as she left, still replaying and reflecting on the morning review with the WorldGov team from Mission Selection.

Johnson had been similarly delighted. *For the same reasons?* Minnus was a true believer in the values of the Saints and the singular purpose of collectively elevating the Race, pushing forward. *Not so sure about Idi's ideology, though.* Minnus still saw the younger man using their endeavours as a vehicle for increasing influence. *Nothing so wrong with that, though.* The whole point of the Saints' Ugandan principles was to develop the Race into a genuine meritocracy, with the members most suited to leadership rising to influential roles. Broadly, Minnus believed that the Race had become such a meritocracy. *So he's the right guy for the job. We should use him. You certainly can't argue with the profile of the telonaut programme in the last decade. Platform, timing, confidence. Idi has given us all that stuff.* However, for all his beneficial contributions, Minnus still felt that Johnson's efforts weren't driven by his belief in the end goal. Rather, perhaps he just wanted to…win? *After all these years, is that what still makes me uneasy around him? Everybody has to validate themselves in some way. So what if he treats things as a game? It's the outcomes that matter, isn't it? Or is it too close to the leaders of the long past. Could it even be dangerous?* Right now, though, it didn't matter. The telonaut programme was doing exactly what it was supposed to do, both uplifting the Race's physical and intellectual achievement and heartening the Race's ambition to achieve more still in the future. Minnus felt good about that. He felt good about himself. As he relaxed back into the chair and closed his eyes, he smiled, recalling a long-ago conversation between two boys on a beach. *All we need do now is decide what to build.*

# Twenty-One

Sero was relaxing outside the Gesponnen base, his constant standardCam companions floating and panning around his home/office/lab. His comfort was a reflection of the audit. Three months on colony, and much had been achieved. With Prid's help, he'd planned and completed a trip between Gesponnen and the reception facility with an average frequency of nine days, making slight alterations in the rail tracks used each time to allow them to visit the activity hubs of the colony. He'd logged details of the cattle kept and harvested on 359D, observing Prid's detailed measurements of their size and shape. He expected that Prid's teasing of some of the less intelligent members of the herd might make the final edit of Minnus's casts. She was fond of using amino soup to draw tendrils in the air, enticing the buffalo to rock along the ground, gobbling up newly created food like demented characters from the Pac-Man entertainment casts of his youth. The pair hadn't yet revisited the Updraft region, although Sero was certain that his first trip there was likely to be one of the highlights of Minnus's first episode. NineCents had informed them that the winds were simply too strong in the region, and no further travel there could be made until the completion of the dissolution.

Zwolf and the other colonists were still unaware of the true reason for his visits back to the reception facility— each time he entered the kill switch room, he ended all outside transmission. He'd also been able to adhere completely to the energy-use projections made following his first request of the colony patriarch. As such, both the planning for the dissolution and his relationship with the old leader seemed to be going well.

Whilst at Gesponnen, Prid and Sero had spent a lot of time at the plate, walking vast lengths along its upper surface and inspecting the areas of the megafauna that made contact with it. They'd camped for two nights on top of the construction, making a bivouac of Prid's own design from the bag of amino soup spray cans they'd taken with them and experimenting with several others, trying to fashion miniatures of Sero's interpretation of the newest style of buildings created on Earth in the period after the first colonists had arrived on the wetworld. He'd interviewed many of the colonists who were most deeply involved in the core-dissolution project itself, including those planning for the creation of the new Gesponnen after successful completion of the plan. The colonists had decided the vibration day would be called Leaf Day, in memory of their fallen matriarch. They'd ceased to refer to the dissolution day as anything other than Leaf Day in recent weeks. Sero had also been trying very hard to speak with a full cross-section of the population, aside from those directly involved in the project. He'd hoped to understand—and represent to the Race—the framework that made this unique colony hold together. Zwolf still seemed a distant leader, guiding this huge project with a light touch—if any touch at all. Sero had hoped that by speaking with many of the members of the society, he'd be more able to understand how this was possible. How were decisions taken and subplans made? Who (or what) acted as the spiritual glue for these people? So far, though, his efforts had been frustrated. The only consistent factors seemed to be that every one of them felt completely empowered to make any decision at all for the good of the colony and that all of them revered Leaf and her plan as a wonderful inspiration. He felt certain that there was more to be discovered, however. *Perhaps the colonists had agreed to present a united front before his reception.* In every social evolution example he'd ever studied, in every colony he'd already audited, it was clear that highly complicated, difficult tasks required either complex organisations of checks and balances (which could be inefficient and were themselves difficult to set up and maintain) or a small group of highly powerful individuals (sometimes only a single person), usually with significant endurance and mental capacity for detached evaluation. In the three months since arriving on NineDee, Sero had seen or heard of no committees or expert panels. There was none of the paraphernalia of government that he'd seen on other fledgling colonies and expected to find here. In fact, there was no deference to anything or anyone at all other than Zwolf and his long-deceased wife. There'd been no pause in work towards the grand plan, no halt for review of progress or subsequent update of all colonists. Sero hadn't even been able to find evidence of the communication routes by which Zwolf discovered the current status of his colony's mission. There were many candidates whose personnel files showed them to be fully capable of being admirable officers to Zwolf's general, and Sero had met several of those individuals himself—including both Divis and Sana, Prid's parents. However, none of them showed any hint of being part of a reporting line that culminated with the colony elder. In didn't seem feasible to Sero that the patriarch was simply consulting NineCents for information in the same way that he, as an outsider, was. Especially not given the enthusiasm and passion the old man had shown for the project during Sero's first interview with him. He simply *must* be more involved with the daily efforts of the project. *But how?* Sero felt sure he was witnessing something new. *Perhaps a new form of social organisation completely. If that were true, how vital might the information be for future expansion of the Race? How critical would it be to understand the conditions under which it arose and what the specific triggers were? What was the method?* He had another nine months to discover the answers.

Sero was also very proud of Prid. Her internal questions over her ability to contribute to the workings of the colony had evaporated. She was regularly coming up with innovative ideas on how to more deeply inspect life on NineDee or present things she was personally familiar with in interesting ways. He had suggested that she describe some of the facets of life on colony to him in a pseudolecture at their base. The evening before each occasion on which they'd set off on an expedition, Prid had performed just such a lecture on the specifics of the region or feature that they'd subsequently be auditing. Sero had encouraged her that it was fine for her not to be able to mathematically describe the thermodynamics of the wind movements or the consequences of the fact that the mass that exerted the gravitational pull of the planet was composed mainly of water. The Race, back on Earth, wouldn't all be able to do that either. What was important was that she conveyed the world around her as she saw it. She was important simply because she was colony born. Her lectures became as much about growing up as a colonist as they were about any specific topic. Sero found her company endearing—he felt he'd formed a unique bond with Prid. He had no children. He had never intended to have any, either. Even in the deepest depths of love, his thoughts had never projected into a future where he had responsibility for the well-being of his own family. Perhaps it might have done, had he found himself accidentally comfortable, if he'd had a little longer. *If she hadn't fallen.* But it hadn't, and she had. Growing close to Prid had resolved something inside of him. *A family? A daughter, even?* Sero had known many men who had become fathers for the first time in their fifth decade.

Even though Sero's body was actually a copy—the eleventh copy, in fact—his genome had been expressed and artificially aged in hyperspace with each copy made. Each of his bodies was biologically identical in age to the age that the previous one had been at the time of its destruction. Sero's personal experience was that he aged like any other member of the Race, at a rate of seven days per week, and even though the Race could map and rebuild individual genomes and the human beings that those genomes encoded, there was still no possibility of simulating every single possible gene expression pattern and meaningfully analysing the results. *Maybe this comes to all men to some degree? Such a model would have evolutionary benefits for tribal groups as older males began caring for offspring in their senior years, having sired them callously in their younger years?* Sero enjoyed theorising for a while and made a mental note to describe his theory to Minnus when he returned to Earth. With a pang of self-pity, he realised that Johnson would likely also want him to describe his musings to an audience using models of monkeys or some such nonsense. *Anyway, where is Prid?*

Just at the moment that his mind had circled around to his young companion, his young companion had circled around the workshop and arrived at his left.

"Hey, Boss," Prid said, "whassup?"

"The sky is up, Prid. And a beautiful blue with it. I'm just lying here watching."

"Why *is* the sky blue?"

*Able to tame speeding halo transports whilst simultaneously wondering why the sky is blue. Why do you find that so admirable, old man?*

"I really don't know. I mean, I *know*, but I don't think that's enough. Sometimes I think it's because of the refraction of light at certain wavelengths and sometimes I think it's to give men like me an excuse to explain things to youngsters like you.

"But enough of my nonsense. We need to prepare for tomorrow." He yawned.

"Hang on, I came to show you something first," Prid said. She handed Sero her tendril bag. "Hold this, and stand still. I just need to adjust it."

When he had taken hold of the bag, Prid began to fiddle with some buckles on her candolier that Sero hadn't noticed before. There were now four clips affixed equidistantly around the sash. She moved each slightly so that they aligned with a tendril spray can on the chest belt.

"OK, I'm ready," she said, taking the bag back from him and slinging it back over her left shoulder, opposite to the candoliered right. "When I get this going, I want you to hold the rope, OK?"

Sero watched nonplussed as Prid forced a clip onto the nearest spray can at her waist height. She grabbed the resulting tendril rope in her left hand before rotating the sash with her right and adroitly clipping open a second can. She wound the resultant additional rope into the first, creating a doubly strong twine. As she completed this move, Prid handed Sero the bulk of both vines and began walking backwards quickly, pulling the plait rope taut. Sero began to get the idea as she moved the sash around again and flicked closed a third clip. By the time she'd added a fourth spraying tendril to the weave, he understood completely what the girl had invented.

"OK, OK, I get it!" he called to the retreating girl. "Come back!"

When she'd turned off her automated spindle and jogged back to him, the smile on her face showed how proud she was that her showcase had worked first time through. "What do you think? Pretty good, eh? I reckon with four vines at once, there's no chance I could get hurt. I could vineseil from the sound satellites in orbit, and I'd be OK!"

Sero couldn't help but smile widely. *Such thrill at discovery!* It reminded him of his own youth. "I think it's great, Prid; a really useful and clever way to make vineseiling both more safe and effective. I'm proud of you."

She beamed on the outside, and his heart bent on the inside. *Wow! Look how much my praise means to her.* He felt happiness at the thought of rewarding Prid with his approval. Sero dwelt on the feeling of pride for a moment before noticing the standardCam again, which was hovering in his vision, focusing on his face. *Dawdling in a hammock and enjoying yourself isn't going to cut it on NV, Novak. You've got a job to do.* "Good work. We need to prepare for tomorrow now, though."

Prid's enthusiasm waned instantly, the beaming smile disappearing from her face. "Yeah, tomorrow. About that…I think I need to say something. I know it's only been a couple of years since Dini went off for training and joined the whole Leaf Day thing, but, well…you see, we were great mates—loved each other, even. Our lives were the same; we both had to deal with distant parents and had lots of time to work things out on our own. But now…" Prid halted again and looked down at the ground. She seemed embarrassed. "But now, we don't speak. And I don't know why. And I still love her. But I hate her. For leaving. And I don't understand. And I don't know what I'll feel like when I see her again."

She turned away from him, and Sero thought that he saw a glimpse of tears forming in her eyes. Without reflection, he closed the distance between them and hugged her to him. She melted against his chest and began sobbing quietly. Her obvious hurt sent Sero's mind racing. At that moment, though, Sero's questions seemed academic, paling in comparison to the insecurity of the young girl in his arms. He squeezed her more tightly.

After a few minutes, they both agreed that they should get some sleep. Sero made sure to take Prid to her bunk and see her lie down and close her eyes before moving to his own pod.

With Prid asleep, his mind returned to the questions he had about her friend. Dini apparently spent almost all her time at the far side of the plate, the oldest section constructed. She was measuring the effects of long-term exposure to the amino sea, assessing how quickly the water movement caused by the growth of the tentaculos might erode or alter the magSteel. Although the nanoBots could repair any damage (and did) instantaneously, it took energy for them to do so. Zwolf himself had informed Sero that if Dini could generate enough convincing data, it might be possible to cease maintenance repairs on vast sections of the plate, in the comfortable knowledge that they would still resonate appropriately when Leaf Day came. A lot of energy might be conserved. Dini's work was therefore very important. This description had only made Sero even keener to interview the mysterious Dini. *How could such an important task be entrusted to a young lady, who'd had only intensive, short-term training? We'll see tomorrow, I guess.*

When he slept that night, he didn't dream.

# Twenty-Two

"**D**'ya mind if we watch this for a half hour?" Joules waved his cSheet at his date.

"Sure, go on. Your buddy?"

"Yeah, he's about to go on. I feel like I should watch. Moral support, ya know? He's nervous. Not his normal thing." Joules unrolled the device and locked it on the bar in front of them, just as the show started. A faint musical refrain found the pair as the words "Moriarty Meets" swam around the screen.

"Oh, I've seen this programme before. She's smaaart."

"Yeah?"

"You can tell she knows where people are gonna go, ya know? Asks a question knowing what they'll say so she can ask another and another to get where she wants to be. Art, really.

"Bit harsh though, maybe. She's smiles, but it's not always smiling along with her guests. Which one is your friend?"

"Guy to the left. Minnus. She's introducing him now."

"And he doesn't normally do this kind of thing?"

"No. His boss convinced him to do it. Minnus says it feels like being chained to a lunatic and left to run the asylum."

"Who's the big guy?"

"The 'God-fearing Jesse Joberan, lead voice of the White Daisy movement.' Not Minnus's favourite people. He says they're a 'cultish right-wing historical throwback with ideas as not far short of crazy, masquerading as intellectual concerns.' Listen to the announcer."

"And debating Mr. Mbeki we have a rousing speaker, Mr. Jesse Joberan. Mr. Joberan has been a legitimising voice for a previous fringe group, the White Daisies. He's managed to focus public debate recently around three key desires: a return to religion (his own, fundamentalist Christian); the removal of the WorldGov earnings cap; and the end of the telonaut programme, which he claims is 'God mimicry…'"

"Woah. That is *out* there," the girl said.

"Yeah, Minnus reckons if left alone with this guy, Inuit would finish up buying ice."

"What's he doing on a cast with him, then?"

"Well, WorldGov weren't even going to respond to these crazies. But Minnus's boss volunteered that the TeloSpace Bureau might be able sort of stand in for them. Publicly show how ill-conceived Joberan's principles were.

"Minnus's boss is a bit of a slime ball. Fancies that he can swing an invitation to join WorldGov, I reckon, if he greases the right wheels. You know, emotional bank balance and all that. He told Minnus he was 'publicly identifiable with the Telospace programme but wasn't senior enough in either the TeloSpace or WorldGov that it would give the Daisies too much credibility'—him talking with them, I mean. That and he lubed Minnus's ego by playing some of Joberan's rhetoric to him. Made him angry."

The show was about to start proper, and Jesse was on screen. Joberan was a relic of a former age. He was tall, white, and Anglo-Saxon. Joules couldn't visually detect any trace of colouring in his skin nor any hint of facial features originating anywhere other than Western Eurasia. He looked different than he'd expected too. Minnus had shown Joules some footage that week, and in all of it, Joberan had been wearing a light-coloured lounge suit—a style harking back at least a thousand years—and carrying one religious symbol or another: a Bible; rosary beads; a photo of his favourite quotation source, the pre-Race Amasian leader Twigg Palin. Today, however, he'd shed this style in favour of a more functional and contemporary coversuit, not dissimilar to Minnus's own. They still looked very different from each other, though. Joberan was a big man, heavy around the gut like his shirt had been filled with pebble ballast, readying him for a concrete vest. His buttocks were like two enormous antique plastic bags filled with water and potatoes. He oozed excess, both literally and figuratively.

"Ugh," said the girl.

"Not in shape, is he? Minnus reckons it might even be a political statement that he's so huge. What did he say? 'An affirmation of the value of accumulation.' Anyway, they've started."

"Thank you. Ms. Moriarty; I believe I will." Joberan spoke with a musical Southern Amasian drawl. Even diminished through cast and cSheet, his words rose and fell and rolled into each other like a cargo of horns being hauled along a mountain surface road.

"Our friend Minnus here represents a project that shows we've gone too far away from honest work and too far towards pretending we are God. We create artificial men on worlds we can't see. I for one don't understand how it's done—or what for.

"Now, I have a brother with a pork-tree farm. Everybody likes pork, and he's a busy man, making sure there's enough. With WorldGov's earnings limit, though, he can only keep so much for himself and his family, and so he contributes millions of Red every year so that we can play at God.

"My niece Billy-Bobette likes animals and would like to have more than the two horses she currently has. But programmes like the telonauts take those horses away from that sweet lil gal. I'd like to ask Minnus what it is that he thinks justifies this."

Joberan leaned into the question, huge elbows on his vast knees, smiling into the camera.

"Ugh," said the girl.

Joules chuckled. "Or in other words, 'Why can't we go back to the past, when things were better for people like me?' Anyway, here's my man."

The screen switched to a close-up of Minnus.

"Will you allow me making a few starting points before taking you on a trip to the future?"

A nod from Joberan on screen.

"This question is more about the Saints' principles than the telonaut programme, Jesse. Do you think you could win the five-hundred-metre sprint at the Olympics next year?"

"I might if I rolled!" Joberan bellowed a laugh and slapped his thighs. When he'd subsided, however, he conceded that it was unlikely.

"OK. What about when you were younger. Were you a good runner?"

"I'd have to say no again; I was never much of a sportsman or even the quickest around the park."

"So even with training, you might not have been able to make it to the Olympics?"

Mock irritation to camera.

"My point, Jesse, is that not all humans are born capable of everything they can think of. No matter our training, I would never have been an Olympic champion, and neither would you. We don't have the skeletal structure, muscle-fibre distribution, and mental capability to generate the speed or endure the trials.

"Similarly, my friend Joules Chavez—who was an Olympic sprint champion—could never have been a programmer, which I know he'd be the first to admit. His mind is not best suited to thinking in the correct way…"

Joules smiled at his date and pulled her towards him. "He's got that right. I'm a people person."

"Or every task or behaviour you can think of, each human begins life with a natural predisposed level of maximum potential. During our lives, we can all move closer to our natural potential in many, many fields, but we can never exceed our genetic inheritance's defined limits. To move closer to our potential, we need security, education, and exposure to the things we're trying to improve in—amongst other things. Access is key. We need to provide access to everything we can, to as many people as we can—to allow everyone to move towards his or her potential.

"So, your brother. I'm sure that he's talented and hardworking. Let's assume he runs the most efficient pork-tree field on the planet. What allows him to do that?

"I think there are lots of factors. He's probably gifted with high intelligence; he is, after all, your brother, Jesse. Not least of the factors are the education and training he's had in the business. Probably his location too. Lots of similar farms in Amasia, therefore lots of infrastructure and trained people to work on the farm. I think we all have to agree that it's not simply your brother's hard work that makes the farm efficient; there are other factors too..."

"I've heard this one before," said Joules. "He's gonna talk about the 'oppression of inheritance' again."

"Of the workers on the farm, perhaps the woman who drives the meat-harvester machine. She's been lucky to achieve development of her intelligence to its highest potential. She has high capacity for endeavour and therefore works hard. She's honest and also a loving mother. Many admirable qualities. Unfortunately, her mind just won't work when imagining the international logistics needed to run a successful farm. She can't conceptualise it in enough detail. In this area, her genetic ceiling is simply too low. She contributes to your brother's farm as best she is able but could never hope to one day own the farm or maybe start her own..."

"She must like him," said the girl. "She doesn't normally let people make speeches. Usually steps in and referees them."

"Finally, I also want to point out that not a single human being on this planet or any other has ever *chosen* either his or her genetic potential or access to capability-improvement systems before birth. In fact, because we know how important variation is to all living ecosystems, the Race has long ago specifically outlawed gene selection in humans beyond the basic Sapien filtering of inherited disease. None of us sit in the sky and say, 'Hmmmmmm, Central Surfaca looks like a fantastic place to work; I think

I'll be born there as a genius, ninja, athlete.' We are simply born as we are, where we are, when we are. Given all these facts, we then need to ask ourselves two questions: How much should your brother be rewarded for his luck at birth, and how much should our imaginary pork harvester be punished for her luck at birth? Should we oppress people because of their inheritance?"

The screen showed a chuckling Joberan, shaking his head. "Are you ever going to take me on your 'trip to the future,' Mr. Mbeki?"

"Here we go. Let's imagine that we do allow your brother to take more profit for personal use than other people—buy his daughter her horses. What happens next?"

"Well, I imagine young Billy-Bobette would be the first to benefit. That little girl's eyes will just light up. It'd be an end to her longing, an end to the need for her father to try to explain something to her that he doesn't understand himself. The world would be simpler. And better. We could teach our children that hard work means their lives get easier, that they can have the things they want."

The cheeks under Joberan's dark-black eyes wobbled slightly as he nodded slowly to emphasise the "rightness" of his words. He turned to the audience and nodded again.

"If you ignore the jowly shuddering, he does make it sound good," said the girl.

"It starts with a new pony for Bill'Bobby. But what if your brother does *really* well? Perhaps he has six great years

189

and is allowed to keep all the Red? What would he do with it all? Ponies will only take up so much of the extra."

Joberan extended his middle finger towards Minnus, pointing it at the floor so that his clenched fist looked like the face of an elephant, stiff trunk pointing out and down from the central mass. The big man jabbed at the air as he spoke in a physical remonstration aimed at his adversary.

"He would provide for his family—the rest of his family, that is. Perhaps his wife's family, he would buy ponies or raceWings; he'd buy comfort, maybe some style; he'd do exactly what you would do!" Joberan raised his voice with the last five words emphasising each of them with slow, deliberate pronunciation and lingering prods to the air between Minnus and himself. It came across well on TV. Confident but not accusing.

"Would he be able to spend it *all*?"

"Hah. First he wants my brother to give all his Red to the hellnauts, and now he wants him to spend *all* of it himself. Make up your mind, Minnus." Joberan rose from his seat and addressed the audience directly as he spoke. "My brother, as am I, is a God-fearing man. A caring man, dedicated to his family. No God-fearing man would waste his income on trivialities. No more than he would see it wasted on the nonsenses of science aimed at reducing God's creations to numbers. A God-fearing man would save that income—make it *capital*, as we did before the world fell away from the truth. With that capital he could provide for *many* generations of his family, be that 'caring man' right through time, even after he had left this Earth for God's kingdom."

Every few words, Joberan adopting a low, rumbling emphasis to his tone, looking directly into the eyes of one of the nearest crowd members and holding his or her gaze before continuing with his pseudosermon.

"He could use the further pursuit of it to give his life *purpose*, to give himself a measure of just how *good* and caring a man he was. He could validate his daily struggles with something more than a small role in allowing the academics amongst us to play in the garden of God at the expense of his labour. He could be the king of his small, God-fearing castle. He could be *empowered*!"

With this there was a ripple of applause came from Joules's cSheet.

"Empowered. Great word," said the girl.

Minnus stayed resolutely silent. He simply looked theatrically back and forth between the still-standing Jesse Joberan and the enormous, Joberan-deformed plastiche chair he'd previously occupied. Minnus waited. After ten seconds of discomforting silence, in which Joberan looked quietly awkward as the only standing person in the room, the White Daisyite lumbered back to his seat and lowered himself creakingly back into the waiting mould.

"Your brother can be *empowered* by accumulating capital? He can be validated? He can achieve worth in the eyes of who? His family? His community? Your God? What of the meat-harvester-machine operator? Can she accumulate capital at the same rate as your brother? Is her life therefore less valid? Valid to whom? Her family? Her community? Isn't her community the same one as your brother's? The community members must all therefore value him more than her? What about her children? Will they be able to reverse the roles and become the owners and coordinators of the farm?'

"Go get him, buddy," said Joules.

Realising he would not be allowed to answer the questions fired at him, Joberan had begun simply shaking his head at Minnus—as if denying the existence of his challenging questions.

"Would your nieces and nephews then work for the new owners? Would they need to work if the size of your brother's *caring* Red legacy allowed them to consume without producing? No? So what then if the roles *aren't* reversed? Your nieces and nephews go on accumulating capital? 'Validating' themselves? Eventually, do they start using their capital to exert power over others? Power beyond the pork-tree field? Perhaps only to make sure that they and their children can generate still more capital and exert still more power? What if it isn't just your brother's family that is behaving this way? What if *everyone* is allowed to accumulate as much 'validation' as they can stand? What happens? Do they begin competing with other families? Fighting them for control of more and more resources, more and more power? More resources than they could ever possibly need or produce?"

Joberan had ceased his head shaking and begun trying to raise himself from his chair. Unfortunately for him, his massive weight seemed to have damaged the memory-form functions of the plastiche. The arms of the man's chair had folded around his gut and were preventing him from rising. Joberan, his awareness of the boundary of his own form dulled by the layers of fat separating his extremities from his spine, was rocking back and forth only a few futile centimetres in some obvious confusion. Seizing the comical upper hand, Minnus leapt to his feet, mimicking the larger man's earlier display for the crowd.

"Is your guy imitating him now with that accent?" said the girl.

"I think he is, yeah."

"Greed. Excess. *Inherited wealth.* These are the portents of the end of society. Thousands of years of social *evolution* have finally allowed the Race to outgrow such *infantile* desires. A move to allow such characteristics back into our society would be a *regression.* A negative step. Today, our earnings cap allows everyone the chance to be the best they can be, without the impediment that the inherited wealth of the *few* would represent for the many."

The hum of the audience's giggling was now coming through the screen. Big Jesse was infuriated, imprisoned in his plastiche cocoon and visibly colouring at the jowls.

"Programmes like the telonaut programme allow *everyone* in the Race to see the fruits of their *personal* labour towards their *personal* peak. Such fruits are borne by our efforts to spread *all* of the knowledge the Race accumulates to *all* its members—regardless of the size of their contribution to its accumulation. We are all *valid*, Jesse. We are valid as one. As the *Race*. We are humanity *evolved*."

Joberan was now hitting the arms of his chair, realising that it was they who were restraining him. Minnus feigned surprise, melodramatically widening both eyes at seeing the huge frame of his opponent unsubtly fighting with the furniture. Minnus's words, mimicry and mocking combined with Joberan's now obvious predicament, had the crowd laughing openly.

"When we were young, before human society grew into the adulthood that the Race represents, perhaps we needed religion to provide firm laws and codes to make things fairer. Ultimately, though, we replaced such blind laws with a new system—when it became obvious that religion was intrinsically arcane and unnecessary. Similarly, we now live in times where we no longer need grievous economics to drive increased living standards. Our society, justifiably, no longer tolerates unequal weighting of worth…"

With a gasp of exertion, Joberan finally wrenched himself from the chair. Reacting quickly, Minnus stepped sideways to avoid the toppling mass that hurtled towards him, launched from its plastiche cannon. Joberan staggered towards the front of the stage, carried by the momentum of his initial burst of effort and his enormous bulk. One well-hidden, fat-swathed knee buckled under the uneven distribution of the angry man's weight. The audience gasped en masse. Joberan knew he would fall. Desperate to avoid crushing the front row of the audience, he threw himself to the floor earlier than he would have reached it naturally, landing just shy of the stage's edge with a comical thud. As he hit the floor, he sprayed spit from his mouth, coating the commSheets of the front row with a liquid dusting. The audience stopped chuckling.

Minnus paused for a few seconds as Joberan rolled onto his back and then sat up ungraciously. Minnus then finished his point. "Because top-heavy things fall over."

The audience burst into loud mirth.

"Society cannot be allowed to be top heavy. People cannot be allowed to attest superiority over others through either ownership of capital or a direct route to a false creator. We are *of* the Race. We are *for* the Race. We are *all* the Race."

Amongst the laughter, applause began. A few hands at first, then rippling and increasing across the audience until all were applauding Minnus's point. Joberan had struggled to his feet to display a luminous pink, sweating face of fury. He turned to the audience that he'd so recently tried to woo into following him and repeated the same elephant point gesture he'd made earlier to Minnus.

"I *know* I am right! The Lord God has spoken to me and made my mind clear. *I* must show you puppets the folly of your ignorance!" Joberan had given up any pretence of composure in his fury and was ranting like any other

White Daisy religionomics crazy. "I will start by showing the power of God's distaste for the spacenauts of hell and their sacrilegious experimentationalisationing!"

With that, God-fearing Jesse Joberan removed his lounge suit jacket, rolled it into a ball, threw it at Minnus's feet, and stalked off screen.

"Well, I think your buddy won the day," said the girl.

# TWENTY-THREE

"**So what should** I expect?" Sero asked Prid.

"I dunno, really. You know how hard it's been for us to get her into the schedule? Well, imagine that you're *not* a once-in-a-lifetime telonaut-auditor-visitor with limited time available. Imagine you're just an old friend. Then imagine how hard it would be to hang out. Dini has become more of a concept for me than an *actual person*."

Sero could see that there was a little hurt in Prid at the changed relationship with her old friend. Many of the ways that Prid had explained what she knew about the colony to Sero involved anecdotes that began, "This one time, me and Dini were…" However, since his reception, Sero hadn't even met Dini. She'd been unavailable, occupied on the other side of the planet.

"She's been gone for two years nearly. It actually makes some sense really. It's such a long way, and we all know how important it is to conserve energy, so the trip back would need to be for something special. You said yourself that her whole reason for being out there is actually to try to save energy.

"She's trying to find a way to redeploy a team of nano-Bots that are on maintenance duty. I researched the details with NineCents. If we can find the optimum point, where ceasing the maintenance wouldn't cause the plate to deteriorate so much as to risk errors on Leaf Day, we can perhaps use the calculation to make similar energy-saving efforts in other areas. We might even be able to delay Leaf Day if we need to," Prid explained. "It's all in here now," she said, waving her bulging, stuffed notebook.

"Maybe even compensate for the energy-hungry visit of one of those oh-so-important, once-in-a-lifetime telonaut-auditor-visitors?" Sero smiled back at Prid with imitation sheepishness. With the exception of the accident with the haloMagnet and the resulting repair effort, Sero and Prid had stuck rigidly to the principle of minimising energy use, even going so far as to on occasion leave Prid alone in Gesponnen whilst Sero made the trip back to the reception facility to download his latest memory fragments and post them back to Minnus on Earth. This was only useful if the trip back was without detour to another site of interest. Prid had of course accompanied Sero when they'd planned routes that allowed them to investigate another location on the way. The quest to be respectful to the needs of the colony and the dissolution plan had become a running joke between the two of them. When they'd planned to visit the herds of cattle grazing on a tentaculo, Prid had performed a mocking calculation of whether it might be more energy efficient for them to send her out to collect a space cow and bring it back to show Sero, rather than for him to go to the cows. Sero had said that it was a good idea, but that in his experience, cows made even worse haloMagnet drivers than he did—even with his record of crashing them.

"She's going to be here soon anyway. I'd better take off. Don't want to break the old man's rules."

Zwolf had been very clear that Prid wasn't to be part of the meeting, citing the old friendship between her and Dini and the limited time available to Dini. Apparently, Dini would be back at Gesponnen for only two months and had lots of work to do in tutoring other colonists on the research she'd been undertaking. The plan was to redeploy other teams to other sites to try to replicate her progress. Zwolf didn't want any distractions. Sero had thought this a little unnecessary and lacking in compassion for both Prid and Dini, based on the stories Prid had told about how close they had been. It seemed more cautious than needed and lacked in humanity, but Sero had been able to rationalise Zwolf's instructions with the logic that if a large family of people have dedicated all the time to such an ambitious goal as Leaf Day, perhaps there should be some expected and understandable myopia. Once the colony was stabilised, there'd likely be a relaxing of focus, and more-normal social relations could resume. Sero was sure Prid and Dini would reconcile. After all, there was now a decades-wide physical age gap between himself and Minnus, but their childhood friendship had continued, regularly reestablishing itself in altered forms across the years. It was usually the things that had brought them together in the first place that catalysed and reinvigorated their bond each time. Shared goals. *The friends you make as young adults are the friends you keep for life.*

"You're right," he said. "You need to give Dini a little space right now, but that doesn't mean I can't let her know that you miss her and want to spend some time with her once this project is all over. Leaf Day is only eight months away now, you know, and I think there'll be a lot of changes on NineDee the day after Leaf Day."

She smiled at him, but the smile didn't touch her eyes. He smiled back but knew that his eyes didn't crease either. As she swung her candolier over her chest and passed him to leave, he placed his hand on her shoulder to gently halt her.

"You know, working out how you feel about certain things and how to deal with things that disappoint you is part of growing into a woman, Prid. You're doing really well. I'm not sure I've earned the right to be proud of you after only three months of working together, but I *am* proud of you.

"Life here on a frontier colony is hard, and that makes the typical sacrifices that all young ladies go through as they grow even harder for you. You're smashing this growing-up thing."

When Prid smiled this time, her eyes did move. "Aw, shucks. Thanks, *Dad*!" she joked as she left him in their lab with only the hovering cameras for company.

Sero waited ten minutes for Dini to arrive, clearing one of the workbenches so that it could be used as a more informal desk, better suited to a situation such as a first meeting. He knew she was waiting outside when the doorframe vibrated. Although the buildings in Gesponnen were universally made of vine tendrils, some of the more useful and practical items such as doors had been built in the city by nanobots, Sero assumed to allow for some social niceties and privacy to remain, despite the interlinked structure of the colony. This meant he could see the silhouette of a woman through his now-transparent door. He straightened his clothing and made a rising motion with his hand to lift the blue light that indicated the bottom of the door from floor to ceiling, opening the door. The woman stepped into the lab.

As Zwolf had also insisted, the standardCams left the lab just as Dini entered. This was the first time they'd left Sero alone outside of the reception facility since his arrival on NineDee. The old man had said he wanted Sero to have some privacy when he met the young scientist. He'd told Sero that she was shy and would feel more comfortable without such obvious observation. At that moment, though, Sero couldn't imagine how or why *any* woman with Dini's form could be demure.

She was stunning to look at. Sero had been expecting someone who looked like Prid. Perhaps he'd created an association between the woman standing in front of him and his younger assistant based on the two female's previous friendship, an association that had prejudiced and skewed his judgement. He'd prepared his questions specifically to discover the differences between a colony-born twenty-one-year-old and an Earthborn girl of the same age. He'd prepared his mind to address those questions to a girl, something less than the preposterously beautiful archetype of womanhood that stood before him. He was, he realised, only half-prepared.

"Hello, Dini. I'm very pleased to finally meet you. You're a very difficult...*lady* to speak to in person. I hope you'll be able to tell me all about the important work you're doing here."

Dini was tall, taller than Sero. She had an asymmetric hairstyle, one cheek cupped by a bob of jet black hair, the other exposed by a much shorter curtain. The revealed cheekbone was high and delicate, formed by a perfect blend of ancestral features from all around the Earth. Her skin was darker than Sero's, her eyes a luminescent green. Sero knew his initial reaction would be noticed by Minnus as he reviewed the images pulled from the spider map Sero would send to Earth later in the week. He hoped he hadn't been so obvious as to embarrass Dini in the here and now, but even two instinctive seconds of lustful assessment couldn't be hidden from a man with the ability to review your memories—especially when those memories would be reviewed from the perspective of Sero's own line of sight. When she'd entered his lab, Sero had been astonished by Dini's physical beauty. He knew his gaze had lingered too long on the flesh exposed by her unusual outfit. She wore a sash as a shirt—a single sheet of material wrapped tightly across her chest from one shoulder to the other hip—continuing the asymmetry of her hair. The other shoulder and both arms were entirely exposed, as was a large swathe of Dini's skin—from just below her breasts to the lowest point of the top of her pelvis, a full seventy centimetres of flawless teak. She was sleek and athletic looking, muscles toned to draw patterns of slight shadow on her body as she walked. She wore extremely low-slung, skin-tight tool pants and tendril boots. The trousers were close-fitting enough that Sero could make out the moving muscles in her legs as she'd entered the room and walked towards him. Realising his inappropriate reaction, he regained his composure quickly enough to focus on her face before she made it across the lab to shake his hand. Here, though, he became lost again. Dini was astonishingly, unattainably pretty. After his experience on Rigil, the change he'd felt within himself after meeting *her*, Sero was a little disgusted with himself for this immature reaction to a beautiful woman.

She laughed slightly and then widened her eyes and smiled. From very old habit, Sero responded in kind until Dini looked down at their clasped hands, and Sero realised he was still holding his guest's palm. She only spoke when he released her.

"We're all doing important work, Mr. Novak—can I call you Sero? Each of us here is furthering the knowledge of the Race. Your own work is even more important; you are the link back to our home world. In fact, I'm honoured to meet you. Perhaps even a little disoriented.

"It's pretty humbling to meet a man of your stature, Sero; you've been to more planets than anyone else in the history of humankind, let alone the Race. You're a pioneer. I have more to learn from you than you do from me."

"A mutually beneficial relationship, then."

Despite her apparent humility, Dini didn't look disoriented. To his surprise, Sero felt his cheeks colour. *Embarrassment? Reticence to flirt? What is going on?* Zwolf had been extremely mistaken, thought Sero. This woman was not coy at all. Perhaps the difference in age between the patriarch and the young woman led to confusion or even highly altered behaviours when they were in each other's presence, Sero postulated. He also knew that when a man has known a woman as a young girl, it was often very difficult for that man to accept the growth of the girl into the woman. At least on an emotional level. *Perhaps Zwolf was simply being overprotective?*

Himself a little disoriented, Sero moved away from his guest under the pretence of collecting a chair for her. He returned with both a lab stool and some restored composure. When they'd settled into a comfortable position on either side of his workbench, he tried to resolve the direction of the conversation to his control. He asked some simple questions about how long it had taken her to travel to speak with him, whether she'd seen her friends and family since arriving back in Gesponnen. Dini confirmed the basic facts Sero had already heard from Prid and Zwolf, explaining that she'd been working on the far side of the plate. She insisted that she now felt wedded to the project and as such had sacrificed all the time she had to it for the past two years. She felt there'd be plenty of time for family and friendship after Leaf Day, when she'd made a success of her project. As she spoke, she regularly used her hand to temporarily clasp her hair back from her face, resting the same arm on Sero's workbench as she did so. Each time she revealed her full face and relaxed her head onto the pillar of her forearm, her head tilted to one side. Although she was dominantly beautiful, the angle of her head made her look somewhat coquettish. He listened attentively, actively paraphrasing the things his new acquaintance explained, but Sero found her demeanour very distracting, so much so that when she challenged him again about his previous audits, he stumbled over his response a second time. *What is it?* Sero quickly tried to understand what he was feeling, reaching for some foundation on which to plan, to improve himself. Something coppery tasting was at the back of his throat. *What does that mean?*

"Maybe that can be the, er…deal between us, then? For every question of mine that you answer, I'll answer one for you about my travels as telonaut auditor. In fact, my manners dictate that ladies should always go first." Sero realised that he had an unwillingly broad smile fixed to his face. He tried to understand why. *Am I flirting?* That wasn't the direction he'd intended to steer the conversation. More of that horrible taste in his mouth.

The look on Dini's face told Sero that he had definitely been flirting with her. *Ugh.* He felt revolted with himself.

"Manners? In a frontier colony? And special treatment for little me! Sero, I have work to do and lots of questions. You, along with the rest of NineDee, might regret letting me probe you. I promise, I can be quite…insatiable."

Sero tried to dispassionately consider how to behave in this unexpected situation. He tried to apply forethought. *If this flirtation becomes something more, what are the consequences? How will it affect the audit? What will the impact on Prid be? How will Zwolf react? Why do I feel so terrible about even considering sex, even whilst I'm on an inept autopilot, ricocheting towards it?* As his mind considered trying to halt his body's dangerous speeding towards emotionally driven behaviour, his body rallied and took control of his vocal chords and facial expressions. *You're a man nearly a century old, a telonaut of half a dozen worlds, a scientist and scholar.* Sero was also a man sitting near to an astonishingly beautiful woman who was clearly impressed by him and interested in more than only talking to him. He reacted with more of the man and less of the telonaut. *Why are women always my weakness?* It seemed so simple to intellectually commit to the progress of the Race above all else and let more base instincts go. In reality, though, Sero was a biological member of the human race with thousands of years of evolutionary instinct already in the bank before the Race existed. That instinct was driving internal physical responses to a blatant advertisement of the availability of a desirable woman. Still, Sero tried to stay in control and think through his words and actions.

"Ha-ha-ha, I was born over a hundred years ago, Dini. More than enough time to learn how to bore young ladies like you into submission with tales of my less-than-derring-do. I think you'll find you'll be running for your wind-created tentaculos hills long before I run out of stories to tell."

Giggling, Dini leaned over and touched the auditor's arm. Sero felt all the hairs on his body lift from his skin and point at the woman in front of him. He was astonished to find he could also no longer comfortably sit with his legs together as blood ran riot around his body, all normal traffic of his circulatory system disrupted, all valves opening in uncoordinated fashion. For some reason, despite his history of ease with romance and sex, this was the first time in his life he'd felt uncomfortable with such a reaction. The first time he'd noticed all the smaller components that made up lust.

"Well, how about you try very hard not to bore me, and I try just as hard not to be bored?"

She left both of her hands on Sero's forearm for a second longer than would have left Sero in any confusion as to her intent, before withdrawing them and arching her back as if to stretch her spine. Her chest thrust towards him. Sero realised that she was doing more than simply responding to his own poorly controlled advances. She was quite clumsily *provoking* him. Perhaps all the time spent in a relatively closed community led to a different level of sophistication in making approaches to prospective partners. However, on other audits, Sero had seen relationship rituals like this operate as perfect parallels to those on Earth— regardless of isolation. A burst of heat from his swelling penis ended his temporary control of his thought processes. He realised he was staring at Dini's carved brown stomach as the muscles beneath her skin strained towards him, following her backwards-falling breasts up, over, and away from him again within the rolling movement of her extending stretch. *Interviewing this woman at any length is going to be extremely difficult, especially in view of how the interviews would be recorded for the Race—through your wandering eyes.*

Finished with stretching, Dini then aggressively adjusted the sash restraining her chest. It had moved as a result of her arching her back. The movement underneath the material told Sero that the single sheet he could see was all she wore. Again, he felt a burst of heat between his legs. Then a noise behind him distracted him from the rapidly rising swell of lust.

"Sero, why are the cameras floating around outside? I forgot my wheel tool for cutting and carving. I'm going to work on some new ideas. I'll be back out of here in a second; don't worry—"

Prid entered their shared base of operations without looking up, casting her tendril bag to one side without care—a level of authenticity that only teenagers can genuinely muster. As she raised her eyes, she saw Dini was already in the lab.

"Oh. Hi, Dini," Prid said. "What *are* you wearing?"

Sero's eyes flicked between the two. Prid looked astonished and embarrassed that she was breaking the rules and perhaps also that she'd spoken without thinking. Dini, on the other hand, looked absolutely furious. The anger in her face and eyes was only momentary, though. Sero recognised a distinguishable change across the space of that second, a regaining of self-control in Dini. It spurred him to regain his own control, putting away the base version of himself and reassuming his conscious self: Sero Novak, telonaut lead auditor. He caught Prid's attention and gave her a cautionary look, widening his eyes and cocking his head slightly. Prid noticed the look, which increased her obvious embarrassment but also triggered a rapid apology and withdrawal.

"I'm so sorry. Childish of me. You look great, Dini. Great to see you." Prid shook and then nodded her head as she spoke, affirming her sincerity. "Ah, here's what I needed." She scooped up her cutting tool from the opposite end of the bench to where Sero and Dini were sat, stepping quickly backwards afterwards before picking up her tendril bag without looking and thrusting the tool inside awkwardly. "I'll leave you guys to it. Sorry for the interruption again!"

Prid turned and quickly walked from the room, leaving Sero and Dini alone again. As she did, the guilt that had been building in Sero reached a crescendo, and he finally understood. *Remorse.* He was feeling physical remorse for being attracted to someone. Someone that he wasn't in love with. Someone that wasn't *her.* He excused himself, went into an adjacent room, and threw up as silently as he could.

# Twenty-Four

"**It's great, dear,**" Nombre said to her husband.

She and Joules had travelled to the South Pole with him. The success of the first NV casts had piqued both of their interest, and so they'd concocted a plan to spend the next few days with Minnus at his place of work. He had shown them around the quarters near to D & P that they'd stay in for the rest of the week and was now giving the grand tour, finishing off at the Postbox facility itself.

"We should perhaps have invited the kids too? They're even more interested in your work than I am—especially now that you're a global debating champion."

Nombre was teasing, but she was probably right. Minnus's children had families of their own, and the whole clan would probably appreciate the access to Telosec that he could provide.

"Yeah, and this is definitely a space that would help me find a lady to start my family too!" Joules said. "This place is grotesque!"

Minnus assumed that his younger friend meant "grotesque" in a positive way, given the reverence on his face.

"I coulda brought a lady here, worn my white coat, played scientist. My athlete shtick is old, and this could give me a whole new angle. A way to help ladies see me as more than some quick-moving meat. You coulda helped me explain the important breakthrough I made for you in setting up the NV casts."

They were walking across the bridge to the Postbox facility, having passed through the Telosec armament and the D & P suite on the way. As there was nobody in the Postbox facility, the bridge linking Telosec to the tall-stalked mushroom-shaped building wasn't in isolation mode—less need to prevent interference with a suspended facility than an active one. So it was a simple matter of walking through the calm, force-field protected tube that was the bridge. That would all change in eight months or so when the final memory fragment from Sero's NineDee audit arrived, along with the latest signal describing how to build his new copy body. At that point, the place would lock down, and not even Minnus would be able to interfere. WorldGov had put clear (and, Minnus thought, very valid) directives in place when the telonaut programme was first created over a century ago. The early history of spider mapping had included a long debate on the ethics of being able to move minds into new bodies. The debate had concluded that the kill switch was the most moral way of deciding whether an individual should want to continue living—in the event of any accident or error in body copying or mind mapping. That way, the individual would be empowered to make a decision, but only if there was certainty that nobody had (or could) interfere with any stage of the process. Once the signal was received, the air-gapped computer housed within the reception facility took over, and the process ran automatically from there. No access from outside the room was possible.

"Invitations are all open if you want to make them. Although I'm not sure Johnson would be too pleased at making this place a dating venue for friends of the staff. He's tightened security a lot recently. The crazy daisies are really fired up at the moment, and we've had some wide-spectrum threats coming in, both here and to WorldGov.

"Given our recent success, Johnson has hired a bigger team to help promote the telonaut programme and telo-space in general, keep the momentum of interest going ahead of Mission Selection elections. One of the lower-level authors received some pretty horrid mail. I think their role is in creating fiction content based on the possibility of new, more distant colonies, trying to generate cultural acceptance in the Race for Red allocation. So they're one of the few people in telospace who still get physical mail, ob-jects that they use as reference material. It's flora and fauna mostly. Anyway, this lady opened a packet at her workstation, and there was a dead vervet monkey inside with a second vervet monkey's decapitated head glued to it."

"That is terrible!" Nombre said.

"*Not* grotesque," said Joules, confusingly.

"Indeed," said Minnus. "There was a message too. Not electronic, not on a cSheet—an old-fashioned piece of paper with ink scrawled on it. Must have been difficult to even source. The message read, 'God didn't make this; I did. I am a sinner. God didn't make your hellnauts; you did. You are a sinner. God will provide a way for all sinners to be cleansed. God is vengeful upon the unclean.'

"There've been other threats too, mainly anonymous messages pushed to the cSheets of team members. So when Johnson heard about this monkey business, he petitioned WorldGov for a higher Red allocation for the next year, until Sero is back. They agreed too. So now there are twenty-five extra people over at Telosec and a couple of WorldGov security investigators looking into it. If I tried to make this place available for your social use, my friend, you might find yourself followed from place to place for a while. Not really the kind of attention I think you're hoping for?"

Joules didn't answer verbally but rather grimaced and shook his head.

Nombre was more analytical. "There are always people who are at the edges of society. For all our progress in the last few centuries, the Race is still populated by normal distributions, with most people's beliefs and behaviours in a typical range in the middle but a small number of people at the extremes. Just because via WorldGov and the principles of the Saints, we've found a better way of organising ourselves to benefit the most people, it doesn't mean that the extremists have gone away. Whatever characteristic we choose, there'll be a minority of people that are so dissimilar to the centre mass that we'll call them senseless and irrational."

"Chopping up monkeys, scratching threats into dead trees, and bundling it all up in a parcel for a stranger seems pretty irrational to me!" Joules said.

"I'd agree, Joules," said Nombre. "But then again, I'm in probably in the central position on the spectrum of reaction to manmade inventions and change. The good news is that because the Race has held together for centuries based on the Saints' economic principles of a profit cap for each individual in any one year, and the inclusion of inherited wealth in that cap, it's unlikely that any single one of these extremists would have enough Red to fund anything much more seriously threatening that the odd monkey corpse in a bag.

"I don't think that there's any kind of an appetite amongst the Race at large for altering something so fundamental to our way of life as the Ugandan principles. Those principles are one of the reasons the Race has continually been able to reduce violence decade on decade for centuries. So don't worry, Joules; the masses will control the crazies."

"So it's just a normal distribution of arseholes, eh?" Joules said.

"As so often, Nombre, you're right," said Minnus, "Although I'm still glad of the extra work that is happening to protect the facility and the project. Imagine if one lone individual—"

"Arsehole," interjected Joules.

"If *some*one did manage to get inside the reception facility, who knows what they might do that could affect Sero?"

Minnus thought of his old friend often, and spending each and every day immersed in Sero's experiences didn't do much to dampen his affection and concern for him. He'd had a very tough time in the Rigil audit. Traumatic, even. No matter the physical age gap between them now, Sero was still his partner in life—even as much as Nombre.

"I love that your first thought is your friend rather than your own safety," Nombre said.

Minnus could see she genuinely meant the sentiment, and there was none of the chastisement in the statement that might have been readable if it had come from someone else.

They were approaching the end of the bridge now, confronted by the large steel door sealing the facility as a raised drawbridge. There was a four-metre gap between the door and the end of the bridge they were on. Minnus could see the blinking red lights that indicated the end of the weather-disruption field in exactly the same place as the end of the physical bridge, aligning the force field and the platform to form a sealed tube with the same four-metre gap from the closed door. He stepped towards the invisible end of the tube and held his cSheet in the centre of the circular window that the lights and the floor produced. Tapping a code onto the unrolled device, he simultaneously spoke his name and a code sentence: "Optimism and perseverance; patience will produce."

Though they couldn't see it from the outside of the building, the locking mechanism unfastened at four heights. Once free of the latch pins that hitched the doors to the inner of the reception facility, the metre-thick panels fell outwards from the building, towards the window from which Minnus, Joules, and Nombre watched. The weather-protecting force field was also soundproof, so they couldn't hear the loud clank that the steel made as it contacted the bridge on their side of the gap, becoming a drawbridge. The final stage of entry was for the halo of blinking red lights to move along the drawbridge to extend the force field protecting them from the Antarctic elements. As they crossed into the Postbox building, Minnus looked down the concrete-and-steel stalk of the building to its base hundreds of meters below. He could still make out the camp that the White Daises had formed there to protest the whole telonaut programme. It had changed in size and shape over the last decade but had always been a presence. Now, however, it seemed more sparsely populated than before. *Perhaps it's just the distance I'm observing from? A misperception?*

He took Nombre's hand and nodded to Joules to guide them through the door.

⅄

"Stark, isn't it?" Nombre offered after a few minutes of technical explanation from her husband. There was nothing new to be explained to either her or Joules about the technical details of blank bubbling. The technology was well established and understood by most of the Race— it was a standard part of curricula the world over as one of the twelve largest Red allocation projects approved by the Mission Selection global elections. Nombre evidently wasn't enjoying the ambience of the place.

"Sero never really explained how plain the interior is. He always talks about the audits and sometimes, like you, about the process. That's not what goes through my mind, though, whilst I'm in this room. What would it be like to wake up in here, all flat steel and dull light?

"I'd always imagined the feeling of awakening after transport to be like rebirth. But this wouldn't feel like that at all. I think I might feel…scared? Like coming around after anaesthesia? Disoriented? It's more like a cell than a birthing chamber."

"It's like a big, upturned metal bucket. We're like spiders, trapped by some giant maid for trespassing in her pantry," offered Joules. "I don't like it either. Feels like we're underground somehow. And I know we just came in on that bridge through the air."

"It's a design choice, guys. Purposeful. Remember, the whole point of the kill switch is that the individual doesn't know whether he or she is the original or the copy. If there were more architectural detail in the postage and reception facilities, there'd be more chance for variation—and therefore more chance of influencing the individual's decision.

"Remember that we want them to make their decision only on *who* they are and *how* they feel. We don't want *where* they are to be a factor. You guys know all this from school."

"Each copy has no way of knowing if the other copy is haler. The quantum-linked atoms can only be manipulated into one of two states, so complex information can't be communicated instantaneously, only simple 'one' or 'zero' signals. 'Yes' or 'no.' You both know that there's an error rate in the blank-bubbling process, even for the original person in the postage end of the process. We are, after all, talking about elevating matter out of 3-D space-time and into higher dimensions, where we think time passes differently—something nobody has ever seen or measured. It *could* be that that once transmission is complete—"

Nombre cut Minnus off with a monotone imitation of the early-grade lecture. "Both the original and the new copy are in worse shape than the original was when he or she stepped into the bubble. If that happens, the only person who has the authority to decide which one of them lives is that person. If a computer or any other individual made that choice, even if it was a medically, statistically correct decision, it would be murder. That's why the efforts to design something minimalist and functional."

Minnus mimed hurt before finishing: "It's also why once the process of bubbling begins, the doors lock down and can only be opened by the individual in the bubble. Every Postbox in the galaxy works the same way."

"Yeah, and all the reflective hard surfaces make the death laser more lethal if you're the guy on the wrong end of the remote-control suicide switch," said Joules. "Just being in here knowing that there's the possibility of a very warm, very quick, very red light show blasting me into a gas and then being cooled into soup to build the next guy is making me very nervous. I think I've seen enough. I'll wait for you guys back on the bridge."

The big athlete left briskly, clearly uncomfortable. He moved out of Minnus's line of sight. He and Nombre were standing at the perimeter of the room, and only the first few metres of the walkway formed by the drawbridge were visible, not the longer bridge itself.

"It *is* a little unnerving in here, darling," Nombre said contemplatively. "Gives me some insight into Sero though. Eleven times now he's stood in an awful tin can like this and decided to kill some other version of himself. After Rigil, he would have known which version he was when he awoke too. The reception copy would've had no physical injuries. He'd have known he was erasing the self that had all that love and hurt happen to it. His last link to her. He'd have made that cold decision in this taciturn room. I wonder how he felt. How he feels now. I wonder if the heartier person really came out of that transmission."

Her musings were interrupted by a loud whooshing sound, and then a blast of air came into the room, strong enough for both of them to need to reach for the wall to steady themselves.

"What was that?" Nombre said, plainly alarmed.

"I don't know. The winds blow strongly at this latitude, especially at this height, but the force field surrounding the bridge should prevent that affecting us in here. I'll check on Joules."

Minnus moved to the door of the room hurriedly. When he came through the doorway, he felt a consistent wind blowing against him. He also saw Joules's back two hundred metres away down the gently curving path of the bridge as his friend sprinted away from them at full speed.

"What is going on?" Minnus whispered to himself.

"L…k ab…ou!" Nombre shouted from behind him, raising her voice to be heard. The wind pumping into the closed tunnel was increasing the air pressure, and Minnus's hearing was suffering as a result. He saw his wife hold her nose with two fingers and blow down it, equalising the pressure in her ears. He did the same.

"Look above you!" she repeated urgently, audible now and pointing to the sky.

Minnus looked up.

There was a wing hovering above them and a second wing heading away from them. As he looked at the nearest wing, trying to fathom what might be happening, Minnus noticed movement on the top of the vehicle.

"Is the passenger on top of that wing?" he suggested, glancing to Nombre for confirmation. She started to respond with "Hmmmmmm…" but then Minnus interrupted her. "He's fallen!"

"No, Minnus, he didn't fall," Nombre corrected. "He jumped." She reached over and took his commSheet out of his hand and unrolled it for him. "We're in trouble."

🙶

As he'd left the postage and reception facility, Joules had wandered a couple of dozen metres back along the isolation bridge. Not far enough that he'd be out of sight of his friends when they left the room but far enough away that he could stop worrying about being zapped by an out-of-control decease-beam. There was no furniture on the functionally designed walkway, so Joules decided to sit on the floor to wait. Within a few seconds, he changed his mind and decided to lie on his back and look at the blunt Antarctic sky thorough the transparent protective field above the bridge. Except the sky wasn't as empty as he'd anticipated. As Joules lay, a wing came hurtling in at high speed, strangely silent on the other side of the sound and atmosphere barrier between him and it. It decelerated rapidly and came to a hover above the bridge, about halfway between the Postbox and Telosec on the other extremity of the passage. Then, astonishingly, the wing's passenger jumped from the wing and began falling towards the bridge. Joules got to his feet and started walking backwards slowly, returning to the Postbox that he'd left Minnus and Nombre in but keeping his eyes on the falling person. *Falling man?* As he backed up, a sheet of a cloth-like material exploded from the dropping figure, opening into a kind of air sack and slowing his descent. *What? This guy is crazy! Why would someone do something so medieval?* It was like some kind of ancient adrenaline sport. As Joules pondered, the madman unstrapped a tube from his chest and pointed it downwards below his descending trajectory. As he did, the tube telescoped out to triple in length. With his arms out wide to hold the long cylinder by wide, earlike handles, the falling man created roughly the silhouette of a pendulous elephant's head, his legs appearing as tusks. The elephant's trunk projected a spurt of light, blinding Joules so that he had to cover his eyes with his forearm.

"Not crazy!" Joules whispered to himself. "A crazy daisy!"

He took off sprinting towards the far end of the tunnel against a wind that hadn't been there moments earlier, racing the dangling, falling man to what Joules now knew would be his point of entry to the isolation bridge.

"That's right," came the voice through Minnus's cSheet. "We have both transports in our sight and have despatched a team from the Telosec end of the bridge. There are only two wings visible on the sensors of the permaSat above Telosec. Both appear to have discharged a single individual each. Wait…confirming…an energy beam has been fired by the first individual. The force field on the isolation bridge has been disrupted! Access is possible. Sir, I recommend that you close down the Postbox now; lockdown with you and your wife inside the facility. We'll sort things out once the situation is clearer. There's a chance that this is an attack."

Nombre looked worriedly at Minnus. "Crazy Daisies?" she mouthed. She saw fury in his eyes.

"I am not trapping Joules on that bridge with two potentially murderous religiophiles. I'm staying here with you, but I'm *not* closing this door until we absolutely have to."

⚲

Joules evaluated who would win the race to the hole in the shield as he ran. The attacker was closer to the entry point than he was, but Joules was moving much more quickly, reawakening the muscle memory of years of training. He was too old to challenge in full-time sport, but he was no passenger. Still, it was going to be close. He had perhaps three hundred metres to cover. Twenty-four seconds in his prime. *Maybe twenty-six now?* He kept his eyes on the downward-floating figure, who had now dropped the weapon he'd used to blast a hole in the walkway shield. *Perhaps if I time this just right?* He pushed on as hard as he could for ten more seconds, giving himself the best chance of pulling off his quickly concocted plan. As he closed to within one hundred metres, he slowed up slightly, trying to coordinate his arrival with the moment he thought that the hanging man would drop through the breach in the field above. If he could conserve his forward momentum, arriving just at the point the man touched down, Joules hoped to barrel the trespasser from his feet and win the fight in the first second by landing on top of the invading man and pinning him to the floor. He closed the distance, modifying his speed as best as his judgment would allow, tracking the slowly spiralling dive of his opponent.

He thought he'd timed it perfectly until, with only ten metres between them, the attacker disconnected from his still-unfurled sail behind him, unclipping some kind of quick-release clasp on the harness that Joules could now see he wore over his dark coveralls. He dropped the last four metres, through the break in the weather shield and to the floor of the bridge. His feet touched the ground with surprising elegance, folding him into a roll. He quickly adjusted up to one knee, bringing up something from his waist to point towards the still onrushing Joules. *Is that a weapon?*

The man in black was now presenting a much smaller target than Joules had hoped for, compact and sturdy on one foot and one knee. Joules had no option though but to try to stick to his original plan and hope for the best, especially as the intruder almost had whatever was in his hand level with the oncoming Joules. The former Olympic five-hundred-metre champion put all his effort into one last push, altering his foot take-off so that he was thrown into a flying horizontal tackle. Joules tried to aim for his adversary's centre mass with his airborne right shoulder, the harness on his chest providing an obvious crosshair for targeting.

Joules's aim was off. The enemy had been instinctively lining up his left eye over the weapon in his left hand. The traverse of his head across to the left side of his mass completed just as the top of the solid mass of Joules Chavez's five-kilogram head arrived in the same spot. The collision between forehead and nose did not go well for the nose involved. Joules's opponent's face crunched loudly under the force of the skull-shaped missile that had careened into it. As the intruder hit the floor underneath him, Joules heard him grunt, his nose exploding with cherry-red blood. Joules quickly picked himself up, feeling the effect of the lucky shot himself. He was disoriented, a little off balance, but not enough to stop him stepping back to the conscious but incapacitated invader and flopping to sit on his chest, pinning his downed foe's shoulders with his knees. Joules had used mixed martial arts as part of his training regime for years but had never thrown any kind of angry strike in his life. He broke that run now, delivering two hard elbows to the temple of the man below him. The assailant dropped limp, clearly unconscious. Joules rolled off him and knelt at his side, relieved that he managed to bring the fight to an end quickly, even if fortunately.

He inspected the item that had fallen from the man's sagging hands. Up close, Joules thought that it was certainly some kind of weapon. It had a trigger near what was clearly a hand grip and a wide cylindrical barrel, about the width of a teacup. Joules picked it up and slid it away from them along the floor, towards the Telosec end of the bridge. As he did so, he saw a squad of security officers running towards him. He waved at them whilst he pointed to the prostrate figure at his feet. Four of the team members at the front of the oncoming pack waved back. *They're not waving, are they?* Then they began to point. Joules nodded exaggeratedly and pointed more obviously down at the man lying at his feet. The Telosec team members continued pointing, though. As they came closer, Joules could see that they weren't pointing at him at all—they were pointing behind him. He turned to see another man in black coveralls drop onto the bridge between himself and the Postbox that contained his friends. The second assaulter was one hundred metres closer to the facility than Joules and probably three hundred metres closer than the security team. Whatever his intent, there was no way that the armed security team would be able to stop him from getting across to the Postbox. Even a long-range shot wouldn't work, the gentle curve of the access bridge itself meaning that there was no line of sight within any range longer than about seventy-five metres. Any projectile would need to pass through the still-functioning sidewalls of the force field twice before reaching the intruder. Joules wasn't any kind of ballistics expert, but he thought that the security team would miss such a shot. He realised that he was the only one who might possibly catch the attacker before he reached Minnus and Nombre. With even more urgency than before, Joules set off sprinting again.

⚔

"Close the door, Minnus" Nombre urged. "Joules is not going to catch that guy. Who knows what he intends to do? What if he has a bomb? If he gets in here and detonates an explosive, we'll be dead, and Sero's reception will be delayed—maybe forever."

The second attacker was sprinting towards them, his objective clearly to reach the Postbox. He was probably two-hundred-and-fifty-metres away now, with Joules in pursuit, having already taken out one of the assault team further across the bridge. The Telosec security team had been quick to respond, but Minnus now saw the security flaw in assuming that any attack on the Postbox would need to come through the Telosec buildings and across the isolation bridge. The compound's own design now meant that the security force were now late to the party, pursuers rather than entrenched defenders. The intruder was only two hundred metres away, but Joules had closed the distance to only a fifty-metre gap between the two of them.

"Nombre, no! I am not leaving Joules out there. If I lock this door, that nut job might detonate an explosive on the bridge. Who knows if the walkway would hold if that happened? We might save ourselves, but by doing so, we might doom Joules and everyone else out there to fall to their deaths.

"The sequence only takes a few seconds to raise the drawbridge. I have it ready. If that guy closes to within fifty metres, I'll raise it. Look. Joules has a chance to stop him; he hasn't been seen."

The gap between the two runners was now only thirty metres, with the Telosec squad closing more slowly a couple of hundred metres further back along the walkway. Minnus began counting down in his head, anticipating the moment the danger would close to the fifty-metre mark he'd set as a threshold for action. *Fifteen…fourteen.* Joule was closing. He was close enough that Minnus could make out the exertion on his face. His friend was pushing himself as hard as possible. *Nine…eight. He's going to get there.* Minnus was an old man, but he decided that as soon as Joules tackled the man, he would leave Nombre in the solid-steel room and close the drawbridge behind him, rushing to help Joules in whatever way he could. *Six…five.* Joules was nearly within grabbing distance of the intruder. Then Minnus realised his miscalculation.

Chasing down a moving target was a lot different to blasting into a stationary one. Joules had closed the distance well but was now unable to tackle the second assailant the way he'd taken out the first. He figured he was going to have to close right up to him and grab him by the throat. He was nearly there. *Just a couple more seconds.* As they both raced around the curve of the bridge, bringing the open doorway of the Postbox facility into clear line of sight with no force field between the foot-racing foes and the Mbekis, realisation hit Joules like vacuum. It sucked the oxygen not from his lungs but directly from his heart and bloodstream. The second man also had a cylinder weapon, and he was aiming into the now-available target of the open doorway as he ran. Joules had no idea what the weapon would do, but he realised in the same instant as he felt panic overrun him that he needed to make his tackle right now. He dove, flailing with his outstretched right arm at the fleeing man's lower limbs, trying to get any purchase he could that might pull the man or the weapon off target. Right at the limit of his reach and only as Joules's chest was parallel with the floor, he tapped the right ankle of the shooter, clipping his legs together and sending the gunman falling forwards. As they both hit the ground, a dull thud reported the discharge of the weapon. Almost immediately an enormous booming wave of sound rolled outwards from the drum structure of the all-steel Postbox room. From his prostrate position, Joules saw the shadowed outlines of his two friends drop to the floor like rocks. Meanwhile, the attacker was recovering, scrambling back to his knees and stumbling up to charge for the Postbox facility again. He'd already made ten metres on Joules. He'd make it through the door in just a few seconds. Joules couldn't catch him.

The athlete screamed a primeval roar as the lack of oxygen in his body became a reason for emotion, doubling his already soaring panic. Then he saw the weapon. As they'd hit the ground, the gun had skittled away from the man who'd just shot Joules's friends. It was lying on the floor just a short way away. Joules dived for the tube, flinging himself from his belly using the knee of one leg, the foot of another, and his left hand. He landed on the weapon with his right hand on the grip, sliding the tube along the ground, pointing it vaguely towards the murderer and firing just as the intruder was reaching the still-open drawbridge. A second booming soundwave rolled down the walkway, and Joules realised that he couldn't hear it, only feel it in his chest.

# TWENTY-FIVE

The patriarch sat across from Sero in a newly fashioned tendril chair, directly underneath the macro sculpture of the NineDee's revered mother, Leaf. Sero occupied a similar seat. The standardCams were set up something like they would be for a talk-show cast back on Earth, one camera in close up on each man's face and a third offering wider shots of both participants in the conversation—a format Zwolf obviously favoured, given the regularity with which the cameras adopted it. Sero found the cameras more irritating than he had on previous audits—perhaps a product of his awareness that they were probably redundant now, perhaps because he was a different man in those previous audits than the one who sat opposite the leader of NineDee. They were engaged in the kind of semiregular interviews that had become a standard part of Sero's audit of the colony—a chance for the colony leader to offer his insight on the most recent sights and sounds that Sero had experienced first hand. This gave Sero, and by extension the Race back on Earth, more perspective. It also helped to smooth out any remaining discomfort Zwolf might have about modifying energy use and schedules to allow Sero to return to the reception facility regularly.

Sero had established early on in his visit to NineDee that the patriarch enjoyed the stage. Their previous conversations had focused on the physical environment and the adaptations that the colonists had needed to make as a result. Four months into the audit, Sero had decided to steer them towards a topic that had been both fascinating and unsettling him since his arrival. He'd already allowed a gentle warm-up, Zwolf updating him on preparations for Leaf Day. The man's capacity for detail was incredible. He'd wax on about the scale and grandeur of the effort and the contribution to the Race, and then he'd wax off about the smallest microcosm of concerns: the song they might sing on successful completion or the potential to alter the colour of the base tendril material to improve the likeness of Leaf that they sat below.

"I've noticed that you don't use NineCents as much as other colonies I've visited," Sero said.

"We don't? NineCents is essential to our work. He's the main processing unit that's completing all the calculus and also helps us to monitor changes in the planetary weather patterns."

"For the regular day-to-day things, I mean, like communications. People here on NineDee tend to simply make decisions on their own—or at least within their small groups. Your 'family' doesn't seem to feel the need to check in with each other as they go about their work. They're perhaps more fully empowered than I've seen before." As always when speaking with the proud duocenturion, Sero was careful to phrase a question as a compliment.

"We have a lot of trust in each other. Is that so unusual for such a tightly knit group as us telonaut colonists?"

"No. You're right. I've seen great teamwork on every colony I've visited. There's no way that any human society in such extreme circumstances can function without a tight sense of the self as a team. But this is more than charisma and a little gallows humour. Perhaps even a breakthrough in how we organise ourselves in such environments?"

"I can see that this is leading somewhere, Auditor," Zwolf encouraged. "You have something to posit to me?"

"Perhaps." *Go gently now. The door's ajar.* "Like all colonies, NineDee is something of a meritocracy in that you're all specialists. As the most expert and experienced hydromics expert, Divis makes decisions in her field, for example. The family units being grouped around similar specialisations seems to work as well here as on other colonies. It allows for small, independent decision-making groups."

*Now show him the failings of others. Make him feel…grander.*

"But for the really big decisions, the ones that might have global physical impact, that kind of diffuse decision making doesn't work elsewhere. Usually, humans need some kind of chief decision maker to arbitrate the really significant decisions.

"Your title is 'patriarch'—a male family head. I notice a lot of characteristics of a family in the organisation of the colony, but not as much centralised decision making as might be expected. I'm struggling to define the social organisation here on NineDee in terms that humanity has traditionally used. I think you might be very special."

Sero noticed a slight smirk from Zwolf as he continued with his blandishment. The man was very proud of the work here, perhaps rightly so, but Sero was beginning to find the regularity with which he had to manufacture obsequiousness when treating with the man personally grating. He was through the door now, though, Zwolf's smirk telling Sero that he had the man's attention, and it was likely that he might open up if Sero could convince him that he'd thought his question through.

"As with many early settlements, it's not possible for the Ugandan principles to operate yet—there's no currency or economic system thus far," Sero continued. "There's also not really anything to trade given the frontier nature and the need to divert all resources possible towards Leaf Day. So you're set up as a more truly socialist group in an economic sense than other colonies. There's not really been any self-interest in the economy up until now."

"Is there a question in there?"

"Nearly there. If anything, I think that *energy* is the nearest thing you have to currency—in so much as it's needed by all to satisfy their personal and professional needs. Given it's also only available in limited amounts, there has to be some process of central rationing or allocation, no?

"I'd originally assumed that either you were making decisions as an individual on behalf of the whole group or that there was some form of council that met periodically to consider things like this."

*Make yourself look dumber so he feels smarter. Ramble a bit.*

"So I had a stab at clarifying things for myself. I discovered during my research with NineCents that you're only sending somewhere between one hundred to two hundred communications via him across the colony per day. With over twelve hundred and fifty souls, that's an extremely low number. So you don't have the communication needed for regular, wider democracy to provide course correction.

"Since I've been here, I've noted that there's no voting on how to proceed on the big decisions. No forums or consultations, I mean. For example, when I asked you for more energy allocation to return to the reception facility regularly, we worked out the details on the spot. No consultation. I figured perhaps your title of patriarch meant you'd been elected or at least had the consent of the wider group to make totalitarian decisions. It seemed to make sense. But over the last few months, I've seen similar important decisions made by colonists with an equal lack of consultation. In economic terms, lots of individuals on NineDee feel they can spend your energy tender without asking how much tender is left, even though you all know that bankruptcy would have lethal consequences for you all and even the planet itself. The thing is, it works! You've made astonishing progress."

As Sero spoke, the eyes of the man opposite him danced. *Is he excited? Evasive? How can one understand the intentions of a man of Zwolf's age from body language?* He was so old he barely moved his limbs, but his pupils subtly flicked around their sockets like a fly in a tiny tether field, trying to escape the gravity well at the centre of the eye. *Just go for it, Novak. Stop overanalysing!*

"How do you create this kind of dispersed empowerment?"

Zwolf was silent for few moments. Despite the eyes that Sero was so carefully pondering, Zwolf had relaxed into a thinking pose as Sero had been elucidating his question, elbows resting to the side of his woven armchair, two index fingers pushed together to form a steeple pointed at the patriarch's forehead. He fixed Sero with a surprisingly penetrating and static stare. *Here we go*, thought Sero, *all aboard the carnival wing; he's at it again. Close up on camera number two!*

"Have you ever been in love, Mr. Novak?"

Now it was Sero's turn for epileptic eyeballs. *Absolutely. With all that I am. All my history mute and meaningless. All my achievements dust and pantomime. Pantomime such as this conversation, as this audit, as this life. What is any of it without the chance that she might be impressed? She's gone. There's nobody else to impress. Only the reflex algorithm of the man I used to think I was and should be. Yes. I've loved.*

"I have genuine love for the Race and the society we've built," Sero insentiently said.

He struggled to meet his interviewee's gaze, but as he glanced quickly at Zwolf, he thought he recognised disgust shimmer across the older man's face like a dimly perceptible wave. It made Zwolf shiver. The shudder was held in check well but not completely. The reaction hurt Sero. *That would've hurt her too. You're better than that.*

"But, yes, obvious statements aside for a man in my line of work, I've loved," Sero belatedly corrected. His shame reaching across the space between the two men, Sero wanted to erase the tremor he'd seen in Zwolf, replace it with the empathy he should've generated in response to a profound question. He gave a more honest response. "Deeply."

Zwolf did seem more satisfied with this. A slight cock of his head showing still slighter surprise at Sero's correction. *Showboating for the audience again?*

"I know. It's clear that you have loved. And lost. I knew throughout your tale of the previous audit on Rigil that this was not a disposable relationship for you. You think of her often, yes? Your partner on Rigil?"

There seemed sincere and unexpected compassion in the patriarch's eyes, and Sero was disarmed. He'd prepared for a question session on political systems. He'd thought that perhaps there was something he could uncover for the Race, some contribution he could make. Something to justify it all. Instead, the stream of conversation was emptying into his dreams. Nightmares. Regrets. He could only speak one word. "Yes."

Zwolf nodded. Concern clear. *For the cameras?* Though his fog of surprise and shame, Sero could still detect a hint of his own suspicion on his palate. Taste an instinctive distrust of the man opposite him. *Why?*

"So, now, let me pose you a question. Imagine your love had a great purpose, an unfulfilled undertaking. Something she cared about so passionately that it almost defined her. What would you do if she died? What would her desire become for you?" Zwolf gave no pause for an answer. "Now imagine that your adoration was not for a lover but a mother."

Zwolf paused now, widening his eyes as though explaining something to a child, the worst kind of coach, asking a question to which he clearly thought the answer was self-evident but just as unmistakably thought his charge didn't have the self-awareness to grasp that plainness.

"Leaf?" Sero offered, reluctant to interrupt but anxious to play a different part in the conversation than stunned, doe-eyed scholar.

Zwolf smiled crookedly. Sero felt more patronised than suspicious. *Perhaps the man is just a dick?*

"Everyone on this colony is either someone who trained with Leaf, lived with Leaf, or was born to a mother and father who loved Leaf. Her vision is inside of each of them. At the core. So, when making decisions, we only need to ask ourselves one question."

The patriarch paused and made sure to be looking directly at the close-up camera that had been tracking him. As he spoke, he rolled his head back to pointedly look up into the sculpture above him.

"What would Leaf do?"

Silent, watching the old man literally and figuratively peer into the projected mind of the long-dead individual that the hollow sculpture above them revered, Sero felt his own repressed wave of revulsion shimmy across his skin. *Religion.*

# Twenty-Six

**M**innus awoke to the sound of unrestrained conversation, near shouting. It was very close by. The shouting was accompanied by a backing track of dull, monotonous, low humming. Like a set of solar-farm inverters or a miniSun right next to his head. Who was it shouting? *Surfacan. It was a Surfacan accent. Really strong. Johnson? Yes, Johnson.*

*Johnson? What is Johnson doing in my house?* He'd just woken up, so he must be in his bunk pod, in his house. Minnus reached out to his left, feeling for his wife. She wasn't there. Nothing was there. Only air. *Where is the rest of the bunk pod? Where am I?*

He opened his eyes and found that they'd become allergic to light. The merest cracking of his eyelids seemed linked to a pair of crampons buried halfway into his temples, some invisible climber taking a further stamp onto his head with each millimetre of movement. Minnus raised his hand to check if there really was something hammered into his head. There wasn't. *Just a lethal headache then.*

With will, he managed to fortify himself against the pain in his skull enough to more fully open his eyes. He was in a room full of people, maybe thirty. He recognised it. He'd been here before. He was in the infirmary at Telosec.

*Telosec! The attack! The crazy Daisy with the weapon!* Minnus remembered the assault on the walkway, everything pouring back into his working memory in a single instantaneous download. *Where is Nombre? Joules?* He forced himself to sit, his pain suddenly irrelevant.

"Nombre!" his shout didn't reach all the way to its targeted volume or pitch, squeaking out of him instead like a pubescent boy.

"Nombre!" The second attempt was better. Louder and deeper. It gained him the attention of the room.

The mixture of security staff and medical professionals all turned towards him in unison. The nearest was a nurse who redundantly called out, "He's awake!" to nobody in particular.

Minnus knew each of them by name; they were all staff in the telospace programme, and he'd worked with them all on one thing or another over the years. Right now, though, he directed his questions at the most senior person in the room and the one that was obviously being looked to for guidance by the rest of them: Idi Johnson, head of telospace.

"Where's Nombre?" Minnus threw the question across the room at the approaching man.

"She's fine. Just sleeping. Just over there. Look." The thin Surfacan man gently pushed the end of the magnetically levitating bed Minnus was half sitting upon, sending it spinning to view the room to his left. Behind a glass wall, Minnus saw his wife, apparently sleeping in the next bed in the infirmary.

"Everyone is fine, Minnus, my friend. It was a close call, but there's no damage to any of our team or the facility. Your friend Mr. Chavez is just in the bathroom. I imagine your wife is just a few moments behind you in waking up, and the force field on the bridge is already repaired. We have a team permanently stationed up there already. They'll stay there, armed, until we can design more structural security to prevent the same thing happening again. This episode is over."

Minnus was still a little disoriented, and the relief that Nombre and Joules were OK had ceased the panic that had momentarily swelled in him. Unfortunately, his body had decided to prompt him to lie down again by giving his head another squeeze between the ice cleats. He submitted, dropping backwards onto his elbows and then shuffling back to the headboard of the bed so he wouldn't need to support his own weight, but he could still see his Telospace boss. He noticed that Johnson was wearing one of his most formal suits, the kind of thing that would normally be reserved for special meetings or events. He was fully preened, hair newly cut into a precise right-angle flattop with not even a nod to functionality in his attire. No coverall, no boots. Everything was slim line and smart. *Wonder where Johnson might have been to be so dressed up when this all went off.* The thought flitted through Minnus's mind before being pushed out by more local concerns.

"What the frak happened?" Minnus said.

"We're still looking in to it. You've only been unconscious for about three hours. We've discovered quite a lot already though with the help of our investigators from WorldGov. They're already out there hunting back down the line of evidence that starts with those rather fancy energy disruptors our two guests brought with them.

"Those aren't consumer items. Their value is set way above the individual annual earnings cap, so either someone has been saving up for a long time to purchase something that should reasonably only be available to WorldGov projects, or someone is cheating the Race economically. Either way, those things aren't easy to get, so Du Plessis and Naidoo have a few clear directions to start off in. They're in the north of Amasia right now, always the first place to start if it seems someone is contravening the Ugandan principles."

Minnus assumed that Du Plessis and Naidoo must be the names of the investigators assigned by WorldGov after the wave of threats recently.

"OK, let's start with something easier. Why are we still alive? The last thing I saw was that guy in black pointing what looked like some kind of cannon at me from his hip. Is that why my head feels like it has been used to pipe clean the near-Earth tether from its clamps all the way up to orbit?"

Johnson looked across the room to where one of the security officers was leaning over a bench.

"Ndulov, please bring that cannon over here, would you, so we can show Mr. Mbeki why he feels so unwell?"

The much bigger man strode over to Johnson and held up the weapon so Minnus could get a look at it from his bed. Johnson didn't touch it or offer to take it from the security staffer, though. He was good at seeming statesman-like and aloof whilst also issuing orders that included the word "please." Disguising them as requests.

"Please explain what you're holding, Ndulov."

*There he goes again.*

"Mr. Mbeki sir. This is a modified mining device called a niobium broom. Its original intended purpose was for use on the Mars colonies, harvesting niobium for use in steel production. It operated as a simple launcher, firing concussive projectiles into caves rich in the niobium sediments that coat their volcanic walls. The specific sound frequency generated by the discharging projectile would dislodge the sediment without damaging the structure of the surrounding rock. This would then allow for drones to fly into the caves and vacuum the sediment easily from the cave floor, harvesting the niobium with as little damage as possible to the Martian environment."

Ndulov made a "let's pretend" imitation of a projectile leaving the end of the device.

"This particular broom has been adapted for a different purpose, however. Its recoil has been dampened, reducing range but making it possible to carry and fire from the hand. As a result, it has effectively been made into a concussion-grenade launcher."

"So you're telling me that my wife and I were shot with a mining mortar?" Minnus asked, incredulous.

"Yeah," a voice called from the other side of the room. Joules had obviously just returned from his trip to the gent's room. There was no mistaking his deep, sonorous voice. "And that's not even the most dangerous part. We were lucky to be hit with only that boom stick."

"*Broom*," Officer Ndulov corrected.

"Not from where I was lying. Definitely a boom. Tell him what the guys I took down were wearing."

Johnson smiled politely at Joules and picked up from Ndulov, dismissing the man with a silent nod. "Minnus, your friend is correct. We were all very lucky today. Each of those trespassers was wearing some high-energy explosives underneath his coveralls. We're quite certain that they were trying to destroy the reception facility and disrupt the telospace programme. We're vulnerable now that we're in the audit-only phase of the programme, and all the Postboxes used in the initial telonaut colonisation surge have been disassembled and repurposed. These interlopers, whoever they turn out to be, seem to have realised that if they could destroy our ability to return Sero back to Earth, they might also disrupt the public profile of the effort.

"We'd need significantly more Red and energy allocation to rebuild a new Postbox. As a minimum, that would allow some to try generate a debate on the best use of those resources. It seems like desperation to me. Perhaps a result of the focus your NV casts of the NineDee audit are generating amongst the Race?"

"Maybe the final straw was Minnus's using conversation and black magic to wedge that heavy fool Joberan into his chair last month?" Joules offered. "That'd've probably fired up the crazies. Folks that follow that kind of guy always seem to take everything personally." He shook his head and then added, "The normal distribution of arseholes."

Minnus half smiled, half grimaced at his blunt friend. Now that he felt he had a grip of what had happened, he was keen to go check on Nombre. He began to get himself out of the bed.

Meanwhile, Johnson picked up the last threads of his tale. "In the short term, given there was no damage done, I think this attack might actually help us. We can quite efficiently protect against a similar attack by stationing more security on the isolation bridge and modifying the field projected around it. Whilst I don't think there's any need to publically inform the Race of the attack, given there's literally no impact on the programme, I can still use the danger we faced today whilst representing us to WorldGov. That should further cement the increased Red allocation we've just received and ensure we can protect the team better."

As Minnus took off his gown and began to dress, he thought that the attack would coincidentally mean Johnson had another reason to spend more time at WorldGov face to face. He imagined that the Surfacan might present this foiled sabotage attempt rather skilfully. Perhaps as a crisis that Johnson was personally handling and resolving rather than a lucky escape where disaster had only been avoided because there was randomly a brave former Olympic sprinting champion on site.

"Joules. You saved our lives today. Certainly Nombre's and mine. Perhaps even Sero's too. Not to mention the future of the telospace programme in general."

Minnus added the last line as an afterthought. Almost automatically. He'd spent so long prioritising the project that he couldn't describe anything as being important any more without referencing back to the overarching importance of the life goals of himself and Sero. Measuring each event's significance on a scale where relevance to Telospace and even the Race's Ugandan principles beyond that were the ultimate markers of success. In the moment though, that wasn't what he considered important about Joules's heroism. He thought about his wife, whom he loved. He thought about his children and grandchildren and how they would feel if he and Nombre had died in such an accident. He thought about his friends Sero and Joules himself. He thought about a day when one or all of them might not be around. He felt overcome with gratitude that the day wasn't today. He loved Joules for that. Without forward planning, he looked to Joules's eyes and hoped everything he was feeling was visible in his own eyes.

"Hey, man, I get it," Joules said.

Minnus knew that he did.

"Also didn't do this guy's career any harm either!" Joules said, playfully slapping the smaller Johnson on the back.

Minnus smiled at his friend's insightfulness and headed into the next room to check up on Nombre.

# Twenty-Seven

"**S**o you'll interview her then? About the project?"

Prid and Sero were in a haloMagnet, gently cruising towards their next inspection site, the second Postbox— the alternative facility to the one Sero had arrived in. The journey had been unusually quiet, with Prid clearly preoccupied with her own thoughts. She'd been much less inquisitive than normal about the intent of the trip and the process they'd take up on arrival.

After it was deduced that NineDee would need an enormous project to be completed if it were to overcome the weather conditions and survive as a human habitat, the second Postbox had seen more usage than any of the other supposedly backup postage facilities Sero had visited in previous audits. Most colonies hadn't even instructed the nanoBots to build the backup facilities. He intended to look over the records of the postages that NineCents had made available whilst sitting in the facility itself recording the experience for NV broadcast by exiting the facility and mimicking the arrival process that each colonist would have gone through. Sights, sounds, and specifics. It seemed though that Prid was more interested in discussing her old friend Dini. Each time they had spoken on the trip, she'd managed to turn the conversation towards Sero's meeting with Dini or some aspect of Leaf Day that was tangentially linked to her. Sitting in the new eight-point tendril safety harness that she and Sero had improvised together following their halo-surfing episode, Prid did her best to look casual whilst pressing him for more details.

After the way in which Dini had displayed such obvious sexuality towards him, Sero wasn't comfortable with answering her questions. Not least because he didn't know what the answers were. He'd bluffed for a while instead. He could see that Prid wasn't for turning, though. *Still, no harm in having one last effort*, he thought, before he pitched into his last attempt to alter the course of the conversation.

"It's certainly interesting, Prid, but I'm not sure we need to focus so specifically on one person. There are plenty of projects around that are underwriting just as much. In fact, Dini is working on something that's more of a fat builder, something that will give extra time to rework things if the truly critical parts of the path to Leaf Day go awry. So we could argue that the work should actually be *de*prioritised." *Or that being around her makes me so ashamed I'm physically sick.*

"OK, Mr. Universe. Excuse my bluntness, but I'm not buying a bar of that. We've been all over this colony, looked under every pile of old tendril, taken the temperature of half the cows on the planet, even had NineCents run through communication logs to see how often we're all talking to one another. There's no way that you would just ignore a part of the plan. Something is going on. Why won't you tell me?"

Prid's eyes were narrowed in suspicion, but Sero felt he could spy some hurt behind the slender slits she was offering him.

"I thought we were a team...friends, even."

*Ouch!*

As was often the case when dealing with women, Sero felt a powerful sweep of guilt press down on him, momentarily shortening the breath in his lungs. *Why is it that every time someone of the opposite sex is upset, my subconscious thinks it's my responsibility to make them feel better?* He knew the answer, though. It wasn't possible to live the life that he'd lived without developing a strong awareness of his own motivations. His instinct, genetically driven he knew, was to try and position himself as an impressive individual, a fixer, to provide solutions, to create resolutions. His emotional reaction was a reflection of the steady state of his ego. *Always need something or someone to fix.* As he looked across the cabin to his young friend, he knew that he did have it in his power to change the sullen look on her face. She was looking away from him, her bottom lip trembling slightly. Sero unbuckled himself from his own harness and walked across the vehicle's passenger area to sit next to Prid.

"Hey."

Prid didn't respond by turning to face him, but her bottom lip trembled still harder.

"*Hey*," Sero tried again, this time gently putting his arm around her as best he could whilst she was in the grip of the safety harness.

"We *are* friends. More than that even. Friends usually only have fun. We've got something even better. We have fun, *and* we work together. Not in a hierarchical way but in a mutually supportive way. We give each other what they need. Do you really doubt it?"

The last sentence caused her to finally meet his gaze. She shook her head slowly, begrudgingly. Perhaps Sero had misunderstood why she was upset.

"It's just that...well, you see..." It seemed that Prid couldn't find the right words. She lapsed into a vulnerable silence again, bottom lip now stilled by the heavy sigh that fell out over it.

Sero decided to fill the space her lack of words left with a story, one that he knew would crack open the door to the room where he'd piled his own vulnerability for storage. It wouldn't be the first time he'd told the tale; Minnus had heard it a hundred times through in the last year that Sero had spent Earthbound. It would be the first time, however, that Sero would be opening his grief to someone who hadn't known him before it happened. For some reason, though, he knew it would be OK to tell Prid. They'd built a genuine bond. If anything, Sero felt he should pass on the way he'd been affected by his grief. Prid was so young and inexperienced. He might protect her by explaining. *Might even cheer her up!*

"Do you remember that day when you showed me how to lasso? Hanging the tendril off the roof of the lab? When we went inside, we asked each other all kinds of questions. I told you all about the colonies I've already visited. You asked me about how people live and which world was my favourite. You asked me how many people I'd met and who was the cleverest person I'd met in the Race."

The change of conversation seemed to have gained Prid's attention, as she was now looking at him properly. Nodding. Engaging. *Better.*

"I think I did quite a passable job of summarising twelve years or so of my life, actually." Sero grinned, reinforcing the lighter mood he was trying to create. "But I wasn't completely honest, Prid. There was one question that I couldn't answer. I didn't know I would ever speak about it with you until just now when you told me you think we're friends. We *are* friends." Sero paused and took a deep, sincere breath. "I could only ever speak about this with a friend."

As the words came out of him, he knew them to be at once true and surprising. As though someone were reading aloud the solution to an equation he'd forgotten the answer to. Reading for him, in his own voice.

"You asked me what it was like to spend a year with people and then to leave, knowing that I'd never see any of them again. I gave you some stock answer about such things being part of my job and my being prepared for it, as I understood how it would work before I even signed up to be an auditor." Prid had relaxed into Sero's one-armed parallel hug now, her young head resting against his chest as he spoke.

"That wasn't true. Isn't true. In truth, I didn't want to leave Rigil, my previous audit, at all. If not for a tragic accident, I would never have left. I wouldn't be here with you now. I'd be married, raising a family at the top of a tree light-years from here."

Prid lifted her head from his chest and peered up towards him, authentic surprise on her face.

"You see, my life changed in a very irrevocable way whilst I was on Rigil, kiddo. I fell in love. For the first time."

As he spoke the words and image came to his mind unbidden of a beautiful women lying naked on a carved wooden bed, laughing filthily like a cartoon dog. Immediately afterwards, he smiled and then felt his throat close with a swell of emotion.

"You see, I'd always been just like my old man, Won, until then. Proud of it too. He was a true Race member, my dad. He wanted nothing more than to leave his species a legacy of discovery. He built a whole life around it.

"I mean, I'm sure he loved my mother in his own way, and he *was* a good father. I never felt alone or unwanted, but he had a focus—a wilful intensity. The importance of everything he did was measured against the scale of his work. His work was about spreading the Race across our galaxy. So everything else couldn't measure up."

Prid was still looking up at him, paying attention in a way Sero hadn't seen her do before. There was a need in her eyes. They weren't just pulling in the light to see but rather pulling in his very words, vacuuming up the moment between them. Perhaps no adult had spoken to her so intimately before. He certainly hadn't seen much evidence of a close family amongst her and her parents—something Prid herself had confessed to. She was fed and watered, but there wasn't any kind of bond he could see beyond the basic exchange of need and duty. As he sat recalling his own father, passing on the only truly emotionally mature bit of wisdom he felt he had, Sero realised that he'd been filling a gap in Prid's life for months. Her parents were just like his father, distracted and driven by a life-consuming end goal. But where he had the whole Race and a millennia-old planet to learn from, she was a teenage girl on an isolated and faraway world. She was without a guide. Even her friend Dini had been lost to Leaf Day. *Can you imagine what your life would have been like if you'd lost Minnus so early?*

"And that was me too. I didn't arrive at the ownership of the link between the Race on Earth and the Race in space by accident. I drove towards it for my entire life. Studied multiple fields, from architectural terraforming to theoretical exobiology. I followed the ethical development of the philosophy of blank bubbling from an early age and made arguments for the safe-guards my father and his peers put in place via WorldGov. I put myself in prominent places, made sure I was maximising my intellect, and I was tireless in pursuing my goal. I had no time for even the family my father allowed."

Prid looked slightly more quizzical at this last statement, raising a playful eyebrow.

"Sure, there were women, but it was *my* world that they lived in. There was nothing shared other than enjoyable relaxation and relief from the pressure I applied to my work. Nothing *truly* mutual that included anything beyond the moment we were in."

Sero paused for a moment whilst snippets of hours of conversations in tall trees passed through his mind. Conversations about futures, family. Happiness.

"And I thought I was happy. I thought that my bringing a record of all of you telonauts back to Earth for the Race was enough for me to end my days, whenever that comes, feeling fulfilled. I was proud. Until I met someone who made me feel differently, who left me wanting something more.

"On Rigil, I met a woman who became everything to me. Comfort. Happiness. Aspiration." Sero felt awkward as he finished his thought. "Desire."

Prid didn't react awkwardly, though; she simply nodded understanding and continued to look right at him with her hoovering, respectful eyes.

"I realised that I didn't want to return to Earth and spend the rest of my life without her, without the family that already existed in my mind—if not in reality. I wanted to build something personal. Something that would be ours. A home. A life for her and me, for our children. For that time, for the first time, I felt that giving all of me to the Race was sterile and calculated.

"Where I'd previously felt an important part of a significant species-wide mission, I then felt foolish, like I'd been missing the point all along, like the child in class who can complete the most complicated mathematics in her head but cannot think of a single way to apply those calculations in the real world. I felt like I hadn't really understood what life was for until that point."

Sero stopped speaking and gently shook his head, regretfully. Taking the time to connect his words directly to the hopeful whirlpools of her eyes, Sero poured as much sincere fatherly wisdom into his words as he could. "Life is for loving other people, Prid."

The young girl reached across as far as she could and pulled him in to a hug, her head back on his chest and her left arm stretched across his stomach in a difficult-to-hold position, restrained by her harness. Sero though he could hear her sniffling into his coveralls.

"She died?" Prid muffled into his belly.

"Yes. She did. She died, and so I left Rigil. I went back to Earth, and I tried to recover. To gain my balance again. With the help of some other people I love, I did. I…" He stopped for a moment to consider his words, not quite sure how to practically describe the emotional process he'd been through. "I reset. Kind of reverted to an earlier edition of myself, one that I can run easily, without much processing power. I went back to work and tried to find the drive that had sustained me before. I came here."

Prid had gained control of her leaking face now and was able to release his midriff from her strained embrace and once again look at him. Sero's feelings of fatherly protectiveness became overwhelming, and he found himself speaking again without forethought. "I'm glad I did, Prid. I found something better than work. I found someone new to love."

He felt a single tear fall down his cheek. At the sight of it, she head butted his abdomen again and buried her face into it, openly crying now. Sero simply placed his hand on her head and let her finish.

Several minutes later, a red-faced and tear-streaked Prid surfaced from his tummy to ask, "And Dini?"

"Well…" *Careful now*, thought Sero. "Well, Dini caused a bit of a conflict for me. A conflict between the version of me that operates on autopilot—the man for whom women are a pleasurable but temporary part of life—and the version of me that loves and is committed to just one woman." *Gently.* "Dini made it clear that she was interested in me. Biologically."

Sero paused for a few seconds to see whether Prid understood. The look of slight unease on her face told him that apparently she did.

"And I'm ashamed to say that part of me reacted to that. The default version of me was 'interested' right back, just for a moment. The guilt that came next, the feeling of betrayal, well, it had a terrible effect on me. I vomited first, babbled nonsense second, and then didn't sleep for several nights."

Prid was nodding slowly again, showing her understanding. Just as he was about to ask her explicitly whether she was following him, she announced her answer pre-emptively. "It doesn't matter how important her project is. Everything you do now is measured by its relation to your love, for the family you didn't have, for the lady that died. You think that Leaf Day is exciting and important, but nothing is as important as her memory. Nothing is worth betraying that memory."

Sero smiled fully at the insightful girl that now held his hand. "Yes."

"What was her name?"

"Aleph," Sero said. "Her name was Aleph."

# Twenty-Eight

"**Y**ou're still you!" Nombre said.

"He wouldn't say that if he were here," Minnus replied. "He'd say, 'Who is this precious old coot, and what have you done with my friend Minnus, the rational utilitarian?'"

Nombre made a tssking sound and shook her head. "You think you were irrational? You were the definition of rational! You assessed the facts available to you and very reasonably drew a risk-and-reward-based conclusion. You took action in line with your thinking, thinking that was broadly correct, I might add. Regardless, the outcomes—and it's outcomes that are always the most important factor in assessing whether your actions were correct, by the way—the *outcomes* were that no damage was done to any of your friends and family, and no harm has come to your life's major work."

The Mbekis were both fully recovered from the incident that had nearly led to the destruction of the Postbox, physically at least. They were back home in Surfaca. Johnson had agreed to allow the algorithm Minnus had written to continue running the editing of the weekly casts as fragment updates were received from Sero, and so Minnus and Nombre had taken ten days to spend time with their family. The whole gang had departed that morning, leaving the most senior member of the Mbeki family alone. Since his children and grandchildren had left, Minnus had been moping around the house, evidently preoccupied. Under compassionate challenge from his wife, he was now in midconfession, trying his best to explain his difficulty in reconciling the experience at the Postbox and his actions with his previously strong sense of self.

"I know. And I'm so happy that we're all safe. I truly am. The realisation that the kids might have lost us and even the idea that you might have been hurt…well…it makes me bodily ill. The relief of it all turning out OK was overpowering; it spun me out of mind for a few days. But it's not the outcomes that I'm upset about. Don't you see? It's the dissonance. I feel like I'm going through puberty again. Finding out 'who I really am' or something equally similarly both moronic and profound."

Minnus knew his wife didn't see. Although she loved him and had listened to him speak about how important the commitments he and Sero had made to each other in childhood were to him, she didn't have anything equivalent in her life. If she had a life's mission, it was a more localised one. She'd aimed to provide support to those around her, to build and encourage a smaller team. Nombre believed in the Race and the hope for progress, just as much as Minnus did, but she'd never seen her role in the Race as anything more than moral support. She engaged energetically in the Mission Selection processes to choose projects and would debate and defeat all comers in any discussion on the merits of the society they lived in. For Nombre, though, simply living in the Race was the end goal—to make sure things were as fair to all as possible and to protect that egalitarian structure but then to enjoy it. Simply to *live* in it. Minnus loved her and the Mbeki team they'd built together. He had strong, healthy children and grandchildren who were all contributing to the Race in various ways. He was proud of all of them, but he'd always identified himself as having a bigger legacy to leave the Race as a whole than only his wonderful family.

"It's about whether I've been deluded somehow. Cocooned in some safe bubble where I've never been challenged enough by circumstance to truly test my principles in the midst of the fight-flight. Sero and I sat on the shore all those years ago and agreed that nothing could ever be a more worthy way to use our span of years than to push the Race forwards, to increase knowledge, to build the species. I've believed that's what we've been doing all our lives. I've believed that we were doing important work. Work that should be protected and was worthy of sacrifice."

"You *have* been doing important work, darling!" Nombre was clearly becoming frustrated with her husband's lack of clarity. "I don't understand. What is it that would have you question these things? You've always been so certain of yourself and your work."

Minnus didn't want to fight with Nombre, and he could see that her frustration was born out of concern. He could've just ended the conversation there, told her that he was probably just tired or still stressed. But he didn't *want* to end the conversation. He felt like he needed to talk about this. "I feel ashamed, Nombre."

Minnus looked at his wife directly as he said the words. Her reaction was probably what he'd have expected from the wonderful woman. She looked initially confused but only for a fraction of a second. Then her face cleared, reset, and became full of loving concern. She took hold of both of Minnus's hands.

"You are a brilliant man, father, and husband. Let's work it out together."

Minnus was filled with love for her. It relaxed him to see the love returned. "Is thinking out loud OK?" he said.

Nombre kept hold of his hands and kissed him gently on the lips. She led him over to the long plastiche chaise and sat him down close to her. "Fire away. What do you think about when you feel ashamed?"

*It's you I think about most when I'm ashamed, darling.*

"So, I think it goes like this," Minnus began tentatively. "If you could've predicted the assault on the Postbox—predicted the way it would play out. You and I inside the facility and Joules off down the bridge fighting an armed invasion force. How would you have predicted that I would've behaved?"

"What do you mean? Were you more frightened than you would've thought you would be?"

"No. No, it's not fear that I'm talking about. I mean in terms of the choices made. What d'you think would've been my decision-making framework in a situation like that? What would've been my preeminent concern?"

Nombre thought for a few seconds before caveating her answer carefully. "I think you'd have lots of things to think about, and you would've considered all of them before making any decisions. But…"

"But?"

"But I think you'd probably be concerned about the facility." She was also tentative. The two old partners were trying their best to not hurt the other with a misplaced word. "The project means so much to you, and with all the threats recently, I think your first thoughts would go to the danger to the project. Not to mention that Sero's life was also in the balance."

She knew him well. He was glad that she'd been able to answer the question in a way that reflected his own assessment. He knew she was confident enough of his commitment and love for her that acknowledging his commitment to his work wouldn't later be taken as some kind of personal relegation for her. Just an honest assessment of where the weight of his conscious self rested most of the time. She was happy enough with the endless attention that his unconscious mind had given her over the years. She knew that he loved her without his thinking about it.

"OK. I've come to the same conclusion. I figured I would've been thinking about how best to protect the programme. In retrospect, probably the physical infrastructure that we need to continue getting the audit reports and eventually to get Sero home again. And I would've been right. I *did* think about it. I thought about it very quickly, processed the options, worked out how to protect the mission, and then…did exactly the opposite thing. I kept the drawbridge open and endangered everything."

"Do you understand why?"

A returned tight hand squeeze prompted Minnus to respond. "Joules. Joules was out there, and he might've come to harm. He was fighting a guy. We might've needed to get to him, or he might've needed to get to us at least. In the moment, fight-flight and all, I chose one friend over the other. I endangered my own lifelong dreams and potential hope and knowledge for billions of souls. Not because it was the rational thing to do. I didn't weight the decision by worth at all. I chose the most immediate problem to solve rather than the most significant problem."

Minnus stopped speaking, looking for a reaction from his wife. He was hoping for some kind of acceptance as he confessed. She gave it, pulling him a little closer and gesturing for him to continue. "And?"

"And that makes me feels some shame. I think because it raises a deeper question in me about whether I really believe in all that the programme has been striving for. I *think* I do. I *think* I'm committed, intellectually and emotionally. But am I *really*? I've been proud to live and think as a principled man. I've been proud of the principles I've tried to live by. Sacrificed for them. What if it's all just a pantomime?"

Nombre looked like she was about to speak, probably to try offer comfort, but Minnus knew he was on a roll and needed to get out all the remaining words.

"I'm nearly finished," he said. "That's only part of the shame, you see? Because there's a part of me that can answer the question, and in answering the question, I generate even more shame."

Minnus paused again, needing to take a full breath in so he'd be able to force out the next sentence. With mental effort, he managed it.

"What about you? What if through my actions, I'd helped Joules but contrived to have you injured or worse? What if I've even taken the other option—closed the drawbridge and protected the Postbox—but somehow in doing so, you'd be hurt or taken? What would *any* of it matter without you? Worst of all, most shamefully, why do I think about this days later and not inside of the moment? Who am I that I'd be so callous with something so precious?"

The tears fell freely now, and Minnus collapsed into the arms of his wife, who held him to her. They didn't speak for several minutes until Minnus regained control.

Nombre lifted her husband's head gently from her shoulder and looked into his eyes intently. "I know who you are Minnus. I'll say it again. You're a caring and loving man. A fantastic father and husband. You've spent your whole life building and protecting a society where people don't *have* to make choices about who lives and who dies.

"The Race itself is trying to make such choices mere abstractions, thought experiments only, decisions that nobody needs to go through any more. And we've largely succeeded. You've managed to be over one hundred years old before encountering a situation like that. Most people never do. Making knowledge the primary focus of humanity, giving the Race a cohesive set of efforts to focus on and aspire around. These are more than admirable and worthy of both of our time and sacrifice. I think that what happened out there was just a product of the speed that the situation evolved at. It was mere seconds between you assessing an unclear environment and making critical decisions. Everything was new.

"You're human, Minnus. Nobody is prepared for a situation they've never expected might happen. The things that you did in that situation don't reflect some 'truer' version of yourself that you weren't previously aware of *or* indicate that the choices you'd made before that day were rendered less correct or valuable. Nothing so fleeting supersedes decades of considered thought like that." Nombre's hands were on his cheeks now, gently cupping his face.

"More than that Minnus, I love you, and I'm proud of you."

She kissed him passionately before standing and walking towards the bunk room. "Now, follow me in here. Now that the kids are gone, I want some private time with Minnus Mbeki, creator of neuroVision, Man One, *my* husband." She began to undress as she walked away.

# Twenty-Nine

The second Postbox on NineDee was different from the facility Sero had arrived at in several ways. Sero's reception blank bubbling had occurred in an underwater room, connected to the colony's main living accommodation and Park 359, adhering to the designs that the nanoBots had been programmed with in the initial launch phase of the telonaut programme. This second Postbox, though, was hundreds of kilometres away from the colony's main populated areas. It had a lonelier feel. Whilst it was still underwater, taking advantage of the miniSuns' ability to create energy by fusion from NineDee's sea, the force field–protected bridge to reach the facility was significantly shorter than the one Sero had jogged down before first meeting Zwolf and the other colonists. There was no need to separate the Postbox from the surface of the planet by anything other than the straightest line, as no colonists had ever lived nearby. As such, Sero and Prid stood in front of a simple steel door on the surface of the tentaculos that they'd ridden across in their haloMagnet. A short vestibule sank into the plane of the tentaculos behind the door, the exterior roof slanting down towards and beyond the land mass so as to look like a wedge of steel ten metres from the haloMagnet track, its hypotenuse twice as long as Sero was tall. There were no buildings from here to all horizons, whether steel or tendril built. Just a steel railroad, pounding away in a straight line, back the way they'd come. Sero and Prid stood at the end of that line, alone for tens of kilometres in all directions. *Eerie.* Before heading towards the door, Sero made some final checks with NineCents.

"You'll still be able to communicate with us in there, I assume, 'Cents?"

"Certainly, Auditor Novak. All diagnostics confirm full communication range."

The steel-vibration-created response came back instantaneously. *There must be a strong relay network from here, despite the distance back to the main processor for NineCents.*

"And my voice-command authority is operational in the Postbox?" Sero asked.

"Confirmed. Full access, as required by my most base of permissions algorithms. You're an authentic Earth auditor."

If NineCents were a human rather than a computer, Sero might have thought he should infer some sarcasm in the response. He knew that the A. I. was simply trying to be reassuring, however. As he buckled on his candolier and tightened his bootstraps, he motioned to Prid to do the same.

"What about Prid? Can she operate the Postbox?"

The response was not instantaneous. It was still quick—certainly within the acceptable norms for a human conversationalist—but it was noticeably slower than the previous responses from the colony-maintenance computer.

"Ms. Pridescent is not on file as a control-permission holder." *Hmmmm. That is a very precise response. Unusual.* Sero stood straight after finishing with his boots and looked to Prid.

"Stay close to me, please. Wouldn't want me to fall and hit my head and leave you locked in a kill-switch facility to get evaporated by superheated light beams."

"I guess I'd just have to die in there if that happened. Helpless." She looked at him like she might look at a turd in her backpack.

*Now there's a sarcastic response,* thought Sero. *She's definitely cheered up, then!*

"'Cents just told you he can hear us in there. Even if I can't get him to open the door, I can still call for someone else to come sweep up your dead body and then let me out. Come on old man, it's only logic. You can do it!" She threw him a smile right back and then came over and tightened his candolier further. "You don't want to have them hang like that. They'll move if you have to vineseil, and you might miss your grip going for the next can."

Prid moved the chest belt around by thirty centimetres and then pulled it tight and pinched it into place. "See?"

"Yes, yes. Come on, Queen Leopold. 'Cents, how long is the walk to the interior door?"

"One-hundred-and-fifty-metres. Less than a minute at your normal walking pace, Auditor." The computer's voice had increased in volume to compensate for Sero's retreat away from the steel haloMagnet rail from which the sound was emanating.

"OK. Open the exterior door, please."

As NineCents responded, instantaneous again, Sero noticed a pair of the standardCams swoop in and hover into a pincer formation, one in front of the two-member auditing team and above the Postbox doorway, one behind them tracking their approach. *The third must be way up high somewhere.* As they approached the doorway, Prid removed her constant companion notebook from the thigh pocket of her coveralls and her tendril pen from her top-left chest pocket.

"Anything in particular we're looking for?" she said.

Sero wasn't sure whether to answer truthfully. The most straightforward answer would be "Anything that isn't a smooth metal box with a pillar in the centre and a single button," but that didn't quite cover it. He had been thinking about the things that didn't quite add up. The lack of communication between colonists, the high birth rate, Dini's complete separation from Prid once she reached adulthood. *Perhaps there's something wrong with the postage? A common transcription error that's giving everyone this unusual au-tonomy? Why doesn't this place function like other Race colonies?* Sero just couldn't reconcile the idea that a pseudoreligious fervour and common goal had unified the colony into a hyperproductive hive mind. Reverence for Leaf just wasn't enough. It didn't fit at all with his experience of other new-worlders. *And I just don't trust Zwolf. His words just smell wrong.* He voiced none of this to Prid, though.

"Observe and record, Prid. We're auditors. We observe and record." *Maybe inspire a little.*

As they reached the open doorway, blue lights at the edges of the steel walkway lit a telescopic chamber, illu-minating a pinkie-finger-sized doorway at the cylindrical horizon. They stepped in side by side, with the first cam-era backing away from them and preceding their passage towards the Postbox facility itself. As NineCents had predicted, sixty seconds later, Sero was instructing the colony computer to open the inner door. As they stepped inside, blue light again activated and bounced around the windowless underwater room. After blinking the bright-ness from his eyes, Sero looked around for any deviation from the dozen-plus other reception rooms he'd been reborn in during his lifetime. *Plain walls. Plain floor. Kill switch. Blank-bubbling platform.* The room was identical to all the others.

He walked the perimeter of the room with one hand outstretched to feel the matte but smooth walls. Standard nanoBot-created steel. No difference. He moved to the bubbling platform and stood in the position he'd always adopted for postage and reception. He looked down at the kill switch. *Perfect. It's physically the same.*

Without more sophisticated tooling, he couldn't do more than an olfactory check, but he was happy enough that there was nothing constructively wrong with the area.

"Well, it's the right shape!" he said to Prid, who had been watching him kick the tires and bend the wings of the room, her pen poised.

The two standardCams had taken up opposite clock positions, orbiting the room. Sero knew they'd be alternately focusing on each of their faces as they circled. *Zwolf's favourite camera dance!*

"OK. Everything is in fine shape physically. She looks unused, even. Only one previous owner!"

Sero threw Prid his best "How funny am I?" smile again. She clearly didn't get his joke, though. No second-hand wing salesmen on colony, of course. Prid didn't say anything or laugh. She stood with her pen held ready and waited for him to continue.

"'Cents. Tell me about the usage history again. When was the last time this Postbox was used?"

"One hundred and forty-six years ago, Auditor."

NineCents at its briefest. *Only the facts, please, ma'am.*

Sero had already read the files on all this and even watched a couple of old video records on the holographic display in Park 359 whilst making one of his weekly trips back to Postbox one. The footage showed exactly what should be expected: fully formed human colonists stepping out of the Postbox facility and running through the arrival protocols. Testing muscles, testing voices. Each one acting out a little surprise at only needing to only walk 150 metres before reaching the planet's surface but then quickly adjusting after meeting the patriarch at ground level. Still, he wanted to talk to NineCents whilst in and around the Postbox itself. *Help me to think.*

"How many receptions did the facility host before that?"

"One hundred and thirty-four, across a four-year period, which is forty-seven point six percent of all receptions, including your own."

*Clever boy, 'Cents, anticipating the next question.* "And the bubbling algorithm. Each time. No anomalies?"

"No, Auditor. None. Mutation minimal sequences were received and corroborated in each case. Nucleotide conglomeration was identical in each reception, and the blank bubble also functioned exactly as designed. The progenitor cells were all shielded from the exobubble environment for the full length of the growth phase of reception, powering joule routes up and down within expected parameter tolerances. All stages were one hundred percent successful for all one hundred and thirty-four colonist arrivals."

"OK. What about the frequency of usage? How long did we give the facility between receptions?"

"There is a range. The longest time between completing the previous and initiating the subsequent of any two arrivals was eight days. The shortest period was nine hours. In each case the factor determining the variation was the replacement volume of miniSuns and nanoBots needed in order to restore one hundred percent efficiency."

Prid had been writing down all the numbers in her notepad. At this point, she spoke up. "Why would we use up more miniSuns on one reception than another?"

"Due to the variations in the environmental conditions on the day, Ms. Pridescent. To achieve blank bubbling, a precise superstring spin pattern is required. The energy delivered via the joule routes must be constant. However, as you know from your curricula, fusion occurs at a very high temperature. Heating the water below us, where the miniSuns are generating energy, has weather effects that affect the environment in which the process is taking place. A feedback loop. In order to maintain energy levels at a precise and unvarying constant, the miniSuns sacrifice some of the linked units in response to that feedback loop, rapidly reducing temperature when needed by destroying a proportion of their number. That number varies as conditions dictate—"

"And so it takes the nanoBots a variable amount of time to replace the sacrificed miniSuns," Prid finished as she underlined something in the notepad.

*So there's a diagnostic step between receptions. We have to ensure the system has fully reset and rebuilt to the optimum specifications.*

*Zwolf was present in all of the videos. Maybe he stayed on to do the confirmations?*

"Did you complete the diagnostics yourself, 'Cents? Was there any corroboration from a Race member?"

"I did. Your question is prescient, though. On each occasion, Patriarch Zwolf personally reviewed the facility and my calculations before permitting the next reception to begin. In those days, we weren't set to standby as we were before your own arrival; we had to confirm the trigger for the next colonist in the queue to arrive."

"He did the inspection personally? Every single time?"

"Correct."

That was unusual. Sero could imagine Zwolf attending the reception of the first dozen or so individuals as leader of NineDee, but once the colony was properly established, he could've delegated the initial greetings and explanation to another senior leader, surely? Certainly the readiness checks...*unless...I'll have to be careful not to give the game away, though...no simulations by 'Cents. Try a little bit of ancient discrete-mathematics practical work?*

"Prid, can I borrow your notebook, please? Your pen too?"

She handed them over with a shrug and a slight lip flex. "Dandy."

Sero scribbled a few numbers at the top of a blank page and then drew a pair of axes freehand on the left and bottom of the same page. On the x axis, he wrote, "Time between receptions (days)." He marked the end of the axis with "9" and notched off several marks in roughly equally increments back down to where the axes met. On the y axis, he wrote, "Reception number (individuals)" and numbered the top of the axis "134" before roughly notching that axis too. His handwriting was awful. He hadn't written more than a thousand words by hand in the last ten physical years of his life. No need. But he could write, as could all Race members.

"What are you doing?" asked Prid.

*Well done, girl. What a wonderful assistant.* "I'm going to show you something. Ever plotted a graph yourself in order to formulate an equation?"

"Erm, no?"

"You'll love it. It's a great tool when you're inventing. I'd bet you've tried to build something and ended up going through too many iterations of a design to get it right before, yes?"

Prid nodded cautiously. "Sure. Took me ages to work out how wide the aperture should be on these." She ran her right index finger across her can bandolier like a glockenspiel. "Too wide and the tendril becomes inflexible, too narrow and it's not so strong. I played about for hours and hours until I found a size that worked."

"OK. Let me give you a tool that will help next time. 'Cents, call out a few pairs of numbers please. First in each pair should be the number of the colonist received, second should be the time it took to prepare the Postbox in days following the previous reception. The colonists shouldn't be sequential, and I'll tell you when to stop calling pairs. Oh, and decimalise everything, please." Sero turned to Prid. "Makes the lesson easier."

"I understand, Auditor. Twenty-five: four point two."

Sero made a mark on the paper during a couple of seconds pause from NineCents.

"Four: seven point eight. One hundred and two: nought point seven."

Two more marks in Prid's book.

"Ninety-seven: Nought point eight."

"That's enough for now. Thanks, 'Cents." Sero flipped the book around to his young companion. "So, notice anything?"

Prid didn't have to look for long before she was clearly ready to offer a suggestion. She held back from speaking, though, offering a subtle enquiring look instead. Sero played somewhat dumb and nodded enthusiastically for her to continue. Taking the pen from him, Prid drew a straight line on the pad from the top left to the bottom right of the graph.

"Excellent. Line of best fit. Only four data points. Any theories yet just looking at this graph?"

"It looks like the more colonists arrived, the less time was taken between receptions?"

"OK. You have a theory." *And so do I.* "Let's get more data. NineCents, please resume your readout."

The computer announced ten more pairs of coordinates for Sero's graph. With each oration, Sero placed a cross on his tool, peppering the straight line Prid had drawn, Xs landing on either side.

"That's enough for now," he told the computer. "So, any change?"

Prid took the book from him and drew another, slightly steeper line on the page, although it was still similar to the original.

"Think it's enough to make a prediction from?"

"Well, yeah, if you want me to just stick dots on the page near to the line we've just made up."

"We don't need to be so random. We can use mathematics to describe the line and give us a way to predict any two points on a line."

Sero quickly added some notation to the hand-drawn chart as he spoke. "For this type of line," Sero said, pointing to the paper:

$$y - y_1 = m(x - x_1)$$

"Where 'm' is the slope of the line, and"—he scribbled again:

$$m = \frac{(y2 - y1)}{(x2 - x1)}$$

"See?"

Sero asked Prid to pick two points on the line to represent *(x1, y1)* and *(x2, y2)* before talking her through the calculations and defining the fuller version of the amateur line they'd created.

"So for our line:"

$$(y - 65) = -20(x-3)$$

"You got it, Prid! Well done!"

Sero hoped his pantomime had been subtle enough that it wouldn't look suspicious under review of the standardCam footage and also wouldn't alert anyone to his line of enquiry should they decide to review his conversation logs with the central computer. As they recorded the halo, he looked down at Prid's notebook in his hand. *No fraking way.*

# THIRTY

**"It was the** God Whisperer!"

Minnus was incredulous. *That fat frak. That ridiculous, dangerous fat frak.* It wasn't often in his life that he'd been so angry, but right now Minnus felt that he could run through walls. "He tried to kill him!"

"Not quite, Minnus. You know Sero wouldn't have died. Just been delayed."

Johnson was much calmer than his Telospace colleague. He was also standing, though, reflecting Minnus's emotions back at him in a blatantly placatory manner.

"Don't split fraking hairs, Idi. Sero's in the air on a timer, and Joberan tried to blow up the fraking runway. Sero's signal is nearly here. There's only a few months left, and it will arrive. Jesse frakin' Joberan knows that. The whole frakin' Race knows that!"

"Well, it's also not certain that Joberan was involved. Only likely."

"Are they here? I want to hear it from them myself."

"Naidoo. Du Plessis." Johnson issued summons towards the private door to his office. The entrance that led to Johnson's private access route into the building opened, and the two WorldGov investigators entered immediately. They'd obviously been waiting outside for their cue. Whilst Minnus knew their names and was aware that they'd been investigating the attack on the Antarctic Postbox, he'd never met either of them. Both were Surfacans by appearance, through and through. They were each missing their two upper front teeth in a cultural nod to their lineage.

Johnson gestured for them to cross the room. "Would you please brief—"

"Tell me what you know!" Minnus was livid. The idea that some deluded, preposterous ideologue had threatened and almost successfully injured Minnus's friends and even family made the old broadcaster furious. "And then tell me what WorldGov is going to *do* about it!"

"Naidoo?" Johnson introduced the woman closest to Minnus, who acknowledged him with a skewed nod and wincing expression.

Naidoo cleared her throat. "Mr. Mbeki. We've basically been trying to find out the source of the niobium brooms and follow any transactions or favours backwards from the potential recipients of the devices. As you know, WorldGov can track and trace all cSheet-to-cSheet Red movements in real time and also back trace for centuries.

We can literally follow each Red right through history from its 'printing' to today. The brooms used in the attack on the Postbox were not brought back from Mars. They've never actually been used for mining. These units are very old and have only ever been on Earth. They were effectively the last run of prototypes used for testing on Earth before the finished product was shipped to Mars for industrial use."

Minnus was impatient, but he could immediately recognise the rigour and discipline in the WorldGov investigator, things he respected. She stood straight and was strictly fact based in recounting her progress. He restrained his anger, manufactured a thoughtful expression, and waited for Naidoo to continue.

"Our last official record of them was in storage in the old SpaceX shop over in Boca Chica, Amasia. We assessed all individuals that have access to the Boca Chica bunker and created a list of only four people who had both the opportunity and reason to favour the brooms along."

"Favour?" Minnus hadn't heard the term used like that.

Du Plessis spoke for the first time. "Exchange an item in return for something other than Red."

The enormous investigator spoke with a classic lower-Surfacan lisp, inserting S's at every opportunity he could. Despite his heated state, Minnus found himself counting the S sounds in the big man's sentence. He thought he'd found five.

"It's complex, as we can only derive likelihoods rather than logged Red transfers, but using cSheet data, we can extrapolate the likely people that might have been the second and third links in the broom-movement chain. It's all only probability based but no less useful for the uncertainty. The processors in WorldGov have centuries of documented precedent to refer to, and I for one trust the guesswork completely."

"Short. Purposeful. Sentences."

Naidoo widened her eyes and cleared her throat again. "It's probabilities. We walk down the list of a person's contacts who might be interested in taking up an illegal weapon, for whatever reason. Red, status, sex, philosophy. Whatever. We draw a web out to seven people using the cSheet data WorldGov holds. Words used, interaction frequency, colocation frequency, and length. Then we walk the web outwards. Cycle one usually has no more than eight people in it. In this instance, only four. We went to see them all and picked a favourite based on the look in her eyes. Round two: seven people based on the algorithm. We saw them all and picked a favourite. On the third go, we got nowhere. No way those guys were into this kind of scale. So, we start again at the top. It's iterative."

Nobody spoke for five seconds as the investigators waited for some acknowledgment from Minnus that he understood.

"Yes. And?"

"Jesse Joberan was on the third level down from our second-choice primary suspect." Du Plessis said.

Naidoo looked momentarily frustrated to have had her brief interrupted. She resumed quickly. "The really telling part is that if we reset the cSheet algorithm with Joberan in the centre and look for people who might want to attack the facility, those two dive bombers you met on the bridge last month show up in the third cycle again. These guys all move in the same circles."

"So where is he now? Where are they all? You've had them detained?"

"It's not that simple, Minnus," Johnson interjected.

"They tried to destroy us! How much simpler could it be? They dropped from the sky, blew a hole in the roof of our building, and started firing grenades around!"

Johnson remained calm. "He means that we only have probabilities. No actionable evidence. There are some links to areas where we might be able to find evidence, but right now we haven't got anything that would convict in a Race-reviewed trial."

Naidoo explained calmly in juxtaposition to Minnus's paper-thin control of his righteous anger. "Remember, the items used in the attack were all favoured along. No Red was exchanged, so there are no cSheet records. Only communication records and proximity logs. We know they've all met in sequence at various times, and we know that they've spoken via cSheet. But we can't show what they spoke about or divine why they met. We're all familiar with the privacy laws that WorldGov instituted centuries ago as a balance against its own power. Nobody is willing to change them to store records of the actual content of conversations between Race members. It's a slippery slope from there, with totalitarianism at the bottom of the hill."

"So they're going to do nothing?" Minnus incredulity wasn't helpful, and he knew it. Naidoo and Du Plessis were just doing their job as best they could, but the impotence of the situation both frustrated and shocked him. "We know who they are and can guess why they did it, but we're not going to challenge them? We're going to let them have another go!"

"No sir!" Du Plessis barked firmly. "We are on them! Nobody in WorldGov can arrest them, but we've got enough data that we can set a team to monitoring them. We've already found some interesting stuff that might one day lead to something actionable. It seems Mr. Joberan is also linked with some groups who've tried to set up competitor currencies to Red so they can circumvent the Ugandan principles. Putting it all together, it's likely that these alternative currencies might have been part of the favouring that led to the group acquiring the niobium brooms."

"So we're going to watch them *until* they do it again?" Minnus said snarkily, disgusted.

There was silence for a moment. Always uncomfortable with silence, Johnson was the one to break it. "WorldGov are watching them, so they can't do it again, Minnus. Right now there's a team in Amasia—Chicago, specifically. Joberan can't do anything other than be a Race member from here on in. He's showed his hand and lost. WorldGov will protect us."

*Not good enough.* Minnus was irate, but he didn't know why. He could process the reasoning behind what he was being told, understand the facts. He couldn't reconcile the emotions that the facts raised in him with the inaction that he knew would come next. He felt threatened, vulnerable. He needed to *do* something. "But what abou—"

"Minnus, please stop." Johnson was still infuriatingly controlled. "I know it's difficult to rely on others when you have so much at stake. That's the foundation of the Race, though. We're all in it together—if we stick to our beliefs. I've also been around WorldGov a lot more recently because of all the good work we're doing here. I can monitor progress personally and make sure you get a weekly update on any new risks that Naidoo and Du Plessis uncover. You have to trust us, Minnus. Trust me?"

Minnus found that he couldn't speak in reply. He didn't know what to say. *Do I trust you?* Instead, he nodded in resignation, took a deep, slow breath, and paused. He looked into the eyes of each of the people in the room and hoped he formed a contract of trust with that look. Then he left without another word.

# THIRTY-ONE

**She was disappointed** in him. He could tell. Aleph was silent. She was just looking at him and sobbing. What had he done do make her cry like this? Perhaps it was something that someone else had done? He didn't understand.

He wanted to embrace her, comfort her. As he stood, his legs felt strange. Too light. Noncorporeal? What was happening? He looked to her to explain and realised that she was pointing behind him. She still cried silently. He turned his body to see what she was aiming at and felt his legs move without his instruction, but too late, delayed by longer than they should have been, as though his feet were rotating on a disc rather than making human movements. Some kind of swivelling observation platform? There was a hill in front of him. No buildings, just a mound with a single dark line running away from him to the horizon, over the summit. He squinted to focus on that horizon and found that someone was walking towards him, down the hill, along the line. He still didn't feel right, though. What was the matter with his legs? His feet felt like they were strapped into something. He looked down to check, but he couldn't see. There was mist or smoke obscuring the floor. Where was he?

He looked back to the approaching figure. It had moved too quickly and was almost with him, covering two-thirds of the distance between him and the horizon as he'd glanced away. That's not possible! Aleph was right to warn him. He turned to speak to her, but she was sleeping. Only a moment ago, she'd been crying at him! Perhaps he was sick. Injured, maybe? Blood loss? Could he be hallucinating?

Prid! The figure was Prid! Bounding, leaping towards him. She covered tens of metres with each lolloping step. He could discern the look on her face as she closed towards him now. Happy. She was happy. Pleased to see him and racing nearer. He felt himself smile too. Aleph would've liked Prid. Wait! Would've? How could Aleph be here with Prid? He turned again to wake Aleph, but she was gone.

And then Prid was on him. Head on his chest and squeezing her arms around him, the bear hug of a koala on a homey branch.

"Father."

⋏

Sero woke in a right-angled sitting position again, his back bolt straight and his heart pounding in his chest. He groaned, rolled out of the bunk, and slopped over to the floor plunge for some water to wash his face. In his heavy-eyed daze, he tripped over his boots, left unorganised on the floor of his sleeping quarters. He cursed himself but avoided falling and instead forced his eyes to open wider than normal, dragging in light and overcorrecting for his lethargy. He found the polished steel that he used for a mirror and did a before-and-after assessment whilst washing his face with the weather-warmed water from the floor plunge. After wasn't much better than before. *Need to sleep more, Mr. Universe.*

Prid had been called back to Park 359 at the request of Divis and Sana. That seemed very fair to Sero. She'd been spending weeks away from them in helping the audit move along, and he imagined that they must feel her absence, no matter how formal Prid thought the family relationships were. Any parents would. Perhaps especially so in a small community like a telonaut colony.

He'd taken advantage of the solitude to work on some of the things that he couldn't figure out about NineDee. As he dressed, his mind reloaded the analysis it'd been occupied with before Sero had finally abandoned the consideration and given in to sleep the previous evening. He had a couple of theories about individual areas of dissonance but hadn't been able to create anything that would unify those theories together into a cohesive whole. He reached his half of the workbench that he shared with Prid just as his internal recap completed. Prid's notebook was open on the bench where he'd left it, his own writing arranged around the journal. Despite his own information collection and the availability of NineCents as a data assistant, Sero had developed a preference for using Prid's notes as an alternative voice to narrate the research back to him. She was a theatrical note taker, often adding her own questions and thoughts in dramatic soliloquy in the margins. During the previous evening, Sero had struggled to break what had become a repetitive and cyclical pattern of thinking. He'd been reviewing data and drawing the same conclusions, the same probabilities, over and again. He missed having Prid around to bounce off. He missed having her around in general. After he'd picked up her book, though, he'd found that her margined perspective was useful in generating creative thought—almost as useful as actually having her there. So he'd run everything through again but using Prid's chronological diary as the base of his review rather than his own more compartmentalised filing. He'd now positioned her journal in the centre of the bench, with his own notes arranged around in topic-based piles in a pattern similar to a clock face, one topic per hour and fifteen minutes or so. He'd spent the previous evening reading Prid's journal and then referring to his own notes as he came across something related to one of his unanswered questions in her pages. He'd added handwritten covering letters to each of his own piles as he progressed. In this way, he'd developed the lists of theories that were placed atop each pile relating to a specific conundrum. Sero was satisfied with his analysis on several of the topics.

Under a note entitled "Families," he'd reasoned that the formal family style he'd observed in Prid's family environment could be extrapolated out into a cultural norm. There was a puritan mentality pervading the colony that may have suppressed individualism but had worked well in arranging the autonomous decision making he'd witnessed. The colonists really did have a creed that was focused on making a single event successful and had been arranged around that Leaf Day–focused system for a generation. Whilst Sero theorised that this norm would change after Leaf Day, with the colonists developing more Race-typical family relationships and social structures, he'd decided he could reconcile the evidence to the theory and accept the two as compatible. After all, if Leaf Day wasn't a success, the colony was doomed, and everyone here understood that completely. What might happen to social structures on Earth if the Race identified some impending threat to the planet at a specified future date? An asteroid impact or supermassive solar flare and subsequent coronal-mass ejection, perhaps. Things would certainly change and probably in ways that Sero couldn't predict on his own. Perhaps with enough computing power, some likely scenarios could be modelled, but Sero had no experience in doomsday research, and, with no access to Earth's information network from NineDee, he could only surmise.

*Why the reverence for Leaf in particular, though, rather than simple focus on the life-threatening event?*

Prid excepted, the colonists had all shown some degree of admiration for a long-dead lady whom the majority of them had never met. Sero hadn't been able to find a reasonable reason for it. At the bottom of the covering note on top of the pile titled "Leaf," Sero had written "Proto-religion?"

Amongst the piles of research topics, there were two further areas that Sero still felt uncomfortable about. He intended to look at those again now. There was also a nagging feeling that the explanations he'd decided upon as most likely for the areas in which he *did* have a viable theory didn't seem to have a unifying theme. There was too much that was reasonable but unlikely. Too many low-probability or completely novel explanations. As such, Sero had an inkling that all the unlikely theories summed together might calculate out to be too improbable for him to accept—too many dubious coincidences. He was sure that WorldGov would put teams of people to work once all the data he was recording was received back on Earth, but for now he wanted to at least complete his thought clock with a viable covering letter for each position on the dial; a theory that he had arrived at through his own mental effort. He walked to stand at the opposite side of the workbench so that the two unresolved-subject-matter heaps were right in front of him at positions six and seven on his clock.

Position six was labelled "Reception Frequency," and the plant-paper tower at position seven was titled "Dini."

There were lots of thoughts about Dini in Prid's notebook, and this was the area that Prid had found the most alternative insight into from reading her research notes. Prid's focus was on explaining why her former friend had become so distant and unavailable after she'd begun her formal training. This interested Sero, but he'd ultimately decided it could be explained by the pervading urgency of the need to make Leaf Day a success. Sero thought that the decision to sideline things that were associated with childhood once an adult takes on adult responsibility and duty of care was one he'd seen before, even experienced himself.

What Sero couldn't explain about Dini, though, was her sexual approach to him. On their first meeting, she'd been almost commercially provocative, testing Sero's libidinous self-control. Prid's notebook had made the subject even more mysterious. Nothing Prid had written seemed to relate to the woman Sero had met. In Prid's mind, Dini was a comic and playful individual; there wasn't a single reference to boys, men, or sex in any way. There were no theories in Prid's journal that a man might have romantically swept Dini away, no jealousy that someone else had Dini's attention now. Only observations that Dini didn't smile anymore and had forgotten her friend.

*If it were just a girl becoming a woman and discovering herself sexually, surely there'd be men here that are her own age that she could experiment with? Why would she throw herself at me like that?*

Sero picked up Prid's pad from the desk and flipped to the point in the book that had been written after the two girls had accidentally reunited in the lab, just after Sero had first met Dini himself. Written in the margin, Prid had scratched the word "COLD" in capital letters.

*Poor girl.*

"Hello, Auditor."

Sero recognised the voice at the doorway and quickly turned over the plant paper at position seven so it couldn't be read.

*Speak of the devil, and she shall appear!*

He turned to see Dini herself, four metres inside the room already. Although he didn't so much see her as inhale the sight of her. For their previous meeting, she'd been impressively sexualised in casual workwear.

She was outrageously carnally dressed today.

She was wearing a single belt of tendril, wrapped around her body dozens of times to form a skin-tight suit, punctured by swathes of skin at the shoulders, hips, stomach, and thighs; her dark, lean skin advertised itself through the windows in her outfit. She noticed him drinking in the details and smiled, turning slowly. "What do you think? I had a little help in making it."

There was skin window on both legs where the cheeks of her buttocks met her thighs. Both were flawless, lean muscle and smooth. There were separated by a twenty-centimetre thigh gap, which drew Sero's attention as Dini rolled onto her tiptoes with her hands clasped above her head and stretched out like an athlete preparing to run. The movement showed every part of her tighten and then relax into the elegant, clean form it had started from. Sero couldn't respond to her question. He simply swallowed.

*Oh no. Here we go again. And no distractions. No hope of salvation by interruption.*

"I like how it makes me feel. Wholly me. Bound up tight. No pockets or practicality. Just me, my muscles, and my...vigour." The last word hung in her eyes as well as on her lips.

Sero stayed silent. His mind turned to Aleph, and he felt the now-familiar unease created by the conflict between his libido and his broken heart.

Dini seemed to see the discord from across the room. She closed the gap between them. "I've realised that you've been avoiding me. I thought we'd had a chemistry when we first met. I know I enjoyed speaking with you. So I was a little hurt when you kept finding somewhere else to be rather than meet for a second date." Her words were softly spoken and paired with bright, round eyes flicking across Sero's face and groin. She completed the sensory triumvirate by wetting her lips as she paused, seeming to taste herself. "Then I heard about your loss. From the patriarch. He told me what happened on Rigil Kentaurus."

Sero was rooted to the spot as she approached, bewildered by the suddenness of her arrival, confused by her knowledge of his internal dilemma, and aroused by her blatant, targeted provocation. He remained silent as she entered his personal space, a surreal observer of his own situation.

"So I came to help. I think you might need some relief. An easy way to rejoin the adult Race. Someone you can be with without having to cherish. I admire you so much, Sero, and I want to be that person for you. I want to be. For. You."

As Dini spoke the final word, she kissed him strongly; pulling his head towards hers. She pushed her other hand down the front of his trousers as she pushed her tongue into his mouth.

Sero knew he'd already given in. His heart *was* broken. He *did* need repair. And this woman was so attractive. A dormant part of him had reawakened and taken control, urging him to be powerful. To take pleasure in being desired. He'd fought it. He'd thought about Aleph. He'd avoided Dini, knowing how lustful he'd been when they first met. He'd decided he could live without the power and pleasure—move on. And then the athletic, supple woman with her hands moving over his cock and balls had come to his room and had given him permissions. Authority to feel again. To frak.

Swelling quickly in her hand, Sero understood what would happen next. He was going to take her, and they were both going to enjoy it. He was going to let go.

Tipping over the edge of reasoning and into inevitable raucous desire, he returned Dini's kisses passionately, urgently, putting his hands on her arse and then chest, exploring a new body for the first time. Dini's hands were meanwhile unclasping his trousers and pushing him backwards towards the workbench. She backed him right up to the desk so his arse was touching it and worked his trousers down to free his dick.

"Up."

Sero didn't understand and looked at her nonplussed. She responded by grabbing a handful of his buttocks with each hand. *"Up."*

He lifted himself backwards and onto the table. Dini then pushed him in the chest, forcing him to lie back and scattering his work. His legs hung below him. She continued to work at his now steel-hard cock with one hand whilst removing his boot and one trouser leg with the other. Once his legs were separable, free from his coverall trousers, Dini lifted them up onto the table, forcing Sero to scoot backwards further into his bonfire of notes as he placed his feet flat on the surface of the bench, his knees bent. When she'd manoeuvred him to where she wanted him, she fell upon his cock with her mouth, making it disappear into her face. The feeling was amazing: the abandon and the power, her keen subservience, the physical pleasure.

*She's fantastic! A male fantasy straight from the mind of an author.*

She worked this way for several minutes, alternately taking his cock all the way to the back of her throat and then working only on its head, slapping it against her face and lips. Eventually, Sero's urge to frak overtook him, and he tried to lift her head from his groin to allow him to stand. She shook her head though and told him to wait. Standing, Dini untied the body tendril at her neck, creating a loose end to the form circling her body. She peeled it away from her skin enough to create a metre or so of slack. Taking his dick back into her mouth, she tied the end of this rope around his cock and balls, just tight enough to restrict the blood flow back out of his genitals. Then, smiling deviously, Dini began walking around the workbench in circles, unravelling her tendril body stocking layer by layer as she moved. She paused after each orbit to play with or suck his cock, teasing him and making certain he was rodlike. Sero strained to watch each centimetre of body revelation from his prone position.

*It's like she's been trained in a harem of antiquity! How does a woman so young and living on an isolated world know how to pleasure a man this way?*

He was entranced by her body. It was literally perfect. Strong. Young. Smooth. Competitive. Only when she was completely naked did she stop circling and stand in front of him, allowing him to rise. They switched positions as Sero tore off the remainder of his own clothes. Dini lay on her back and opened her legs to give him access. Sero eagerly buried his face in her lips, finding her raised spot immediately and working away in quick, firm flicks of his tongue. He let his saliva drip copiously from his mouth as he moved, coating her. He'd decided to have her finish like this, reciprocating her generosity, but she wouldn't wait for him to take her to climax. Dini pushed his head away and deftly turned over onto her knees. She raised her arse into the air, away from the table, and put her face flat to the surface amongst the scattered papers before looking backwards.

"I. Am. For. You. Frak me. Frak me, Sero—frak me."

So he did.

The relief was immense, his involvement in the occasion total. He fraked her as though he'd fallen from the ceiling, each stroke whipping the tendril tail tied around his testicles, keeping his fingers between the lips of her genitals and driving through her, tip to hilt, with each thrust until he felt her tighten around him. When she did, Sero emptied his abandon into her, lust, surprise, shame, and all.

⋏

"I could arrange it again, if you're worried?"

They'd had sex four times that morning. Each time was better. Once he'd committed to the act, given into his lust, Sero had thought only of pleasure for himself and his new partner. Striving to enjoy himself but also to impress.

*The first time is always the same. Everyone giving the best performance.*

He'd succeeded, he thought.

Dini had continued to be generous and supple, sometimes taking control and sometimes demure. With the first kiss and Dini placing hands on him, a flood barrier had been broken. Sero's stored lust had broken out over him and swallowed up Dini in the process. She was a willing vessel for it and had accepted the barrage eagerly. But then something had happened. Sero noticed that as his libido became near to satisfied, he felt other emotions replace his dwindling desire. Chief amongst them was guilt. It had begun as a trickle. An uneasiness as be pounded away on top of Dini. A feeling of his focus on his own pleasure slipping away, to be replaced by a spotlight aimed at more mechanical sexual performance—a task to be completed. He'd still managed to finish and even timed his climax to coincide with Dini's, but he'd immediately felt the need to go over to the floor plunge and wash. He was cleaning away more than the juices of passion, he knew. Now, lying adjacent to a still-naked Dini, Sero's mind had become fully occupied by guilt.

*Why did I do that? Why couldn't I just say no? Calmly leave the building? Who am I?*

Dini seemed not to notice his distraction, though. She was persevering with an attempt to arrange a repeat of the encounter.

"I know Divis and Sana well, and they're always happy to have Prid at their home. I can arrange for her to be away again, and we can spend some more time easing you back into manhood." She spoke with a coquettish smile as epilogue. "I've still got another month before I must return to the other side of the plate to complete my work."

Sero did not want to arrange another meeting. After cleaning himself up and then lying in thought for half an hour, feigning intimacy in the aftermath of their rutting, he was horrified with himself. He couldn't explain that to the young woman beside him, though. He couldn't bring himself to be that heartless. She'd seemed to genuinely think that their lovemaking might help heal him somehow, and she'd committed to it fully. She'd been every heterosexual man's dream partner. "Thanks but no thanks" wasn't the gentlemanly answer to give in this situation. *What about Aleph? You loved her. What is this in comparison to that? Nothing. You're a fool, Novak. A fool.*

"How about we eat lunch, and then we can talk about it?" Sero said.

He got up from bunk pod, unpeeling Dini's limbs from their coil around him. He began dressing again as he spoke, wandering around the room to collect his clothing, discarded that morning to different corners of the room.

"Sure," Dini responded. "Can I, erm, borrow some coveralls, though? Unless you'd like to help wind me back up into that thing?"

She gestured to the tendril rope now circling the workbench in the centre of Sero's lab. Despite himself, Sero smirked. He went across the lab into the room where Prid slept whilst she was here and returned with a set of her coveralls. They'd be tight on Dini, but Sero thought that they would fit well enough for her to be out in public whilst wearing them, especially when he considered the outfit she'd arrived in. When they were both dressed,

Sero moved over to the kitchen area and began preparing a beefsteak and some vegetables. Being out of the bunk and dressed had helped relieve his guilt a little, and now being busy was more completely returning him to a state of rationality, rather than a regret-wracked mute.

He felt he could small talk whilst he cooked, but didn't know where to start. In similar situations in his life, he'd previously spent this afterglow period strictly locked into performance mode, displaying wit and modesty, moving through the cycle of joke to compliment to question on repeat. *Perhaps I should just stick to the question part?* Before he could think of something suitably benign to ask though, Dini returned to the topic of scheduling.

"We could definitely make it work. Maybe we could even save some energy whilst doing it? I need to be at Park 359 next week. Don't I remember the patriarch telling me that you need to go back there every so often and visit the Postbox? Maybe we could coordinate? Divis and Sana are already there, so Prid could stay with them, and you could come visit me in my quarters."

*The patriarch has explained my fragment-download schedule to Dini? That's strange. Why would he mention that to her?*

"When is the next time you're going to be there?"

Sero noticed the veil over the question. It wasn't about sex. *A direct question on my movements?*

Something clicked in Sero's psyche. He felt it. A revelatory barrel dropping into place inside the lock that the Dini puzzle had represented in his mind. *She's a spy! That's why she's been so keen to ingratiate herself to me, so forward. Her agenda isn't sexual; it's reconnaissance.*

Sero managed to control the outward reaction to his insight, gently lifting the beefsteaks onto a plate to rest and bleed. His guilt and discomfort had been instantaneously replaced by intrigue. If he could get information from Dini, perhaps he could decipher the unanswered riddles that the bonfire of paper on his workbench represented. With nothing more than that—an internal realisation and microsecond of reactionary reflection—Sero was back in the game. All thoughts of wrongdoing banished from him. He'd been played, and now it was his turn.

"Four days from now, if I remember rightly." He tried to appear unconcerned about offering the information. "Does that work?"

He added the vegetables he'd steamed to the plates and brought them over the table, where Dini had seated herself, casually putting them down and sitting opposite her.

"Yes!" Dini said excitedly. She tapped her feet rhythmically on the steel floor of the lab. Rat-a-tat-tat.

Sero was immediately distracted by a sense of déjà vu. *That seems familiar.* "Yes, I'm certainly going to be there. We can perhaps spend more time together too? Talk some more about you and your extraordinary life? Maybe even how you're feeling about NineDee? You know, before, after, during…"

Dini grabbed herself proactively, unsubtly reconfirming what she was bringing to the meeting.

*How did I not spot this before? It's bloody obvious, you arrogant old sod. She's been hired out to infiltrate your audit, and she using her body to do it.* He forced another smirk from his lips, hoping it wasn't too transparently painted on his face. "I think that's a fair swap." He tried to make himself sound like he was flirting. "What do think about my cooking? I'm no expert, but I always liked to think I could cook a good cow."

"Mmmmm. You're Mr. Universe. Of course I like it!"

Dini was chewing enthusiastically and making purring sounds as she swallowed. Her obsequiousness seemed amplified to Sero now he'd realised that there was motive behind her method. She was wolfing down the steak as though she'd never eaten. A clumsy, almost childlike show of appreciation of his cookery. He simply thanked her, though, before clearing the table and moving to his workbench. He began to reorganise his research, which had been victim to their first assault upon each other earlier in the morning.

"You look busy. Need to get back to work?" Dini took the hint but didn't seem suspicious of Sero's renewed preoccupation with his desk.

"Let me get out of here."

Dini spent a minute or so coiling the tendril she'd been wearing as a suit earlier and hung it on her shoulder around her torso. "Waste not, want not!" she said.

Sero forced another smile from his face. He felt a cold and calculated actorly instinct come over him. "Thank you. See you in four days?"

Dini nodded silently.

With the agreement made, Dini kissed Sero on the mouth passionately, grabbing his crotch as she did so in a gratuitous good-bye. She turned and walked towards the door but stopped just before she left. "I absolutely cannot wait to see you again, Mr. Universe." She excitedly tapped her feet again then disappeared through the exit.

Rat-a-tat-tat. Again.

"Rat-a-tat-tat?" Sero mumbled to himself.

And with that small musical percussion, all Sero's assumptions about the colony of NineDee came crashing down in his mind—a cacophony of realisation that plummeted out of his brain and through his chest, squeezing his lungs and heart to a stop as it passed. The feeling settled in his stomach as a horrified sickness.

*"She" isn't hired out to infiltrate the audit. "She" has her own agenda. "She" isn't even Dini!*

# Thirty-Two

"**I**t's not the algorithm, Idi."

Minnus was in Johnson's office again at the telonaut bureau. In the three months since he'd last been in the room, Minnus had to admit that Johnson had been right about WorldGov's ability to prevent further attacks on the Postbox and Minnus's family. Nothing untoward had happened at all. Nombre had gone back to her normal routine. Minnus had been working from home a lot more, in part because he wanted to stay close to Nombre, in part because he felt that the Telospace bureau had become a target. However, the work itself was going well. There'd been no disruptions to the schedule and no further dangerous incidents or attacks.

Perhaps the audit of NineDee that was being sent out to the Race could even be said to be going too well. In the last two months, the NV broadcasts had become vanilla to the point of being dull, and the enthusiasm that had been built up in the initial phases of the broadcasts was ebbing. Minnus had been working to review the algorithm that processed Sero's memory fragments and then produced the highlights that were broadcast in NV to the Race. He'd looked things over every way he could think of and couldn't find a problem.

Johnson wasn't taking the news well. Minnus had been operating out of his apartment in Surfaca for a month. He'd even set up a download mirror that would automatically send the latest weekly memory fragment received from Sero over to his home. The algorithm still did its work automatically and broadcast from the Antarctic Telospace base, but he could store and use the fragments if he needed to. However, although he'd spoken to Johnson every week via cSheet, he could no longer placate the bureau head remotely. Minnus had therefore agreed to fly in that morning by wing.

When he'd arrived at Johnson's top-floor office, the younger man had been waiting for him. It'd looked to Minnus like Johnson had just finished a cSheet call. His communicator was lying on his desk in an unusual position. Perhaps it had been pushed away along the surface after a difficult conversation rather than being rolled up and placed in a pocket, as most people did? That would seem to fit with the attitude that Johnson was displaying towards his employee. If he hadn't been a man of over one hundred years of age, Minnus might have thought that he should feel told off.

"So are you telling me that Sero has decided to only experience dull things? Mr. Universe has decided to go local? In the last two months, all you've given us is parades and propaganda! It's like looking out of the eyes of a streetlamp. There's no context, no excitement. It's just a parade of stately presentations. There's barely even any science!"

Johnson was clearly flustered. Minnus couldn't recall a time that he'd ever seen him raise his voice like this. He tried to reason with the younger man.

"I hear you, Idi. It isn't like Sero. But it's not the algorithm. I've checked and rechecked. The algorithm is working. It's keyed to the same seed memory as it was before. It's editing the same way. It's just that the events we've been witnessing through Sero in the last few months are the ones he associates with the big project now. "Leaf Day.""

"Without an alternative point of reference, I think we only have two options at this point. We could revert to the previous method we used—pause the NV broadcasts and wait until Sero himself arrives back here along with the standardCam footage. We'd then need to manually edit the footage. So we're talking about holding off on sharing with the Race for about a year. Six months for Sero's final signal to get back and six months to edit.

"*Or* I can start at the beginning and watch Sero's memories in near real time. Experience everything that he did; perhaps try to find another seed memory that will make the algorithm do the work for us again. Worst case, I'd be able to see the differences between what we've already broadcast and what Sero actually experienced."

Minnus positioned the words as options for Johnson to choose from, but he knew that Johnson didn't really have options. There was no way the ambitious Idi Johnson would submit to pausing broadcasts, not after the way he'd used the last six months of success in garnering Race focus and positioning the telonaut programme well in the eyes of WorldGov. Not to mention elevating his own credibility balance in the respect account he'd been building with WorldGov. Stopping the NV broadcasts would likely delete that credibility instantaneously.

"Minnus…" Johnson spoke as though to a son or daughter: respectful, controlled, but clearly expecting respect and attention. "We cannot wait for another year to begin sharing with the Race again. There are other concerns here beyond this single audit."

Minnus was unsure whether to be self-satisfied that he'd interpreted the situation correctly or offended that Johnson was still holding a pretence that his motivation was other than to build enough of a public platform to be elected to WorldGov. It was obvious at this point. Months of moving carefully in the correct circles of power and networking with those already in WorldGov through his roles in the Telospace. *Years, even?*

It had become clearer in the last few months as Johnson had spent less and less time running the bureau itself and ever more time in or around WorldGov advertising his record of success. He'd used the audit of NineDee as a promotional tool for Telospace, and he'd done that well. There'd been a swell of interest amongst the Race, and it looked almost certain now that the programme would be refunded in the next mission elections in a year's time.

Johnson had also been running a parallel promotional campaign, though, promotion of Johnson, by Johnson, for Johnson. Whilst Minnus had never held any personal political ambition, he was aware enough of the process to become a candidate for WorldGov that he could divine how Johnson likely approached the task. He could see his younger boss in his mind's eye, walking the corridors of power, impressing existing GeoReps with his work and gravitas, ingratiating himself so as to be thought a potential successor.

Once recommended as a benefactor by an incumbent GeoRep, Johnson could become active in speaking directly to the Race about his experience running the bureau and why that made him a great candidate to represent whichever geography he'd targeted. Surfaca, perhaps? With only twenty geographies to choose from, Surfaca would make some sense, but Minnus imagined Johnson would be more calculating than to position himself as a future GeoRep for his homeland simply because he was born there. He'd campaign for whichever region he thought he could most likely succeed in as a candidate. *That's why he's so flustered. He's linked his personal capability to the success of the audit—made NineDee his evidence-based credentials to govern. He needs people to vividly remember the audit because he's going to make it the centrepiece of his upcoming campaign.*

Minnus held his silence along with Johnson's eye. Whilst he had no problem with Johnson running for WorldGov, he didn't like the lack of transparency that he felt he was experiencing now. So he held his tongue and dared Johnson to continue to hold his own. If Minnus was going to have to work both himself and by extension his friends and family like dogs in the sun, he was damn sure going to do it for a clear reason. He wanted that reason out in the open.

It took ten long seconds of silent staring at each other before Johnson broke. In doing so, he seemed to regain more of his usual composure. As though the telling of his truths gave him back some of the power and control that the unexpected slowing of the audit pace had taken away from him. Minnus could see the change on Johnson's face as he spoke—from ruffled to ruthless as he moved from a topic around which he had no firm plan to a subject about which he'd been planning for years.

*This man's long-term plan is too entirely entwined with his sense of self. That could be dangerous for the sanity of a person. What if that one overarching design slips away? What does the architect of the plan become then under self-reflection? Some other person? Two people?*

Minnus decided to let Johnson speak without interruption.

"I've been representing us at WorldGov, as you know. The Race is our benefactor…as it should be.

"We need their support, and as head of Telospace, I have to think about how to maintain the Race's support long into the future. How would we complete the audits or even expand them without the Red and energy we're afforded every five years in the mission elections? You know how we've slipped down the priority list. At inception centuries ago, this programme was the top priority for the Race, funding hundreds of transmissions and blank bubbles here on Earth. Telonauts have consistently dropped down the Race's mission priorities ever since, to the point where we can now only fund a single auditor and a couple of blank bubbles per decade here on Earth. The energy and Red are being used for other things. Do you want to risk losing touch with the colonies altogether? Becoming only cousins to fellow Race members out there in the cosmos?"

The rhetoric was familiar to Minnus. He'd seen Johnson and his predecessors use it regularly during campaigning for mission elections in previous decades. They'd always succeeded in getting enough support amongst the Race to continue with the programme. Minnus thought that this kind of long-term view was intrinsic to the culture that humanity had built up over the centuries since the inception of the Race as an organisational creed. He didn't think there was much genuine risk of a swing in voting now. People wanted to know about their brave frontiersmen relatives out in space, and there'd always be dedicated people like Sero and Minnus eager to bring them that knowledge. Johnson was simply campaigning to an audience of one. Minnus didn't answer the rhetoric.

"Well, I don't. I think I have found a way that I can best protect us. Best protect you, Sero, and your work by extension. Whilst I've been representing us to WorldGov and completing all the required proofs and procedures to show that we achieving great things with the Red surplus afforded to us, I've learned just how influential those few GeoReps are upon our benefactors. Their position gives them credibility and respect. Despite the egalitarian base of our society, we're still a meritocracy.

"These people have risen to represent the interests of hundreds of millions, sometimes billions of people. They're elected by the Race as a whole to help con-struct the future of humanity." Johnson paused before delivering his summary questions in a changed pitch, hushing as though giving away a vital secret. "What if I could become a GeoRep? How much influence would I gain? I could use it to remind Race members just how important our work is here. I could secure the future of the programme. What a legacy we could continue to leave."

"When and how?"

Johnson seemed to sense that Minnus was going to help him—that he'd developed a potential ally and sup-porter but only if he sealed the deal appropriately. He be-came more enthusiastic as he gained even more control of the conversation and himself, positive dynamism replacing the aggressive energy that he'd exuded when Minnus had first entered the room.

"I've been asked if I might consider running as the replacement for GeoRep Breen of Eurasia. She is aging and intends to step down within the year to spend more time with her family. We've spoken many times, and she's offered to formally nominate and support me in the replacement elections. The ten-week campaigning limit means I'll probably be speaking to the Race whilst the audit of NineDee is still being broadcast. It's a key part of the message I'd like to convey: evidence of our ethos, work rate, and record of success. I'm concerned about the speed that Sero seems to have slowed to, but even a ponderous broadcast would be better than none at all. That's why taking NV offline isn't a good option for us."

Having shared his plan, Johnson quite accurately sensed the need to stop talking and allow Minnus some space to react.

*Maybe he wouldn't be a bad GeoRep. He does get things done, even if I don't like his personal manner sometimes.* "Thank you for your honesty. I've often thought you might desire to become a GeoRep."

Minnus felt some sense of small victory in the sentence. Honesty was important to him as a principle, and bringing Johnson to a place where he saw the value of straightforwardness gave him some internal satisfaction, but he'd chosen the word "desire" specifically as a challenge to Johnson's announced motivation for standing for election. In reality, Minnus would likely have agreed to the long slog of trying to manually review the NineDee audit anyway, but for his own reasons rather than the faux protectionism that Johnson was espousing. Working out how to self-edit spider maps and offer Race members true person-to-person experience sharing was the proudest achievement of his life. He genuinely thought that kind of mutual experience could bring about an even closer unity amongst the Race and increase empathy. He wanted it to be available to everyone. He'd happily put in whatever work was needed to build a more compassionate Race. Still, Johnson hadn't been sure of that, and his uncertainty had brought about a little more honesty in the world. *Making Johnson a little more honest could only be a good thing if he's going to be a GeoRep, couldn't it?*

⅄

Minnus was halfway back to Surfaca in his wing, deep in contemplation over how he would begin working through the spider maps Sero had sent each week to try to "correct" the memories that were being pushed out to the Race each week. As he pondered, he noticed his cSheet flashing to show an incoming comm from Joules. The two friends hadn't seen each other much in the last month or so. Minnus had been spending more time at home, and Joules had been taken up with a new mysterious love interest. He sent Minnus a few written comms and audio messages about the lady, but the two hadn't had a verbal conversation about it. *Perhaps it's all gone wrong, and he needs a shoulder?* Minnus answered the call.

"Hey, Joules. How are you?"

"Amazing! Fantastic!" Joules's face had appeared in hologram form, projecting from Minnus's cSheet to replace the main viewing window in his wing.

The smiling face of his friend caused a miniature smile cascade onwards to Minnus. The change in his face must have been more noticeable than he'd have guessed, though, as Joules immediately picked up on it.

"Woah! And better than you, it looks like!" What's up, man? My cSheet says you're in your wing, but your face looks like you just woke up. Everything all right?"

Minnus loved the natural compassion of his long-time pal. Whatever news Joules had that'd made him feel "amazing, fantastic" had immediately evaporated from his thought and speech reel and been replaced by concern for a slightly frowning old man.

"I'm OK, mate. Just a lot happening at work that needs my attention and time right now. Just came from a meeting with Idi that's changed my direction a little. I'm still processing it. I know you'll still be watching the NV casts. What do you think about the last few weeks?"

"Seems fine to me? Pretty samey, I guess, but then again, I always think that. I love what you guys do, and I'm proud to be involved, but I've got my own life to sort out first, and I'm probably not ready to commit the way you do. I'm a passenger, I guess? As long as everyone's safe and ploughing on, I don't think about it too deeply." Joules had won the five-hundred-metre Olympic sprint titles but was still consistently self-deprecating. "What do you mean? Is there a problem with it?"

"Yeah. 'Samey.' I think that's an accurate review. Long story short, we think something's up with the memory fragments that are coming back. The algorithm you helped me create is working fine but seems to only be generating uneventful footage. Nobody at the bureau believes that Sero would've just stopped looking around at the things that interest him and started following what looks like a propaganda script on behalf of the locals on NineDee. So I've got to look into it more closely. Probably means hours and hours of manually watching and listening to Sero's memories at double speed lie in my immediate future. I'm just trying to work out a cleverer way to do it."

"Sounds like you're going to be incommunicado for a while."

"Maybe. Perhaps inspiration will strike. Anyway, I don't think you called to listen to me process. What has got you feeling 'amazing-fantastic'? I'm going to guess that she has a name?"

Joules smirked across Minnus's viewing window.

"Yes, she does! You're going to love her, Minnus. That's why I'm calling. I want to bring her around to meet you and Nombre. I think she might be the one."

"Wow. That's great," Minnus said, although he was a little unsure.

He'd heard similar pronouncements from Joules in the past, pronouncements that were followed quite quickly by separation and the heartbreak of either rejection or self-recrimination. "Tell me about her? Perhaps start with her name?"

"Maree. She's called Maree. You might even know about her already. She was an athlete too. Swimmer. Made some finals about ten years ago and set a couple of worldies in smaller competitions. Was well known because she was the fastest in the field at the time but didn't quite get it right on finals days. Doesn't matter now, anyway; she's impressively over it. Namale. Maree Namale."

The name did strike a bell for Minnus, but he couldn't bring a face to mind. He made a mental note to look her up via his cSheet once the call was over. He needed a distraction anyway to clear his mind before he dived into what would likely be a long stretch of contemplation. Meanwhile, Joules was continuing.

"Just find some photo and video coverage, Minnus. She's a bloody amazon. Two metres ten, ebony marble for skin, and stacked like a tower of tigers."

Minnus laughed at that image, imagining a gestalt of big cats writhing into the form of sculpted woman.

"And this is why she's the one? Because she ripples like a bag of twisting cats?"

Joules breezed past the joke. "Because she gets me, and I get her! When I'm with her, it's like starting from the beginning again and remembering everything via someone else. She's the same, you see? After sport, we both didn't know what was next. It's not possible to compete at the highest level after forty-five, and we've both been trying to work out how to fill our lives knowing that we've got a hundred years in front of us but no more challenges. All the women I've been with since I stopped racing, they didn't get it. They tried to fill up our lives with aspirations and alternatives, but they couldn't understand properly. With Maree, we can help each other because we both have shared experiences. Do you see? Speaking with her about her time since she stopped swimming is like speaking with me in a mirror—watching my own NV cast. She's a version of me, and I'm a version of her. By combining our stories, we get double the lifetime to learn! And I really feel like I'm learning more about myself when I try to learn about her. She says she feels the same about me. You'll see, Minnus. We just…pop!"

Minnus had often thought that Joules could be accidentally profound, but there was a sentence in his last response that had plunged the old man into a spinning wheel of rapid thinking. "It's like starting from the beginning again and remembering everything via someone else…"

*Starting from the beginning again.*

*Sero is experiencing other things beyond what we're getting out of the algorithm; we're receiving a normal volume of memory fragments with each weekly download. He's just not associating those other new memories with the colony. So what is he associating them with? Perhaps I don't need to watch everything manually; I can just set up concurrent instances of the same algorithm, each using a different seed memory as the start for a cluster? If I can find the likely candidates for alternative seed memories, I can speed up the viewing process. I can get the algorithm to "remember" everything on the audit again, but viewed through a different contextual filter. If it works, perhaps I might even be able to intertwine more than one memory cluster to form a more representative NV cast!*

"Joules, I'm thrilled for you. She sounds truly 'amazing-fantastic,' and I can't wait to meet her. Why don't you call Nombre and set it up? I'm going to head back to work and set something going that will mean I can be fully present when I meet Maree. You've just given me an idea."

The two old friends said their good-byes via a few more playful jokes and bantering smiles, and then Minnus spoke to his cSheet, directing his wing be rerouted back to Antarctica so that he could begin working on his reremembering notion.

# Thirty-Three

*Frak me! What now? How could I possibly confront a colony of this size with this kind of challenge? I'm dead!*

Sero was terrified and horrified in equal measure. After Dini had left, he'd spent the rest of the day reviewing his research notes and cross-referring them to his new universal theory of NineDee. His conclusion was that his new suspicions were likely correct and that with enough time to do the analysis, he probably already had enough data to prove it. If he'd felt able to ask NineCents a few questions, Sero even thought he could have built a proof that afternoon.

But Sero didn't feel able to ask NineCents any questions. He didn't feel able to ask *anyone* any questions. If his suspicions were correct, giving the colony any inkling that he'd deduced the reasons behind the unusual society on NineDee would likely end his life.

It seemed Sero had unknowingly spent the last six months in the midst of genocide. The death of one more visiting auditor would mean nothing to the inhabitants of NineDee. The realisation that he was likely impotent in guiding the next course of events was generating a panic in Sero that he'd never known before. Each wave of disgust was superseded by even greater horror as he extrapolated his analysis to include the impact on the Race back on Earth as people discovered what had happened here—the impact on the children of the colony if they discovered who—what—their parents really were. The layers of abhorrence were manifold.

And then there was Prid. Sero couldn't see any way to save her. He couldn't even fathom a possibility of *protecting* her. In every scenario he could imagine, she was doomed. Even more so than he.

There were some scenarios that he could imagine in which he might maintain a pretence of ignorance through to the scheduled end of the audit and only divulge his true suspicions once he'd arrived back on Earth. If he did that, he could possibly make it out of this mess whole if not entirely hale. In no scenario could he see a way to prevent Prid's death by taking her with him though. *Surely taking her with him was the only way to ensure she endured?* The knowledge that she was going to cease to exist, that all her hopes for the future were moot—had always been moot—was devastating. Even more devastating as Sero had realised immediately that she was truthfully more than an assistant or a friend. She was a surrogate for the life he'd imagined with Aleph. A young and inspired mind to which he could pass his accumulated wisdom. A soul that he might watch grow and guide. A daughter. *His* daughter. He didn't want to be an explorer any more. He wanted to be a father. Her father. And she was going to be wiped from existence. There would be no legacy for her, not even an individual remaining who truly knew her, nobody who could tell tales of her and fondly remember the experiences they'd shared or insights she'd offered. Unless Sero worked out how to save them both.

*Nothing has ever mattered really, Sero. Faced with it, you know that all your worthy hopes for contributing to the Race are vanity in comparison to this one challenge. Saving this girl. Protecting her. And you're sitting here in panic. Your life's meaning has grown upon you across the galaxy, from Aleph to Prid to this moment. And you're running from it. Despairing. What use is that? Hopelessness?*

Sero loathed himself. *Mr. Universe? Mistress to the Universe, more like.* He moved over to the floor plunge and wash area, his first visit since earlier in the day after he'd copulated so fervently with that *thing.* He looked into the polished-steel mirror at the face of a man who'd had what felt like decades of thought experience in the intervening four hours. He saw a familiar face look back out at him. It was the face of the man who'd lost himself after Aleph had died, the man who'd given up and operated on automatic pilot for months back on Earth and depressed his friends. He'd met this man before. He didn't like him.

*Come on, Novak! You know what that kind of desolation feels like. You know what it results in. And you've beaten it before. Can anything be worse than the loss of Aleph? Snap out of it, and take control!*

The internal monologue became external as Sero began repeating the words to himself in the mirror.

"Take control. Take control. Take. Con. Trol. You have something to fix and someone to protect. You have purpose. Take control!"

With the rapidity of a lighting element changing state, Sero was back on. Digitally reversed from despairing to inspired. Usefully bipolar. His mind began whirring through the options he had available to craft escape for Prid and himself. The face in the mirror changed to one of determination and mechanism. Sero made a mental image of that version of himself. This resolute man would be the self-image he'd carry with him. This unwavering resolve to guide the world around him would be his primary characteristic. This is how he'd protect her. By being intelligent and resourceful and never, ever giving up.

"Optimism and perseverance."

Sero left the mirror and returned to his bunk pod, his ego image redefined and reinforced. He perched on the edge with his legs apart and rested his elbows on his knees, adopting a Rodinian thinker's pose and listed his advantages internally.

*I want only positive thinking here, Novak. You've done all the risk assessment. Now let's give that some balance.*

*They don't know that you know what's going on. So you can play this dumb and continue as you have been. If you've got the stomach for it—the will. And you do. So, advantage number one.*

*They're all going to die if the dissolution on Leaf Day isn't a success. That's leverage. If you can manipulate that to your advantage, you have something to trade.*

*You've got power over your movements. They think that you've got to report to the Postbox at Park 359 Central once per week to prevent a new blank bubble siphoning off all the energy they need to get through to Leaf Day. You've never told them the routine exactly because there isn't one—you made it up. So they need you onside. If you decide to not "report" one day, they think a new blank bubble will be formed, and Leaf Day will be doomed. That's the second big advantage. I have something that they need. I can threaten to with-hold it. Provided they don't realise that there actually is no schedule for preventing bubble formation, and I'm really only downloading memory fragments back to Minnus for NV serialisation. They must believe that there is the chance that a second bubble might appear, or why would they send Dini to seduce me? The schedule is probably what she's tasked to discover.*

*Wait a minute! I'm downloading memories to Minnus. Why not download more than only* my *memories? We're getting somewhere now.*

Sero took Prid's journal from the table and began completing a few manual calculations using pen and the final page of the book. The first seeds of a plan had begun to sprout in his mind.

⅄

Four days of relative seclusion later, Sero approached the home quarters of the people he'd been introduced to as Divis and Sana, the parents of Prid. He'd had NineCents call ahead to explain his arrival time and ask that Prid be ready to leave with him for only the afternoon, implicitly making sure that he publically left enough of a free time window to keep his prearranged date with Dini.

He didn't know if he could trust NineCents and therefore needed to maintain a logical set of possible movements that wouldn't alert the colony computer if it had been tasked with observing him for signs that he'd had any kind of epiphany on the subject of the colony. He'd explained that he and Prid had formed a method of using each other as proxies for the Race. In some conversations, Prid would take on the role of intrigued observer; asking questions so that Sero could explain things to her but also allowing the Race to understand things through Sero as he verbalised explanations for Prid on camera footage that would be viewed on Earth in the future. Sometimes the roles were reversed, and Prid would be the one explaining details of colony life to an inexperienced Sero. Sero had offered to Divis that this methodology was a good way of allowing a wider proportion of the Race access to the details of the colony's achievements; a straightforward explanation of something given by a young girl was less threatening than a lecture delivered by a multidoctored hydrobotanist. He'd then explained that on the next trip to the Postbox, he'd like to have Prid accompany him on the walk all the way to the door so they could talk about the telonaut process on camera and in context for the benefit of the Race.

It had seemed a pretty robust explanation for his desire to have Prid come with him to the Postbox. At least at the time he'd described it. It also seemed Divis had accepted it. *Which means everyone on NineDee has accepted it.*

As he arrived at the door to the home, a familiar blue light rose through the doorway from floor to the full height of the entrance without Sero even announcing his presence. The "family" was clearly expecting him, as he'd hoped. Sero took a longer-than-normal breath and ground his teeth as he reached the doorway, steeling himself for the pantomime drama that he knew must follow. He stepped through the doorway and into the house, smiling wilfully.

A standardCam whizzed into the house ahead of him to focus on the interior. Prid was stood in the area between rooms that served as a hallway, fully dressed with candoliers loaded and two packed bags at her feet.

"Hiya!" Prid called out enthusiastically.

She stepped towards him with arms swinging upwards into a hug. Aware that he was likely being watched but equally aware that any moment with Prid might be the last they'd share, Sero returned the embrace with all his heart. He held her as long as her dared before resetting to be as businesslike as he thought his colonial hosts might have expected.

"Good to see you, young lady. You look like you're all packed up and ready to leave. You know we're not setting off back straight away though, right? We're just going to the Postbox now, and then you're coming back here for a

while." Sero was speaking in part to Prid and partly for the
benefit of any other prying ears.

"NineCents did say that, yeah, but I thought it might
be a mistake. What else are you going to do here once we're
finished in the box? Don't we need to get back to get on
with our work?"

"We do, and we will. I've just got an interview to do.
The person has requested some privacy." Sero hated lying
to Prid, but he'd already decided that he'd protect her from
the truth until the last possible moment. That meant keeping her away from Dini.

"Dini." It was a statement rather than a question.

"Yes, Dini. But don't worry, Prid. It'll only be an hour
or two, and I'll come straight back here to collect you.
Then we'll be off again."

He could read the heartache in Prid's face as she pondered over whether she was missing out on something
by being excluded. *The innocent fears of a normal teenager—in
amongst all this.* He didn't need to further explain himself,
though.

Divis entered the hallway from one of the adjoining
rooms to interrupt them. Sero knew that she'd come from
a stark recreation room. He had interviewed Divis's husband, Sana, in the house on an earlier visit and had used
the steel-furnished room as the location, padding the seats
with some of the tendril minimattresses that Prid used to
make her own space in the house more comfortable than
the tastes of her housemates allowed. He'd thought at the

time that the house was unusually barren for a family home. *Not a real family.* Sero suppressed a shudder.

"Hello, Auditor. Pridescent is fully prepared. How are you today?"

Divis was formal in tone, but Sero didn't think that made it necessarily true that there was suspicion behind the formality. He couldn't help but filter all his interactions with colonists through an instinctive wariness, though. Whether he'd taken control or not, the risk of discovery still existed, and he was nervous. He forced a less-formal response from himself, wanting to appear calm and focused only on the next task. "Hi there, Divis. I am dandy, thanks! We're over the halfway mark of the audit now, and like everyone else, I'm looking forward to Leaf Day. It's really starting to feel close, isn't it?"

"Five months away. We're really just tightening the screws now. There will be no more research until we've dissolve the tentaculos bounded by the plate, only drills and drills to mitigate any scenario we can envisage during the day itself. But yes, it is very exciting. Decades of work have been required for us to be ready for the process."

"We'll be ready," Sero used the plural with intent. "Whilst we're talking of planning, though, perhaps we need to discuss Prid's role on the day sometime soon, Divis? I'll be observing the dissolution from Gesponnen to record the moment for the Race and posterity. Do you have any notion of whether Prid might be able to accompany me?

I'd like that but don't want to interfere if you have a more integrated role planned for her."

The small-talk rigmarole was a requirement of Sero's pretence at normality. He'd figured that speaking about Leaf Day in supportive and awed notes would be wise in general and specifically looking farther into the future might reassure the colonists that he had no immediately destructive intent. Perhaps more than that, though, he felt that he needed to get the colonists to do most of the talking when he interacted with them. He was in control of his plan and fully intended to execute it, but he didn't completely trust his mouth to not betray the rational half of his brain with some kind of accidental but revelatory Tourette's-like tic.

Prid stayed quiet whilst Sero and Divis talked for a few more minutes, Divis given charge of the conversation and driving plans for both Leaf Day and more regular returns to the home for Prid. Sero could detect the intent below the subterfuge. The colonists wanted him to spend more time alone with the spy Dini in the hope that she be able to use that nuclear body to spin particles of information from him.

*That's good, though. It means they're carrying on with their own deception that Divis and Sana are really Prid's parents and have a duty of care over her. Which is further evidence that I'm not suspected, right?*

Sero maintained his pleasant attitude throughout the exchange, despite noticing Prid's unsubtle distaste for the idea of unnecessary visits to her original quarters. He also thought he detected some resentment in Prid that he'd asked Divis where she thought Prid should observe Leaf Day from rather than asking the young lady directly. *Going to be harder and harder to keep up to this pretence for five more months. At least without hurting Prid's feelings.*

Sero's resolve wavered minutely at the thought of directly causing upset for Prid. *Take control of the situation, Novak.* With an internal reminder of the stored image of his own resolute face, he was immediately back in character.

When Divis seemed satisfied with the commitments Sero had made to help Prid return home, the two-member audit team left the home quarters and headed out along the steel path towards the Postbox as usual. All three standardCams were deployed in formation, one high above them tracking progress and two orbiting the pair as they walked.

"What was that all about?" Prid asked.

"Hmmm? What?" Sero returned innocently, continuing to walk.

"That weird chit-chat back there; you were behaving like you work for her or something."

Sero gulped gently, his thoughts immediately moving to question whether Prid might not be the only one who'd noticed some tension in his conversation. He needed to manage Prid's expectations for the future, though, and so continued with his guiltless demeanour. "It's not so bad to respect the wishes of others, Prid. We all rely on each other in the end, wherever in the galaxy we are. Earth is no different; each individual is a cog interlaced with other cogs in a larger machine. Saying please and thank you, even if it's unnecessary, is just a way of smoothing the natural friction between cogs. There's no superior-inferior relationship inferred by saying please and thank you."

It was a generic bluff and didn't directly answer Prid's question, but it was also something that Sero genuinely believed, the kind of fatherly common-sense wisdom he'd hope to pass on to Prid anyway in another situation. *Hopefully the current state of affairs won't end up devaluing everything I tell Prid once she knows the truth. I'm going to need to lie to her for...*midthought, Sero was distracted by something unusual. They'd made it to Park 359 and had begun crossing the larger open space towards the platform that gave entry to the underwater bridge leading to the Postbox facility. Sero had made this walk more than two dozen times in the last six months on previous trips to download his memories and parcel them off to Earth. Something was different this time, though.

The standardCams weren't following him in their usual way. The two standardCams that would usually set up in diametric orbit around him and Prid had pulled back and were now static near the entrance to the park. Sero looked up for the third camera and found it was also retreating from its elevated oversight role, returning to join its teammates. They were all moving to stay behind, too far back to be recording the pair's movement across the park for any future broadcast. Prid had observed Sero's head movements and had now also noticed the unusual camera behaviour.

"Did you arrange for there to be no cameras?" she inquired.

"No," Sero responded gruffly, his eyes flitting across the horizon, looking for any other unfamiliar occurrences.

In his atypically anxious state, he thought he might simply be overreacting to an easily explainable situation. *Maybe the cams have a standard default position if they encounter some kind of programming anomaly? A "return to base" instruction? Perhaps... perhaps not.*

As he strained his perception to focus on the opposite side of the park, Sero spotted three silhouettes climbing the stairs to the platform that overlooked the area. One of them was definitely the form of Zwolf, hunched slightly and moving more slowly than most would've. The second was significantly bigger than the patriarch but not someone Sero recognised immediately by sight. There were several hundred bodies on site that he hadn't yet spoken with at any length, so one unfamiliar physique wasn't so unusual. He recognised the third shadowy figure instantaneously though. Dini.

The three were moving to a position between Sero and Prid and where they desperately needed to be to enact the first, most crucial part of his plan. In his assessment, the trio looked like a barrier. *How far away? Two hundred metres? Maybe two minutes at this pace? If NineCents is listening, none of it will matter anyway.* Sero made a split-second decision and began speaking very quickly.

"Prid, listen to me. We're in trouble. It's really important that you hear what I have to say before we reach the entrance to the Postbox."

"Erm, OK?" The girl hadn't grasped the urgency in his tone fully.

"Prid! I am talking about life or death. This conversation is the most important one you've had in your life up to now. Are you fraking listening?"

That did it. Prid visibly recoiled at the neck in surprise at Sero's cursing.

"Good. You need to trust me. We have less than two minutes at this pace before we reach the platform, and the slower we move, the less chance this is going to work; there'll be too many of them. So listen hard. I'm only going to be able to say this once."

For all her surprise at the sudden change of pace and solemnity in the conversation, Prid had quickly gathered herself. The look on her face was now one of deep concentration.

"No physical reactions, OK? Just walk as you're walking. Don't look back at the cameras, and don't make any extreme or surprised arm motions."

"Uh-huh."

"Everything you think you know about the adults here on NineDee is a lie. In fact, I'm not even sure we should be referring to the colony's adults in plural. Truly, there is only a single adult mind. Zwolf's."

Prid didn't understand. She kept on walking and didn't slow, but her face cycled through several similarly quizzical expressions in quick succession.

"I don't know why, but I think I've worked out how. I think that he learned how to modify the bubbling process early on in the colony's history. Remember that we reviewed the receptions at the second Postbox? Zwolf was visiting in between each new arrival to 'personally greet' them. Except he wasn't. He was checking that his mind had been copied into the new body, and he was preparing the next reception to do the same. That's why there's no chain of command. Everybody—male or female—they're all him."

Prid controlled her reaction as he'd asked, but Sero could see her mind humming behind her eyes, joining the dots and coming to the obvious horrific conclusion.

"But that would mean—"

"Yes. It does mean that. We'll talk through the parent situation later, though. Right now, we have to stay alive. I think that the only reason that I wasn't overwritten on arrival was because the Zwolfs didn't know the auditing schedule. The first time they knew I was going to arrive was when the facility received the signal and began the blank bubbling automatically. Once my copy body was complete, I think the Zwolfs had no choice but to let me begin the audit and try to assess whether there was any risk to their plan. His plan. Whatever."

"But—"

"Prid, we're going to be there within a minute. We're nearly within earshot."

"If this were true, why am I me?" Prid blurted the question out, rapid fire.

"One question only. Best guess? I think the overwriting process can only work on adult brains. Full sized, I mean. Makes some basic geometric sense, really; I'd guess that trying to fit more neuronal connections into an immature brain than the brain is sized for might alter the outcome. Maybe the resulting child-Zwolf isn't Zwolf enough? Probably that's why 'training' begins so late—why you've noticed such a change in Dini since she began her 'training.' She's not Dini any more. Look, you're going to have to decide. Right now. Do you trust me?"

The two stood still for a fleeting moment. In that pause, half a year of daily emotional human interaction crested, nascent familial longing suffusing and overcoming both of them. It was a final, silent seal to their relationship, a crescendo that became a contract. They were family now, and they both knew it and understood what it meant. Not just intellectually but at their cores—in their human souls. They would sacrifice all for each other to preserve one another. They each knew that the other individual's survival and happiness was more important to them than their own existence. They committed these assurances wordlessly, with a single cavernous inhalation each and an exchanged nod.

His heart bursting with love for his brave young adopted daughter, Sero used his last few seconds to outline the barest of plans that might give them a hope of survival and building on this dear embryonic family's beginnings.

"We have to get into the Postbox. We can work the rest out later, but we *must* gain entry. If we don't, I can't see a way out of this."

As they stepped onto the bottom slat of the metallic staircase, Sero added, "Use your cans," in a hurried whisper.

They reached the platform together. They were both calm and level, both smiling. At the summit of the stairs, the three colony bodies were positioned in a roughly equilateral triangle, Dini-Zwolf on Sero's left; Zwolf-Zwolf on Sero's right, and a huge man that Sero had never seen before behind the more familiar colonists. *Rhino-Zwolf?* The man was enormous. Perhaps two and a half metres tall and 180 kilograms. Immediately on seeing their faces, Sero knew that there would be no artful language, no fencing in verbal shadows. The Zwolf trinity had decided that the game was up, and there would be no more simulation. Zwolf-Zwolf spoke first.

"Well, at least I can stop speaking in that ridiculous accent now."

"I kud haf a try!" said Dini-Zwolf in exaggerated style, whilst Rhino-Zwolf chuckled behind them. "See ivf he kan stil be svayed?"

Sero's response was disdainful. "Frak you, Zwolf. All of you. You're a gang of fraking monsters."

*Keep them looking at me and hope Prid has some inspiration on how to use the distraction.*

It wasn't much of a hope, but he figured that the Zwolfs were more likely to underestimate Prid than him, and Sero had to work with the tools available to him in the moment. So he amplified his rant. "You're genocidal. You've killed a thousand people, stealing their bodies for who knows what reason. How many of the Race's best, exactly? Do you know?"

He began strolling around the platform, walking in short, animated circles that left him slightly closer to Dini-Zwolf with each oscillating circuit. Meanwhile, Prid had decided to play clueless.

"Sero, what are you talking about?"

She was very convincing, fixing a perplexed expression onto her face and walking backwards slowly. Sero noticed that her edging was in a direction though. She was heading towards Zwolf-Zwolf. *OK, targets set. Old man for you, young woman for me. Splendid.* Prid had hooked her thumbs under the chest sash of her can bandolier. It wasn't a posture Sero had seen her adopt before.

"Yes," said Dini-Zwolf. "And each one of them has made an enormous contribution to your Race. A step change in evolution."

Sero snorted his further contempt but continued edging ever closer to the female-bodied Zwolf. He wasn't completely sure what he would do once within arm's reach, but he knew that between the efforts of him and Prid, the trio of Zwolfs would need to be brought down long enough for him to get to the Postbox and close the door behind them.

"How did you know I'd worked it out? You sent the cameras away, and you're here with Rocksteady over there."

"You. You changed. You went to Prid before coming to me when you arrived here at the park. I've lived a long time, Mr. Novak. No man that has ever lived would wait four days for a repeat showing after the morning we spent fraking like hooked dogs. They certainly wouldn't be worried about their ward, asking a child's mother whether they might chaperone her to the prom. The Divis body agreed. So there's only one logical thing to do. If you have discovered our progress, we should talk about it."

*A little more.* Sero glanced over to Prid. They were both three metres or so away from their respective targets, Sero feigning unreasoned fury—if only slightly feigning—and Prid still looking on apparently uncomprehendingly at her mentor, reversing towards the old patriarch's static frame.

The Dini-Zwolf shim continued her speech.

"It's funny how your preferences can change, you know, once your mind takes on a different physiology, I mean. I actually thought I might enjoy prostituting this body a little more—"

Sero had closed to within two metres using his circling, pacing distraction when he threw his haymaker. He wasn't a violent man and had been in less than five fights in his life, all but one of those as a precocious child. Now, though, with the life of his adopted daughter and his own life on the line, Sero Novak, Mr. Universe, threw a dam-busting right hand that began in his left leg, twisted up through his rotating hips and shoulders to whip down his right arm at full extension and drive the nose of

Dini-Zwolf, his sexual partner of only last week, up into her face. The shim dropped like a shot goose, plummeting backwards with the grace of a slaughtered cow. The strike sent everyone else on the platform into a whirlwind of motion. Zwolf-Zwolf seemed surprised by the direct physical attack. He was initially frozen in place, likely not helped by the older physique in which he was encased, but then he began a motion to step forward and close the distance between himself and Sero. He had only made a single half step, though, before Prid was on him. She had immediately removed her can bandolier when Sero had sprung and had reversed it so that the tendril spray cans were facing inwards on the loop. Deftly, Prid then flicked a clip on the reverse side of the can holster, dropping a hammer in place on the release nozzles of four of the eight cans on the belt. The hammers held releases in place, and the cans began shooting tendril rope towards each other in the centre of the circle. All this had happened in less than a second. As Zwolf-Zwolf had begun his movement towards Sero, Prid had pounced upon his back and slipped the still-spraying tendril sash around his shoulders and chest. The spraying cans increased the volume of biomass inside the loop, pinning the patriarch's arms in place but also holding the band more firmly in place like an ever-tightening plant girdle that couldn't be easily slipped off. The momentum of Prid landing on his back as he stood on only one foot threw Zwolf-Zwolf off balance. With no arms to hold out in front of him to protect him from the fall, the physically oldest member of the Zwolf troika fell forwards hard, smashing his face into the steel platform. He was dazed momentarily but was beginning to roll over, perhaps to rise, when Sero's right boot connected with his temple at as full a sprint as the seven metres or so running start would allow. Zwolf-Zwolf didn't move again.

*Two down! Maybe we can do this.*

Sero turned back to look for Prid and was hit in the right cheek by what felt like a caber tossed from orbit. His face whipped around, and he felt shock at the force of the blow, but he managed to stay on his feet and didn't lose consciousness. His surprise meant that he didn't defend himself, though, as Rhino-Zwolf approached for a second assault. Sero realised that his arms were by his sides, and he was an open target. He felt fear as he looked at the bigger man but realised all at once that something was wrong with this fight.

*I should be lying on the floor in pieces by now. In fact, why did Gigantor over there only hit me once and then back off?*

Rhino-Zwolf was delaying, despite his size, weight, and reach advantage. *Because he's a 210-year-old scientist inside the body of another man. He's probably been in fewer fights than you. He doesn't know what he's doing.*

Just as Sero made the breakthrough in understanding, though, Rhino-Zwolf barrelled towards him, crashing his arms around Sero in a clumsy but aggressive bear hug. The momentum of the giant threw both men to the floor with Sero finishing lying facing the Rhino on his left side and being crushed in a rock-solid embrace, his arms pinned at his sides.

Whilst clearly not an experienced fighter, the big man had worked out that his strength would be all he needed from this position. He began to squeeze. From his prone station, Sero had no defence. He immediately felt the air begin to be forced from his lungs and struggled to get a breath back into them. He looked up at the eyes of the behemoth that was crushing the life from him. There was fear in those eyes too, but no pain, only the fighting response of a man who feels threatened—the bellowing instinct to kill. Sero felt his own eyes begin to close as he heard his murderer bellow again, screaming as he applied pressure to Sero's ribs. Then Sero saw Prid's face appear over Rhino-Zwolf's shoulder, a narrow can of tendril spray in her hands. She stepped over towards the struggling pair, tying the can with a second tendril as she walked.

Sero's eyes closed further as the oxygen in his head ran out, but when he opened them again, fighting sleep, he found he could breathe a little more. The Rhino had relaxed his grip. Sucking in a big breath, Sero saw why. Prid had approached Rhino-Zwolf from behind, unseen. She'd reached around and rammed the narrow can into the big man's mouth midscream. It was set to autospray, and he could see the panic in the man's face as the canister shot endless streams of tendril vine down his throat. Prid was clinging to the can as best she could from behind, trying to hold it in place, hoping to suffocate the bigger man. There was just enough give in his hold that Sero could break out, which he did—although still with some effort.

Seeing the opportunity to escape, Sero reversed the hold, whipping his arms out together and wrapping them around both his opponent and his ally, who was still flailing around on the ground behind Rhino-Zwolf, just managing to keep the still-spraying can in place. By reversing the bear hug, Sero hoped to hold down the Rhino's arms just long enough that Prid's tendril can could do enough incapacitating damage for them to get up and get away. The vine must be clogging his throat by now, reaching into his airways even, stopping him from breathing.

*Just hold on.*

Now there was definitely fear in the man's eyes as he began to choke. But the fear drove adrenaline, which drove strength. Sero felt his arm lock give way as Rhino-Zwolf panic-heaved his own arms up and out, breaking the hold. With his hands free, the giant immediately reached up to grab Prid's wrist with one hand and the can with the other. He threw both as far as he could before falling to his knees and projectile vomiting thick tendril spaghetti onto the platform below him.

Sero was already up. "Run!"

Luckily, Prid had actually landed closer to the bridge entrance than Sero, and he reached down and hauled her to her feet as he passed. "Into the Postbox! Now!"

When they made it inside, Sero gave instruction to NineCents to close the door. He wasn't sure whether the computer would obey, so he gave the highest level instruction he could—to prepare the facility for blank bubbling and postage. Once that instruction was given, the only person that could reverse it should be himself. Either because he had aborted the launch or because he had been successfully transferred to his destination and pressed the kill switch. The door shouldn't be operable from the outside. *If that doesn't work, and the Zwolfs have such a level of control over the colony computer that they can override a blank-bubble isolation instruction, then all is for nought anyway.*

Sero and Prid both slumped down on the floor, backs leant against the now-sealed exit. They didn't speak for a few minutes as they caught their breaths. When they'd recovered, it was Prid who spoke first.

"OK. OK. Three things. One, that insanity outside has me pretty convinced about your theory. But how did you know? Two, what's the plan now that we've locked ourselves in a room with no food, no water, and only one exit? Three, 'fraking like hooked dogs'?" Prid looked at him with equal humour and disgust, like any teenage daughter might look at a father who she's found out is sexually active.

Despite himself, Sero laughed gently at Prid's ability to focus on traditionally teenage preoccupations despite the deadly scenario they were embroiled in. There had been an element of gallows humour that made things more bearable when he and Minnus had spent so much time working through Sero's grief over Aleph. He found some of that spirit returning to him here in an arguably worse situation. First things first. Sero shuffled closed to Prid and put his arm around her shoulders. This was going to be a tough ten minutes.

"OK, soldier. I'll get to your questions. I'm going to tell you everything; I promise. But before that, I need to say well done. You were amazing out there. I know that was a difficult thing to accept in no time at all, but you did brilliantly. You were inventive, resolved, and fearless. I'm really proud of you. We wouldn't have made it without you."

Sero gave Prid a tighter squeeze across the span of her shoulders, and she returned the gesture with a pillow strike of her cheek on the shoulder of his enveloping arm.

"Let's start with Dini. She was your friend, after all, and probably the one whose murder you'll feel most keenly once this all settles in. I'm going to call her Dini-Zwolf from here on in, though, unless we're talking about your actual friend from before. Your actual friend is dead though, Prid. Do you understand?"

Prid nodded silently and swallowed, and Sero could tell that she did understand. He supposed it might be easier to accept the news given that since being overwritten, Dini-Zwolf had behaved like Zwolf, so an element of grieving had already happened based on the social distance that had grown between the two females.

"OK. Good girl," Sero said, giving her another hopefully reassuring sideways hug. "So, Dini-Zwolf seems to have been busy working on something related to Leaf

Day. In all likelihood what she told us about trying to save energy is true. No reason to lie about that, really. However, I think she was recalled because the Zwolfs thought that her body might be the best one to use to infiltrate our audit."

"What do you mean? Infiltrate? We're pretty open already—there's a set of cameras flying around everywhere with us."

"True. But those cameras don't know when and where we're going to go. Specifically, they don't know the schedule for me to return here to the Postbox."

*Careful now, Sero. Prid doesn't know why you come back here either. You still have to keep some secrets in case the Zwolfs try another route to protecting the energy they need for Leaf Day. Better that you're the only one who knows the full truth.*

"And they know that if I don't return here according to a specific schedule, another blank bubble might be created with another copy body of me inside to replace me. They can't afford the energy for that. Leaf Day might fail as the extra energy used in blank bubbling would push the colony over the tipping point of no return.

"I think they were looking to Dini-Zwolf to discover that schedule so that they could force me to complete it if I ever discovered what they've been doing here."

"OK. But why Dini specifically?"

"I'd spoken with Zwolf-Zwolf about Aleph. He knew I'd had a history with many women. Knew something of my character and my recent loss. I think that he saw that as a weakness to exploit.

"There's also the fact that Dini-Zwolf is a male mind inside of a beautiful female body, which means it has level of insight into how a man might want that beautiful female to behave when around him. I'm afraid men are all ultimately suckers for beautiful women, Prid. It's part of our genetic makeup. Dini-Zwolf was banking on the idea that her body might be enough of a distraction that I wouldn't question some of the inconsistencies. They were nearly right."

"Fraking like hooked dogs?"

Sero was a little embarrassed to recount the whole morning to Prid. He gave what he thought was an appropriate version instead. "That was Dini-Zwolf trying to disgust me. They'd seduced me as part of the infiltration attempt. That's why they kept arranging for there to be no cameras and no you, Prid. They wanted privacy for the seduction. It wouldn't have worked otherwise. It nearly *did* work, but by being closer to me, Dini-Zwolf opened itself up to closer observation. Ultimately, that was what helped me realise what has really been happening here."

"How? Did she accidentally tell you something?"

"Not verbally, no. It was actually a mannerism. It taps its feet absentmindedly in a certain rhythm when something is going well. I realised I'd seen and heard the rhythm before in several places—including Divis-Zwolf and Zwolf-Zwolf. Once that realisation happened, it was a short series of thought experiments cascading towards the truth. Your journal helped a lot, actually, Prid."

"My parents aren't my parents."

Sero gave a few seconds of silence to the young girl before trying to clarify, though he knew that he'd need to give her as much information as he could now. In even his best-possible scenario, Prid may not remember anything once they left the room. *May not* want *to depending on just how crazy the Zwolfs are.*

A wave of nausea passed over Sero as the possibilities sprouted like multiple mushroom clouds in his mind. What would they do in order to preserve their vision? *Take control, Novak! Affect what you can, and ignore the rest. Take control! Optimism and perseverance.*

"I think that they are very likely your biological parents. If my theory about overwriting adult spider maps onto immature brains is correct, the Zwolfs would need to continue to procreate if they were to expand and enhance the colony. They still need people, and their current bodies will all die of old age eventually. I'd guess that they have figured that the best way to develop healthy bodies and brains in the replacement generations is to raise them in family units, a solution tried and tested through millions of years of human evolution. So they form monogamous couplings to produce and raise children."

"But I don't get it. Why wouldn't they let us in on the secret? It's not like we're going anywhere off colony. What could we do?"

"Well, I think that perhaps they worry about developing normal brains and bodies. Who knows what damage might be done through self-inflicted harm by a child hearing this news that wasn't as strong as you? But I also think that there's a lot you might do to change things—if you did it together. How many people are there on NineDee who haven't yet undergone 'training'?"

"About three hundred, I think."

"Properly led, that sounds like enough for a resistance force, don't you think?"

Prid didn't answer, but she did extract herself from Sero's hug and stand up, the mention of resistance finally sparking anger inside of her. Her world had been revealed to her: murders, deceit, disgust. Her anger seemed focused, though, rather than the flailing resentment at the newly revealed world that Sero might have expected. Sero admired the brave young woman standing above him, looking up to her both literally and philosophically. Now was the hardest part, though—the remainder of his plan.

"OK. It's up to you and me. What do we do?"

"Well, I've had a few goes at thinking this through. Here's how I see it.

"We know that their primary goal is Leaf Day. We know that they can overwrite adults. I don't know how, but they can. The only reason they won't overwrite me is that the need me to prevent a new blank bubble being generated and therefore using too much energy to allow their primary goal to be achieved—which means that, at least until Leaf Day, we have some leverage. We also know that they don't overwrite immature brains. I reckon they need as much manpower as they can get, and after investing years into your growth, I don't think that they'll risk losing the investment by trying to overwrite you too early. So they might restrict our movements, but they won't wipe us."

Prid nodded slowly to show that she was following Sero's train of thought.

"We also know that they've spent a lot of time actually using the cameras to record my audit. I'm guessing that means an element of pride in what they've built here. I think they actually *want* to send the footage back to Earth. I think they want the Race to see it. But they must know that if the Race truly understood that there'd been a genocide on NineDee, there'd be a response. Even if that response was years in coming and required the launch of hundreds more quantum-linked kill switches and nanoBots to create new reception facilities so that the Race could send a police force up here to correct the problem. The response would happen. So they must be intending to send the footage back along with me.

"Clearly, if their plan is to work, I can't arrive back on Earth. I'd just correct the Race's interpretation of the audit footage immediately."

*Not to mention that if Minnus's new tech works, the Race will have already seen all of this through my eyes before I arrive.*

"So that means I will likely be overwritten sometime after Leaf Day but before the scheduled end of the audit and my return to Earth."

Prid had begun pacing in slow circles as she listened but was still nodding her understanding.

"So, my original plan was to keep running the audit as normal but find a way to get you into Postbox one and me into Postbox two at the same time. If we activated the blank bubbling for postage to Earth, nobody could interfere. Our signals would be queued back at Earth, as there's only a single reception Postbox there, but it would work.

"Setting aside the complexity of getting us both into separate Postboxes at the same time, the problem would be that if we did this before Leaf Day, we'd be abandoning the colony, including the three hundred innocent kids that live here. This means we would have had to maintain the charade until after Leaf Day and hope that I wasn't wiped immediately. We'd have had to look for a window to post ourselves back to Earth after Leaf Day but before the scheduled end of the audit."

"None of that will work now, Sero. They know that we know."

"Yeah. Once I realised that they'd decided to break the charade, it did cross my mind to get you in here and post you back to Earth immediately. I'd starve in this room, locked in after the blank bubble formed, but you'd be safe."

"And we'd have condemned those same three hundred innocent children to death."

Sero nodded grimly. "So, plan B. This one is even tougher. When we've finished this conversation, we're both going to take spider maps of our minds as they are now and store your DNA coding too. Mine is already well known. I'm going to try hide the information in the next signal that is sent back to Earth. Then we're relying on my friend Minnus to work out what has happened and make a plan to revive us.

"This will be difficult. We won't be in a blank bubble here, as we'll never have been posted. Only the Sero-Zwolf will be posted. So there'll be no body built for either of us. Who knows what will happen in the intervening years?"

"That's not much of a plan, Sero."

"It's the best one we have right now. If we do this, we can step out of the door with at least some backup and then try to negotiate or trick our way back to plan A between now and Leaf Day. If I'm right, and the Zwolfs do want to send a record of their 'glory' back to Earth, they'll have to let us out into the wider colony to show continuation in the audit footage. There might be a way to control where we go and what we do to move things to our advantage."

Prid looked thoughtful but only momentarily. "OK. So, you're probably going to die inside the next six months, and I'm almost certainly going to be dead inside a few years. Our best hope is to wake up possibly decades from now in new bodies in a different place with no memory of anything that happens beyond ten minutes hence, although there's a slightly slimmer chance that we might be beaten and tortured for six months before escaping to wake up years hence somewhere else. At which time we *will* remember the torture and beatings. Have I got it about right?"

*Gallows humour again. How I love this tough young girl.*

"Yes, Prid, you've got that pretty much bang on the nose."

"What are we waiting for?"

# Minus Three

She's never going to leave him, is she? Not now. Not with a child to consider. Ugggh. The thought of her allowing Zwolf inside her makes me sick. I should be inside of her. I already understand her emotionally so much more than he. I should understand her physically too. Yet here we are. She's pregnant, with Zwolf's child. Not mine.

Oh, for a minute to be in his boots! If I could just have her look at me once in the same way she looks at him, misguided though she is, to feel her love. I have earned it, haven't I? All those hours spent together. The assessment process for colony selection, staying chaste for so long and waiting for her feelings to catch up with mine. Then betrayed by that usurper Zwolf. It won't stand.

I will not allow it.

*I saw the coils and springs of love and the altera-
tions of death, saw the Aleph from everywhere
at once, saw the earth in the Aleph, and the
Aleph once more in the earth and the earth in
the Aleph, saw my face and my viscera, saw your
face, and I felt dizzy, and I wept, because my
eyes had seen that secret, hypothetical object whose
name has been usurped by men but which no
man has ever truly looked upon: the inconceivable
universe.*

Jorge Luis Borges, *The Aleph*

# MINUS TWO

**P**oint-to-point surface postage. That's the answer.

If I plan this correctly, I can make it work. What do I need?

A single hard line for the kill switch. I'll have to run it across the surface of the colony, but the computer can help with that.

I'll need to copy myself into the reception box via spider map too. Have to do that in advance and modify the programming at site B to boot. Make it splice my spider map with Zwolf's copy body.

The rest is just timing, I think? I need to do this as soon as the latest blank bubble is complete. As soon as the next colonist steps out of that facility, the signal from site A needs to be the next in queue for bubbling. Otherwise we'll be missed, and I won't be around to talk them through it.

I need to say good-bye to this body too. There's no way of doing this and keeping it alive. If I'm not in the Postbox when he bubbles, then he won't go through with it.

It will be worth it, though. When I step through the door as her husband, her lover.

Whatever shell I happen to be in.

# Thirty-Four

"**H**e's being tortured, Idi." There was no other way to say it. Minnus could scarcely force the words from his mouth. He couldn't convey the sense of revulsion that he felt. He didn't have the eloquence. Instead, he simply slid the NV headset across the table and gestured for Johnson to put it on.

Minnus had already hard loaded a sequence into it for Johnson to see. The sequence showed that the sapienCam, Sero in this case, was tied to a steel chair in a darkened room. Several big men took turns to beat him in sequence—on the thighs, on the upper arms, around his kidneys. Never on the face or forearms though. Preserving his looks; hiding the cruelty from customary sight. The sounds in the NV footage were particularly distressing. Dull thumps followed by groans, whimpers, and wheezes. After a few minutes, the view changed automatically to a memory of Sero's young assistant Prid being paraded up and down in front of him. Uninjured but naked and clearly being manipulated into displaying herself. Sero could be heard throwing up on the NV footage.

The final cut was to a sequence where Sero explained the reason for his capture to Prid. A split-second decision, it seemed, as his enemies closed in. The conversation was broken by a fight at the entrance to the Postbox on NineDee. Sero and Prid barely made it through to the safety of the facility, and then the telonaut lead auditor continued explaining the terrible situation to Prid.

Johnson sat in silence as he experienced the footage, which was just over fifteen minutes long. When it was complete, he removed the NV carefully and laid it on the desk in front of him.

"That is awful, Minnus. I really don't know what to say. I'm so sorry for Sero and for you."

Minnus nodded grimly. He had no idea what would happen next on NineDee. He'd first seen this footage late the previous evening. He hadn't slept since, and now, having been awake for thirty hours, he was starting to feel noticeably muddled. He'd watched Sero's summary assessment for Prid a dozen times in that space of time, though. He shared his friend's assessment of the situation. There was little hope that Sero would be returning to Earth hearty and hale in three months' time. The best outcome that they could hope for would be to secure a change in the law that would allow Telospace to build a new body for his friend and map on the mind that had been received three months ago as part of Sero's back-up plan. At least then his friend wouldn't remember the torture.

"How did you find it?"

"Huh?"

Minnus thought this was a strange question to ask. He wanted to talk about when they were going to announce things to the Race so that they could begin a campaign to secure the authority to create new bodies for Sero and Prid. Using the NV sets to distribute some of the horrible memories would likely be the best way to generate support, Minnus thought.

"Erm, seed memories. I used the same algorithm we've always been using but altered the seed memory on each occasion. Then I looked at the length of the NV footage that was generated by each different seed memory. I figured that there might be some overlap, but by sorting by memory volume, we'd be more likely to fill in the gaps that weren't being shown to us in the first cut NV that we've been broadcasting. I was right. Everything you just experienced came from the highest-volume NV package by hours."

"Perhaps not the time for compliments, Minnus, but you're a brilliant man," Johnson said.

There was something reluctant in his voice though. *Like a police officer who knows he's about to give bad news?*

"What was the seed memory?"

"Aleph. I used the same memory that I had been working with in the original algorithm design. The one that gave us the NV-edited version of the Rigil audit as proof of concept. Do you remember?"

A nod came from Johnson.

Still not reacting the way Minnus might have expected. When the news of the situation on NineDee got out, Johnson's aspirations of becoming a GeoRep were going to take a serious knock. *Why is he so calm?* "I think it might be the way Sero has processed the whole thing. In his mind, there was the plain subject of the audit: cold, clinical data gathering about Leaf Day. Separately, over time, he was processing a second subject—family. The seed memory of Aleph is about family. I think because of the threat to Prid, he's associating all the horrid events that are not just facts and figures with the love he felt for Aleph and with her loss.

"There are some parallels, although not absolute. It gives us some insight into how the brain works, actually. But enough of this; we need to get this new information out to the Race.

"I can only see one option now, really. I think we have to disclose everything and then wait to see what happened at the end of the audit. As long as we keep getting weekly memory fragments, we can observe progress. If and when a final postage signal arrives at the end of the audit, we can decide what to do about it. Legally, I mean, depending on who or what is in the signal.

"Most importantly, we need to start a campaign to change the law and allow Sero and Prid to have new bodies built back here on Earth, just in case Sero's mind doesn't accompany the final signal back here to Earth. I've reviewed the packages he sent after that fight you just NVd, and the data *is* there. We could do it if we could get the energy and Red allocations. And if it weren't illegal, of course."

Johnson leant back from the desk and pushed the NV set even further away from him, back towards Minnus. He made a pointed temple of his hands, joining the fingers of opposite hands together to form a spire, his elbows resting on the arms of his plastiche chair. He was silent for a long time. Perhaps ten seconds of consideration. "We're not going to do that, Minnus."

"What do you mean?"

"We're not going to disclose just now."

"What?"

"We're not going to disclose. Yet," Johnson repeated his intent.

"What are you talking about? Didn't you just see that NV footage! A madman has murdered hundreds of people on a Race colony. He's torturing others!"

"Sero isn't *being* tortured, Minnus. He has *been* tortured. All this took place over eight years ago in another part of the galaxy. We're just retro voyeurs, looking back through time. We can't help him. We can't help any of them. You know this better than me. We're just passengers here. Whether we get the real Sero back or not now is not something we can affect. The signal either has been sent from NineDee, or it hasn't; it's either in transit here, or it isn't; it either contains Sero's mind, or it doesn't. Whatever scenario is true, it's inevitable at this point. Announcing all this now in an unplanned way might have unintended consequences."

"You are out of your fraking mind!"

Johnson looked at Minnus distastefully. "I understand you're grieving here, Minnus. Sero is your oldest friend. To watch that footage was harrowing for me. For you, it must have been near torture itself. But I'm not crazy. I'm the one most likely to be rational in this room—most likely to think of the Race as a whole."

Minnus's fury was building. He hadn't expected even an iota of challenge to his plan to rebuild Sero and Prid once he'd showed Johnson the NV footage. He was shocked and outraged. Something struck him about Johnson's statement, though. He *was* grieving. And he hadn't slept for a long time. The kernel of doubt about his own ability to reason was enough to curtail his fury slightly. "Go on," he said though clenched jaw.

"I think you're right. We should be making plans to try to change the law so that we can legally build Sero and Prid new bodies here on Earth. Based on what you just showed me, it seems that neither of them will be relativistically alive by this point. The only chance they have to live is probably to build them copy bodies. So the question becomes, 'What is the best way to do that?' Think about it, Minnus.

"This is not an insignificant change in the law. We're talking about allowing the birthing of humans directly from a bubble—not a transport, a *construction* of a human. That is illegal for a reason. From that point, it's a slippery slope down into genetic design. We've set the Race above other animals in law in that we don't allow construction of human beings. You created animals yourself as a child as part of Sero's father's business. You've told me about it. Won Novak could make a living from that business exactly because you owned the creatures that you created. We don't treat humans the same way so as to protect against the charge that one human could claim ownership of another. It is a heavily guarded and emotionally loaded piece of legislation. To reverse or even modify it will take a very careful campaign and will need some very senior WorldGov support. Right now, we don't have that—"

"But we could. We could have you."

Despite the logic of Johnson's argument, Minnus found it hard to keep the distrust out of his voice. It didn't matter that Johnson might be right. Johnson wasn't making an argument because he was motivated to save Sero. He was making a conveniently aligned argument for maintaining his trajectory towards WorldGov.

"Yes, but only if I'm successfully elected. Breen is going to go public with her retirement announcement and succession recommendation next week. If we broadcast in-head NV footage of a man being beaten before then, who knows what the consequences might be? We could end up with no chance of influencing the Race to save Sero at all. Given how dull the NV is that we're broadcasting now, it's already a closer thing than I might have liked. I'm not sure our chances will stand any more uncertainty."

*"Our." A contractual agreement specifically loaded into a single word.*

The machiavellian telospace bureau head sat passively in front of Minnus, his case made. Minnus knew that he would have to acquiesce. He knew that he'd have to agree to stay quiet until the election was over at least, whether Johnson won or lost. But he was not going to just sit idly by and wait for the future of his friend to be decided by fate and politicians. He was going to do something. He had to.

"OK, Idi. You already know your case is solid. I'll wait. But I won't wait idly. I'm going straight from this room to the editing suite, and I'm going to begin reviewing all the edits again. I'm going to find the very best sets of footage to demonstrate the specifics of our case, and I'm going to have it ready for the moment you're elected. I want this discovery to go public at the same time as your confirmation."

Minnus spoke clearly and forcefully, fatigue and emotions driving his urgency, his need to be actively engaged in doing something to help his friend.

His boss's reaction was less animated. Johnson returned to his thoughtful reclined pose, arms forming a church of consideration in front of him. Another ten seconds or so. "No. I think you need to take a break from work here, Minnus. Separate yourself from the stress of this situation. I want you to go home to Nombre. You can come back in after the election in a few months' time. There'll still be a few days until the blank bubble process should finish for Sero's return reception, assuming that whatever happens still happens according to the original schedule."

"No. Fraking. Way."

"Minnus, be careful, please. I'm your ally here. There's no need for us to weaken our relationship. We have too much to do together! Respect my wishes in this."

"I will not sit by and rely on the machinations of WorldGov to save my friend!" Minnus was shouting now. "Sero is more than a friend to me, Idi. We grew up together, but the time he's spent in transit means I've experienced so many more years of life than him. When he came back from Rigil, he was traumatised. The time I spent with him, bringing him back to society, it taught me something. I haven't been to half a dozen worlds. I haven't experience teleportation, but I *have* experienced more emotional life than Sero. I've married, had children and grandchildren. I've grown emotionally in a way that he is only just beginning to. He's not just my friend anymore; he's a target for me pass my emotional wisdom on to. He's a younger man with the chance to live and learn that all of us should have by right as members of the Race. He's as much a son to me now as a friend. I. Will. Not. Be. Idle!"

Johnson sighed. He didn't seem exasperated but reluctant to do something that he knew he must. He stood and walked to the door of his office, opening it with a word before standing adjacent to the exit. "Minnus, I'm very sorry, but you're fired."

# THIRTY-FIVE

*Four months. Four months of being beaten and demeaned by night and performing like a circus animal by day, jumping through his hoops. No window of opportunity. Not even one. And I am a pitiable, worthless fool.*

Sero was weak. His assumptions about how the Zwolfs would handle the situation had been largely correct, but his assumptions about how he would handle incarceration had not.

He hadn't anticipated such physical and psychological brutality. Four months had passed since he had left the Postbox with Prid. His speculative hopes of turning some serendipitous situation to his advantage had been spent, like air leaking from a slow puncture in a child's balloon. For every night of those four months, Sero had been held prisoner, the Zwolfs holding a joke audit with the standard cameras each day before moving him back to this steel cell and trying to beat a confession on the timings of the contact sequences that needed to be made to prevent a new blank bubble forming.

During the daytime masquerade for the cameras, Sero and Prid had been vastly outnumbered. They were briefed each morning on exactly what would happen and what was expected of them. Every briefing finished with a threat to kill Prid if the Zwolfs' expectations weren't met. Whilst Sero didn't think that the Zwolfs would actually carry that threat out due to Prid's value as a future host body, he couldn't take the chance. There are some things that a man doesn't gamble with, no matter his assessment. The life of a child wasn't a viable stake with which Sero would test fortune—especially a child whom he cared deeply for as an adopted daughter.

So whilst there had been slight windows where he had thought that he might've been able to make a break for it, he hadn't devised any way in which he could break both himself and Prid free of the Zwolf overwatch, whether planned or impromptu. Everything would require too much synchronised spontaneity. There'd been chances to jump from halos and try to sprint away on foot, the guard units being smaller whilst in transit as each halo could only berth a small number of heads. But Sero hadn't taken action.

The Zwolf-culture was also still displaying confidence in their plans. One day, they had taken Sero and Prid to a more remote section of the plate than Sero might have guessed they would. Their pride had given another opportunity as Sero had been delivering his prepared lines in the staged interview with Dini-Zwolf over her energy conservation work. With a knock to her head and a deft bit of vineseiling, Sero might have been able to rappel down to the tentaculos and the foot of the plate. He'd never seen any of the Zwolf-culture vineseil other than Prid, and he guessed that he might've gained a large head start whilst they worked out how to get down to retrieve him. But he hadn't taken action. He hadn't found a way to signal Prid as to his exact intentions. Without a coordinated stroke, Sero felt that the chances of them both getting away were too low to gamble the possibility.

Whereas his hopes for daytime escape had ebbed away in frustration, Sero's belief in his personal will and strength to endure at *all* had dwindled by night. His only nocturnal contact for the first two months had been with large, physically strong, male versions of Zwolf barking about the need to "avoid the replacement protocol" as they pummelled him. Of course, Sero couldn't divulge any schedule to them because there was no such thing.

When they'd realised that they couldn't beat answers from him, thinking perhaps that Sero possessed some kind of Sisyphean brutality endurance, they had begun to leverage Prid in an even more abhorrent way than threatening her life. For the last eight weeks, they'd been parading young Prid naked in front of him in his cell, one Giganto-Zwolf prodding her forward whilst a second held Sero's head forward and eyes open, whispering about what they'd done to her body the previous night and what they were going to do again that night if he didn't give them the schedule. The escalation to involve Prid was much worse than the beatings, and Sero knew that the Zwolf-culture could tell that they were making progress. Logically, he didn't believe what they were saying. His reading of the situation was still that protecting Prid's fragile young mind and body would be a great concern for the Zwolfs, knowing that their mind would one day inhabit her. But after months of cruelty, Sero's rationality was depleted. His reserves of will had been consumed through the effort of spending every day scanning for opportunities to escape and every night retreating inside of himself as a method of withstanding the anguish he felt at her situation.

His reactions had become emotional. As Prid was paraded in front of him, he'd sob and then be furious and strain at his chains, ranting at his captors. For two months, he'd been unable to honestly "break" for them to stop the torment; he couldn't give them what they wanted. But the previous evening, the door to his cell had been left open, and he had caught sight of Prid sobbing too. The image of her swollen, red face puffed up with despair and grief together with the gentle whimpering sounds of her despondency had combined to send Sero over the edge of an emotive cliff. His tears collapsed into anguished wails from which he couldn't escape. He'd shaken and yowled until his tormentors had finally given up on their policy of only beating him on skin that could be hidden from camera during the day. Out of frustration, one of the gigantic

Zwolfs had struck him so hard in the temple that he's been knocked unconscious instantly. The regular beat-Zwolfs had become very good at delivering painful, accurate blows. Trial and error was a good teacher of violence, it seemed, when there was enough time and a static enough living target upon which to practice.

When he'd awoken, Sero had no longer felt compelled to scream and instead had sat chained to his chair in silence until morning, when a Zwolf had arrived to treat his bruised face. That had been the same day. They'd cleaned and then powdered his face so to mask the purpling on the side of his head before taking him out to read his script for the camera session's performance. Now he was back in his cell again, force-fed and watered and dreading a repeat of his shaming.

He didn't look up as the light in the cell changed, which always happened when the door was raised.

*Three more big brutes coming to talk about fraking your daughter. Why waste time lifting your head? Politeness? Frak off.*

"I think it's about time that you and I have a proper chat. Off camera, I mean."

The voice was that of the man Sero had previously known as the colony patriarch but who he know thought of as the double-barrelled Zwolf: Zwolf-Zwolf. The change in routine was enough to motivate Sero to at least lift his head. The old man that he saw when he did so was still dressed more theatrically than his Zwolf comrades, still playing the role of an elder statesman, even without cameras to observe him. His voice was different, though. No Eurasian accent. No colloquial pronunciation. Despite his situation, Sero's investigative instincts took over, and for a flash, he found himself theorising about why the old madman might fake an accent, whichever way around that fraud might run. A crooked smile from his adversary jerked him back into the moment, though, and he shut off the thought, simply staring at the Zwolf-Zwolf in silence instead.

"I have to say, I much admire your resilience. We've worked quite hard on loosening your tongue. Much harder than I might have expected would be necessary."

Sero continued his mute gaze. Whilst he knew that there was really no difference between the individuals in the Zwolf-culture, as they all had the same mind and memories to the point that they were copied into their current body, Sero harboured more resentment towards this individual version. As the oldest and original Zwolf, Sero couldn't help but see it as a leader and therefore more guilty than even those bodies that had beaten him so badly and tortured poor Prid over recent months.

*If there's a progenitor of evil here, a maleficent queen bee, this thing standing here in front of me is it.*

"I don't think that you're ever going to give us your schedule. I think we may have developed a stalemate—an impasse of situations, at least for now."

Sero still glared at the old man in baleful hatred, wishing he could leap from his chair and do his oppressor harm. Sero wouldn't speak to him unless he'd been was fully broken, unable to summon the will to disobey. It was as though the appearance of the seed of evil here in his cell represented some kind of victory for Sero. The change in approach had suddenly increased Sero's resolve, precisely at the time he'd felt broken. If Prid had been ushered into the room rather than Zwolf-Zwolf, and he'd seen her eyes again, Sero thought that he might have given in and told his captors the whole truth in the hope of some leniency for her.

*But that would have been them winning. The fact that they've changed things, that this old frak is here in front of you, well, that means that you're winning, Novak. You, not them—you!*

"There are really only two things we can do to you to coerce you into telling us what we want. We can threaten and then hurt you, or we can threaten and then hurt people close to you. You've managed to make both of these options a little toothless by withstanding both our physical and... psychological persuasion. I think you have worked out that we'd be loath to improve young Ms. Pridescent earlier than is medically advisable and that we're even more loath to simply kill her in revenge for your noncooperation. These new bodies take literally years of effort from our little team.

"So you figure you just have to hold on until some kind of opportunity arises that you can manoeuvre to your advantage. As long as you're both alive, there's always hope, right?"

*Condescending old bastard.*

"But in order to stay alive, you have to maintain your only bargaining chip. You have to withhold your expected schedule for manipulating the kill switch. Your threat of automatic initiation of another blank bubble intimidates our entire civilisation; such is the tight timing we've created for our journey to energy and food independence here. You've proven that you understand that this is your only leverage, and you've also proven that you're able to withstand everything we can throw at you to protect it. See? Impasse."

Zwolf-Zwolf began pointing and wagging his right index finger at Sero as a Race curricula teacher might to an inattentive student. "But you see, Mr. Novak. It's only an impasse if we don't both start prioritising. I've come to explain some of the prioritising we've done and make you one final offer before we take this to the next level. If you're the sensible, loving man I think you are, then the next level of this process won't be necessary."

Sero's resolve was dented by the confidence in the tyrant's eyes. *What more can he do? Is he really going to kill Prid? He's made the threat so many times; what does he think saying it again will change? It must be something else.* The old man stood in his own patch of silence and appraised Sero as though he could look into the telonaut auditor's mind itself and see the spinning wheels that were frantically trying to power his traumatised psyche to divine what it was that he might still be vulnerable to.

"I'm going to make her frak you." Zwolf-Zwolf's matter-of-fact delivery was faultless, a nailed dismount from a difficult vault, an awakening slap from hysteria. *Practiced. Deliberate. Intended to shock.* "I've decided to sacrifice some efficiency by improving her body a couple of years earlier than our previous history suggests is optimum. It'll likely create a weak hybrid. An incomplete version of my mind inside too confined a space. But it will be functional enough to carry out my intent. Not only will her mind be gone from this realm, but her body will become mine to use, and I will use it to break you. I will abuse it to break you. And you will help me do it. Do you understand?"

Had he been able to stand rather than tied to his chair, Sero felt certain he'd have been able to improve on the haymaker he'd used to fell Dini-Zwolf outside the Postbox. The hatred he held in his heart for the leering man opposite him would surely amplify the power in his fists. *This fraker is stupid, Sero. He's spent too much time alone with himself. He hasn't thought this all the way through at all. But you have.*

Sitting in isolation, Sero had long ago worked out the impasse, but his conclusions were not the same as Zwolf-Zwolf's. For the first time in many weeks, Sero smiled. "You are an idiot. How extraordinary that fate would have such a moron made capable of replicating versions of his mind. You've literally dragged down the intelligence distribution of an entire planet singlehandedly by making the entire population as dumb as you."

Sero let his barb sink in, enjoying the chance to strike what he felt were probably meaningful blows upon the ego of the author of NineDee's horrific, genocidal monoculture.

"Sure, there's an impasse, but you're understanding things poorly. The impasse is precisely *because* Prid and I are alive. You were right in judging that you can hurt me by hurting her. But you were more right than you seem to understand in judging that we will both endure whilst there's hope of us making it out of here together. Don't you see? If you take her away from me—kill or mutilate my *daughter*, end all hopes of recovery or rescue—then I'll have no need to persist in fighting you or preserving myself. You stupid frak! You can't escalate your threat level to be even more grotesque and think I'll break and give you what you want. By escalating, you'll only get escalation back.

"Look into my eyes. If you hurt Prid, I will suicide. All I need to do is simply not return to the Postbox at the allotted time. A new me will be built, and the energy required by that process will destroy your entire civilisation. No questions will be asked. There will be no opportunity for intervention and negotiation. You will all die with me. And I won't care in the slightest. There is *nothing* more important to me now than family. And Prid is my family. Do you understand? Nothing!"

Sero spat the last words out with venom, hoping that the forcefulness of his performance might hide the lie that he felt was obvious.

*Will this megalomaniac realise that I'm not morally capable of dooming three hundred children by my own inaction? Does he even still believe that there is a "replacement protocol"? Your entire threat is a bluff, Novak! He could just murder you here and now. As far as he's concerned, the Race would never know what happened to you, and he could make up whatever story he wanted once some new auditor arrived in sixteen or seventeen years' time. If he doesn't believe your story about automatic replacement anymore or even is just more willing to gamble that it's not true than he's previously been, given how he's observed you in the last months, then he'll win. Your only way to persevere is to give him enough belief that the potential losses are catastrophic for him. Make it so that he dare not take that risk. Make him believe.*

Sero and Zwolf-Zwolf stared each other down, each reading the other man. Sero desperately fought to keep the internal doubts in his heart from advertising their presence on his face. Retaining control in his dilapidated state was stretching his remaining will to the limit. In contrast, the patriarch's face showed no sign of what was occurring inside the mind it represented. The two men held the glaring contest, Sero becoming increasingly nervous as time passed but unwilling to break gaze with his opponent. Then Zwolf turned his head and stood more fully upright.

"Daughter, eh? I think we might need to return to that. But I think we have the makings of a balanced arrangement here. We will not execute our threats. You will not execute yours. *We* will police this arrangement by not allowing you the window of escape you seek."

"And how am I to police my half of the arrangement? I need to know that Prid is Prid and that she is well. She has been through enough already with your disgusting efforts to break my will. This conversation has made me realise that I'm willing to punish your entire planet of arseholes if I think for even a minute that you've treated her badly from this point forward."

*Make him believe, Sero. You've got him on the run. Push. This could be the start of turning things to your advantage. This could be a way in.*

The patriarch's body looked contemplative for a few seconds before responding. "You may speak to her for five minutes each evening on return from the audit processes. However, I will be present for each meeting. This should be no problem, as wherever we are, whichever cell you are restricted to at the end of each day, I will be with you. I will be accompanying you every day from now until the end of the audit. I wish to be present as we record what will become the image of our achievements in the eyes of the Race."

"Agreed," said Sero, trying to prevent the elation he felt inside from seeping into his speech. As Zwolf-Zwolf left the room, Sero added a thrown chaser to the conversation. *One for the road?* "Perhaps you and I can talk afterwards too then? About how this all started? Maybe you can make me understand?"

Zwolf-Zwolf said nothing and simply left the room.

*A long shot, Novak, but this has already been the most successful day in months. Keep firing!*

# THIRTY-SIX

"**I don't trust him**, Nombre. He might never let me back in.
We need some insurance in case he tries to bury this."

Minnus, Joules, and Nombre were seated around the
largest table in the Mbeki home. Minnus had called both
his wife and his friend on the flight back from Telospace,
asking that they be at the house when he made it back.
Fortunately, they were both in the area and so had made it
back before him. In the previous hour or so, Minnus had
recounted the whole tale; including letting them watch the
edited NV that he still had stored on his cSheet. Whilst
he couldn't broadcast to the whole Race without access to
Telospace and the equipment he'd set up there, he could
still manually hard load a data set from his cSheet to their
home NV sets.

He had thought about trying to disperse the footage virally but knew that Telospace would just pronounce the footage a malicious fake and move on if he did. Johnson might

even leverage it to his advantage by portraying himself and his project as strong in the face of unwarranted attack. He also still held out some hope that his agreement with Johnson would be productive and that the Telospace head really would help Sero if elected as a GeoRep. He couldn't burn those bridges yet. But he did need a second plan, something to fall back on if his suspicions about Johnson were proved correct, and, once a GeoRep, Minnus's ex-boss simply walked away from the problem. So here he was, asking those closest to him for help and advice.

"Geez, Minnus," Joules said. "It's rancid, man. This Zwolf guy is sick in the face!"

"Yeah," said Minnus.

Nombre was more considerate than Joules, however. She'd processed Minnus's actual statement, whereas the athlete was still only processing the NV experience he'd just had. "What kind of insurance?"

"The way I see it, we need a way to make sure that he has to confront it. Something that makes him stick to the plan of at the very least campaigning to change the bubble laws."

Minnus had run through a few options in his mind on the way home, but he was so tired and emotional that he'd not been able to form much in the way of coherent strategy.

"I'm not sure what that would be, though. Maybe we could virally release the NV footage we have, and I could make an announcement in support of its authenticity?"

"I don't think that would work, darling. Assuming bad intent on Johnson's part, I mean. In the scenario we're talking about, you'd be setting yourself up in opposition to a GeoRep—your word against his. I'm sure you'd convince some people, but wouldn't you run the risk of ending up a fringe group like the Daisies? Sitting on the outside, throwing stones at the big house?"

"The fact that he got shot of you this evening means he can also pitch you as a trouble-making disgruntled former employee drone," added Joules, catching up with the conversation.

"You need something that carries the weight of authenticity. Independent of you, Minnus." Nombre had a look of deep thought on her face.

"What I need is for him to just go through with the plan."

"That's actually where my mind was headed, dear. Do you have anyone inside Telospace that you could trust to make a broadcast on your behalf? From Telospace itself, I mean. If an NV cast went out from the proper facility, it would certainly be hard to explain for Johnson. He'd have to confront the issue, wouldn't he? That's as far as we need to take it. Once the truth is out there, it would seem to me that Johnson's options become limited. He kind of *has* to go through with your agreement to campaign for a law change. If he doesn't, he'll look weak. Not to mention that there'll be valid questions about his competence to represent any geography if we manage to make it known that he was aware of genocide and didn't share it with the Race immediately."

Minnus thought about it. Was there anyone who would do this for him? Anyone who he was close enough to that they might risk opposing Johnson? He realised that there wasn't. He'd treated his work at Telospace as a mission, not a lifestyle. He came home to Nombre, lived his emotional life outside of his vocation. He was proud of his work and still felt it had moved the Race forward in a worthwhile way, but he didn't use his work as a catalyst for the formation of meaningful emotional relationships. He had enough of those in his life already. *Have I been closed off to new friendships?* Either way, he didn't think there was anyone he could reach out to with something as serious as this. "No. I don't think so."

The three sat in silence for a minute. All considering. Joules had slumped forward so that his torso and chin were resting on the table in front of him. Minnus's fatigue was beginning to overwhelm him, and he was considering adopting a more relaxed position himself when he noticed Joules's eyes open wide. *Alarm? Realisation?*

"What is it, Joules?"

"Maybe we don't need someone on the inside. Maybe we just need to get on the inside ourselves. People have gotten in there before. Amateurs. They didn't even know the facility like we do."

Minnus and Nombre were silent.

"I'm just sayin'. If it's important that we get in there to make the broadcast, maybe it's worth speaking to the people who were able to get the tools to get the job done last time."

Minnus looked at his friend and then across at his wife. He found himself thinking about his life as he did so, recalling a conversation with Nombre from a few months earlier about whether he truly lived according to his principles in times of great stress. Joules's suggestion that they ally with a group that diametrically opposed those principles in order to save Minnus's friend pushed a whiplash of déjà vu through his chest. *What do I really believe? Can I work with those people? The very people that had endangered my family and friends before—the people with such a detestable deficit of logic and empathy?*

He knew the answer before he'd even ordered the thought in his head. Of course he could. Minnus had meant what he'd said in Johnson's office about Sero being as much a son as a friend now, although he hadn't known that the words were true until they fell from his lips. Still, they were true. He'd do anything to allow Sero the chance to grow and experience love the way he himself had. He wanted to see him become the fullest version on himself; leave behind a singular existence focused on an ideology and instead live as a loving and loved man. *Live!*

Minnus knew what he had to do next. He had three months to make it happen.

# Thirty-Seven

They entered the cell almost together. Prid was just in front of Sero as he'd taken a position to separate her from the older Zwolf-Zwolf that was following them as chaperone. A small thing, but Sero couldn't help himself from taking every step possible to protect her. She'd been through so much.

The cameras had left them five minutes previously, and they'd just been subjected to the same nightly body search Sero had endured on every evening of the previous 120. The Zwolfs were very careful. With the rigmarole completed, Sero could now converse properly with Prid for the first time in months, and his eyes were already filling with tears.

Although he'd thought about nothing else in the previous twenty-four hours, he still had doubts about the best way to proceed. He desperately wanted to hold her reassuringly and tell her that he was going to find a way out of their situation. He wanted to comfort her. Who knew the emotional consequences of what she'd been through though? Who could predict how physical contact might make her feel? Especially from a father figure that she'd been forced to parade around nude for. She was fifteen years old, and she'd been made into a victim.

Rather than go with his gut, Sero had decided to be more controlled. He wouldn't run to her. He wouldn't hold her. He would simply show her that he'd forged an agreement with the Zwolfs that meant she wouldn't be used in the same way as she had been for the previous fifty nights. He'd decided to take control of the room but only through the spoken word and presence. There would be no fight; there would be no feeling; there would be no fury. Not today. When they made it into the room, and Zwolf-Zwolf closed and voice commanded the door sealed behind them, Sero addressed their captor rather than immediately speaking with Prid.

"We have five minutes. I will use those five minutes to speak with Prid. I will consider anything you say and any delay you cause to be an interruption to those five minutes. As such, anything you say will directly extend those five minutes. I will consider any slight to these terms a slight to our agreement, and I will act accordingly. Are we clear?"

Cleverly, Zwolf-Zwolf remained quiet and simply nodded slyly with a silent, cancerous smile on his face.

Feeling he'd established a tone of control in the room, despite the impenetrable exit door, Sero turned to Prid. He'd fortified himself against this moment but could already feel his eyes leaking and his chest tightening. He was able to force out the words he'd rehearsed though, accompanied by a broad and heartfelt smile of compassion.

"Hey, Prid. This old amoeba and his gang of brothers have finally realised that they can't make us talk by hurting us. But they know I can end *them* by suicide. So I've negotiated that they stop mistreating you, and I get to check how you're doing for five minutes each day. Make sure they're running a straight line through their end of the deal, you know?"

Sero's voice began to crack, struggling to deliver the concise and precise summary that he'd rehearsed. He didn't quite make it all the way through the last few words without lapsing into a barely audible croak. "Kind of like an audit." Sero checked the tears, stemming his eyes through will alone. "How are you?"

She ran at him, throwing herself into a hug; plunging her head into his chest. She clung on, squeezing as though Sero might disappear if she didn't maintain contact. He was overcome, and his barely staunched tears began to roll freely down his cheeks. He could hear Prid's own sobs in sync with the rhythm of her chin rising and falling, pressed tightly to his sternum.

His plans to maximise their five minutes evaporated as he held her, hoping there would be some of her left following the release of the moment. Some of *his* Prid. *How long? Three minutes? Four?* They might have only five minutes each day for just thirty days. Their time together was precious. He didn't care, though. He'd longed to provide her reassurance. If what she needed now was silence and solid embrace, then that was what he would give her, time and space be damned. He knew that their five minutes would be over soon, but he held on tight and felt Prid's tears subside. Her arms released him, and he reciprocated, allowing Prid to step away from him slightly. She tugged down the sleeves of her coveralls so that they stretched halfway down each hand before wiping the saltwater away from her eyes and cheeks.

Then Zwolf-Zwolf took a step forward and made a simple statement. "Pridescent, you will be leaving us now. The auditor and I will speak alone."

To Sero's surprise and elation, Prid spoke the first genuine words he'd heard from her in months. "I am *more* than fine. Tomorrow?"

Sero smiled and nodded at her. "Tomorrow."

With no further words, Prid turned and stalked from the room, achieving an admirable elegance in her stubborn and rebellious teenage gait. Sero's heart leapt again. Five minutes was enough.

*What a tough young woman. What an inspiration. What can I do to be worthy of her admiration?*

Zwolf-Zwolf closed and resealed the door after Prid's exit and indicated that Sero should sit in the chair that had been provided. It was the same chair he'd been tied to on previous evenings, but there were no restraints on this occasion.

Initially, Sero didn't know how to respond to Zwolf-Zwolf's suggestion to sit, overcome as he was with the confusing and conflicting emotions of despair, hope, pride, and shame. The five-minute embrace with Prid had left him disoriented, and it took him a moment to recalibrate himself into the room. When he did, it happened in a moment, his mind accelerating rapidly up to competitive speed from an emotionally clouded standing start.

This was an opportunity. He was in a room with his chief captor, and rules of the conversation were stacked in Sero's favour. There was a lot that he didn't yet know about what had happened on NineDee. He had a skeleton of the facts but no idea of the motivations behind such an atrocity. He also had a good chance of getting the information back to Minnus and the rest of the Race based on the "replacement protocol" ruse that he'd managed to maintain. At worst, he could find out details that might prevent this from occurring again. He might be able to arm any successor telonaut auditors with important information that would allow them to redress the tragedy. At best, though, he might save Prid. *Take control. Just keep him talking.*

Sero took a seat, allowing the Zwolf-Zwolf control of the room once more. *Not control of the conversation, though.* "Why are you here?" A direct question. Sero thought he had the measure of the man's ego. His assessment was quite simple at this point. The Zwolfs *wanted* him to believe in what they were doing. They'd gone to so much effort to continue making a record of his audit using old standardCam technology, even after Sero and Prid had been captured. They'd displayed such reverential vanity in describing the monument that they would build to Leaf. They'd undertaken extreme measures for Sero's confinement and torture, in the abuse of Prid. There had to be a deep-rooted motivation behind such commitment, an emotion driving the action, even if the actions presented as megalomaniacal insanity. Sero guessed that the old man was here because he *wanted* to talk—*wanted* to be understood, perhaps even validated. Sero would let him talk, at least.

"I wish to divulge my evil master plan in a single monologue, of course." Zwolf-Zwolf simpered down at Sero. "How else might you be dazzled by my brilliance?"

"Shall I just enjoy the show, then?" Sero fired back, aiming for a playful but not insulting sarcastic tone to combat the geriatric murderer's acerbity. There was no response from the colonist. The silence stretched, and Sero became nervous, wondering whether he'd misjudged his approach. Silence didn't help him; he needed the old man talking if he were to discover anything. "Perhaps not a show then. You do want to explain some things to me, though, don't you? Maybe more like counsel. Why not tell me more about what happened here? It might give you a chance to think, if nothing else. Can't be easy having only yourself and other people's children for company."

Sero couldn't help but add a slight barb to the end of his statement. He wanted Zwolf talking, but he also felt the need to fight against his captor in some more tangible way. Petulant side-long insults were all he had in his armoury.

"You really do think I'm evil? I used the word partly in jest, but you believe it, don't you?"

"I don't think I believed in the concepts of good or evil until I met you. I had only ever previously observed people with differing motivations who were assessing events from different perspectives. If there *is* such a thing as 'evil,' though, I think what has happened here on NineDee would be the closest my experience has come to defining the word."

"Why, Auditor?"

Sero felt that his response was critical. It could open up a line of dialogue that might lead the conversation to areas that might aid their escape. It might equally illustrate the differences between the two men, which Sero thought were vast. If Zwolf-Zwolf felt no bond at all with Sero, why would he want to share further? Years of diplomatic experience on different colonies helped Sero to craft his answer. "From the perspective of an impartial observer, it might seem *malicious*?" Sero added a querying tone to the final word of the sentence, trying to soften the impact of his assessment in both word and intonation choice.

"My rough calculations have around seven hundred consciousnesses as the toll fee for whatever progress has been made here. Minds—independent, free-thinking, sentient personalities, all of whom have been sacrificed. It might seem malicious because it's difficult to understand how that sacrifice can be proven to be worthwhile to leave your effort in a better position than the nearest viable alternative, which an impartial observer *might* assume to be the previous plan of establishing a colony of many individuals. There's precedent for that. I've visited half a dozen colonies that represent that precedent. The colonies can be established without such a toll."

"So you think that the entire enterprise was planned from the beginning? That I knew exactly how everything would conclude? That all action and consequence was foreseen and accounted for?"

"No. But then again, I don't understand how this would even begin at all. There must have been a first time—a moment when you decided that someone would have to die. There must have been a point when you could've chosen to proceed or to desist. To kill or not to kill."

*There's the hook, in the water. All you have to do now is ask the right questions and hold the correct silences, Novak.* "You know when that moment was, don't you?"

"You told me you have been in love, Mr. Novak. You told me you have lost that love—grieved. Can you remember what that is like? I want you to hold the memory of those feelings in your heart as I offer you a tale, for perspective."

The last word was a riposte to Sero's earlier statement on the reality of evil.

"Do you recall the personnel files you studied on the colonists that were originally transported here? Perhaps you can name the first three for me?"

"I can. You, Leaf, and a quantum physicist called Zahir."

"A good memory—useful, I'd guess, in your role as an auditor of new Race worlds. Yes, those were the first of us to pass through the doors of this world. The first to arrive here and the first into the training programme back on Earth too. We were all three young, ambitious, and talented—hungry for life. Do you remember the feeling of ambition, the desire to achieve something stupendous, to be significant?

"I think you must. Nobody would arrive in your position without having embarked with that goal in mind. Your life is no accident, Mr. Novak. Perhaps we are more alike than you might think?"

*Silence.*

"No matter. There were three, all brilliant and driven. The best the Race had to offer in the truest meritocratic sense of fitness for purpose. And I was one."

Zwolf-Zwolf had ceased to look at Sero whilst he was speaking. His eyes were rather looking to the corner of the cell in contemplation. Even without the spoken words, Sero would've been able to read the pride in those eyes, twinkling away in the semidarkness as their owner foraged through his recollections. Then the eyes changed, became more sullen.

"But of the three of us, she was greatest. Brilliant? Yes, but more than a mind—a wit, a bard, a beauty. So dazzling that all who spent time in her orbit were pulled in, her character so densely packed with intrigue and splendour as to represent a multiverse of attractive mass. But there were three of us.

396

"We trained for this mission together for five years preembarkation. We knew all of every part of each soul: every mannerism, every desire, every insecurity, every flare, and every foible. In such fires families are forged. Love, lust, and longing. But there were three of us. And I was one…" Zwolf-Zwolf's face changed again, going beyond brooding contemplation and into morose remorse. "And they were two.

"I'd noticed it before we left. They had tried to hide it from me. Leaf was a special lady. Extremely perceptive but caring too. She knew how I felt about her. I think she knew what we could've become too. But he struck first. Distracted her—wooed her in the most classical of senses. He lacked only a horse and a thunderstorm through which to ride.

"She must have convinced him to be subdued in victory and to delay any announcement of his conquest. Perhaps she'd hoped that I might find myself distracted once we had arrived here, maybe that my work would become my wife. She never gave me any explanation that I believed as to why she would've been with him, let alone why she would hide it from me. Perhaps his hold over her was more specific than that. Maybe he had some form of leverage. A command, even. I do not know. But they *did* hide it from me. I had only suspicions until we arrived here on NineDee."

Bitterness swam over Zwolf-Zwolf's face, dragging all of his features towards his chin.

"They were humble and respectful in explaining. I think that must have been her influence, her fight against him to achieve some parity in the relationship. They took me to the first quarters. We'd set up a shared living quarters to operate from as we began first assessment of the wetworld. It was before any of the cattle were transported to us, so I chewed on a tendril as they explained, casually oblivious to the impending end of my world. Sat in a *kitchen*!

"There were some subtle references to the need to procreate on a colony such as ours, some less subtle references from him about love. She couldn't have denied him. Not with him sitting there in the same room. Anyway, they had decided to leave the shared quarters, set up their own home...Leaf had been working with the tendrils and had some ideas on how to use them for construction to build something of her own design. I nodded. Smiled. I laughed even! As if it was fine. But I *knew*. It cannot be possible that a man might love a woman as I loved Leaf and that love not be reciprocated. She knew that. For whatever reason, she had been trapped into a commitment to him. I had to rectify things."

There was a new hush. Sero felt that the old man might be looking for some confirmation of the morality of his story, an indemnity for whatever might come in the next chapter. *Could this genocide really be about a single man's amorous rejection?* He had nothing genuine to offer but wasn't going to jeopardise his hopes of getting some insight just because of a misplaced need to chastise a genocidal maniac. *Lay on, MacDuff.* "How did you begin to right the situation?"

Zwolf-Zwolf responded to the question almost as though it were an interruption, an alarm sounding to remind him that there was someone else in the room. His head moved a little too quickly, recognising Sero in his stark chair. With the movement, the Zwolf's manner seemed to change too, appreciably resetting into a default bearing of superior defiance.

"I took control. Moved the situation to my advantage. I intervened." The so-called patriarch retrieved himself from propping up the wall and stepped closer to Sero, peacocking himself to fully upright and lowering his voice an octave. "We were alone. At least a hundred years until any kind of Race authority might come to inspect our progress. I realised that I might *be* the authority. I might change the rules if there were a significant enough reason. Why should I not be in command? There was a very significant reason to act, and I was the only person left not complicit. I had a moral duty to act. I took myself away and assessed what resources I possessed that might be employed to correct the situation. To allow all things to be achieved, both the continuation of the colony *and* the emotional and intellectual fulfilment of Leaf and I.

"Leaf was an honest and loyal woman. There would be no success found in simply bludgeoning him over the head with a steel brick. If he were found dead or went missing, she would have to grieve for him out of respect. Perhaps she would have even been forced to consider her feelings for me, knowing that I may have been involved in the rescue attempt. It wouldn't do. So I decided to protect her from such a position by making it easy for her to uphold her promises to the body she was sharing a home with.

"I simply decided that my mind would be inside that body rather than the trickster who had stolen her from me. We had everything we needed here on NineDee already. Two Postboxes, which could be used one as a delivery and one as a reception facility. Each was equipped with the spider-mapping equipment to copy and rebuild a mind. I only had to have one send a signal package that included the genetic structure for a first parent individual and the neurological structure and therefore memories and character of a second."

All at once, Sero realised the truth of it. The person in front of him, the "Zwolf" was no "Zwolf" at all! He was a Zahir. Zwolf had been Leaf's chosen partner. Zwolf was the one who had set up home with her. Zahir was the murderer. Zahir was the mind occupying all the adult colonist bodies; there had been no Zwolf mind on NineDee for over a century. That's why the old man had stopped speaking with a Eurasian accent when he'd been discovered. He'd been playing the role of Zwolf all along in order not to draw suspicion.

The revelation didn't answer all questions, though; Sero still didn't know how the complete conversion of the colony had been achieved. Discovering how the security put in place in the telonaut system could be circumvented was a critical piece of information to get back to the Race

too. He now had two reasons to keep the Zwolf-Zwolf—
*no! The Zwolf-Zahir!* He had to keep the Zwolf-Zahir talking.

"So, Zahir, how did you make it happen? I thought the
blank-bubbling technology was fool proof. How did you
work out a thwart method in isolation? You were only one
man, at least then. Surely that's impossible."

The old man smiled at Sero's choice of name or perhaps at the unsubtle flattery.

"I'm a quantum physicist, remember? To answer that
question fully would be too complicated and certainly too
protracted for this initial discussion. Suffice to say that I
devised a method to momentarily partially deblank the
bubble in the reception facility, a combination of reducing
the strength of the force-field envelope that surrounds the
bubble and altering the conformity with which the strings
spin so that information can penetrate the bubble. I then
only had to preprogramme the reception facility to use that
deblanked window to send an override spider map to the
gestating copy body. Which wasn't hard at all, given I wasn't
modifying any machine code. I was writing completely *new*
code to run only in certain situations—something I had
full authority to do given were we all trained on how to
best adapt to whatever conditions we might have encountered once we had arrived on colony. In this instance the
new situation that activated my mind overwrite-out inser-
tion code was the exact change in joule-route conditions
that I had used to deblank the bubble in the first place.
Very neat, I think you'll agree. I called it MOOI."

"So you convinced Zwolf of the need to transport from one location to another—invented some reason that he found suitably persuasive and enacted your plan. But once you'd made the first successful attempt—once you'd adopted the body you wear now—you couldn't turn it off, could you? The intervention programme, I mean—MOOI. The Postbox began overwriting every new colonist's arrival with your mind didn't it? Automatically."

"Very astute of you, Auditor. I invented some diagnostic data that showed a problem with the second Postbox and explained to the cuckoo that we needed to test it before we went to the trouble of allowing new colonists to come through. Thinking that he had the safety of the kill switch protocol as a fall back, he agreed—volunteered, even. But yes." The superior and defiant tone of the geriatric wavered. "Ultimately I couldn't properly deactivate MOOI, and it led to my failure." The Zwolf-Zahir fell silent.

"She worked it out, didn't she?"

A pursing and wetting of lips from the old man was the only reply. "Did she realise immediately? Were you able to get any happiness at all from your scheme?"

"Three days. For three days we lived together in bliss, as man and wife. All was as it should be. We talked of her plans for a tendril city, a civilisation built on a single main resource, used ingeniously. We walked the silent planet together, hand in hand along empty, echoing corridors and unspoilt natural plains of vegetation. We made love. It was ecstasy and yet obvious: extended hours of purest clarity, fuelled by love and hope for the future."

Despite his palpable regret, there was little sadness in Zwolf-Zahir's tone. Instead, there was a taint of anger, his teeth tightening gradually together in a clench as he built through the description. "But I made mistakes. I'd planned to tell her that there'd been an accident that explained where 'Zahir' had gone to; why he—why *I* had disappeared. I didn't do it well. I took too long, focusing instead on playing the character of Zwolf. When I played my hand after those first idyllic three days, I was clumsy and inconsistent. Her reaction was only more evidence that she had always really loved me, of course. She was distraught at my 'death' and began investigating what had happened. She used NineCents as an assistant, and I had to work hard to mist the data, make the possibility of what I'd done look even more remote than it might have seemed even initially. I may have been able to get through that difficult phase with the ruse intact—"

"If it hadn't have been for MOOI?"

"Yes. MOOI." There was a look of bitter resignation. "When the next colonist came through, we went to greet her together. We ran through the normal protocols, but it became clear to me that my mind was inside the body of the twenty-five-year-old woman we were interviewing. I've since discovered that the miniSuns need to adapt to the changing weather around the Postbox much more significantly than I'd first calculated in order to maintain the blank bubble.

"MOOI reads the joule-route fluctuations as the same targeted energy change that I'd programmed it to search for in the first instance. It reacts accordingly. As the Postbox thought that every transmission at the second facility had been successful using my additional code, it made that additional code undeletable, as though it were part of the original Earth-designed code. The best I was able to do was to upversion the spider map to be a new version of my own mind each time a new colonist arrived."

"Leaf and I never regained our idyllic pace. She became consumed with identifying what was wrong with the colonists arriving at the second Postbox. Why were they fully functional human beings and yet had recall problems with their named specialism? For a time, I was able to improve the new arrivals' initial answers to early protocol questions. I had access to both the personal files against which the answers were to be checked and the question sets too. It was clear after a while, though, that the new colonists couldn't do their job. They didn't have the background they needed.

"My new minds set about frantically trying to learn all they could in new specialist fields, but the effort took too much time and was too noticeable to Leaf. Eventually she confronted me."

Zwolf-Zahir's eyes glazed over, and he began looking through Sero rather than at him, his voice in the room relating the story but his mind absented away to a long ago time. A tear rolled from each of the old man's eyes.

"I told her everything. Explained why—tied everything back to those perfect three days and the dreams we had for the future. But it was too much for her, too shocking to hear all at once. She asked to be alone for a night to think."

*Silence.*

"I found her hanging from a roof tendril the next morning, her chair kicked away underneath her."

The cell lapsed back into silence as the patriarch returned to the moment of the discovery of his lover's suicide, his eyes focusing a kilometre beyond the rear wall of the room. Supposition and logic finished the tale.

Sero imagined the distraught Zwolf-Zahir flanked by a new colony made up of 50 percent equally distraught Zahir minds in copy bodies and 50 percent true colonists from Postbox one. In their grief, the Zahirs decided to build the monument city of Gesponnen to their lost love but knew that the genuine colonists wouldn't allow resources to be used that way without some more logical thought. So the Zahirs would have needed to begin reposting all the true colonists from box to box to get them overwritten and therefore members of their Leaf cult. Maybe they even came up with a credible cover story to induce the real people to do it voluntarily. Inventing a "contaminant" in the atmosphere that had killed Leaf, perhaps, something that they could protect against only through the germ line of the progenitor call, pretending the Postbox would be used as an expensive gene-filtering machine during point-to-point surface teleportation. It would explain the vast disruption to the weather on the colony since the first transportation too. The Zahirs might have used double the blank-bubbling energy needed, causing the now understandably outsized effect on the planet's wind systems. The exact method didn't matter. It was clear to Sero that this genocide was no accident. It was a decision made by several grief-crazed copy minds. An *active* decision to kill followed by repeated, active decisions to kill *again*. This was the selfish depigment of other souls; the deprivation of others' chances to feel and to love; their chance to fight, to struggle; their chance to be part of a family. The hatred boiled in Sero as he sat in silence. There would be other times in which he would try prise information from this Zahir—other evenings. In that moment, Sero didn't trust himself to speak even a single word for fear of that word baring others and creating a cascade of chastising, righteous anger that couldn't be stopped. He needed to help Prid, and that meant he couldn't alienate the monster in his cell. He stayed quiet for a long time before standing and leading the decrepit murderer to the door and gently patting his back in an artificially comforting manner that disgusted Sero to the core of his being.

# THIRTY-EIGHT

*The most noticeable thing is that the people in every public space all look so different from each other.*

Minnus was in Chicago. The old city was the strongest vestige of the old world and the philosophical, if not literal, capital of Amasia. He'd taken the time to research and dress himself in a manner that he'd hoped would allow him to pass unnoticed amongst the city's residents. His research had led him to draw some inaccurate conclusions. Given who he was trying to visit with, he'd based that research on a particular demographic. His lifelong experience had told him that fashions in dress and hairstyle would be localised, despite the global nature of access to pretty much everything in contemporary culture. People still liked to identify with a particular group, be on a specific team, self-actualise. In Chicago that was still true but not in a homogenous way like in Surfaca. Here there were hundreds of small groups, each distinguishing themselves from the other. As he'd strolled throughout the city, people on every block corner were dressed differently than the group on the previous and the next corner.

They often still had themes amongst themselves: one group of exclusively young men with holoTattoos floating and moving over their faces, some with pictures, some with written text; a mixed-sex group all dancing to some obviously synched and embedded music that only they could hear, effort in silent unison with some unheard melody; a group that seemed to be learning from a street-based teacher, huddled around as he stood on a simple portable magLev platform, probably carried with him underarm from wherever he'd started the day.

This was all new for Minnus. He was surprised that in the age of the Race and global admission to information on the smallest detail of life on other planets, he had been able to avoid learning about and understanding this region of his own world and at least surprised that he'd *been* surprised by what he saw on arrival. And he was dressed as some kind of Olde English cattle owner. *Surprised that I can* be *surprised, I suppose.*

The variety of self-expression wasn't the real bug down his back, though. It was the clear variation in levels of access here. Through the veneer of individualisation, of self-definition, Minnus thought he could see and even feel the reactionary snarl of people living out forced choices. He imagined he could even taste it in the air. It had taken some time to clarify in his mind, but he was certain of what was unnerving him now.

His search, using the information that he'd gained from the assistant at the castCo, had been difficult. When he'd lost access to Telospace, he'd also lost access to Naidoo and Du Plessis. His next best alternative to find his quarry was to go through the production company that had prepared him for his debate with Joberan. They'd come back with only cryptic information, but it was enough to get him started. There were no public digital street signs here that his cSheet could interpret for him to help move him to where he needed to be. The info he'd sourced had almost anonymised the address into riddles. He'd been pinged a knot of cryptic slogans and testimonials, the young researcher clearly excited by the idea of surreptitiously liaising with a controversial but respected former guest but also clearly representing people that he thought were dangerous. The production assistant was clearly aware that he had to respect his internal instincts of self-preservation. *"If you know what Milton knew, then you are CAN DO!"* and *"Capital? It's only Human."* Most helpful, though, was *"Rockefeller and Saieh can see us; can you?"*

Clearly, the people he was looking for only wanted to be found if they wanted to be found. Still, Minnus had been able to find information in the WorldGov repository that showed that there was a pair of buildings in Chicago six centuries ago that were physically close and named after two then-contemporary capitalists, John Rockefeller and

Alvaro Saieh. One was an old worship centre for monotheism, a "chapel," and the other was, as far as Minnus could work out, a pseudoreligious educational building focusing on economics at the University of Chicago. Using old photographs and geolocation data, Minnus thought he was now somewhere close to the two buildings. So he'd stopped to eat in a building that felt like it must be at *least* six hundred years old. It was not well maintained, but Minnus could see the grandeur it might once have rendered so long ago.

Sections of depleted granite-coloured stone walls stood above him, still roofed with (probably faux) red ceramics that evoked an old-European sensibility. Next to the counter stood a full modern-height cartoon statue of a clearly ancient Nurfacan king. *How old is that?* There was a weather-protection field cutting out a large section of the wall opposite where Minnus sat. Through the field window, Minnus could see the remains of what once might have been a place of deity worship but now looked like a place where pagans might worship death spirits. There were stone remnants lying around in piles that looked like the organic remnants of some calcium-crapping behemoth. Certainly enough stone to have previously formed the tower of one of the chapels Minnus had read about but now looking like randomly placed burial mounds.

On the way to the spot, Minnus had just recently passed a still-standing tower with a carved inscription across the lintel of the lowest arch that read "Saieh Hall for

Economics." From here on in, he was looking for clues on the ground to meet with his target. This was as close to the newly underground Joberan as his clues could take him. *Just your nose now, old boy; let's see if you can sniff out an overfed fraker.*

As he sat quietly eating a duck sandwich and watching passers-by to see whether he could identify someone who might be a likely link to his quarry, he'd begun to notice the things that would solidify in his mind the difference between different and *different*. Clothes that didn't fit. Not as a statement. Not with intent. Just clothes that didn't fit, over and under. People on the street asking to borrow things—commSheets mostly, but even asking for transport help, like a ferry to another location. Most tellingly, though, there were some obviously unhealthy people here. Not unhealthy through age as all of the Race eventually became. Unhealthy through accident and lack of attention. Thin. Fat. Stooped. Slow. Low. Unhappy. Less than their maximum. Left behind. Such sorry people simply didn't exist in Surfaca or anywhere else that the Ugandan principles held sway.

The woman he was watching now was pitiful when contrasted with her surroundings. Despite the ruined nature of the piled stones nearby, this area was still one in which life was thriving. There were new businesses and homes built in and around the dilapidated skeletons of former businesses and homes. It was organic, the infrastructure repurposed to whatever use someone might think it fit. Some people were selling, others serving those who came to buy; still others trying to divert the shoppers long enough from their missions to be distracted into purchasing whatever they had to sell.

Here Minnus now sat in a small but comfortable eatery with seats overlooking a ruined church and a walkway and contemplating how the obvious lack of a design to the area hadn't really made it any less efficient than something more functional and purposeful back home in Surfaca.

Down the walkway passed people of obviously differing wealth, some with all the attributes that a maximum salary might give. Occasionally, Minnus thought he detected some evidence of people that seemed to be too young and carrying too much wealth on their person to be justified by even a maximum salary. Too tailored, too much jewellery, too much attention from others, assistants?

In contrast, there was the woman he was watching. She wasn't a passer-by. She was passed by. Minnus had been seated for thirty minutes, inspecting the crowd for people dressed similarly to him, people that therefore might be dressed similarly to his intended interviewee. His sandwich had been prepared from scratch, to order, so he'd waited alone for a while. All that time, the woman had been begging. Not metaphorically begging, like when his wife emotionally stressed her desire to visit a particular place during the afternoon. Literally begging: a person with nothing pleading for a person with much more to share something with her.

Minnus knew why, of course. He'd read about the city-scale microeconomies in Amasia. Ideological rebels against the Ugandan principles setting up alternative currencies and trading norms, groups stating that WorldGov couldn't intervene to limit their earnings if those earnings came not as Red but as tomatoes or meat. The groups would then make the logical leap that accounting for tomatoes using tokens and lists was simpler than moving so many tomatoes around. So a new currency would be born. WorldGov allowed these microcurrencies as a nod to freedom of speech and expression. It did intervene, though, to ensure that no pseudocurrency in any one city could be exchanged for a different form of money from another currency start-up somewhere else. The only form of money that travelled was Red. In this way, it became difficult for any one person to egregiously exceed the earnings cap in any one year. They might earn too much locally in relative terms, but they could also only spend it locally, as their money wasn't good anywhere else and wasn't exchangeable for anything other than Red. It was a compromise that had worked to maintain calm—offering economic extremists some measure of control, whilst still ensuring that no economic system could globalise sufficiently to destabilise the progress the Race had made. However, as Minnus could clearly see from the shameful health of the woman sitting cross-legged in the walkway in front of him, for every slight local-currency winner, there was at least one local-currency loser. As the woman went through the futile motion of again asking whether a suited man passing her might spare some food or offer her some work, Minnus decided he'd had enough and got to his feet. He pinged the table he'd been sitting at with his cSheet, leaving a deposit in Red, and then he strode out onto the walkway and sat next to the woman, crossing his own legs as he lowered himself gingerly to the floor.

"I never did like duck much, anyway," Minnus said as he offered the second half of his sandwich to his new street-level companion. "How about you?"

The woman looked surprised but wasn't so surprised as to be suspicious of the offer of food. She took it quickly but gratefully with a smile and a nod. "Duck is my favourite. Not often I get to eat duck nowadays!"

Her accent was broad and local. *Someone who has been here her whole life.*

As Minnus watched her take her first bite, he noticed that her skin was loose around the neck and along her forearms, which protruded from her short-sleeved shirt to grasp the sandwich in a bony clamp. She was light skinned, although she had obviously spent quite some time unprotected in the sun. Outrageously, she was also actually dirty! Not in an accidental, "I've just been working outdoors" kind of a way but in a grimy, frictioned-in "I've just been *living* outdoors" kind of a way.

"If you don't mind me saying so, from what I've seen in the last half hour, it doesn't look like you get the chance to eat enough of anything nowadays."

From the way in which her face changed, some suspicion finally creeping in, Minnus knew he should course correct. He didn't want to upset the poor lady. "Tough crowd today?"

"Tough crowt effyday," the woman returned though a hundred grams of duck, bread, and balsamic glaze. She was clearly ravenously hungry and had decided that whatever else Minnus might be, he wasn't enough of a threat to slow her eating.

"I've been watching your progress from the eatery over there. Thought perhaps I could help. I'm Minnus. What's your name?"

She made a whirling motion with her right hand, pointing at her jaw to indicate she would finish chewing before answering. Once done, she rinsed the last of the duck-bread barrier from her mouth and swallowed. "Jenny," she offered. "Jenny Parker."

"OK, Jenny Parker. What I know about you so far is that you're hungry, you like duck, and you've lived in Chicago for a long time. I'd've bought you dinner anyway, but it strikes me that you might be able to help me too. Do you fancy some more duck and a chat about some of the people that ignore you out here every day?"

Jenny Parker tore off another bite of the duck sandwich before putting it carefully into a pocket on her jacket and standing up. Brushing off the street dust, she started walking straight back towards the eatery from which Minnus had watched her. "You coming?" she called back over her shoulder. "This is our first date, and you're already late?"

Jenny Parker sat opposite Minnus, still tucking into her second duck meal of the day—this time a whole roast bird accompanied with vegetables and hot sauce. She'd slowed some, though, and could at least now fully form words.

"Yeah, there's often a guy comes through here dressed like you. Mustard pants, pastel shirts, blue blazer, always in brown shoes. I notice shoes more from down there on the ground. Big guy, right?"

"Right," replied Minnus.

"He's actually pretty generous. Quite often gives me local dough, never Red—my kind of thinker. But there aren't a host of people around here giving me any help at all. So yeah, I remember him."

Jenny Parker had turned out to be much less pitiful than Minnus's first impressions had extrapolated. Sure, she wasn't in top physical shape, but she was as sharp a conversationalist as Minnus had come across, and he'd actually become distracted from his mission for a few minutes as they chatted over her second lunch. He got the feeling there was perhaps more he could learn from her than some best-guess coordinates for where to head to next.

"The people round here really don't help you? Surely there must be some of them that know you? *See* you every day, at least? How is it that you're even still here, asking for help, after so long? What was it you said earlier? A year?"

"Yep, somewhere around that. A loooong, sad story." Jenny Parker smiled ironically as she rolled her eyes to indicate just how long "loooong" was."

"I've got about three months before my literal deadline comes up," said Minnus.

"OK. Where do you want me to start? I'm happy to tell the tale. Not often I get to chat with a *Race* member anymore."

She emphasised membership of the Race as though it were rare and special rather than something available from birth to every human alive.

"Well, I know you grew up here; your accent alone tells me that. What I can't figure is how someone so intelligent, who seems to have something to contribute, ends up side lined like you are—living here for the last year." Minnus then hurriedly added, "If you'll forgive the question."

"Sure, I'll forgive quite a lot nowadays." She put down her utensils and clasped her hands. "OK. Part one: I was born, I grew up. In Chicago. Part two: I met a man. A sexy, distracting man with dreams, ambitions. I wanted to impress him, so I started to get into what he was into. What he was into was economics, philosophy, and changing the world."

"What was his name?" Minnus asked.

"Surname 'Important,' first name 'Not.' He was just a gateway drug."

*Nice metaphor.*

"Anyway, so he was a gateway to a different lifestyle. I'd grown up in Amasia, but my parents were real Race members before they died. Took great pains in the decision-making process every time the mission-election questions came around. Felt like global Red was all theirs to redistribute. Believers, you know?"

Minnus did know. He was a similar "believer" guy himself. His kids would probably make similar statements about their own childhood.

"When I met this guy, I felt the same as the olds. I'd finished my curricula, found something I thought I might be able to make some Red from. Even get near to the earnings cap eventually." She waited. "Socialising! I was running a meetHouse when I met him. He came in one night, drinking alone. I was working behind the bar, by myself, alone too. You know how it is at the beginning? Do it all yourself, and prove you're good at it?

"Anyway, when it came to closing time, he was the last one in the gaff. I thought he was out*rage*ously hot. So I asked if he wanted to stay late, close the door, like, and just be on an...impromptu date. I did things like that then."

Minnus smirked ever so slightly at the irony of the word "then."

"So it turned out he was so distracted with his own day that he didn't notice that I thought he was smoking hot. Or my strange posture pointed at him. But we got chatting anyway, and he told me about what he did."

Jenny Parker stopped speaking. She looked at Minnus as though she expected him to continue the story. She was easy to listen to, but that didn't make her easy to interpret. He really didn't know where this was going. Maybe this guy stole from her? Beat her? Left her here somehow? Minnus didn't know how to complete her sentence for her though, so instead he merely raised his eyebrows and nodded to show he'd understood so far and was still listening, maintained engagement. After a couple of animated mouthfuls of roast duck, Jenny Parker continued.

"So"—she swallowed the last duck mush—"he was a currencist."

The blank look on Minnus's face evidently indicated to Jenny Parker that he didn't know what the occupation of "currencist" was. Evidently because she raised her own eyebrows in a way that despatched more incredulity towards him than if she'd looked down her nose and said, "Reaaalllly?"

"He wanted to *compete* with Red—to set up another, alternative system of trade, something that could be used to subvert the earnings cap; something extra; something people could *keep*. For them*selves*."

There was then a gravid pause. Minnus read the expression on Jenny Parker's face as a pointer that she felt what she was about to say was, in her mind at least, some line of revelation.

"He wanted to allow people to be *rich*!"

Through the dirt and the bagging skin, the lack of nourishment, the year living on a Chicago street, Minnus could see how the word excited Jenny Parker. Rich.

"He explained that he thought some people were just naturally better than others and that this superiority wasn't their fault or choice, so why should they be burdened with a duty of care to others? To be fair, he also had some crazy 'God' stuff in there about the better people being chosen or worthy or something, but at the time I didn't really listen to that. What I heard was, 'If you're so good at something that people will give a part of themselves to you as reward, why shouldn't you keep it all?' After all, who knows better than me how to distribute my earned rewards?

"It was the first time someone had explained to me that there was a philosophical question that the Race didn't answer in the curricula: 'Why isn't the most productive use of the fruits of my labour to elevate my own comfort?'"

Minnus could tell that Jenny Parker was delivering the question to him in the same manner it had been delivered to her, expecting the response to be an internal inspection. She was proselytising.

"He told me he was going to be around for a couple of weeks and was staying in a bunkHouse across the street. I was interested in the idea, so I decided to do some research the next day and have some questions ready for him the next time he came into my meetHouse. Just to show how expansive and interesting I was." Jenny Parker paused and smirked again. "Plus I wanted to have sex with him," she finished.

"How do you research something like that?" asked Minnus.

Jenny Parker banged over a look of similar wonder to the one she'd pushed at him earlier. "Well, when you run a meetHouse, the world brings information to you. All you have to do is decide which pieces you want to put into your head. Geez! You're a *Racey*. All 'communal knowledge' and 'shared experience.' But you don't instinctively think I might ask some of the one *thousand* people that came through my doors each day?" She shook her head, wide eyed, before continuing. "Angels and fools, man, angels and fools."

Minnus wasn't sure what her last comment referenced, but could tell he wasn't coming off well during his limited slices of the conversation. "Sorry," he said. "I'm just getting involved in the story—trying to put myself in your place. You see?"

He could see what she thought of him pretty clearly for himself though. *This guy is sheltered to the point of anaesthesia.* She persevered nevertheless. "So I asked some people, most of the people that I met that day, to be honest. At least, anyone who was waiting for someone alone or had more than one drink right up at the bar. Or the people that were dressed a bit like he had the night before. Or were staying in the same bunkhouse.

"I found out some stuff that I'd just never known. Turned out that at least half the people I spoke to had two forms of money in their cSheet. Red, of course, but also Miltons. Back then, Miltons were kind of new. I'd certainly never heard of them. I was late to the game, though. I made up for it, though. Boy, did I!

"So I learned that whilst one Milton would buy you less than one Red, nobody was tracking how many Miltons anyone was earning in any one year, at least not WorldGov. And there were lots of places and certain circles that were using Miltons as well and even exclusively in the *stead* of Red. I figured guys that promoted and tried to facilitate Milton usage were probably currencists.

"During the day, It became apparent that Fit Boy wasn't the only currencist in Chicago and certainly wasn't the most prominent. Most of the people in the place were talking about a lady named Pryce. A local bird that'd started Miltons from a cSheet programme shop in the old Near South Side. That's how I slept with him in the end."

Minnus was putting it all together as she dove back into the roast duck. *She ran a social establishment…lots of visitors…knew lots of people…knew someone who knew Pryce…a meeting with Pryce would be valuable and impressive to her target…Jenny Parker impressed her "Fit Boy" by offering access to Pryce when the gentleman came back into her meetHouse.*

"So I went straight over to the bunkHouse and told him we were going down to McCormick that night to meet the inventor of Milton." Jenny Parker said midchew. "He was impressed! We went down there, and she spoke with us for a half hour or so. When we got back to his bunk-House, he was very grateful." Swallow. "Access is a great aphrodisiac."

"And that got you to here, today, how?"

"Oh yeah, right, well, the half hour!"

"Pryce convinced you to lean into the Milton?" he offered.

"Oh. Yes. Yes. Oh."

"A persuasive orator, then?"

"A persuasive decorator. Her place was astonishing! Like a queen of old. Just, well, *above*. You know? My parents had been at the earnings cap for a couple of years. They had some friends that had been there for a couple of decades too, so it wasn't like I'd never seen what wealth looked like. But this was different. This was…opulent," she said with a dreamish smile.

The archaic word surprised Minnus. Jenny Parker's face was a screaming beacon that told him she'd used the word as an ultimate aspiration, a positive desire—as opposed to the corrupting, negative connotation he'd assumed was the widespread interpretation of the word, given the history of the Race.

"She had four houses. All knocked through into one. She didn't have a big family. No exceptions of allowances to justify the size. It was just *her* space, *her* stuff. There were enormous curtains. No blackFields or even colourGlass, but ten-metre-tall material curtains of handwoven, patterned cotton and wool—from real sheep, she said.

"Pryce had clothes. Not a set of shimmer cuts that vary patterns day to day as you choose via your cSheet like your wife or my former self might wear but hundreds of real, authentic dresses. All individual, all physical, all different.

"But the thing that sold her lifestyle to me, the real clincher that changed my life, was power. There were people in her house, at least ten that I saw, who all worked to make her life simpler. They did things for her. They were willing to demean themselves just to get some of her obviously ample Miltons. They fetched and carried; they cleaned and pampered; they pretended love." The stern look returned to Jenny Parker's face. "And I wanted that for myself."

"So you started to use Miltons in your meetHouse?"

"I did. And I worked with a renewed purpose. Once I had an idea that I could be rich—special!—it gave me a whole new drive. Do you see how that would've worked? If I could keep all profit, why wouldn't I increase my ambition? Before that night, I had been happy to run my single house, earn enough Red to stay comfortable, just live my life like everybody else. Happy enough but right in the middle of the bell curve on every measure I could think of. But Pryce, she showed me that I could be more than that. That *I* could be 'above,' if only I could increase my ambition."

She was still very clearly proud of her moment of revelation, giving off the air of a cultured citizen explaining the wider world to the family back at the farm. "So I started competing. Pretty simple stuff at first. I'd use my cSheet to assess the ad hoc Red-Milton exchange rate in Chicago and then make sure my prices were set to incentivise customers to have a Milton account and pay me from it. I advertised nearby on all the local cSheet corner hubs, pinging directions to the 'cheapest and best Milton meetHouse.' It started slowly for a week or so, but then word got around, and my 'Milton meetHouse' became a destination, somewhere people would go by preference. I guess it was partly through price preference, but I was also pulling huge volumes of people through the door. Triple the footfall than when I'd been a Red-only shop. That's the whole point of a meetHouse in the end, isn't it? Meeting people?

"So it became a virtuous circle. Cheaper prices mean more people; more people means more money; more money means cheaper prices. Anyway, six months later, and I'm literally programming Milton into my cSheet myself. I'd taken the equivalent of twenty times the Red earnings cap in Milton profits in the preceding six months. Twenty years of maximum wage. Can you imagine? I'd used my cSheet balance to buy cheaper and better booze supply and then expanded to five more venues. I'd franchised Milton meetHouses. It was wonderful!

"I barely even had to go to the venues anymore. Just monitor the Milton-Red price, automatically adjust my prices to maintain my position as the cheapest and there-fore best, and then let the guys I'd hired manage the operations. I was also paying them in Milton, so I could afford to get some really great guys to keep the customers happy. The money just kept coming."

"So you bought some stuff? Ambition equals reward, right?" *No, it doesn't. Not if ambition leaves you with piles of a product that has no intrinsic value and isn't linked to anything that does have intrinsic value.*

"Sort of." Jenny Parker winced. "Miltons were still a young currency, and whilst it was *possible* to buy the big things with them, like houses and the amazing things Pryce had, it was still pretty niche. You could only earn and spend Miltons in Chicago. WorldGov are marvellous keen on preventing any genuine Red competitor from establishing itself. So I converted enough of my Milton back to Red each week to live the best life I've ever known, but it wasn't possible in only six months to change it *all* to Red. Even the conversions I'd made had pushed me to the earnings cap already in that year, which meant I was spending Miltons too. Chicago loved Miltons, and I had lots of them, so I could eat at the finest places every night and stay in the best hotels. I was a face around the town for a month or two."

Jenny Parker's face took on a suddenly wistful perspective. "I set up a rental for a supersleek racing wing, paid in Miltons; I shopped in the local boutique stores for bespoke clothing that I had them make personally for me, paid in Miltons. Well, you get the picture?"

"I do." Minnus winced himself, feeling genuine sympathy for the naivety of the storyteller.

"And then the Milton died?"

She looked down at her nearly but not quite empty plate and then put down her fork, seemingly losing her appetite suddenly.

"Let me try to finish," Minnus said. "Milton got the attention of someone at WorldGov. Too much trade in something other than Red probably has the ability to affect global budgets and programmes even when limited to one city—if that city is big enough. It's not like global Red output grows or changes each year. Chicago has a population of fifteen million. It's big enough. So they decided to intervene and shut the currency down."

Jenny Parker looked at him sullenly.

"Maybe they started charging very high Red prices for things that couldn't be sourced in Chicago? Things that couldn't be bought in Milton? That would bias the exchange into Red and make the local currency worth much less over time. Or perhaps a mandatory cSheet application that ceased the ability to convert into Red at all?"

A grim nod.

"So, nothing to underwrite the local currency and no way of exchanging it for another. You had a microcosm of the hyperinflation that caused the end of old-school capitalism. Too much imaginary wealth, which wasn't based on anything worthy. And when that wealth became worthless—"

"I'd already earned and spent a full year's worth of capped Red. The meetHouses went immediately. I owed suppliers and staff money and only had Milton to pay them with. Which they found as near to worthless as everyone else after the Red became delinked. Even if I could start taking Red again as payment, nobody would've come. The places were completely associated with Milton. Even named after Milton.

"Without a price differential to pull people in, they had no real incentive to be in my places above anyone else's. So that left me with global black marks for credit. Just the personal debt I still owe for the working value of the goods in my old supply chain would take me ten years of full Red cap earnings to pay off. That debt is linked to both my DNA and every cSheet in the world. I can't earn anything in Red without immediately having to give it away. So…welcome to my home." Jenny Parker opened her hands and gestured around the two of them. "Because I'd already met the earnings cap, I couldn't even sell the stuff I had. If it'd been nearer to the end of the year, I might've been able to hold on to my stuff and sell it in the next year to earn more Red for myself. But with six months of the Red year to go, I had to trade my stuff well below its value in return for the basics. Managed to trade my household contents for two months of rent and my wardrobe for enough food for about the same time, but then I was out, undesirable. Here is where I landed."

"I'm really sorry for you, Jenny Parker. It doesn't seem to me like you've been treated fairly. This is not what the Ugandan principles are supposed to do."

"Don't you feel sorry for me! I choose to be here! I could acknowledge my Red debt and go work in a pork-tree field somewhere if I wanted. I could be hooked back into the Race under one of WorldGov's 'right to contribute' schemes. But I won't be, because it *wasn't* my fault—it was WorldGov's and the systems and the Ugandan principles and the whole frakin' thing. Their fault!

"So this is my protest. One day, someone is going to come along and break us out of this repressive 'solution' to our history. Someone is going to rise up and give us humans a chance to strive and win again, rather than just reading and watching about other people striving and winning. When that happens, I'll walk off this street and begin pushing again. But I'm not going to play at making a success of a business, just because some faceless ancestors have decided my inheritance is their predictive wisdom on my own limits and appetite." She spat the last sentence with clear resentment and bitterness.

"I can see now why I thought you were so strong when you started speaking to me," Minnus said gently. "Your decisions and positions come from passion and...principle. I've never wanted the things you do, but I've held clear principles my whole life. Ideas that I've lived my life according to—at least once I'd worked them out for myself. I admire your ability to stand by your code."

Jenny Parker calmed somewhat at Minnus's attempt at diplomacy. "You know, I wouldn't have thought that anyone who is so obviously a committed Racey would've been able to see my perspective. Especially not Man One," she said with a knowing smile.

As she stood to leave the table, she looked at him directly. "Come back this evening at about seven. I'll let you know if I've seen your guy, and I'll try find out where you might look for him next. Maybe I'll even speak to him."

When she was five metres away, she called back over her shoulder. "You were wrong about one thing, though, Racey. I don't think WorldGov killed Milton. I think it was Pryce herself. Head down to the old Near South Side this afternoon, and see what you think."

⅄

*She's probably right*, Minnus thought to himself as he walked. There was no way that anyone could be living the way Pryce was living unless they had access to more than their fair share of wealth. There was definitely no chance at all that anyone whose wealth had been sunk into a dead currency and the technology around it could be apparently relaxing comfortably in such outrageous, decadent style.

Minnus had taken up Jenny Parker's suggestion and spent an hour wandering around the old Near South Side in Chicago. There was an old sports stadium, unused and crumbling but made from concrete and steel and so still remaining as a monument to former cultures. There were plenty of newer buildings too—a good mix between commercial and domestic properties. Quite normal really. Until he'd found himself on a road called South Prairie Avenue.

It wasn't a tall street. There was only a single layer. Such planning was pretty rare in a big city like Chicago. Not really fair to allow only a few people to use such a big surface area for their living space, especially with modern technology and the heights that the Race could build to with the sound-based traction beams that had filtered down into regular use from the near-Earth tether project over in Houston.

It wasn't the squat, selfish nature of the building that told him it must be Pryce's. It was the flaunting transparent front: not even a field but glass. The original street-facing exterior of the old houses had been removed and replaced with a new facade of wholly transparent glass. There were still some ostentatious original architectural features breaking the front elevation into sections, left behind to remind the observer that the houses were old and originally separate abodes, but from the street he was walking along, Minnus could see right through the glass front wall and into the home. All the furniture, the staff busying themselves within, every floor. The place was like an enormous child's playset, a doll's house for behemoth of a toddler. It was filled with shameful, baroque furniture too. Like a museum dedicated to some ancient oversized and anthropomorphised chair society. The house was purposefully designed to shout the wealth of the occupier into the street beneath it.

On the back wall, above a ridiculous bunk pod with room for ten people side by side and complete with its own individual bunk-sized ceiling, a giant holo screen pushed a name into the room, identifying the house like the dog-tag application in a cSheet might when it sensed the death of its owner. The word was "Pryce."

When Minnus had returned to meet with Jenny Parker that evening as arranged, he hadn't told her that he thought she might have accurately guessed at the cause of her poverty. It didn't seem helpful to reinforce an emotion that might give her an enemy. So instead he asked some questions about whether she had any more duck that day and if he was in a bidding war with anyone for her duck-based affections. Did he need to start breeding ducks again? She'd laughed and he thought at least appreciated the familiarity. *Must be difficult for someone who used to run a meetHouse to become semi-invisible.* No harm in being nice to someone for the sake of it. In return, though, she'd been nice to him. She'd found him some information on where he might meet Joberan.

So now he stood outside a small, old red-brick building, also at street level, immediately adjacent to the tower he'd passed earlier in the day that had the inscription Saieh Hall for Economics. There was a smaller sign here, projected onto the wall of the building in very short writing by a cSheet hub. The Becker Friedman Institute. Minnus pinged the hub with his cSheet and waited for a response.

After half a minute, a voice was returned to him from his cSheet.

"I ain't easily or often shocked, Minnus Mbeki, but today appears to be one such day." Even through the replication of the cSheet, Joberan's deep voice was clearly identifiable.

"Hello, Jesse," Minnus said carefully. "You're a difficult man to find."

"For some," the cSheet confirmed. "Although I'm easy to find for those who I expect might want to find me. For you, well...that's different."

"I have a good reason to search for you, Jesse. Something I think will interest you. I think you might be right, and I might be wrong..." Minnus paused for a few seconds to let his admission have an impact on Joberan, and then a rising blue line on the steel doorway indicated it was about to open.

⋏

The room was large and plush. There was a masculine leather theme with chairs covered in old animal back and front and even mirror and picture frames bound to match. No plastiche in sight. The floor was an old, polished hardwood. Minnus's heels had echoed clicks and slaps as he'd made his way through the walkways. The room was too dark, lit sparsely by wall lights that were angled to point upwards to the ceiling. The cave-like interior felt intimidating. He scanned the room but couldn't see the person he was looking for—couldn't see anyone at all, in fact. He headed for an exit in the rear wall. As he reached a spot level with several high and wingbacked chairs facing each other in rows, he heard a voice call out.

"In here, ol' man."

Minnus was startled, already uneasy in the dark and old-fashioned environment. He turned towards the voice and saw Jesse Joberan sitting alone in the furthest armchair at the end of a row. He had been out of sight, unviewable from the easiest route through the room. He was sat in front of a fireplace, a cSheet embedded in the arm of his chair. The fire was a real wood-burning one, crackling away and giving off licks of light and shadow across the dark spaces in the room.

"You're wrong about it all, Mbeki, not just one thing. You're only slow to realise it. Still, I'm interested to hear what epiphany has brought you all the way here to seek me out. You found God? Been saved?" There was sarcasm in his tone, but his voice still rolled and boomed as though he were speaking to a full chamber of people rather than only Minnus.

Joberan was more loosely groomed than last time Minnus had seen him. His beard was less well kempt, and he wasn't wearing a suit. Today he wore a long coat over a more casual and unmatched shirt and a pair of trousers. He wasn't completely dishevelled and would certainly not be remarked upon in public, but he was untidier looking than he'd previously been. If it were possible, he was even fatter than he'd been earlier in the year. He had an amber drink in his hand in a short glass filled with ice. There was a bottle on the table in front of him, half-empty.

"Drinking alone?"

"You don't count yourself as company?"

"I've only just arrived."

Joberan appeared slightly irritated but answered Minnus's question anyway. "My meeting has finished, and my associates have either left or are elsewhere in the building. I'm simply relaxing. Will we debate my freedom to do even that now?" He took a swig of his drink for emphasis. "Don't worry you lil self; they'll be back."

Minnus gestured to the chair immediately opposite Joberan, asking for permission to sit. The big man simply shrugged and waved towards the seat with his clinking glass.

"No. There'll be no debates tonight, I hope." He knew that talking Joberan around into helping him might not be easy. He'd hoped that the preacher might have shrugged off any embarrassment that he had felt after their joint appearance on Moriarty Meets, especially as Naidoo and Du Plessis were so sure he'd been active in taking revenge in such an extreme way—taken control, as Joberan might have seen it. The first exchanges between them seemed to indicate enmity on the fat man's part. *Not helpful.*

Joberan seemed to sense Minnus's fear and readjusted himself in his chair to be more upright. As his girth resettled around him, Jesse Joberan's presence appeared to double in size again. He was a truly enormous man. "Good. I am no longer a man of words but one of action," Joberan said, watching Minnus's face carefully. "But I think you know that already."

The implication was clear: *Yes, I did attack your facility. Yes, I am capable of threatening you with violence. You are on my turf now.*

Perhaps with that made plain, Joberan felt more able to relax into a familiar persona, one of control. He placed his glass on the table and rested his arms on the sides of his chair, throne-like. Rather than the open antagonism of a few seconds earlier, Minnus felt superiority ooze out from Joberan. Neither position would help Minnus to get what he needed. He wanted to ask his critical questions in an environment of balance. He needed the tone of the conversation to be adult to adult, rather than allowing himself to become a junior participant. *Stall a little. See what happens.*

"What is this place? It looks like a member's club."

"Of sorts. It has some significance to people with similar beliefs to my own. You might say we're all members of a lil club, I suppose." His smile turned into a smirk; he was clearly enjoying his own hints at mystery. "But I'd prefer to think of us as an organisation. A group of people with a purpose. 'Club' sounds a lil too insignificant, don't you think? Like a pastime. We have more considerable aims than to pleasantly amuse ourselves. We chose this environ for its…inspirational qualities."

"It was a school, wasn't it, before the Saints?"

"More than a school. *The* school where the more important work was done, work that divined many of the principles that our organisation holds dear."

"Economic principles, I'd guess, based on the sign above the door."

"Yes, originally, that would be true. Although as you know, those are not the only values that I hold dear. They're a good start though. There's enough common ground amongst my associates and I on the topic that we have forged ahead in other areas too. Brotherly-like. Shared interests will achieve much in difficult times."

As Joberan was speaking, several people entered the room from the rear, taking up seats nearby. There were around a dozen, both men and women. They didn't speak, but they were clearly coming to witness the conversation. They didn't open cSheets to read or even pour themselves drinks. They simply sat and observed the two conversing men. Minnus decided to ignore the newcomers and press on. Joberan's last comment on shared interests was an opening too good to miss.

"I agree. Banding together to get things done is something I've always believed in. It has brought the Race success. It has brought me success. And access. It has brought me power." Minnus paused to allow the last word to sink in, reminding Joberan that he might be on the preacher's home ground, but Minnus was a part of a programme that reached the minds of billions worldwide. "And now it seems that you and I might be able to help each other."

Joberan looked unexpectedly uncomfortable, disarmed by the suggestion that the two men might be allies rather than opponents.

*He's realised that I'm not here to berate him about the earlier attacks.*

Meanwhile, still more people were joining the room. Some had moved chairs to come and sit closer to the fire. Minnus and Joberan were beginning to seem like they were on a stage, with an audience clustered around them.

"There are limits to the folks I would collaborate with, Mbeki. We, or at least most of the folks here, despise your hellnaut programme and the travesty it represents." Joberan gestured to his new and growing audience around the room. "It's a perversion of God's creation, funded by an unfair system of theft from the brightest of us. I struggle to see what shared aims we might have that would allow us to overcome that plain-as-cow-kak fact."

Minnus breathed deeply. "I need you to help me infiltrate Telosec and steal evidence that the telonaut programme has created murderous monsters on another world."

The room was entirely silent. All eyes were focused on either Joberan or Minnus. Ten seconds passed, then twenty. Minnus didn't take his gaze from the man sitting across from him. The big phony rector retrieved his alcohol from the table and sucked a cold dram back through his teeth, looking pensive. He smiled as he returned the glass to the table and then added voice to the smile, chuckling to himself first and then projecting the chuckle out into the room towards his spectators. "Let's talk about a few other things first. This is revelatory. I'm interested to know how far you have fallen from your tower of certainty." His Southern

Amasian drawl was exacerbated by the tongue-loosening effect of the alcohol.

Minnus offered a single nod of acquiescence.

"Let's talk about your beloved Race, shall we? Surely that's a good starting point? Why don't you simply go to WorldGov and explain yourself?"

"I have no evidence, and there are powerful people who oppose me. Without evidence, I'd be wasting my time. Time that would be better spent planning an independent remedy."

"Independent? Surely not. We long ago identified that the best solution to all big problems is to pool all resources and launch globe-spanning programmes. What good can 'independent' action do? No, there's no place for that here."

Minnus wasn't ready to play an endless game for Joberan's amusement. He needed something that the fat frak had, but he wouldn't lie down and be kicked around just for kak and giggles. "I see where you're going with this. I understand your point. It's valid in part, but this situation is an unusual one and doesn't discount all the progress we've made together. Surely even you can admit that the achievements we've made as a species since the start of the Race are grandiose enough to validate collectivism?

Joberan chuckled again. "Advancement? Look at this thing," he said, flicking the cSheet on his armrest dismissively in a performance for the acolytes in the room. "Do you know how long we've been using these devices as our primary communication tool, Mbeki?"

Joberan stared straight through Minnus, suddenly full of conviction. Minnus stayed quiet. "Hundreds of *years*, with barely an improvement, barely a modification! What about in-atmosphere travel on Earth? When was the last time we invented a new means of transport? Again, hundreds of years ago. The last improvement was the wing. You know why, don't you? You know why we have rates of progress comparable with the Dark Ages?"

There were murmurs of agreement from the now heavily populated room.

"Because we're making more worthwhile progress in other endeavours. Our attention as a species is focused on the bigger things," Minnus said.

"More worthwhile? Who gets to decide that?" Whether through performance anger or genuine frustration, Joberan's voice became a terse bark.

"We all do, Jesse. We all vote to select the projects that the Race will support with our collective excess Red. You can be part of that." Minnus turned his head slightly so that it was clear he was addressing the room. "We all can."

It was clear from the mumbles of derision that the audience didn't share the view.

"Pah!" Joberan scoffed. "After you've suppressed our earnings, stolen from the future of our families, and horded our efforts in your vaults, do you think allowing us a tenth of a billionth of a share in the decision-making process is a fulfilling way to express what we think is worthwhile?"

"Are you saying that colonising Mars via local space flight and providing a new home for our expanding number is not worthwhile? If you were solely accountable, would you have ceased research on the diamond nano-threads needed to build the near-Earth tether and allow us to literally climb into space rung by rung, without the aid of rocket propulsion? What outcome would've been different?

"Even if we discount specific projects and assume that you would have found something just as worthwhile to pursue, what of the *social* progress that the Race has made? Jesse, we've almost eliminated inequality. There is no income gap between groups. Men versus women, skin colour versus skin colour, place of birth versus place of birth. We're all able to begin each life afresh and forge our own success, with nobody disadvantaged by the whims of fortune. Isn't that more important than the egos of a few people who feel that they should be more significant than the system allows them to be?"

Joberan's eyes closed to slits, like a dog preparing to bite. He raised his finger and pointed to his opponent in an accusing style. "I see you still have some thinking to do, Mbeki. Despite events changing your view of one of the Race projects, you've yet to consider all the other flaws and constraints in your way of life. You're simply not thinking things all the way through. We cannot help a man who refuses to think for himself." Joberan's hands returned to his chair in the same throne-like position as earlier, and he straightened his back again as though to make a royal decree. "It is a truth available to the soul of all men that some of us are born more capable than others. You know this and were keen to use it as a defence of your Ugandan principles last time we met. You see it as a problem to be solved—an error to be corrected. But by pursuing your egalitarian ideals, you neuter the hosts of potential philosopher kings in our midst. You replace those giants with mediocrity, a majority of fools.

"In doing so, you suppress the potential of all of humanity. In the era of your Race, what incentive does a genius benefactor have to strive, to fulfil his potential? What is the result when that wise patron cannot use the fruits of his brilliance to provide for and protect his friends and family for years to come, cannot distinguish his name in history through wealth and succession, cannot leave a legacy for his children and the followers of his creed to work with? The result is that his efforts are undeveloped. His worth is diminished. His life is unfulfilled. For him, there is no value in innovation. So the rest of the majority of fools use centuries-old technology every day just so that the privileged minority, suited to just a few particular tasks, get to experience the thrill of struggle.

"Do you not see? God made us so we could re-create ourselves through our families. God made us competitive so we could find the best solution and maximise our potential. Without the possibility of bettering our own lives versus our peers, without the natural competitive drive to prove our own worth is more than the next man's, we become stagnant as individuals and sterile as a society. Through setting all families in competition, we both impel the brilliance of brilliant men and propel families closer together, just as God intended. Your Race reduces the importance of family. That can only be wrong."

Until the very last point of Joberan's recital, Minnus had been mentally preparing his response. He'd heard such arguments many times and had always refuted them. But not this time. Not now.

His mouth hung agape, his intended words recalled just before he spoke them. To deny pure capitalism was automatic for him after years of repeated and genuine thought on the matter. He knew his own mind on the topic. It didn't warrant any further thought. *Did it?* To talk about a celestial plan from a divine being was equally non-sensical. *Surely if there is a divine plan, then everything we do is part of it, and trying to influence the outcome of anything is a waste of time. Stupid.*

But a single word had expanded like a gas in Minnus's mind, though, taking up all available space. Family.

*Is what I'm trying to do so different from what Joberan is talking about?* When all the distracting talk about natural competition and divinity was set aside, when Minnus got down to the nub of his motivation, he wasn't here to educate or warn the Race about the problems on

NineDee any more than his actions during the attack on the Postbox down in Antarctica were about protecting the telonaut programme.

Then, he'd been most interested in protecting Joules, whatever the risks. Now, he was here to save Sero, to give his friend the best chance possible to live, find love, and prosper. As an older and perhaps more sage man than his childhood friend, Minnus knew that with life experience came wisdom: true understanding of humanity and one's place within it. A deeper—however flawed—understanding of *love*. He was here to protect Sero, to give Sero a chance to experience those things. *He's right! Joberan is right.*

With some alarm, Minnus realised that he was, beyond doubt, willing to make unilateral decisions about the fate of the telonaut programme in order to protect his family. He knew he was. Frak Johnson. Frak WorldGov. Where did that willingness to arbitrarily decide things lead to? Logically, it meant that the differences between Joberan and himself were not so large. The two men merely used a different currency to assess the worth of a selfish act. Joberan used family wealth propagation and belief in his own natural superiority to justify self-interest; Minnus used family experience. The men had different motivations but the same outcome: the outcome of trying to take personal control rather than deferring to Joberan's "majority of fools." They both ultimately held the belief that an individual might know what best to do, even if there were a majority of others that disagreed. The will to act on that belief was what came next. *Frak me. He's right.*

When Minnus had opened his mouth to speak, he'd expected to refute Joberan's argument. The microsecond-later realisation that he didn't want to contest it left him agog and in focus of the group. He turned to see three dozen pairs of eyes looking at him. They'd arranged themselves in loose rows, mimicking the layout of the recording studio on Moriarty Meets. *Perhaps intentional? Lure me in here and then surround me to watch me be humiliated by Joberan? Some redress against our earlier episode?* It didn't matter now. They weren't going to humiliate him. They couldn't.

Minnus began to speak. He didn't know where his stream of consciousness might lead, but he knew that for the first time in his life, he genuinely understood a part of the viewpoint of these people. *Perhaps that will be enough.* "When you let me in here, Jesse, I told you that I'd realised something. To tell the whole truth, I don't think I was able to articulate what I've realised until just now. You see, something happened to me that shocked and scared me—something that made me reassess my responsibilities, who it is that I hold dear, and what I'm willing to sacrifice for them."

The crowd had begun to mumble, talking amongst themselves a little at low volume. Joberan seemed to sense that Minnus's mood had changed, though, and gestured for the room to settle.

"I had thought that I had the answers. But I've come to realise that you're right about some things, Jesse. My perspective *has* been skewed. I *am* one of those privileged few who have been able to truly engage with the grander aspirations of the Race. I've been challenged and driven by that engagement for my whole life, believing that others might feel the same pull. Perhaps you're right. Perhaps it's not enough for those who live comfortably but without challenge to watch the achievements of the Race that they are part of from afar.

"Perhaps the intellectual distance between our successes and their daily lives is a problem to solve. Perhaps one I can help with given my background in NV casting. I don't know. What I do know is that when my family was threatened—when my family was recently placed in danger—my viewpoint changed. There is nothing I can think of that is more important to me than my family. Nothing. That includes the telonaut programme. That includes WorldGov, and that includes the Ugandan principles. If I need to fight against any or all three of them to protect my family, I will."

The room was now completely noiseless but for Minnus's monologue and the crackling of the fire behind him.

"*Whatever* it takes. Now, I'm not a man of faith. I don't believe in your God. I also don't believe that a return to unfettered capitalism is the answer to your desires. But I do believe that we can work together to get something we all want. If you help me with my plan, you'll be able to prove to the Race that Telospace has accidentally created the monsters you've been warning of via your White Daisy arm for so long and perhaps even use the facts to open a debate about how much Red should be centralised when the consequences of allowing a 'majority of fools' to decide how it is utilised can be so heinous."

"And you? What would you gain from this plan o' yours?" Joberan interjected.

Minnus felt a tear well in one eye involuntarily, but he expertly blinked it away and swallowed. "I get to protect the future of a man who is like a son to me."

The two men held each other's gaze.

"Well, y'all, that *is* a fortunate turn of events." Joberan stood slowly, hefting his enormous bulk out of the leather wingback chair. He scanned the room before settling his eyes at the very rear of the space. "Pryce? What do you think?"

All in the room turned to face a woman in a tight purple dress at the back of the group. "Yes. I think yes, we'll fund it, but I want to know everything first."

Although she was barely visible all the way at the other side of the room, Minnus could tell that she was looking directly at him. "Come with me."

# THIRTY-NINE

"**W**e're not getting out of here, are we?"

It was the first thing she said when she entered the cell. The question made him ache in his soul. All the hopes and dreams of a young girl, crushed into one despairing question on the hopelessness of their situation.

She'd refrained from asking it for thirty nights. Each night, they'd spoken about a different topic. Each evening he had told her more about Earth, the history of the Race, and even pre-Race achievements. She would come the following night with a new question, usually some tangential thought from a previous evening's conversation or occasionally her own conclusion on a figure's ambitions or motivations. In this way, they'd spent their two and a half hours of contact: episodic lectures on the thousands of years of civilisation and momentous decisions by long-dead kings, prophets, and leaders. Such decisions as had led them to there and then, to that room and the realisation for Prid that good, innocent people have died all throughout history on the whims and inconveniences of madmen and women.

The pain of her losing hope was crushing for Sero. After so much suffering and abuse, after such a brave and resolute fight to maintain hope and dignity, Prid was suffering a collapse of will on the final evening before they knew they'd be separated. The realisation made Sero's lungs freeze.

"I mean, not together at least. You're probably getting bubbled tomorrow, and I'm probably staying here until I'm older, right? Ready to be overwritten?"

Sero wanted to offer her more hope, restore her resolve against despair. Zwolf-Zahir was watching from the doorway, though, monitoring their conversation. Even if he had not been, what plan could they have made? The following day was to be the day of the dissolution, Leaf Day. Once the process of disbanding the tentaculos encompassed by the Gesponnen plate was complete, there would be no need to manage the colony's energy usage anymore. No need for the Zahirs to retain Sero at all, "replacement protocol" or not.

Even if the dissolution process failed, their situation would be no better. In that case, the colony itself would be doomed to collapse into an uninhabitable storm planet. Who knew how the damaged minds of the Zahirs would react to that? *Not with love and forgiveness for us.* The reality didn't matter though. Right now, Sero had a helpless young girl in front of him. She needed hope. He wouldn't let her down.

"Do you remember me telling you about my old man, Won?"

Prid looked up at him, surprised by the obtuse answer to her question. "Yeah, started this whole telonaut thing with his mates. Brilliant guy."

"I took a lot from him, you know? A lot of my values. He wasn't right about everything, of course. If he were here with us now, I think I could teach him some things about love and family that he never discovered when he was alive, but there were three truly insightful words that he drilled into me. Words that have never left me. Words that have never failed me.

"Whatever the problem, whatever the crisis or co-nundrum, I've never needed more as a guide than those three words, and I don't see how this situation should be any different." He held out his left hand in a clench, extending a finger to count off each of his three words as he said them.

"Optimism. Perseverance. Patience.

"We've done the optimism part, and we've damn sure persevered. All we need now is a little more patience." Sero put his arm around Prid and hugged her to his chest. "Can you do that for me, soldier?"

A silent returned hug.

That was fine with him. He drank in what might be their last moment of genuine contact and joined her in con-templation, exchanging love in some kind of broken, over-balancing osmosis between them. He knew that she would need more, though. Especially if the worst happened, and she was left alone here without him, fully aware of the fate that awaited her. A cuddle and some kind words wouldn't get her through it. She needed a mission—a purpose.

"I'm going to require an answer, Prid. An opportunity will come. Whether that is an opportunity for me tomorrow or one for you in six months, a chance to redress things will come. You need to tell me you can be patient, persevere, waiting bravely for your window. I need to know that when that window comes, you'll still be *you*, able to respond—ready. So can you do that for me, please, soldier?"

"Your time is up, Auditor," Zwolf Zahir called from the cell entranceway.

"Prid?"

She stood, looking down at Sero, who was propped against the wall, and raised her right hand to her temple, clenched into a fist. She mimicked Sero's word accounting as she spoke his own mantra back to him, forming a proper three-fingered salute as she did so.

"Optimism. Perseverance. Patience."

"Good girl."

"Auditor," Zwolf-Zahir stressed again from the doorway.

Prid ignored him. "I have three words for *you*...Father." Her eyes filled with steel as she spoke. There was no waver in her voice, no hint of a crack. There was only determination and honesty.

"I love you."

Sero had only time to nod before she turned and left the room.

Despite his madness, even Zwolf-Zahir had the sympathy to wait a few minutes before speaking. He left Sero in the cell and moved to stand just outside the doorway, perhaps expecting an outpouring of emotion from his prisoner. Sero was not despondent, though. He was rejuvenated, his spirit reawakened by the very same advice he'd given to Prid. He would persevere. He would find a solution tomorrow. And he'd save Prid. Right now, Sero would finish the other half of his self-appointed mission. *Take control.*

In working out how to write his mind onto Zwolf's body, Zahir had discovered a way to send information through a blank bubble to a targeted location on the other side. *If that could happen from one Postbox within our own dimension, perhaps it could happen from two locations in our universe at once? He had built a possible way to create wormholes—joining two points in 3-D space-time together by folding through a higher dimension—which would mean we could make teleportation instantaneous.*

The implications were astounding. The Race would no longer need to send pencil-beamed light signals in order to transmit information over long distances in the universe. The multiyear delay that the Race currently experienced between sending telonauts out to a colony and receiving word back would be made immediately moot by the use of the blank bubbles themselves to transmit information and—with enough research—perhaps even matter itself. There would *be* no more delay. The Race could expand colonies exponentially in both span and population. They could fire out new solar-sail-carried nanoBots at the universal speed limit and then begin the flow of telonauts as soon as the bots had finished construction of a reception facility on a new world. In a couple of millennia, the Race might establish a civilization spanning thousands of worlds. There were, after all, over sixty-four hundred stars within a two-thousand-light-year range of Earth. A truly *connected* civilization, with *instantaneous* communication.

Yet the human specimen that stood three metres from Sero had not used his discovery for any such grandiose civilisational splendour. He'd tried to use it to relieve himself of his base jealousy and had contrived to murder hundreds of people instead.

But Sero would try to salvage that position. He'd gain the last pieces of knowledge that he could from Zwolf-Zahir on how he was achieving the targeted postage of information through the blank bubble, and he'd make sure that he sent a final memory fragment back to Earth that night, before the leverage to do so was snatched away from him by a successful dissolution. Zwolf-Zahir reentered the cell.

"I'm aware that this may also be our final conversation. I'd like to make sure that whatever the outcome of Leaf Day, I understand the subtleties of your methods. If I die, the information will die with me, but at least I'll understand.

"How did you penetrate the blank bubble with information to change the information already within it even though that information was already described in higher dimensions? Do you realise that you've possibly created a way to physically rather than biologically teleport? It might be the single greatest discovery in the history of humanity…"

Zwolf-Zahir smiled haughtily and moved to sit in the single chair in the room.

# FORTY

"**I can still see** and decode the spider map fragments that have been coming in. I can even edit them here at home to give a better representation of the truth. I just can't broadcast them to the Race."

After several weeks of waiting, Minnus had finally gathered the critical stakeholders in a single place. He was astonished to see that Jesse Joberan and the woman he knew only as Pryce were sitting in his kitchen along with Nombre and Joules. Not only because of the previously unlikely nature of the team-up but also because of the seemingly unrealistic aim of evading a pair of WorldGov-sponsored observation teams that Minnus knew had been trailing Joberan and Pryce.

Their need to avoid being seen entering the Mbeki's apartment was the biggest reason for the delay in gathering together. If WorldGov, more specifically Johnson, knew that Minnus had made contact with a group that had previously tried to break through Telosec and into the last remaining Postbox on Earth, it wouldn't take him long to realise that Minnus had decided that the enemies of his frenemy were his brand-new friends. Who knew what Johnson would do if he thought someone with such detailed information about the inner workings of the facility was inviting proven threats into his home?

In the end, all Minnus had needed to do was to get in his wing as normal and fly to his apartment, entering at living height as he always did, directly from his wing. By that point, Joberan and Pryce were already in the hold area of the wing, having been placed there whilst it was undergoing a seemingly routine maintenance down on the coast. Minnus understood that Pryce had paid a lot of money in Red competitor currencies and called in the help of several of the Daisy movement's quieter but influential supporters to provide enough distraction and cover for the two of them to slip away from their respective reconnaissance teams and attend the rendezvous. Now that they were all here and had seen the footage for themselves, Minnus felt that they truly understood the travesty that had occurred. The horror on their faces had been so readable as to curdle the air in the room.

"So the transfer procedure that you have already installed at Telosec only works one way? You can't transmit the footage your new algorithm has edited here at your home back to Telosec and have it replace the NV cast? It has to be physically taken to the facility and hard connected to the system?"

Pryce was clearly an intelligent woman and had been driving the planning session forward with her clarifying questions and paraphrasing since they'd begun several hours ago. There was an incisive quality about her that threaded through both her succinct yet descriptive speech and her personal styling, which was elegant and purposeful, if perhaps a little baroque.

Minnus was tired, but he felt the hours had been worth it. Not only did Joberan and his financier clearly now believe that this we no honey trap intended to lure them and then capture them in some illegal act, but they also believed in Minnus's own anger as his motivation. Minnus had shown them something they understood: revulsion at something so different.

"You got it," said Joules, who was clearly even more fatigued than Minnus. "*So* we need to go in there, take over the broadcast facility, and send out the truth."

The retired sprinter wasn't equipped to deal with a multi-hour strategy session like the one he was trapped inside of— too many short-twitch muscle fibres. He was ready to climb the walls and possibly the ceiling of his friends' home.

Joberan picked up on the youngest person in the room's impatience. "OK, there. Bull's-eye. Just hold on a jiffy. If we're financing this invasion, we need a plan for what happens after we go in and *hopefully* get out. We're with y'all on this. The situation is an ungodly travesty, but we need to think further than kicking the door down. What comes next?"

"What do you want to achieve by broadcasting the reality of the situation on NineDee?" Pryce was direct in her speech and pointed in her mannerisms. She looked only at Minnus when asking the question, clearly thinking of him as the leader of the group. However, after a few seconds of the Mbekis passing a silent football of reply around the room through the smallest of facial gestures, it was Nombre who answered Pryce.

*She'll be better at hiding what the last few fragments showed us. Imagine if they knew we'd be broadcasting the details of instantaneous teleportation by using another dimension as a data route. "Hellnaut" wouldn't cover it!*

"We want Sero to be rebuilt here on Earth, along with Prid. We have a genome and spider map for each of them," Nombre said, believably.

"You want to break the governance for teleportation. You want a special ruling from WorldGov that allows the creation of new life outside of your kill-switch protocol." Pryce was calm in her paraphrase.

Joberan however, placed at her left and crushing the largest plastiche memory chair Minnus possessed, was not so calm. "The whole point of our opposition to this devilment is that it is un*natural*. Now you want us to help you remove even the small unsatisfactory safeguards that *are* in place against your Race playin' at being life builders! I will not allow it!" The big man folded his arms on his mammoth chest in frustration at not having a desk to pound on.

Pryce remained calm, however. "Jesse. I asked what they wanted, which is not the same as it being in my power to give them what they want. Even if we help them here, there's a long way for them to go before they get to that aim. We're not here because we agree on our end goals; we're here because right now, we might be able to find a mutually beneficial relationship."

"Relationship!"

"OK, not a relationship. A transaction. We give them something, they give us something. What we each make of our halves of the transaction afterwards is up to us."

Pryce adopted the pose of a curricula teacher, waiting patiently for her students to quieten and acknowledge her authority. When she raised her perfectly shaped eyebrows at him after fifteen seconds of this silent posturing, he reluctantly nodded his acquiescence. It was clear who the senior partner in *their* "relationship" was.

"OK, understood. For the short term, your goal is only to release the truth. You want to use it as propaganda to change a law in your favour. We want to use the truth as propaganda to change the economic system in which we're all imprisoned. I see no conflict in the short term. In the longer term, as Jesse states, we may once again become adversaries. That does not affect today."

Joberan hrmmphed but didn't contradict Pryce.

"We'll each make our own plans for swaying Race opinion after we win this round. Agreed?" Pryce moved swiftly on through the deafeningly silent lack of opposition. "How do we win this round together, Minnus?"

Minnus and his wife passed the silent ball between them again for too long.

Joules's impatience overcame him. "The same way you got in here. We get people on Minnus's wing in the hold, in secret. He gets his wing in through the top level of Telosec, bypassing all the layers of security from the ground up— same idea as you guys had last time. But this time we don't need to draw attention until the final moments."

Joberan glanced at Pryce guiltily, but the younger woman gave no sign at all that she acknowledged or even understood Joules's accusation.

Minnus took up the narration of the proposal. "I don't want to involve more people than necessary. There will likely be consequences in law for whoever is ultimately associated with the project. No matter the outcome, I don't want anyone harmed—especially Johnson. If we create a martyr, neither of our groups' subsequent plans to propagandise will be successful. Agreed?"

The pair of Daisy affiliates nodded silently.

"Security for those entering at the highest level of the building is low. Johnson *does* need to give a special clearance, but there are none of the metal- or explosives-detection systems that we'd have to negotiate if we entered through the front door. Johnson doesn't like to inconvenience the very meritorious persons that might want to come and inspect the facility. All we need is for Johnson to OK my wing to land. I'll cover that.

"Once we land, Joules and I will walk calmly into his office. We'll need a way to immobilise him and stop him calling for help but also leave his voice capable of giving commands to the central computer and probably the site-wide announcement system too. I need my access reinstated.

"Once I have access, I'll simply walk to the Postbox, open it, and use the normal interface to upload the true NV cast. After that, everyone will know pretty quickly what really happened on NineDee."

Joberan looked unconvinced, a tiny amount of exasperation visible in the centre of his massive head.

*If his head were normally proportioned, he'd probably look furious.*

After an undignified snort, the indignant preacher offered his counsel. "There are several problems with that idea. First, even if you do get your access reinstated, someone along your path is going to question your sudden restoration. I reckon your old boss wonna been singin' about your good grace all these weeks since he fired you. Someone'll react. What will you do? Convince them with logic? Cuss words?" The centre of the fat man's face puckered, like a whale's arse might if it had the runs. "Second, if Johnson has some kind of call-in—like, he presses a button every five minutes or something to confirm he's OK— then disabling him won't help. It'll draw attention to you eventually, and then you'll have one idealist sprinter against an armed Telosec squad." Joberan looked at Joules. "Not even you can run that fast."

Joules glared back at the irritating behemoth but didn't contradict him.

"Third, you have no way out whatsoever. How do you intend to do your propagandising if you're locked up awaiting trial? By puttin' yourself in the middle of this, you automatically expend all your credibility."

"We'd thought of your second point," Minnus responded as flatly as possible, no sign of the distaste he felt for Joberan's manner. "That's one of the reasons you're here—in addition to being the procurement arm of the operation. We figured that some of your men might escort me, with nonlethal weapons. Just in case."

Nombre and Minnus passed the mind football around again. For the second time, Nombre was the one ended up in possession and who stood up from her stool and spoke. "The last part is my place. I'll be immediately ready to speak to the media. I'll make sure to be first to the microphone. We already have some connections through Minnus and Joules's earlier casts, along with Moriarty. She'd take this in a picosecond if I offered an exclusive. Especially once the NV cast goes out. It'll be my job to make the Race see that Minnus and Joules had no choice."

Her jaw was set, and Minnus was proud of how determinedly she spoke. He knew from their earlier conversations, though, that she didn't want this outcome. Despite her set facade, an element of her hopes slipped through. "But if we can work out a way to get Minnus and Joules in and out unseen, I would of course prefer that."

Pryce and Joberan now exchanged their own thought ball through exaggerated expressions.

"You thinkin' what I'm a-thinkin'?" the enormous preacher asked the currencist.

Pryce acknowledged that she thought she probably was through a frown and slight chin oscillation. "Remote dead man?"

Joberan nodded his enthusiastic agreement. "Yes, ma'am!"

"The only way you're going to get him out unseen is to kill Johnson and wipe the records of who was approved to land that day. I'm guessing you're not going to go for that. Doesn't help your case anyway to leave bodies lying around, as you said—and eventually WorldGov would work it out. But we *can* get Minnus out, and nobody has to die, if you have the stomach for it."

"Go on," Minnus said.

Joberan took over earnestly. "Dead-man's switch. We let everyone know that you're carrying a trigger to a bomb, and if you're killed or incapacitated somehow, the switch will trigger the bomb. An old technique—something mechanical that you have to maintain a strong grip of to prevent the trigger from firing. If the bomb is in a significant-enough place, they'll let you walk out of there and get back on your wing without evening raising a hand to you."

It was Minnus's turn to look unconvinced.

"How would we get a bomb into a significant place in Telospace? All the systems are heavily guarded. We'd need the frontal assault that we've just explained that we want to avoid."

Joules, however, was quicker on the uptake this time. "I'm the bomb."

Minnus and Nombre looked at each other in dawning horror and then still amplified horror as they realised what would be needed.

"No," Minnus said emphatically.

"Minnus—" Joules began.

"No!" Minnus shouted back at him. "What if someone does accidentally shoot me? Frak! What if I trip and drop the frakin' trigger? I'd have murdered you and Johnson both!"

"Minnus," Joules started again, "I *want* to do it. Think about it. It gives us almost a guarantee that you make the upload. Johnson knows you ain't gonna destroy the Postbox. Frak, we can even *tell* him exactly what you *are* going to do before you leave his office. He won't suicide just to prevent an alternative cast going out. He's in this for his own power; killing himself would defeat everything he stands for. He'll order you and the team untouched. On top of that, if we can get out of there after we've done this, we can still run. Give you enough time to mount a campaign from the outside. It's a better idea, Minnus."

"And if I drop the trigger and kill you both?" Minnus retorted.

"You won't," Joules said simply. "Frak, tape it to your hand, man; then all you need to do is keep squeezing!

*Tape it?* An idea came to Minnus suddenly, and he jumped up. "What about faking a bomb? Wouldn't that have just the same effect?"

Joberan just smiled and shook his head.

Pryce answered the question, though. "The moment you get Johnson to make a pan-announcement that you're to be allowed to walk to and from the Postbox, every Telosec pair of eyes, sensor, sniffer dog, and mirrored lens is going to be pointed at his office. They'll know exactly whether you're bluffing or not before you even reach the Postbox."

"Good news is ya wouldn't need any of our guys for this plan. Bomb boy here is all the ammunition you'd need!" Joberan piped up.

Minnus sat down again, deflated. He looked to Nombre, who returned a noncommittal look. "I will back you, darling. This is the life of your Sero. I know what that means."

"It's only worth it if we get Sero back. To do that, my escape needs to increase our chances of starting the Race talking about him, talking about saving him. I wouldn't even know *where* to run to, never mind how. I'd anticipated being interviewed from prison when we came up with this. It's not worth the increased risk. There's no corresponding increased benefit."

"I can help with that," Pryce said. "I can set you up somewhere where there's a local currency that we can use to hide you. If you don't spend Red, and you don't use *your* cSheet, you can disappear. Trust me. I've done it. Several times."

"Why would you do that?" Minnus asked distrustfully.

Pryce's response was emotionless; matter-of-fact. "Because then we'll have power over you. We'll help you get your friend back, but you'll have to also start a conversation about the morality of the telonaut programme as a whole. You'll gain for us a much bigger slice of Race credibility than we can on our own. You're Man One, after all. Who better to represent us? Once that's done, whatever the outcome, our transaction will be complete."

Minnus dropped his elbows onto his knees and his forehead into his hands, massaging his creaking moral engine. He tried to weigh the options in a balanced way, but his mind simply didn't allow him to process such a level of risk to his family and friends. Sero versus Joules? The chance of Nombre being without him versus the chance of everyone dying? His children's opinion of him changing? He couldn't process the emotional consequences of making such a decision alone. All he could think to do was to ask those he was closest to in the room to make the decision for him.

He did it silently by raising his eyes to them in turn. When his eyes met Joules's, the athlete simply said yes. Commitment came easy to a man who'd gone through the physical dedication it took to win an Olympic five-hundred-metre-sprint gold. When he turned to Nombre, her own eyes were glazed with sheen. Crimping off a smile that nearly pushed the sheen out of her eyes and down her cheeks in rivulets, Minnus's wife said only, "I love you."

And with that, the decision was made. They would do it together, him and his family.

Minnus stood fully, his need to be upright entwined with a need to own their choice, to move it from a decision made to an action taken. He shook off his doubt, awakening his resolve by focusing on the clarity that the movement from thinking to *doing* always gave him. "OK," he said to the room. "Let's do this."

# FORTY-ONE

The standardCams swooped and sailed past each of the colonists.

All twelve hundred of them were lined up atop the
Gesponnen plate. They were all ceremonially dressed, tendril crowns adorning their brow that were similar to the
giant one on the monolithic statue of Leaf in Gesponnen
proper. Even Sero and Prid wore the vine-ringlet hoops
in addition to their standard clothes, maintaining the visual continuity that joined their earlier audit to the later
sections recorded by the standardCams in between their
nights of captivity. Sero was in one of the original black
outfits he'd been given on arrival, with a few knowing ad-
ditions of local creation: tendril boots and a belt with a
spray can and a cutter looped onto it. Prid was dressed in
her usual coveralls and still had her bandolier of tendril
canisters draped across her body. Zwolf-Zahir was wise
enough to know that she needed to be in the standardCam

footage for there to be no questions raised back on Earth. If she was to be in the footage, then of course she also had to look the same as she did in earlier recordings, especially when Sero had made such a focus of the inventive ways she'd used her tools. So here they both were, backs straight, standing at the front of a group of Zahirs as the focus of one of the standardCams whilst the other two soared around the plate.

They were twenty-five metres above the tentaculos floor, standing on the plateau ring of steel that encircled the soon-to-be-destroyed megafauna. The previous fifteen minutes had been filled with them each reciting the lines that had been given to them that morning by Zwolf-Zahir, asking him questions about the order of the day: What could they expect? How long would the process take? Now they were each standing in a prechoreographed formation that the Zahirs thought offered them all a fair view but also looked the most impressive for the circling cameras.

NineCents was vibrating a countdown into the steel below their feet so that they could all hear how close they were to the beginning of the steel quake and the hoped-for culmination of their collective decades-long efforts. With twenty seconds to go, the crowd had hushed into a nervous quiet; each stood alone, but all focused on the impending moment. As the countdown reached ten seconds remaining, Sero took several sidesteps to his right and took hold of Prid's hand. It was off script, but he figured that they had nothing to lose now, and the Zahirs were all too fixed on the approaching critical moment to notice anyway.

NineCents's voice was rolling around them, emanating from the steel beneath the feet of all twelve hundred colonists so it could be heard universally at the same time. The effect was like standing on the skin of a gigantic talking drum.

"Four. Three. Two. One."

Immediately as the computer finished the countdown, a deep, booming hum filled the air around them as the orbiting satellites directed soundwaves into the steel deep beneath their feet, causing the entire circumference of the kilometres-wide ring to vibrate at the same frequency and at the same time. There was no "steelquake" as such—no huge shifting of the plain on which they stood. Only an unsettling feeling of pressure, something additional to the atmosphere, as though there were something between the molecules in the air that wasn't usually there, taking up space that was normally bare.

Prid and Sero stood and watched the horizon together. The diameter of the ring was so great that they couldn't see the opposite side; the horizon was somewhere around 75 percent of the way across the ring. The background hum of the vibrating plate was so loud that they couldn't have been heard if they'd tried to speak, so they each instead wordlessly looked for symptoms of the tentaculos disintegrating in front of them. For several minutes, there were none. The briefing from Zwolf-Zahir for the benefit of the cameras had surmised that there should be some visual disintegration of the tentaculos within just a few minutes. Sero began to consider whether the dissolution might not be successful.

As his mind wandered towards the contingencies he'd tried to plan for such an outcome, Prid squeezed his hand and pointed away to their right. At first, Sero couldn't see what she was aiming at, but when he squinted his eyes into farsight, he could make out a bubbling of water appearing on the surface of the tentaculos about five hundred metres away from the plate wall. Prid pointed again, this time away to their left. Very quickly, dozens of small fountains began sprouting all across the plain. *It's working.*

Despite the difficulty of their situation, Sero found it hard not to be drawn into the moment. Even if the scheme had been hatched and reared by a slaughterhouse lunatic, the ambition of creating an inland sea in this way still held romance. The concept had such scale that Sero found himself giving in to natural human awe.

His contemplation was broken by a sound that was even louder than the background hum of the vibrating plate. He snapped his head back around to the right, in the direction of the first fountain to spring. In its place, a huge jet of water had erupted, almost matching the height of the steel wall on which they stood. Several of the Zahir audience had jumped backwards, surprised by the aggression of the upsurge, even though it was half a kilometre away.

Sero noticed that a space had opened up around him and Prid. It was only a few metres, but that was a few metres more freedom than he'd had at any time in the last few months. *And Prid is with me!*

He looked around. Each one of the Zahirs was transfixed by the beginning of the fruition of their dream. Not a single one of them was looking at Sero or Prid. With no real idea of what would happen if they managed to flee from the Zahirs right at that moment, Sero made an instinctive decision. *The first step is to get away from them. We'll work the rest out later.* With so many of the Zahirs on top of the plate, though, there was no chance that the extra distance would give Sero and Prid enough of a head start to reach two different transports and make it back to the two Postboxes. If they got away, they'd be escaping to live in the wilderness of NineDee, perhaps forever. *Doesn't matter. Prid will live.* Sero leaned in as close as he could to Prid's ear, trying to be heard over the roar of jetting water and the ring of humming steel.

"Prid, when there is enough open space below the plate wall—enough clear water—we're going to run and jump off the plate."

A mute, surprised, and questioning look.

"It's the best chance we have to get away from them. I don't think they'll jump after us en masse, and we might be able to fight off only a few of them. The water will be a good leveller."

Prid seemed to consider this for a second before slowly nodding. She tapped her candolier. "Yes. I've got this cutting tool too. We have some resources thanks to Zahir's obsession with prepackaging the camera footage for the Race."

The two held eye contact for a single second. In that one second, Sero imagined a lifetime of choices that they might make together, problems that they might overcome. Prid was so young, so unready for death. She was still less ready to have her body stolen from her as a parting gift for her road to the void. Sero could stop that. He could help her. He'd never wanted anything more than to protect the precious young woman in front of him now. *Daughter.*

"You ready?" he said.

Prid nodded subtly again.

"OK. I'll squeeze your hand to count. We go on three. Sprint a dead-straight line to the edge of the plate, and then we jump."

He surveyed the scene around him. There was still a gap between him and the nearest Zahir. About fifteen metres. The distance to the edge of the plate was around fifteen metres too. If they managed to maintain the element of surprise, he was sure they could make the edge of the cliff before any of the Zahirs even reacted. He watched the tentaculos break apart in front of him, jets of liquid acting like pressure drills to divide the tentaculos into small islands on the quickly forming lake and then retreating back into the water as they holes they formed became too wide to produce a spurt through pressure.

Sero was too far back from the edge of the plate to know whether a pool of water had opened up directly under where they'd be jumping. He didn't want to risk jumping blind unless they absolutely had to. *Not going to swim very far with broken legs.* They had to wait as long as possible to give the best chance that their jump wouldn't have lethally debilitating consequences.

As subtly as he could, Sero also tried to watch the closest Zahirs for any sign of them closing the gap between himself and them and, with it, closing Sero and Prid's window of escape. It was a game of brinksmanship.

Meanwhile, the water jets seemed to have passed their peak intensity and were now much fewer in number and lower in height. In his peripheral vision, Sero noted that some of the Zahirs had begun walking towards the edge of the plate to look over the edge. *If they cut us off, we have no chance.* Worse than that, the two nearest Zahirs seemed to have noticed how far away they'd become from their captives and were edging back towards Sero and Prid as they regarded the near fully formed lake.

The two nearest happened to be large males, well over two metres tall. Feeling there was no more time, Sero decided to take a chance. He didn't know for certain that there would be a soft landing once they leapt, but if they didn't move now, there might be no opportunity to jump at all. He squeezed Prid's hand slowly and firmly, making sure she couldn't mistake the signal. One, two, three! They bolted for the lip of the plate, still holding hands as they ran.

Although the distance was mere metres, the journey seemed to Sero to happen in slow motion, each step plodding and insufficient. He willed himself towards the edge in his mind. *Come on!* After an infinite pair of seconds, they'd reached within two long strides of the point they'd leap. Sero felt the muscles in his legs coil beneath him, ready to push both him and Prid out into empty space. He felt Prid tighten her grip on his right hand as she also prepared to spring. *Nearly there!*

Just as Sero began to unleash the power bent at his knee, he was tackled from behind and to his left by two flying metres of onrushing horizontal Zahir. The impact threw him off balance and cancelled his attempt to propel himself off the plate. Instead, he fell to the ground unevenly just shy of the rim. Prid had not been tackled, though, and had made her jump. When they came to rest, it was with Sero pinned to the plate by the hefty Zahir smothering his legs and Prid hanging out over the plate rim, dangling from Sero's arm, their hands still tightly clasped together.

Panicked, Sero began to buck and kick, trying to remove enough of the Zahir's weight that he might slip out from beneath it and slide off the plate and into the water that he could now see was definitely below Prid. The Zahir held fast to him though, for long enough to be joined by the second male, who quickly sat astride Sero's lower back in a mount that Sero knew he'd never be able to escape from. He was caught. Rather than despair, though, the realisation seemed to free Sero from panic. *I can protect her. I can free her.*

He looked down at Prid, and the world around him returned to slow-motion hyperreality. She was tugging and swinging at his wrist with both hands as though she thought she might jerk all three men over the edge of the plate and into the tentaculos sea with her. She couldn't. For an instant, Sero's mind returned to another precipice, light-years away. He saw a different love swinging from his desperate clinch. He thought he smelled the bark of trees and the coppery taint of blood, felt something sticky and slick in his palm. *Aleph.* A shudder of regret passed through him and centred into a lump that was forming in his throat, closing it to air. Then a scream from Prid returned him to the present.

"Sero!"

He looked directly at her, twisting his head and body as much as he could under the force of the men pinning him down so that he could get the best eye contact possible. Under the still-buzzing roar of the vibrating plate, Sero mouthed the words "I love you." Then he let go of her hand and dropped Prid into the water just as the Zahirs got enough control of him to drag him away from the edge.

He didn't see her hit the water.

⩓

They didn't beat him. It seemed to him that they weren't even interested in him. After the two big Zahirs had dragged him back from the edge of the plate, they'd been joined by another dozen colonists, and Sero had been surrounded and marched down the ringlet staircase and off the plate in near silence. As he was removed, he'd noticed some of the Zahirs looking over the edge of the plate where Prid had escaped, but none of them had seemed to react as though they could see her. Certainly none of them had made the leap to follow her into the water. As Sero stood in the haloMagnet transport, hands tied, he smiled to himself. *She might have made it. She might live.* He felt good.

He was accompanied by Dini-Zahir, Zwolf-Zahir and the same two tall Zahirs who had foiled his own escape. The haloMagnet wasn't big enough for five of them, and they'd made him stand for the entire three hours it had taken to travel back to the main colony Postbox at Park 359. Throughout the journey, the Zahirs had spoken only of Leaf and how the success of the dissolution had opened the way for them to create wonders in her memory—five previously identical minds speaking to themselves in self-referential, reverential tones. Sero had ultimately tuned them out.

He did not have even a passing interest in their schemes and ambitions. His thoughts were only of Prid and his hopes for *her* future. He imagined her swimming to freedom, climbing the plate wall in some remote location using some ingenious tendril construction, building a home. She had a chance of life, and he knew that even if that chance was slight, she still existed. She was still an independent, free-thinking individual. Prid was still Prid.

Throughout the course of the journey, Sero had daydreamed about the future for her. Maybe she would steal into the colony one night and free other youngsters. Perhaps she could co-opt NineCents somehow and improve her odds. He was awoken from his hopeful contemplation by NineCents announcing their arrival at the park.

Zwolf-Zahir instructed Sero to get out and begin walking towards the Postbox with a minimum of fuss. There was no pretence at making himself understood in any deeper way. He simply gave Sero an instruction and expected it to be followed. The threat of forced compliance was implied with little subtlety. Nobody spoke again as the group filed across the open space of the park and then down below the surface of the tentaculos and across the force-field bridge to the Postbox, but Sero noticed that the three standardCams had emerged from the transport with them and were following them as they moved. They didn't seem to be recording, though, following in flat formation only rather than adopting differing perspectives of the scene.

When they were halfway through the underwater tunnel to the Postbox, Zwolf-Zahir began to speak. "This will be the end of you, Auditor." Still detached and businesslike.

Sero didn't speak. He only nodded his understanding.

"We have decided to adapt MOOI once more. We've been working on the programme since you arrived here, in fact. You'll enter the Postbox as normal—although accompanied by my brothers here. They will ensure you begin the transportation process, forcibly if necessary. You will never leave the blank bubble again, though. The latest copy of my mind will travel with your body signal, not your own spider map. As you know, once the signal is received, blank bubbling will begin on Earth, and nobody can interfere in the growth process. My mind will awake in a Sero Novak copy body on Earth, which will press the kill switch, evaporating all material in the postage facility here on NineDee."

One of the lanky twins spoke up. "We will die of starvation long before the lasers come, but our sacrifice will be worth it. Our brother on Earth will further build Leaf's glory by showing the Race what has been built here and explaining the footage we've recorded. She will be known throughout history as the inspiration for our efforts—truly the mother of a civilisation."

"We tell you this as a courtesy," Zwolf-Zahir finished. "We are not so different, you and I."

Sero could feel the look of surprise at the statement take possession of his face. He withheld the snarling, venomous response that immediately came to mind though. *Pointless. Prid is free and has a chance now. My own chances depend on Minnus. No value in philosophical argument here. What am I going to do? Change their mind?*

"Oh, I see you flinch at the idea, but if you look inside yourself, you'll see that I'm right. We're bred of the same template, each of our gene sets combining to produce organisms with the same taste and preference for purist social advancement. The original brain from which all of our spider maps on NineDee came was not so dissimilar to yours, Mr. Novak. We are from very similar segments of a phenotypal 'normal' distribution, you and I. But for happy accident, it might be you standing in my place and me in yours."

Sero remained silent and stony faced until the Zwolf-Zahir shrugged and led the group on to the Postbox. When they arrived, the false patriarch lowered the drawbridge to the postage facility and went inside alone. Sero assumed the old bastard would be spider mapping his mind.

The Dini-Zahir had said nothing since they'd left the transport. With Zwolf-Zahir alone inside the Postbox, it took its turn at leading the conversation. "You have nothing to say, Auditor? That seems like something of an anticlimax for one with so storied a history as you. Surely you'd at least like some last words, even if they're unrecorded and heard only by us?"

Sero considered this for a moment before he decided to speak. What would be the point in correcting them? What value would his perspective offer to a megalomaniacal creed such as had been built on NineDee? He felt disgust for the creature in front of him and its entire kin. He felt horror at the way these monsters had treated Prid. He felt anger on behalf of all the lives snuffed out by the wicked mind that had stolen their bodies. But most of all, he felt pity. In the end, it wasn't his anger or disgust that drove him to speak but rather his disappointment. Sero was disappointed in humanity. For all its creations and discoveries, even with the climax society that the Race had developed to manage the worst instincts of man, Sero wondered now whether humanity could truly be deserving of any future at all.

The Race held individuals who could destroy on the scale he'd seen there in NineDee. Normal distribution or not, if the human species and the social construct that the species had developed to control the extremes of that distribution could still manufacture such evil—could still destroy the happiness of others by making selfish choices, could still delude itself of its own self-justifying worth, would yet steal, do murder, and lie to its own membership—then what answer should the universe give in judgement? Sero spoke to Dini-Zwolf only out of pity for what it represented.

"All that you think you've built, all that you've accomplished, and all of your dreams for the future are but wet paper facades in a hailstorm. You claim love as your motivation, devotion as your propulsion, and yet you've entirely missed the point of love. Your relationship with Leaf wasn't a mutual sharing of selves. You didn't exist only for each other's happiness. You were rejected by her. Spurned.

"Ultimately, Leaf killed herself rather than be trapped on this planet with a hundred versions of you. Out of that tragedy, you built a religion. A blind and endless debt to a woman you had pressed into the most despairing of choices. No matter what you build here, no matter whom you tell about it, you can never atone for the murders done or the suicides driven.

"When you tire of your great project, when the final building is erected as attempted recompense to the woman whose life you destroyed, you will not feel complete. It will not secure for you the love you crave. All of this is not about Leaf. It is about you. There will only ever be *you* in your life now. No others. So there can be no sharing; there can be no sacrifice; there can be no love.

"I've known love. In knowing it, I've learned why we exist as a species. I've dreamt, as you also claim to, of advancing our knowledge as a race; I've hoped to be significant as a member of a noteworthy species in our universe. But I've learned that significance is not sufficient. If nobody is close to you—if there is nobody independent to grow with and to share with, to teach as an individual—then there is no point in significance at all. You exert your will over a host of selves, no one of them worth any more effort than a dallied internal conversation in the mind of a madman. Without your being significant to another person on an intimate level, you'll only ever be a brick in the path that the truly significant walk upon.

"You're no human that I understand or could ever admire, whatever you build. On behalf of the Race, I strip you of the title of 'human.' You have devalued it. I pity you."

As the Zwolf-Zahir reemerged from the Postbox, Sero strode past him without a word. Once inside, he completed the familiar formalities that initiated a transport in similar silence, watched by the two goon-Zahirs, their fists balled in readiness for any attempt he might make to alter their plans. Sero didn't make any such attempt, though. He calmly remapped his mind and sent it on to Minnus as his final fragment download, pretending for his audience that he was merely doing this to initiate the blank-bubble process.

As the drawbridge closed behind the furthest guard, Sero stepped over to the spot where the blank bubble would soon form. He didn't look at the Zahirs, didn't hear any of their threatened commands to stay where he was and wait. He thought of Aleph and Prid, his family. He felt proud to have known them. Although he might have been about to die, he did so in the knowledge that he'd fulfilled his purpose as a man. He had loved, he had been loved, and he'd passed his belief in love on to a younger generation.

Sero closed his eyes and thought of the future that might have been as the bubble shimmered into vibrating isolation around him.

# Forty-Two

Everything was prepared. For all his dislike of the White Daisy organisation, Minnus had to admit that they were controlled and committed. Once the deal had been forged between himself, Pryce, and Joberan, it had taken less than two weeks for the equipment they'd need to be literally delivered to his door in the same way that Joberan and Pryce had themselves been smuggled in and out—in the hold compartment of his wing. He and Joules had carried the boxes of "groceries" into Minnus's apartment the previous evening and were now running through how they worked using the instructions that had arrived with them—conveniently stored on an air-gapped cSheet.

"OK. I think I've got it," Joules said as he gingerly lifted the harness away from his neck and placed it carefully back in the steel-and-ceramic box that had been disguised as a fruit delivery. "It's actually lighter than you might think. I wouldn't like to try it, but I think you could run in this thing if needed. We'll probably need to at some point, right? Anyway, I can arm the bomb with this button that's connected to the vest. I'll trail that down my shirt sleeve here and have the button in my palm when we get into the office."

"Remember that it's single use, though, Joules. Once you press it, you're armed, and only my trigger switch can disarm it."

"That's a good thing though, right? Means that they can't force me to turn it off if they storm Johnson's office. They'll have to comply and let you keep on walkin'."

Joules seemed to even be enjoying the preparation. He had always been more comfortable with an objective to achieve. It seemed that a potentially suicidal infiltration was no different from knocking two-tenths of a second off his personal best. A simple causal chain. *We need to do x to achieve y. Why are we still standing here talking? X needs doing!*

Minnus took stock one more time before packing his own equipment back up. He had taped the dead-man switch to his left hand as Joules had suggested. He tested the strength of grip he'd need to keep applied. It wasn't so much, but Minnus could imagine that he might still fatigue if there was any kind of delay. He had also received some protective clothing that could be worn under his shirt. It was a form of adaptive plastiche armour that moulded to his figure once activated. All pretty simple to use and hopefully unnecessary, but the items were unfamiliar to

Minnus. He wanted to be sure that using them wouldn't be a problem for him in a high-stress situation. *Ready as I'll ever be, I guess!*

As he was removing the armour, his cSheet flashed and alerted him that his house computer had finished a task. It was the NV algorithm. It had completed the processing of Sero's latest memory fragment. Viewing the fragments had become something of a morbid ritual for the Mbekis. In the last month, as he had been around so much, Joules had also taken to sitting in their home and viewing with them.

"Is that the latest one?" Nombre asked as she entered the room, already moving to collect the three NV sets that were stored in the wall bay on the other side of the workshop in anticipation of Minnus's answer.

"Yep," Minnus called after her, himself hurriedly removing the tape at his wrist to free the trigger from his hand. By the time he'd untied himself and activated his NV set, Nombre and Joules were already seated, and the latest memory segment from Sero was queued up and ready for viewing. As soon as he had the set in place over his eyes and ears, Minnus activated the stream.

Together, they watched the condensed final day from Sero's perspective. When they began watching, they didn't know that it represented his final day on NineDee, a torrent of tests and traumas.

They saw Sero's reference to his father, Won, when comforting a terrified Prid, and they heard his voice as he spoke the old man's mantra to her: "Optimism. Perseverance. Patience."

They all cried as they heard Prid call Sero her father for the first time, as proud of her spirit as Sero himself must have been.

They marvelled as they heard Zahir explain the fullest details yet of his ability to send information into the already formed blank bubble, thereby making possible the concept of instantaneous teleportation.

They saw the dissolution of Leaf Day begin through Sero's eyes and were shocked as he and Prid ran towards the edge of the Gesponnen plate.

They replayed Sero's decision to drop Prid several times through, all agreeing that it was an intentional and desperate attempt to free her.

And then they saw Sero dragged into a transport and held down.

*Oh no!* Minnus flung off his NV set and leapt to his feet. "Frak!"

His two viewing partners we're clearly surprised, removing their own NV sets more slowly and looking askance at Minnus.

"Joules, seal that crate! We have to go. Right now!" Minnus was hurriedly strapping the plastiche armour back to his chest as he spoke.

"Darling. What do you mean? What's wrong?" Nombre asked.

"No time!" Minnus shouted, flailing with the tape he'd previously used to test his dead-man trigger device.

"Hey, buddy, calm down," Joules suggested.

"Don't you see? Their project worked. They don't need to keep him alive anymore. They have no more energy problems! Sero's threat is powerless now. In the footage we just saw, they were taking him to the Postbox!"

Joules didn't look like he understood, but he'd already begun following Minnus's flustered request to pack up. "Meaning?" he asked as he clamped the ceramic rim of his bomb case closed.

"Meaning that we're on a clock. If they went straight to the Postbox and began postage, we could be only hours or even minutes away from reception beginning here on Earth. They might have sent his body back ahead of schedule. And it might not be Sero's mind that's mapped into that body when it's built. Just as we feared."

Nombre then seemed to suddenly understand what Minnus was trying to communicate. "And if reception begins, the reception facility will automatically lock up. It doesn't matter what power you gain over Johnson— nobody can open that door from the outside."

Minnus saw the same horror that he felt inside fill the eyes of his wife.

"I have to get in there right now. I need to occupy the facility until we get some help from WorldGov. The only way to prevent reception beginning is to put a person in that room and have them not leave. The transmission protocol won't allow the blank bubbling to begin unless the reception facility is free of other humans. It might be Sero's only chance."

Joules now also seemed to fully grasp the situation. He lifted the bomb crate from the floor gently and sprint-shuffled out towards the wing outside the apartment, waddling at controlled speed. "I'm on it. See you outside." He kissed Nombre on the cheek as he passed, hugless due to his explosive burden.

Minnus had meanwhile hurriedly docked his cSheet into the arm of his workstation chair, downloading the remaining, unviewed NV footage into it via physical connection, completing the set of "real" NV episodes for broadcast.

"Nombre—"

"I know."

"I might not be coming back for a long time. If I have to wait there until this is resolved, it might be weeks. Longer."

"I know"

"I—"

"Minnus. I love you. You've given me everything you could. Our children, our family, our friends. All of them. You've been there. You've built us. Go give your friend a chance to build his own family. That girl might still be alive up there."

Minnus couldn't help but be overcome by her support. All those decades together. She truly did understand him better than he understood himself. "I love you, Nombre."

"I know, old man. I've felt it every day for a lifetime." She stepped to him and threw her arms around his shoulders, kissing him passionately. "Now go!"

Minnus sprinted for his wing.

⋏

Once in flight, Joules removed the bomb vest from the carry crate and began preciously dressing himself in it for the second time that afternoon. He was in the rear of the wing, hidden from the sensors on the front-facing dashboard above the primary passenger.

In the primary passenger's seat, Minnus had given the wing instructions to move with maximum speed to the Antarctic location of Telospace. Having buttoned his normal shirt over the body armour he now wore, he had dialled up Johnson on his cSheet, using the dash sensor to project an image of his own face to Johnson's cSheet. Surprisingly, Johnson answered almost immediately, and Minnus had just barely composed himself before he was being broadcast into Johnson's office. He could picture the ostentatious hologram that Johnson preferred to use when on a cSheet call, likely magnifying Minnus's head and shoulders to an unnecessarily large scale on his office table.

"Idi. No time to explain now, but we're coming to see you. You have a problem, old friend, and I think I might be the only one who can help you."

"Hello, Minnus," Johnson said pleasantly, if a little cautiously. "Are you OK?"

"Yes. No. Well, you'll see when I get to you. You don't know it, but you need my help!"

"I do?" Johnson was clearly suspicious, answering slowly and uncertainly, but he was also too sly to reject a potential ally in the event of an as-yet-undescribed crisis—a characteristic Minnus hoped to lean on. "How so? This is all a bit abrupt, Minnus. We haven't even exchanged a hello. Everything looks fine from my perspective."

"No, it's not. I'm bringing something to show you. It's dangerous. For you and for me. Evidence. If it gets out, I'll never get Sero back, and you'll definitely never be able to stand for a representative position in WorldGov."

"Evidence? Evidence of what," Johnson said in an affected manner, playing up to his self-defined standard of plausible deniability. *He's not soft. He's concerned about being recorded or observed.*

"You must know I've been watching the fragments as they arrive...this is the last broadcast, Johnson," Minnus said. "If you run the most recent fragment through my new algorithm rather than the one you're still using, you'll see. If what I think might happen next does indeed come to pass, there'll be no election for you...and I'll lose my oldest friend."

"I see," Johnson said calmly, despite what Minnus knew must be the liquid fear of loss filling his lungs.

"Look, I'm heading to you now at maximum speed. Joules is with me. We watched the fragment edit together. We'll be with you in fifteen minutes. Just make sure we can land at your office. I've got the details physically loaded onto my cSheet. I can explain once we're inside. This isn't something we should stream.

"I've got to go, Idi. I need to make a few last checks on my calculations before we get to you. There isn't much time."

With that last injection of urgency, Minnus gestured for his cSheet to close the connection, hoping he'd layered enough political risk into his communication to interest Johnson in allowing him access to the top floor of the Telospace facility once more. Minnus had been fired just a few months previously. He didn't have a plan B to fall back on if he and Joules couldn't get close to Johnson. *It has to work!*

"Joules," he called back through to the wing's hold. "He's gone. We're alone again. Come up here?"

Joules Chavez walked carefully into the front section of the wing ten seconds later, his expression grim but determined. He was in the competitive zone, Minnus knew, pre-visualising the success of what he was about to commit to.

"We're…fourteen minutes out. Let's watch a ten-minute version of what's remaining of the NV cast. Better to know it all now before we broadcast."

Minnus instructed his cSheet to project a two-dimensional conversion of the remaining unviewed edit of the memory fragment onto his dash display. The two men watched Sero's final sombre walk to the postage facility and conversations with the Zahirs in the forbidding silence of the hurtling vehicle. As the wing arrived into a landing cycle at Telospace, they saw the final image from the fragment. It was of two large colonists staring at Sero as he walked towards the spider mapper. They were both standing inside the Postbox, with the facility door sealed.

⅄

It looked like Johnson might even make it easy for them. Minnus's wing autopiloted in to land on the designated spot fifteen metres from the door into Johnson's office. Minnus could see Johnson waiting outside the door, alone. *Maybe I convinced him? Maybe he's keen to talk privately?* If Johnson was truly alone, their plan had a much higher chance of success. They needed it to be easy too; any delay might mean that the reception of the Sero-Zahir might have already begun by the time Minnus made it to the Postbox. He wanted to focus on the rough mental arithmetic that his subconscious was trying to force him to calculate. *How long do I have? If they began postage immediately after Sero uploaded the last fragment, how long before the bubble would have formed? When will we receive the signal here on Earth?* Minnus couldn't concentrate on the mental work, though. It didn't matter. He just needed to get to the Postbox as fast as possible.

"When we set down, we walk with urgency, but we don't run. Don't worry him until we're inside. Can you cover the bomb vest properly?" Minnus asked Joules.

"Yeah, we're good. Just get us inside, and then I'll take over. I know what I'm going to do."

There was no time for further discussion. The two friends simply had to trust each other. They hugged in silence as the wing door began to open, forming a short ramp. Minnus was aware enough to break the hug before they were visible from the outside, and when the ramp hit the floor, he was already walking towards the Telospace head, seemingly standing sentry at the entrance to his office.

Johnson called out to them as they walked, easily audible across the distance. Unusually for Antarctica, there was no noticeable wind. "What is this about, Minnus?"

"It's not him, Johnson. I have proof."

"What?"

It's not *him*," Minnus replied with more emphasis. He and Joules had now crossed the space between the Wing and Johnson's position outside his door. Minnus was waving his cSheet for emphasis on exactly where his evidence was. "It's not Sero. They're going to send back a signal, but it won't be Sero. I have it all here. An NV record of a confession."

"So what?" Johnson said. "If they send back a colonist on a return journey instead of Sero, we'll just receive them and wait for Sero in the next signal." There was a questioning tone to his response, still suspicious.

"You don't understand, Idi! It will be Sero's body but not his mind! You won't be able to hide that amongst all the publicity. Who knows what Zahir intends to do once he's here masquerading as Sero? Look, it's all on here. You need to look at this NV edit right now so that we can decide what to do!" He held the cSheet right in front of his former colleague.

Minnus wasn't sure if the younger man was buying what he was selling. Johnson had always been difficult to read, and this was no different. Minnus's impatience had almost driven him to break with the plan and attack Johnson. He needed to get in there immediately! Without looking back across his shoulder, he could feel that Joules was similarly eager to act. Nervous tension filled the space around them. Just as Minnus shifted his weight slightly on his feet in preparation for a lunge at Johnson, his former boss turned and waved at the office entrance.

"Follow me."

Minnus moved to follow but was pushed aside by an onrushing Joules Chavez. Minnus could barely follow the movement as Joules stepped close behind Johnson and reached under his target's arms and around his waist. The big Olympian grabbed a fistful of Johnson's jacket in each hand, just above his belt on either side of his midriff. He yanked hard on the material, pulling it backwards and upwards, chic old-fashioned buttons popping and spilling onto the floor as he did so. In a fraction of a second, Joules had the tail of Johnson's jacket lifted over the back of the Telospace chief's head and down hard over his eyes. Surprised, Johnson began to turn, likely to ask Joules what the frak he thought he was doing, but Joules only let him make a quarter of a turn before swinging his giant sprinter's leg around and tripping the disadvantaged executive to the ground as he flailed blindly. A further fraction of a second after Johnson hit the floor, Joules landed on his chest. By the time Minnus joined them in the office just a moment later, Joules was sitting on Johnson's sternum, the big man's knees pinning the smaller man's arms to the ground at the biceps.

"Dead man!" shouted Joules.

Minnus slipped the trigger from his pocket and squeezed it tightly closed. "In place!"

Being restrained by a 110-kilogram athlete shouting about dead men didn't have a calming effect on Johnson, who began bucking underneath Joules. In response, he received a sharp jab to the nose from his assailant.

"That's enough, Joules!" Minnus intervened before a second blow could be delivered. "Idi, just stay still and listen."

Minnus walked over to the pair and opened Joules's jacket for him, which allowed his partner to maintain the downwards pressure of his body anchoring Johnson to the floor. Minnus wasted no time in getting right to the heart of his ultimatum.

"This is a bomb. It is big enough to kill you, Idi." Minnus pointed to the vest now visible across his friend's chest. "This is the trigger to the bomb," he said, waving his left hand and showing the dead-man switch. "The two are rotating on matched frequencies. If I drop the trigger or release the pressure on the switch, the bomb goes off. It is in your interest to make sure that doesn't happen."

For the final message, Minnus leant over his prostrate former boss and stared hard into his eyes.

"I am going to the Postbox to save the life of my oldest friend. I will not stop. Your job is to make sure I get there still holding this switch."

He gave a quick glance at Joules and then walked quickly to the elevator at the far end of the office and through the door.

⋏

The descent was over quickly—less than ten seconds to drop the one hundred metres to the level of Telosec that allowed access to the bridge—but Minnus heard Johnson's voice before the doors opened. He was broadcasting to all cSheets in the facility.

"All team members. This is Idi Johnson. Our colleague Minnus Mbeki is with us today and is heading to the Postbox on an urgent mission. Do not delay or assail him in any way."

The message was unusual, and Minnus was sure it would create some consternation amongst the staff, but it was unambiguous at least. As the elevator doors opened in front of him and he set off running as fast as his aging legs would allow him, he noticed that Johnson had also instructed that the doorways and access points between him and the bridge all be opened. He could see almost clear through the office and medical areas right through to the bridge itself.

Freed from the concerns of getting access to the facility, Minnus now had the time to do the calculations he'd been putting off. He ran over them in his mind as he bodily ran towards his goal. *Final fragment ninety minutes ago...editing took a half an hour...twenty minutes of us watching...ten minutes packing...Flight time of twenty minutes and another ten minutes to get to this point. How long would it have taken to divert enough joule-routes on NineDee to create the blank bubble? Three hours?*

The Postbox wouldn't have sent the signal unless the bubble was fully formed, so there would be a finite but significant gap between the arrival of Sero's final memory fragment and the arrival of the signal to begin building a new blank bubble and copy body. *Most of the transmissions on Earth had formed a bubble in two hours or even longer, but they were sharing energy capacity with the rest of a fully populated planet. NineDee had no such constraints and was a wetworld. It might have happened more quickly.* Minnus knew he could be cutting his arrival very close.

He'd made it through the offices by this point, dozens of heads staring at him as they watched a 120-year-old man sprint-shuffle through the walkway between their stations. Minnus caught glimpses of some of their faces as he passed. Some of them seemed shocked, some amused. A couple of the faces seemed scared. Minnus imagined them wondering what terror might make an old man hurry like that. *Life and death, kids, life and death. Nothing more important to an old man.*

He pushed on past the medical facility as quickly as he could and moved straight out onto the bridge. He passed four armed Telosec agents as he crossed the bridge threshold, but none moved to stop his progress. Once beyond them, Minnus felt immediately alone.

The force field protecting the tunnel barely refracted the light of the windless Antarctic day so as to offer Minnus the illusion that he was exposed on the high-up connection bridge. There were dots visible against the reception facility at the far end of the bridge, which Minnus assumed must be similarly stationed guards protecting the entrance to the facility itself, but from the hundreds of metres away that he was at that point, they were nonanthropomorphic smears of shade against the open doorway of the facility. He pressed on harder in the isolation of the skywalk but knew he was slowing. Despite being in good health for a centenarian, he was no endurance athlete. His lungs were beginning to signal their displeasure by sucking in less and less of the oxygen he needed to keep moving. Minnus's pace dropped. He simply couldn't keep going at that level of exertion. His maximum speed after two minutes of running was much lower than his initial maximum speed. He kept forcing one foot in front of the other through the will of a desperate man.

As he fatigued, he glanced more and more often at the dead-man trigger in his left hand—he hadn't had time to tape it since leaving Johnson's office. It felt secure, but his tiring gait had him worried that he might slip and accidentally murder his friend and the ultimately innocent Johnson.

He'd made it just over halfway along the bridge, driving as hard as he could whilst trying not to focus on the risk of becoming a double murderer, when he saw the problem. In between the four Telosec guards, arranged in their two rows, Minnus could see that the drawbridge to the Postbox was lifting, rising back onto the facility to seal the entrance. *It's starting! The signal is here!*

He tried to spur himself on faster and managed a spurt for a few seconds that raised his pace back above the canter he'd settled unhappily into, but that was all it took for him to gauge the movement of the door against his own pace and realise he wouldn't make it. In desperation, Minnus began screaming to the guards.

"Get inside! Get inside the Postbox now! Get inside!"

If they could hear him, they made no move to act on his plea. He began waving his arms as he ran all too slowly towards them, trying to mime that they should dive for the lip of the draw door and pull themselves in. *Just one of you! Please!* But the agents didn't move towards the door. Instead, the nearest one began running away from the door and towards Minnus. Despondent, Minnus fell to his knees and screamed, completely emptying his lungs of the little air they had left.

Sero's life flashed before Minnus's eyes. It wasn't enough. Sero had seen seven worlds, looked through eleven pairs of different eyes, delivered on all the dreams of his childhood. But it wasn't enough. Minnus had watched Sero grow into the man that a younger Sero had hoped for, but what a low limit to place on a life—to have achieved what a twelve-year-old boy thought important.

Minnus had seen so much more, been afforded so much more learning through his family. Despite his many lives, Sero hadn't lived. And now, he was dead. His physical presence in the universe was reduced only to a mind stored on a permaDrive. Something that would look and sound like him would soon step from the doors of the reception facility, and Minnus would likely have to confront the despot that would wear his friend's face. Somewhere elevated into other dimensions, that face was already owned by Zahir's mind, waiting in cold, still stasis for the joule routes feeding the blank bubble here on Earth to safely power down and pop its contents back into sapien space-time.

Realisation exploded through Minnus, his skin goosebumping in waves. *There's still a way.*

He picked himself up from the floor, no doubt confusing the Telosec agent who had almost reached him, and began running back the way he had come.

⋏

"Joules. Give me the vest!" Minnus screamed wheezily as burst from the elevator doors. The athlete had already removed the vest as requested via the breathless cSheet message from Minnus that he'd collected a few minutes earlier, delivered whilst Minnus was running back along the skywalk. Joules now held the vest up in one hand like a water polo player faking a shot. He still sat on Johnson's chest, pinning him to the ground. Minnus was exhausted—at the limit of his physical capability. He knew what had to be done though. *Nearly there. Just a few more metres.* He stopped moving as he reached Joules and took the vest from his outstretched hand, slipping one arm through a sleeve opening and leaving the rest hanging from his body. Without saying anything more, he headed over to the exit door."Minnus!" Joules called after him urgently. "What's going on?""I can still save him, Joules." Then, as he disappeared through the exit, Minnus turned and said, "Thank you, my friend. Make sure that the NV edit on my home permaDrive gets out there. I imagine it'll be pretty easy to find someone who'll be asking questions about it in about ten minutes' time. Look after Nombre for me. I love you."

Then he turned back and headed out to his wing, still docked outside.

Minnus ploughed up the ramp, laying the bomb vest on the floor next to the primary passenger seat, which he flopped into. First, he instructed that all safety and collision avoidance software be deactivated, and then he gave the craft the course he wanted to follow. The wing told him the route would take three minutes before arrival at the destination. *Three minutes. Too long and yet not enough time.* He instructed the wing to move and begin a visual countdown to destination on the main dash. Then he snapped open his cSheet, telling it broadcast to Nombre's commSheet and make sure her unit would record his transmission no matter whether she answered or not. He began speaking.

"It's the joule routes, honey. There's only one way to save Sero now. It's *all* that's left. You know how this works. The blank bubble is sending someone into another dimension to be 'built,' one where time doesn't pass like it does here in our universe. We use the energy funnelled to the blank bubble by the joule routes to literally move matter into other dimensions; we preprogramme the matter with a description of what to do, how to grow. Then we move it all outside of time. When we drop the blank bubble, we move the matter back again—back to our timeframe.

"So he's already there, Nombre. Zahir has already done it. He already inhabits a copy body of Sero, just blank bubbled away from our space-time—and only for as long as it takes to safely wind down the joule routes from the amount of energy it needs to generate the blank bubble in the first place. The only way to stop him coming through and pressing the kill switch is to interrupt the depowering process. To interrupt the joule routes—encased inside the concrete stalk of the Postbox. So I guess you'll know by now what I need to do."

Minnus's voice broke as he moved from technical description of why his plan was needed to how he felt about it, cracking into a croak as tears began to fall from his eyes.

The wing had soared upwards in a curving arc and had reached the pinnacle of its parabola. The dash timer showed that there was a single minute to destination. Minnus spoke on through the tears. His voice was clear and strong again, recovered through flowing sincerity.

"Once, when we were young and before we'd learned enough to know better, you told me that you admired that I wasn't the kind of man who would 'settle.' You loved that I wanted to be significant—wanted to build something. I want you to know that the greatest thing I built wasn't cultural or technological. There was no contribution to the Race that was worth more than what we built together. We built love. We created truly shared experience and emotional interconnectedness. We build a family; we taught them, tested them, and wove them into that interconnected love.

"In doing it, we both learned that love is really all there is to make humanity worthwhile. The Race, for all our constructs and achievements, would be worthless without the web of sacrifice and encouragement that love gives. We did it together, you and I. We loved and helped others to love. I'm proud of us."

He didn't wipe the tears from his cheeks. He didn't even try. He carried on with his message, knowing that it would be his epitaph. Thirty seconds on the dash.

"Sero has a chance, Nombre. A chance to experience love again. To build something more worthwhile than all our projects and plans could ever have let us understand. Prid might be alive up there on NineDee. If I can return him to her, he can grow too and help her to grow just as we did. I can not only save his live, but I can give him a chance of a life that means more than he and I dreamed of when we were children. And I love him too. So I must. Please explain to the children. I know you understand because I know you so completely."

The screen of the wing became transparent as the vehicle approached the stalk of the Postbox, the only safety feature Minnus had left active. The screen counted down the final five seconds as the concrete of the structure expanded to fill the image in front of him. Minnus's final words were instinctive and unplanned.

"We did it all together," he said.

Then he let go of the dead-man switch.

# FORTY-ONE

*Blue...blue...blue...blue...blue.* The light circled, appearing on the left of his vision, too bright for him to keep his eyes open but still recognisable as colour. Aware of his feelings of longing and hope, Sero focused on the memories that sprang to the front of his awakening mind, using the emotional echo to imagine the shape and extent of the soul they powered. Two blues passed. Sero smiled. As blue became cyan, then black, his eyelids rose, lifting the curtain of darkness to reveal the semidark of the bubble's interior. The bubble wall parted as it had nine years earlier, and Sero could see that the room was bare but for the two perfectly preserved but wastrel-thin corpses leant against the far wall in a sitting position. They were holding hands. In front of them, like an underground sundial, stood a shadowy line of cabling and a pedestal. The kill switch.

Sero fairly slid from the bubble as soon as it dissipated. There was no following of protocol, no testing of muscles.

He flopped onto the kill switch like a free-falling walrus, urgent and uncoordinated.

"Welcome back to NineDee, Auditor Novak."

The voice wasn't NineCents. It was female.

"Look at the door, and say your name."

"Sero Novak. Telonaut lead auditor."

The drawbridge fell slowly open. Immediately on the other side, silhouetted by an underwater scene of tentacle-like plants, stood a woman in her early twenties. She held something that looked like a weapon in her right hand and reached out immediately to him with her left. "Come on!" she urged. "We don't have much time before they find us!"

# Minus One

**S**hould I do *it? It feels right. It feels important enough to break the "rules" for. It would be the start of a family. What could be more important than that? When I think about what we could build together. Together! How far might we take the Race if we could join* together *truly? I know she loves me, and I worship her. What is the sacrifice, really? The loss of a single unworthy man, an outlier on the normal distribution of our species, a negative influence. Not like us. Not like her. Not like me. Could any unforeseen consequences outweigh the value of me being with her, and her being with me, together? Family.*

Still to come in Infonaut, the second part of the Teloverse series:

> *Sero Novak awakens on the Race colony of NineDee to be confronted by a woman who claims to be the older version of his adopted daughter Prid, leader of a planetary resistance force opposing the Zahir monoculture. Is this woman really Sero's beloved daughter?*
>
> *Meanwhile, Sero hears rumours of a young child born of Dini-Zahir, his former lover and the new matriarch of NineDee, whilst on Earth, an unlikely alliance is formed between those who mourn for the loss of Minnus Mbeki, who each have their own agenda in collaborating to mine the NV footage of Sero's NineDee audit for a way to fold space-time itself.*

### Did you like this book?

Let everyone know by posting a review on Amazon. This is the best way to get your view out there. Just search for TELONAUT in the Amazon search bar on then click on the review link

### Want to give me (the author) feedback?

If you're reading on Kindle, the next page will be a 'before you go' section for quick rating TELONAUT. Why not participate and share your thoughts with your friends using the easy social media links? I'd really appreciate it.

Made in the USA
Columbia, SC
31 July 2017